continued . . .

D0544069

More praise for *Unbreak My Heart*

"A poignant family drama . . . gut-wrenching."
—*Midwest Book Review*

"A truly compelling novel of finding and letting go of the past so that the future can be lived to its fullest potential. Have a hanky handy."
—*Rendezvous*

"A moving family drama that touches the reader on several levels. . . . Fans will fully enjoy."
—*Affaire de Coeur*

"With the same unerring ability she displayed in *Twelve Days*, Teresa Hill finds the reader's heartstrings and isn't afraid to pull. . . . She had me in her grasp right from the prologue and didn't let go until the final page. . . . Make sure you have a few hours at your disposal before opening *Unbreak My Heart*. . . . Let this master storyteller pull you into her world."
—The Romance Journal

"Proof-positive that author Teresa Hill is a talent to be reckoned with. Her ability to paint stories that use vivid and complex emotions is a special talent that is sure to be an audience pleaser."
—*Romantic Times* (Top Pick)

Twelve Days

"Take a leap of faith and read this book. *Twelve Days* will touch your heart, make you smile, and remind you that Christmas miracles really can happen, if only we reach out to others and believe. Teresa Hill spins a tale that is pure magic. *Twelve Days* is the best Christmas story I've read in ages."
— Catherine Anderson

"Dramatic and emotionally uplifting."
—*Romantic Times* (Top Pick)

"Teresa Hill provides the audience with an early Christmas present. . . . The poignant story line catches the audience early on and never eases the emotional throttle until the novel is finished."
—*Affaire de Coeur*

"The warm fuzzies of Christmas thread their way through this theme of love and hope like a string of twinkling lights. . . . This is a heartwarmer. Ms. Hill hit all my buttons with her warm characters, beautiful setting, and moving story."
—*Old Book Barn Gazette*

"An insightful relationship drama."
—*Midwest Book Review*

"*Twelve Days* is magic."
—The Romance Journal

More stories of the McRae family

Twelve Days
The Edge of Heaven

Also by Teresa Hill

Unbreak My Heart

Bed of Lies

Teresa Hill

AN ONYX BOOK

ONYX
Published by New American Library, a division of
Penguin Putnam Inc., 375 Hudson Street,
New York, New York 10014, U.S.A.
Penguin Books Ltd, 80 Strand,
London WC2R 0RL, England
Penguin Books Australia Ltd, 250 Camberwell Road,
Camberwell, Victoria 3124, Australia
Penguin Books Canada Ltd, 10 Alcorn Avenue,
Toronto, Ontario, Canada M4V 3B2
Penguin Books (N.Z.) Ltd, Cnr Rosedale and Airborne Roads,
Albany, Auckland 1310, New Zealand

Penguin Books Ltd, Registered Offices:
Harmondsworth, Middlesex, England

First published by Onyx, an imprint of New American Library,
a division of Penguin Putnam Inc.

First Printing, March 2003
10 9 8 7 6 5 4 3 2 1

 REGISTERED TRADEMARK—MARCA REGISTRADA

Printed in the United States of America

PUBLISHER'S NOTE
This is a work of fiction. Names, characters, places, and incidents either are the product
of the author's imagination or are used fictitiously, and any resemblance to actual
persons, living or dead, business establishments, events, or locales is entirely
coincidental.

To Gail Virardi and Vicki Hinze,
Two of the wisest, kindest,
most generous women I am blessed to know.
I would not have made it through 2001
without you both.

Chapter 1

She was standing in the foyer of the most elegant restaurant in town, Steve's arm resting lightly at her back, her future in-laws by her side, her new life firmly in place, when she saw him.

Customers were heading in and out of the front doors, clustering at the hostess stand, heading off to their tables, everyone going every which way at once, while she stood frozen in place.

There he was, Zach McRae in the flesh.

For a moment it was as if Julie Morrison's life were a movie playing out on the big screen and someone had just hit the pause button.

No . . . as if they'd sent the tape in reverse, and in an instant she was seven years old again, scared, lost, and trying to hide in a quiet corner of his parents' house, wishing she never had to go home.

Zach turned, saw Julie, and walked right up to her, shoulders wide and squared, a too-familiar smile on his face—as if he's last seen her yesterday, not more than eight years ago—and said, "Hello, Julie."

"Zach," she managed to say. "What are you doing here?"

What she really wanted to say was, *Please don't say another word. Please don't ruin anything.*

"Business." He was still smiling. "And you? Is this where you disappeared to? Memphis?"

She laughed. What else was there to do? A part of her was surprised, maybe even hurt, that he'd recognized her so easily. She thought she'd come so far from that girl she used to be. Especially standing in the lobby of one of the finest restaurants in Memphis, a discreet—and yet she hoped stylish—designer dress wrapped around her body. Steve's ring—a tasteful family heirloom passed down through the generations—on the third finger of her left hand.

And yet, at the same time, she realized there was a part of her that was immeasurably pleased that Zach had known her right away, even after all this time.

"You disappeared?" Steve asked as his arm tightened around her, bringing her back to the present.

She realized they were all looking at her, Zach and Steve, as well as Steve's parents. Both in their sixties, tastefully gray and discreetly looking of old Southern money, they'd never been happy at the prospect of welcoming her into their family.

Calm down, Julie told herself. All she had to do was stay calm. *And get rid of him.* Stay right here in this carefully constructed world. It was hers now. No one could take it away. No one could make her go back to what she used to be.

Steve's mother cleared her throat and gave Julie a pointed look.

"I'm so sorry," Julie said. "I was just surprised. . . . Steve, this is Zach McRae, an old friend of mine. Zach this is my fiancé, Steve Land, and his parents Barbara and Joe Land."

As they all shook hands, Julie couldn't help but notice that Zach, all grown up, was just as straight and tall and solid as she'd ever imagined he'd be. He had dark hair, thick and clipped short and neat, even darker eyes, a strong, determined jaw, a beautiful smile.

And a decidedly kind heart. She remembered that well.

"Old friends, you say?" Steve asked him.

"Yes," Zach said, not taking his eyes off her. "And neighbors."

"Oh?" Steve's mother sounded interested all of a sudden. "You're from St. Louis, too?"

"St. Louis?" Zach asked, blank faced.

And just like that, Julie felt the treacherous ground she was standing on shift this way and that.

Julie jumped in, begging him with her eyes to just let it be. "He used to be. It's been ages since we've seen each other." She smiled up at Steve in the end. He wasn't going anywhere. He wanted to marry her, after all. Then she turned to Zach and uttered a bold-faced lie. "And your family moved to . . . Where was it, Zach? Ohio?"

He took a breath, his jaw tightening. She could just imagine what was running through his head: *Just like old times, huh Julie?*

Years ago, he wouldn't have hesitated to call her on a lie. She held her breath, waiting. . . .

"Yes." He finally nodded, not taking his eyes off her. "I'm surprised you remember."

All the lies, he meant.

She hung her head, realizing he had the power to shame her, even now.

"And you two know each other because . . . ?" Steve asked.

"Julie and my little sister Grace were inseparable for

years when they were younger," Zach explained. "I'm sure she'd love to hear from you. In fact . . ."

He slipped a hand into the inside front pocket of his jacket and pulled out a small case. Taking a business card out of it, he scribbled something on the back, then gave it to her.

"Do that, Julie. Give her a call."

His look said, *Or else.*

What? He'd track her down? Not that it would be difficult. She'd never bothered to change her name. At the time she'd been tempted, she hadn't had the money, and once she had it, she realized she hadn't left anyone behind who'd care enough to come looking for her.

She took the card, promising to call.

The hostess, sleek and elegant in a slim, black floor-length skirt and a crisp white blouse, joined them, nodding respectfully to Steve's father. "Your table's ready, Mr. Land."

Steve's mother asked for a moment, then turned to Zach. "You've just arrived in town, Mr. McRae?"

"Yes, ma'am," he said.

"Alone?"

"Yes. I was supposed to have dinner with a colleague, but he got tied up at the last minute. He'd talked so much about how wonderful this restaurant is, I decided to come anyway and try it on my own."

"Well, we can't have you eating dinner all alone. Why don't you join us? We've met so few of Julie's friends, and with her not having any family left . . ."

Zach gave Julie another one of those looks. "I'd love to join you. If that's all right with everyone."

Barbara Land looked gleeful, as if she'd read between every line and knew Julie was hiding something and that Zach might well be the key. Steve gave Julie an odd look, his arm tightening once again at her waist. She could feel all those not-so-subtle male signals rolling off him. *Hands off. She's mine.* As if Zach had ever seen her as anything but a lost little girl or a troubled teenager.

There was a short, awkward silence before Steve conceded. "Please, join us."

Moving through the crowded restaurant, Zach caught her by the arm, drawing her back from the rest of the group, and whispering to her, "Got rid of the family again, huh, Julie?"

She'd spent most of her high school years claiming to be an orphan or the sole child of a father who was off building a bridge in South America and hadn't been home in years.

"Wouldn't you, if they were yours?" she asked.

"No, I wouldn't."

"Of course not," she admitted as they wove their way through the myriad tables and chairs. "You've probably never lied about anything in your life. Or done anything wrong."

"I never claimed to be perfect, Julie," he said, still too close.

"No," she said, the years falling away and bitterness she'd hoped to never give in to again, rearing up. "You just have a perfect life."

He caught her arm and stopped her right there in the middle of the restaurant. "You know that's not true."

Yes, she supposed she did. It was something she'd forgotten so many times over the years, because he certainly seemed like a man who'd had everything. But that wasn't the case.

She hadn't believed the story the first time she'd heard it whispered about the neighborhood. About Zach and his two sisters found abandoned in a motel on the edge of

town at Christmastime one year. His mother found weeks
later in a ditch outside of town, where she'd been left for
dead. Not long after that, she *was* dead, Zach's father in
prison for killing her.

It hadn't seemed possible. His adoptive family seemed
as close to perfect as any she'd ever known. But she'd
asked Grace, who'd confirmed the whole story.

Zach had talked about it once, telling Julie he knew
what it was like to be alone and scared. He told her because he knew she felt the same way, and he knew how
bad it was, something she'd never wanted anyone to
know.

And here he was, seeing through her all over again.

In the center of the restaurant, they stood staring at
each other, his hand still on her arm. He was so big and
broad shouldered now. There was heat coming off his
body, the smell of warm, clean male skin and something
subtle and enticing that emanated from his freshly shaved
jaw. She shook her head, dismissing that momentary
flash of awareness, and stepped back.

"Zach, please . . ."

He didn't let go, but his voice changed, going deep and
so familiar it hurt. "Why don't you just tell me what's
wrong, Julie."

As if that were all she had to do—pour out her troubles to him, and he'd fix everything. He might be able to.
Things that seemed impossible to her were no problem in
his capable hands. But then the world just worked for
Zach McRae, other than that odd little blip in the first five
years of his life.

"Come on, Julie. It's me."

Maybe she should tell him. Just so he'd know she was
okay. Because even after all this time, he probably still

cared. He knew her better than almost anyone ever would, and he still cared.

Before she could open her guilty mouth, Steve showed up. "You two get lost?"

His arm came around her waist, possession and tension evident in just the touch of his hand. Julie stood sandwiched between them, her past on one side, her future on the other, both of them crowding her until she almost couldn't breathe. Steve's jaw was tight, his cheeks flushed. He glanced down pointedly at Zach's hand on her arm.

If they'd stood there one more minute like that, Steve could have grabbed her other arm and they could have played tug-of-war with her. The testosterone levels were soaring. She'd never seen Steve behave this way.

"I'm sorry," she stammered. "We were just . . . just—"

"Talking about old times," Zach said, as he let his hand fall to his side and stepped back, as if to cede that territory to Steve, ignoring all those not-so-subtle signs of a challenge. "Emma's pregnant again. She's my older sister. She and Rye are hoping for another boy this time. They already have two girls. Grace—my younger sister—studied art in Paris for several years. She loved it there, but now she's home."

"And your parents are well?" Julie asked.

"Couldn't be better."

"I'm glad. They were always so kind to me."

They arrived at the table to find Steve's father standing, pointedly waiting. Steve's mother was already seated. Steve held out a chair for Julie, one that put her squarely between the two men and staring at her future in-laws all through dinner. *Wonderful.* Barbara Land seemed overjoyed, possibly thinking tonight she'd find a reason to object to the engagement.

Here Julie had been thinking she was home free from the moment the ring had gone onto her finger. But she wondered now if there'd ever come a point where she felt safe and secure. That's all she'd ever wanted in her whole life. It meant everything to her.

She slid into the chair, placed the crisp white napkin on her lap, and looked around the table from one set of inquisitive eyes to another. Her composure slipped another notch. She was scared. Not just the little, low-level buzz of anxiety that seemed to permeate her life, or those little spikes of fear that came from time to time when things got really bad. This was full-fledged fear. It had been a long time since she'd felt that way, but she'd never forget the feeling.

Another week was all she needed. She and Steve would formally announce their engagement then. A month after that, they'd be married. Even if at some point in the future Steve found out everything, he wouldn't just walk away. Marriage vows meant something to him. Maybe he wouldn't care about her secrets at all. He claimed to love her, after all.

No, he claimed to love the person she was pretending to be.

"Ma'am?"

She looked up. The waiter was holding out a menu to her, probably had been for a while. Everyone at the table was staring at her. She took the menu, studying it intently, wondering what would be easiest on a stomach turning queasier with every passing moment.

She gave a little start when the busboy leaned over her shoulder to fill her delicate crystal water glass. When she dared to look up from her menu again, he was gone. It was just the five of them sitting around the table. Silence fell, an awkwardness settling firmly into place.

It was amazing. Zach had hardly said a thing, and yet they all seemed to know something was wrong. A flash of panic ripped through her. It hurt, deep in her abdomen. She put a hand on that spot and winced.

"Are you all right, dear?" Steve's mother asked.

"Yes," she claimed, forcing a smile across her face. "Just a little muscle twinge. I think I pulled something in my side at the gym this week."

"You'll have to be more careful," Barbara said.

"Yes, I will." She dropped her gaze, afraid everything might show in her eyes.

"So . . . you're still in Ohio, Mr. McRae?" Barbara Land asked.

"Yes," he said.

"And what brings you to Memphis?" Steve's father asked.

"A case," he said.

"Case?"

"I'm an attorney," he said.

Oh, no. Julie was afraid she knew the case.

She'd scanned the front-page headlines this morning as she'd rushed out the door. Even in a rush, she'd thought about Zach for a moment. Because she knew what he did. She'd stumbled across his name in the paper months ago, when he was defending a boy in Texas, trying to keep him off death row. Next thing Julie knew, he was on the television news. Zach McRae, right there in her living room, the first familiar thing she'd seen in ages. She'd drank in the sight of him and the sound of his voice, and then had gotten caught up in the passion in his words.

"You're defending that boy, aren't you?" she asked. "What's his name? Tim? Tom?"

"Tony Williams." Zach's gaze settled on her, once more seeming to see right inside of her.

She couldn't tell if he was surprised or pleased. Obviously, she'd been keeping up with him, might as well have taken out a billboard announcing that fact.

Oh, Julie. You're a mess tonight.

"That boy who shot his father?" Steve asked.

"He's been charged with that," Zach said.

"Found standing over the body with blood on his hands, I heard," Steve's father said.

"You're defending him?" Steve sounded incredulous.

"Yes," Zach said, managing with just one word to issue a challenge.

"Why?" Steve asked.

"Let's see." Zach settled back in his chair, getting comfortable. "Because he was fourteen when it happened. Because he has only a marginal IQ. Because he's been abused in ways I doubt you could begin to understand. Because no one ever helped him, not in the entire time he was growing up, and now all society has to offer him is a jail cell and a lethal injection. Yes, I'm defending him. Someone should have shot his father long ago. Tony would have been much better off if someone had."

Steve's mother almost choked. She covered her mouth with her hand and coughed, Steve's father patting her on the back, politeness obviously beyond her at the moment.

"Well," she said a moment later, recovering her composure. "How very interesting. This is the sort of thing you do?"

"Yes," Zach said.

And did it very well, from what Julie had found out. Honestly, it was just too easy to find information about people these days. She had ever-so-innocently typed his name into her favorite internet search engine, and there

came story after story, pictures often, of Zach McRae, the
crusading lawyer.

He worked for a legal foundation based in Cincinnati
and took on increasingly higher-profile cases. Hopeless
cases, most of them. Brutal ones. Usually involving kids.

How did he do that day after day? What sort of toll
must that take on a man?

"And you'd put that teenager back on the streets?"
Steve asked. "Knowing he could do anything?"

"I don't hold out much hope of him going free, but I'd
sure like to see him get the help he needs," Zach admitted. "I don't quite see what society has to gain by putting
him to death."

"So, you're an opponent of the death penalty?" Steve's
mother tried.

"No," Zach said. "I'm all for it in certain cases."

Julie almost laughed, as horribly inappropriate as that
would have been. She felt sorry for the Williams boy.
Honestly, she did. There was nothing funny about his situation. It was just that the comment was so Zach. He
knew exactly where he stood, what he believed in, and
he'd never been shy of telling anyone. She'd always
thought if they'd just put him in charge of the world, the
whole place would run a lot more smoothly.

Steve's mother was making that little choking sound
again. The things Zach had likely seen over the years, the
kind of chaos Julie had lived with, were obviously as for-
eign to Steve's mother as a man who spoke his mind as
openly as Zach. Once more, she felt like an outsider looking in on her fiancé and his family. One more time, the
lost little girl inside her nagged, *You don't belong here.
You never will.*

She turned to Zach, a pleading look in her eyes once

again. "Is your mother still working in stained glass, Zach?"

"Yes," he said.

"Barbara's great-uncle did, too. He did the windows of their church here in town—"

"The one where we're going to be married," Steve interjected.

"Yes." If she got through this night, they just might. "They're absolutely beautiful, and Steve's parents have a few of his pieces at their home. I was . . . Well, I thought of your mother when I saw them. I hope her work is going well."

"Couldn't be better," he said. "And it looks like Grace is going to follow in her footsteps, working in the glass."

"Oh." Julie smiled, a genuine smile, for the first time all night. "I can see her doing that. And your father? Zach's father does wonderful restoration work," she told Steve. "They used to live in the most fabulous old Victorian house."

"Still do," Zach said.

"Good." She was just starting to relax a bit when she realized what he'd just said. She wasn't supposed to have ever seen the house the McRaes still lived in, the one they allegedly moved into after leaving St. Louis, where she claimed she'd known them.

Julie held her breath and scanned the faces around her, waiting for someone to pick up on that little inconsistency, but no one said a word.

The waiter came and rescued her, rambling on about the night's specials and getting into an extended discussion with Steve's father about the quality and vintage of the different champagnes offered, until he'd settled on just the right one.

"We're celebrating," Steve explained, taking Julie's

hand and angling it so that the big diamond ring he'd put on her finger was practically under Zach's nose. "Tonight with my parents, and next Saturday they're throwing us an engagement party."

"Congratulations. I hope you'll be very happy together," Zach said, not taking his eyes off her.

I will be, she wanted to tell him. *I'll be just fine.*

She told herself to stop seeing disaster around every corner. Her life wasn't like that anymore. Then Steve's mother turned to Zach and said, "Yes, we're planning a lovely party. You simply must come."

Julie nearly choked. She watched helplessly as Zach smiled and said he would love to.

The endless dinner continued, Steve simmering angrily, Barbara Land looking like a woman who would not give up, now that she sensed she was onto something. Zach was as charming as Julie had always known he would be when he was all grown up. Julie picked at her dinner and mostly just stared at her glass of champagne, touching it to her lips when forced to for each toast, but nothing more. She wasn't sure, but she thought Zach was doing the same thing.

He finally excused himself, saying he had to be in court early. She and Steve said good-bye to his parents at the front of the restaurant, and then faced each other in the parking lot on the warm summer night.

"Well." Steve made a show of pulling out a cigarette and lighting it, drawing one long, hard pull of nicotine into his lungs, something he seldom allowed himself. "What was that?"

"I don't know." She stared right back at him. "What was it?"

"Who is he?" Steve tried again.

"I told you. A neighbor. The older brother of a girl I used to play with."

"What else is going on, Julie?"

"Between me and Zach? Nothing. There's never been anything between us except friendship, Steve, I promise."

"But there was something between you. You were jumpy all night, right from the moment you spotted him."

"I was just so surprised. It was like stepping back into the past for a minute. I haven't done that in so long, and you know the memories aren't good ones."

"What else?" Steve asked, unrelenting.

"I don't know. It seemed odd that he would show up here tonight, don't you think? I meant, this is the beginning for us, of something wonderful, I hope." She searched his face, needing to know he felt the same way, something she hadn't had to do in a long time. "I don't want anything to mess this up."

"That's it?" Steve kept his distance while he drew in deeply on the cigarette.

Put it out, she wanted to say. *Stop looking like you're so far away, and hold me.* But he stayed there, uneasy and maybe still angry. It was unsettling. He was the most easygoing man she'd ever met. It was one of the things she loved about him the most. How even tempered he was, how capable, how solid, how reasonable.

Tears slipped out of the corners of her eyes. She looked off to the side, hoping he wouldn't see. "It just . . . It seemed like a bad sign. Him showing up now."

"I don't believe in bad signs." Steve tossed the cigarette butt, crushing it out with his foot.

"You're right," she said. "I'm being silly."

Except it didn't feel silly. It felt bad. She thought about just going to him, slipping her arms around him and hanging on to him, asking him to hang on to her. She tried not to do that too often, tried to hold the feelings at bay.

It wasn't working now.

She went to Steve, her head bent low and coming to rest against his chest. She grabbed the edges of his suit jacket, to hold on to what they had, and her breath caught until his arms reluctantly came around her.

Acquaintances of hers, upon meeting him, said he didn't seem very exciting, that he was a bit set in his ways. They'd done everything but come right out and call him dull, but Julie had never thought that. He was stable, something she'd craved her whole life.

Then there were the friends who'd implied that she might be willing to overlook certain shortcomings of Steve's because of the money. He wasn't rich. Just comfortable. That's what Steve called it. Julie had so seldom been the least bit comfortable and never in the way he meant it. She hadn't gone after him because of his money, but at the same time, she knew they wouldn't ever have to worry about losing things, like their home, or wonder where their next meal was coming from.

Steve's family had been here for nearly a hundred and fifty years. They had roots and staying power, the likes of which she'd never known. Steve hardly ever drank. He didn't have a temper. He didn't flirt with other women, didn't belittle her or discount her opinions or yell. He didn't lie. He didn't cheat. He didn't bet on ball games or horses. He didn't hit her.

He was the epitome of calm in a world she often thought was crazy. It had been the first thing that attracted her to him. They'd been in a meeting room full of screaming people, facing a major crisis at one of the stores the Lands owned, and Steve had been the picture of calm. He'd gotten everyone to settle down and solved the problem. They'd all gone on with what they needed to do, and she and Steve had gone on to dinner and then to dating for a full year and now to being engaged.

She meant to hang on to him for dear life.

"Sorry," he said, his arms finally tightening around her, his body relaxing against hers. "I just don't think I've ever seen you even appear to be interested in another man—"

"In Zach?"

"You hung on to every word the man said."

Because she was scared of what was going to come out of his mouth.

"He's never been interested in me that way, Steve. He never would be."

"And why not? I happen to find you very interesting."

"You didn't know me when I was twelve." Thank goodness.

"I would have found you interesting at any age," he claimed, easing back all too soon. "And you're still tense. You're sure there's nothing wrong?"

"I've just been rushing all day." She'd come straight from the office, and he'd come from the other side of town, from the town house they'd share after they were married.

"You could still come home with me," he said, his lips finding hers.

She closed her eyes and tried so hard to fall into that kiss, to let it take her so far away from here, make her forget every fear, every bit of dread lurking deep inside of her.

Come on, she thought. *Take it all away.*

But as much as she tried, she couldn't. The business card Zach had given her was practically screaming at her from inside her purse. She eased away from Steve, head down low. "I'm sorry. I can't."

"You look so sad, Julie. What is it?"

She really didn't want to lie. She'd never set out to. It had just happened, and now it was too late for anything else, wasn't it? "It's the engagement party, the wedding, all those decisions still to make."

She felt bombarded by it all lately.

"I know my mother has certain ideas about how things should be done," he said. "I've usually found it easier just to go along with her, but then I really don't care whether we have beef or seafood at the reception. I couldn't care less about what kind of flowers are in the church that day or what the organist plays. I just want to marry you."

"And I want to marry you."

"Good. The rest really doesn't matter, does it?"

"No, it doesn't," she said, liar that she was. "I'll see you tomorrow afternoon? After the final fitting for my dress for the party?"

She wanted to look just right, like the kind of woman Steve Land would marry. She wanted to be that woman.

"All right." He gave her a quick kiss, helped her into the car, and waited, watching as she drove away.

Once Julie was out of his sight, she pulled out the card Zach had given her.

On the back, he'd scrawled out the name of his hotel, the phone number, and his room number.

She turned south, toward downtown, and his hotel.

Chapter 2

His hotel was one of those apartmentlike complexes set up for people on extended trips, which she took as a bad sign.

Murder trials took a while, didn't they?

Julie worked up her courage and knocked on his door. A moment later, it swung open to reveal Zach, minus the tie and jacket, white dress shirt open at the collar, sleeves rolled up nearly to his elbows.

"Julie." He stepped back, gesturing for her to come inside.

There was a small living room with a tiny kitchenette. Through the open doorway in the corner she could see a slightly rumpled bed, pillows piled up against the headboard, a pile of papers strewn off to the side. There was another pile of papers, equally as big and messy, on the coffee table by the floral-print sofa.

"Sit down." He pointed to the sofa as he cleared away papers from the coffee table. "Sorry about the mess. It gets worse the closer I get to trial, especially when I'm running out of time."

She felt that way, too, like time was running out.

"I shouldn't have taken the time out for dinner," he

said, "but it's gotten to be a pretrial tradition. The last decent meal before insanity sets in."

Julie wished so badly that he hadn't been at dinner. She thought about all the little fibs she'd ever told him and wondered why she'd even tried with him. He'd always seen right through her.

"Zach?" She stood there, ready to beg. "I don't know how to say this without sounding totally ungrateful for everything you and your family ever did for me." They'd been a refuge of calm in a chaotic childhood. "But this . . . My life, now, it's . . ."

"None of my business, huh?" He leaned back in his seat and smiled slowly.

She nodded, making herself meet his gaze.

"Okay." He shrugged. "If that's the way you want it."

"It . . . Well . . ." It was, wasn't it? Wasn't that the way it had to be?

"Look, I just wanted to make sure you were okay. You seemed so nervous at the restaurant, I thought . . ."

"That I'd gotten myself into another mess, and you were going to come rescue me?"

"I would have," he said quietly.

All the breath went out of her at the understanding look in his eyes and the promise of the words.

She believed he would have, even after all these years, and to someone like her, who'd never really had the kind of family she could depend upon, it meant the world to her, knowing that.

And she was kicking him out of her life at practically the first sight of him in years? It sounded crazy when she thought about it like that. It wasn't like she had a lot of people in her corner.

Julie sat down, her legs trembling, her hands, too.

Zach leaned to one side of his chair, his elbow resting

on the arm, chin resting on that one hand, just waiting for whatever she'd say next.

It was an old trick of his. He sat and stared at people, and they confessed everything. She used to squirm and look at the floor and tell herself to just get up and walk away. But she didn't. She'd found herself telling him the hardest things, the things she'd most wanted to hide.

"That's it?" she asked finally. "You're going to let me off that easy?"

"You want me to give you a hard time, I will," he said with a grin.

She laughed, couldn't help herself. It was so much better than crying. She could do this, couldn't she? It was the right thing. What she'd always wanted. Security, stability, respect. This was everything.

"Let's see," he began. "If I were to give you a hard time about this, I'd probably say something about it being a mistake to lie to a man you're going to marry. But I doubt you need me to tell you that."

"No, I don't." She'd told herself that very thing time and time again. "And I told him, Zach. I did. I told him there were things that happened back home—"

"In St. Louis? Did you ever live in St. Louis?"

"No," she admitted. "But does it really matter where I was?"

"It seems to. To you."

She let that go. Honestly, it wasn't important. She'd just felt safer, thinking if anyone ever went looking, they'd go there and not find anything. Because she'd never been there.

"Anyway," she went on. "I told Steve I hadn't had the greatest childhood, that there were things I wasn't dying to talk to him about, and he's okay with that. He said I didn't have to tell him anything I didn't want to."

"Okay," Zach said.

But with his tone, he managed to say he didn't think it was.

"Everything is different for me here," she tried. "I'm different."

"Are you happy, Julie?"

"Yes," she insisted.

Zach put his feet up on the coffee table, like he was settling in for a nice long chat. "Talk to anybody back home lately?"

"No." And she liked it that way. Honestly, she did.

There was something so nice about being in a brand-new place and starting over completely. She could be anyone she wanted to be. So she was surprised to sit here with him and realize how nice it was to be with someone so familiar. It seemed there were a million memories stuffed into her head that came flooding back, tiny little things she'd done and people she'd known that he would know, too. It might be nice to sit here and chat and catch up, but it seemed dangerous, too. Like opening a door she might not be able to close again.

And she liked having that door closed.

"Your mother and stepfather are still there," Zach offered. "Your little brother, too."

"Half brother," she said, as if that were some excuse.

He'd be thirteen now, and she barely knew him.

Zach waited, ready, it seemed, to tell her anything, but she didn't ask.

She could just imagine how her mother was. The woman would never change. Julie had never really cared about her stepfather, and he'd certainly never cared about her.

And her half brother? She had to turn away for a moment. There'd been a time . . . a you-and-me-against-the-world kind of time, when Peter had been so little and the house had been loud and crazy. When things had scared him, and he'd come running to her.

But that was a long time ago. Her stepfather had seen what was happening and hadn't liked it. She'd never known exactly what he'd said or done to change things between her and Peter, but they had changed. Not that it mattered now. The damage had been done a long time ago.

"Zach, there's nothing back there for me anymore."

"Okay."

He waited, as if he thought she might change her mind. She wouldn't.

"Look, it was good to see you again," she said, knowing she couldn't afford to linger. She grabbed her purse, dug for her keys, then remembered one more thing. "About the engagement party . . . You don't really want to go, do you, Zach?"

"What if your parents were in some kind of trouble, Julie? What if Peter was? Would you want to know then?"

"No," she insisted, that little voice inside saying, *Go now, while you still can.*

They were a mess no one could fix, and why should she even try? She'd survived all on her own, and she'd be damned if, now that she'd built a new life for herself, she'd be drawn back into theirs. If that made her selfish in Zach's eyes . . .

It did. She could see that.

But then, she'd disappointed Zach McRae so many times before. She'd disappointed herself, but she could live with that. The distance kept her safe—and halfway sane.

"I really have to go," she said.

He nodded once again, still watching her in that quiet, unsettling way of his. She would not let him make her feel bad, and she wouldn't defend herself to him.

She wasn't going to let herself think that this meant she probably wouldn't see him again or about how safe she'd once felt in his arms. He was just a tiny part of what was back there, one of the very few good things she remembered from a time of too much pain.

"I'm sorry, Zach," she said at the door.

He stood leaning casually against it. "I hope this works for you, Julie. I hope it makes you happy."

But she knew he didn't think it would. He thought it would all backfire in her face, and everything she was trying so hard to hide would come out.

Eight years, she thought. She hadn't been that girl in eight years, and it was so nice not to be her anymore.

She wouldn't let him or anyone else drag her back.

She hurried home, kicked off her shoes, and took down her hair, working out the soreness at the back of her neck and head that came from piling it up the way Steve liked it. It was such a small thing, putting her hair up. She was willing to do a lot to make him happy, because he was giving her so much.

She checked her voice mail and saw that he'd called to say good night and was wondering where she was. It didn't take that long to get from the restaurant to her apartment, and he knew that.

She'd say she was in the shower, she decided.

One more little lie.

What was one more on top of all the others? And it was such a small one.

Julie sat down on the chair in the corner and didn't bother with the lights, didn't bother with anything.

She was tired. It was hard to believe sometimes how tired she could be, and she was only twenty-six. It seemed it must grow impossible to go on at some point, if, at twenty-six, she could feel this worn down and . . .

Hollow. That was it. Empty. Like the set of a movie. They made the outside look so good, but inside there was nothing. How could she be a good wife to Steve when she felt like this? What did she have to offer him, if there was nothing inside of her?

Her phone rang. She jumped at the sound, rushed to swipe away tears running down her cheeks, and then grabbed the receiver in the dark. "Hello."

"Julie?" Steve said. "What's wrong? You sound upset."

"I'm all right," she said, thinking *lie, lie, lie.* And then, she just couldn't do it anymore. Not tonight. "No, Steve, I'm not. I went to see Zach."

"What?" Steve asked, his voice sounding the way it had earlier that night when she'd thought they were going to play tug-of-war with her. "Why?"

"To ask him not to come to our engagement party." That was part of it. "I saw the way the two of you were together. You were tense and uncomfortable—"

"You said there was nothing between the two of you," Steve reminded her.

"There isn't. Steve, he probably still thinks of me as a little kid."

"You don't look like a little kid anymore, Julie. You're a beautiful woman, and no man who looks at you can miss that."

"Well . . . so what? Even if he did look at me and think I was attractive, he'd probably find that as odd as . . ."

"As what?" Steve asked. "You finding him attractive?"

"That's not what I said at all."

"You don't think the man's good-looking?" he asked incredulously.

"I suppose he is." A picture of him, as he was now, flashed through her mind, along with those few moments in the restaurant when she was suddenly aware of him as a man. "I just don't think of him that way, Steve. I was thinking of what he'd been like as a boy. He looks the way I always expected him to, and I suppose he looks good. But what does that have to do with anything? He's just a guy I used to know."

"Who had you nervous as hell from the minute you laid eyes on him, and then, when you're supposedly too tired to come home with me, you go rushing off to his . . . Where did you see him, Julie? Did you go to his hotel?"

"I was there for five minutes. He has a suite. I sat on the sofa, and he sat on a chair. I said it was nice to see him again, then asked him not to come to our party."

"Why?" Steve asked.

"I didn't think you'd enjoy having him there." Certainly true, but not the whole truth. "It's supposed to be our night. We should be able to enjoy it, don't you think?"

"What else, Julie?"

"Your mother's dying to get him into a corner and grill him about everything he knows about me," she tried. "You know that, don't you?"

"So? What's he going to tell her that has you so afraid?"

"Oh, Steve, please . . . You said it was okay. You said there were things you hadn't told me, either, and that nothing really mattered except who we are now. Don't you believe that anymore?"

"I just know I hate the idea of you leaving me to rush

off to see him." Steve sighed. "Did you know you were going to him when you left the restaurant, Julie?"

"Yes." She closed her eyes, all the breath going out of her. Telling the truth was just hell. This was why she so seldom did it.

"So you stood right outside the restaurant on a night when we're celebrating our engagement and lied to me. Then went off to another man's hotel room."

"It wasn't like that. He never touched me. He never has. I can't imagine him ever wanting to. I don't see any reason why I'd ever see him again. I told him that I was happy for once, and that my life was none of his business."

"Then why are you so afraid?"

"Because I don't want anything to mess this up. You and me . . . This is the best thing I've ever had in my life. I can hardly believe it's real sometimes. That you love me and you want to marry me."

The truth poured out of her, and she felt so odd in the aftermath. Like she'd been stripped raw. That was the trouble with words. They tumbled out of your mouth, and then there was no taking them back.

"And what did he say? When you told him to stay the hell away?"

"That he hopes you and I are happy together. Steve—"

"I don't like this, Julie. You can tell when there's something between two people. It's like that with you and him. I felt it."

"Well, we've been through a lot together. Steve, I used to play with his sister. You have a sister. She must have had friends. You know what it's like with a girl who's a friend of your sister's. The year I turned thirteen, he went off to college. He dated cheerleaders and sorority girls. I used to see him on holidays and maybe in the summers.

Think about it, Steve. There was no time for anything between us, even if either one of us were so inclined, which we weren't."

"And you just happened to run into him at that restaurant?"

"Yes."

"And you're not going to see him again?"

"No. I'm going to marry you. I won't be seeing any other men."

"Julie, if you're not sure. If you have any doubts . . ."

"You're the only one I want," she said.

"Then stay the hell away from him," Steve said.

Then he hung up.

She didn't think he'd ever done that, ever even lost his temper. He didn't have one. It was one of the things she loved about him.

He'd never been jealous, either. She'd never given him any reason to be.

She'd just stay away from Zach. How hard could it be?

She was getting married. She was going to be happy. She thought about it, curled up in the chair by the phone in the dark of her quiet little apartment. She thought about her quiet, calm little life and all the plans she'd made, tears that she didn't understand streaming down her cheeks.

Zach told himself Julie Morrison's problems were none of his business, but that wasn't getting him anywhere. He poured himself another cup of coffee, regardless of the hour, and reached for the phone. His sister answered on the second ring, her voice soft and a little sleepy.

"Wake up, Gracie, it's me," he said.

"Zach, don't you ever sleep?" she groaned.

"Sure, when I'm not in trial."

"Are you ever not in trial these days? Mom said you practically went straight from Texas to . . . I can't remember now. Where are you?"

"Memphis, I think. Barbecue. Elvis. The river. You know the place?"

"I know the place. What are you doing there? You were supposed to be home, at least for a little while."

"Something came up," he said.

"Something always comes up lately, Zach."

"No, something really came up. Brian Welch's wife got creamed by a Suburban on her way to pick up the kids from school."

"Oh, my God. Is she all right?"

"She will be. It's just going to take a while. But there was no way Brian could have stayed in Memphis for three or four weeks for this trial."

"Okay, I'll give you that. But you're not the only lawyer at the agency."

"But I'm the best," he claimed.

"Zach—"

"I like this kid, okay?"

"It's always a kid. There's always one more, and they're always in some kind of terrible trouble—"

"They're going to fry him, Grace, if I don't help him."

"They're still using the electric chair?"

"No," he admitted. "Lethal injection. But dead is dead."

"So he killed someone, right? This kid you're defending?"

"Yeah, his old man."

"Perfect."

"Hey, the guy deserved it."

"Tell it to the judge, Zach. I'm your sister. You need to come home."

"I'll come home after this trial."

"That's what you said before you went to Texas."

"And I needed to be in Texas."

"You liked that kid, too, right?" she asked.

"He was just a kid," Zach said.

"And you can't save them all."

Leave it to Grace to cut through it all, just that easily.

"I liked it better when you couldn't even talk," he said. "When you just babbled and sucked on your fingers and grinned. You were so cute back then."

"Well, I'm not two years old anymore. Sorry."

"Yeah." This was what happened to sisters when they grew up. They gave a guy six kinds of hell, and they were better than anybody at it, because they knew him so well. He had one older, one younger, and he adored them both.

They were closer than most siblings, due to the way they'd grown up, and the last few months hadn't been the easiest ones they'd ever lived through, but they were tough. They had each other and the best parents any kids could have. Every advantage in the world that mattered.

Life still sucked sometimes.

But not as much as it had for Tony Williams.

"I'll come home when this is over," he said.

"Promise?"

He hesitated. It had been an automatic statement—that he'd go home when he was done.

"I'll try," he said. Shit, he was playing word games now. He sincerely doubted he'd try to go home. To distract her, he asked, "How's everybody?"

"Not happy that you're not here," she said.

So he'd catch hell from his older sister, his mother, and maybe his father, too. Suddenly everyone seemed to think they knew what was good for him, when he'd always been perfectly capable of taking care of himself.

Perfectly happy. Perfectly in control.

That was him.

He'd somehow lost that side of himself, and he couldn't get it back.

Like dropping something on the floor and hearing it rattle and roll and just not being able to find it. He felt like he was on the floor, feeling his way in the dark, simply unable to find all the parts of himself that he'd lost. Everything that made him work.

"Come home, Zach," Grace said.

Oh, hell. They already knew. They just hadn't been able to corner him about it because he was hundreds of miles away.

"I'll try," he said. And he would. He just doubted he'd succeed.

"If you don't miss us, I'd think you'd at least come see Gwen every now and then."

"I do see her." Every now and then. "In fact, I was thinking I might get her to fly down for a quick weekend."

He could talk through his trial strategy with her — she was as smart as she was gorgeous, and a lawyer, too — and then they could make up for lost time from the Texas trial, the time they'd likely lose to this one and her father's reelection campaign. He was in the U.S. Senate, and Gwen, as always, would have a big role in the upcoming campaign.

One of these days, they were going to find time to get married.

Maybe they could find a way to stay in the same city most of the time. That would be nice. Especially when he walked into a restaurant and found himself blown away by a pair of legs in a snug little skirt on another woman.

Which reminded him . . . "You'll never guess who I saw tonight."

"I doubt I could," she said. "I don't think I know anyone in Memphis."

"Yeah, you do. She was more your friend than mine. Neighbor," he said. "Your age. Practically disappeared off the face of the earth eight years ago?"

There was a pause, then, "Julie Morrison? You ran into Julie Morrison?"

"Uh-huh."

Except she wasn't little Julie Morrison anymore.

She was a woman with long legs and trim curves. It had been disconcerting for a moment—the reality of little Julie Morrison all grown up. But hell, a man couldn't help noticing a pretty woman, could he?

"Where?" his sister asked.

"I walked into a restaurant to have dinner and there she was."

All legs and what he'd bet was long brown hair that hung maybe to her waist. He'd always been a sucker for long legs and hair. She had the hair piled on top of her head in a way that showed off the sweet curve of her neck. She wore a short, loose silk jacket that concealed just about everything on her upper body, but the skirt showed promise. Just snug enough to show off the shape of those trim hips, short enough to allow just a bit of very shapely thighs to peek out beneath it.

Zach had fiddled with his tie and tried to look away, and then the woman had turned around and somehow turned into little Julie Morrison.

Julie, who'd panicked at the sight of him, the little liar.

"So what's she doing?" Grace asked.

"Having dinner with her uptight fiancé and his parents. All three of them stuffy as could be."

"Julie with a stuffy guy?"

"I know. Last thing I expected, believe me. She swears he's just what she needs. I don't believe it for a minute, but I doubt she cares what I think of him."

"How is she?"

"Same as always, it looks like. Lost, worried, swearing everything's okay." *Same old Julie,* he thought sadly.

She'd probably told him a thousand times that she was okay, and he'd yet to believe her once. He sure didn't believe her now.

"You got all this out of her at dinner with her fiancé?"

He'd gotten that just by looking at her and figuring out the snow job she'd given her fiancé about her past, and he'd hated to see it.

As a kid she'd alternately made him so mad he could have spit or scared him half to death. There were times when he'd really hurt for her, she kept things so tightly locked up inside.

He'd wanted things to be so much better for her, and he was afraid they were about to get worse.

"Look, it's a long story, Grace, and I really do have a ton to do. But I remembered Mom saying something a few weeks ago about Julie's parents being in some kind of trouble. I don't think Julie really wants to know. But just in case . . ."

If he saw her again. If she decided lying to her fiancé just wasn't the way to go. He hated to think of her doing that to herself, even now.

Give it up, Julie.

"I think I heard about a problem at the bank where Julie's mother works," Grace said. "But I don't know any specifics. I could try to find out."

"Shit," he said.

"Yeah. Did you get Julie's phone number?"

"No, but she works with her fiancé. His family owns a chain of department stores based here in town, and she does PR for them. Find out what you can, and I'll track her down." She had to stop running one day.

And, he supposed, someday he'd have to stop, too. Go home. Face down his own demon.

But not just yet.

Right now, he had a kid in Memphis who needed him. And once that was over, he wasn't sure what he'd do.

He'd never run from trouble before in his life.

Chapter 3

Julie sat in front of the antique dressing table in a guest room at Steve's parents' home, her shaking hands making it difficult to fasten the antique pearl-and-diamond earrings he'd given her. They were seventy-five years old, originally his great-grandmother's, the match to the delicate pearl necklace with the diamond clasp now draped around her neck. The set was the most elegant jewelry she'd ever owned and probably the most expensive. They looked just like the kind of thing Steve Land's future wife would wear.

Julie stared at her image in the mirror, the smoky white dress that draped softly from shoulder to shoulder, dipping just low enough to show a hint of her breasts, and left her arms bare. Tight at the bodice and the waist, the skirt flared and swirled around her feet as she walked and looked like something a movie star out of the '40s would wear.

She felt like a complete impostor in it, but she'd bought it anyway. Because it, too, seemed like something Steve Land's future wife would wear. Steve had confirmed that himself, telling her it was perfect. She had the image down pat.

It was the woman inside that was the problem.

She heard a light tap on the door and called out, "Come in."

Steve, clad in a crisp black tux, leaned into the opening and said, "Ready?"

"Almost." She dropped the back of the earring one more time and swore.

"Those can be tricky." He walked into the room and bent down to find it. "Let me. I used to do this for my grandmother once her arthritis set in."

Julie folded her hands in her lap and kept her eyes down, feeling him watching her in the mirror as he bent close to fasten the earrings.

"I'm sorry about all this," she began, as his fingers closed around her earlobe.

"Me, too. He's not coming tonight, is he?"

"No. Of course not."

"Good. All done." Steve let go of her and straightened. "So, maybe we can forget about this and have a good time."

She glanced warily at him in the mirror. He'd been uneasy all week. She'd worried he'd call the whole thing off, despite how it would look to cancel at this late date. Of course, he could always break the engagement later. Even once they were married . . . Well, marriages ended all the time.

Julie had just wanted one place in the world where she'd feel safe, and she'd thought it would be with him. Tears flooding her eyes, she asked, "Can we do this, Steve?"

"I'm angry and unsettled by the whole thing, but I still want to marry you."

"I want to marry you, too. I want to be a good wife and make you happy."

"No more surprises?" His hands closed over hers at the words.

"No more surprises," she promised.

It went well.

She smiled and nodded as she made herself walk through the crowd on Steve's arm. He introduced her to everyone, a hint of what she hoped was pride in his voice. The Lands' home was a showplace, a Georgian mansion of white stone, complete with Doric columns that spanned three stories. Tonight it was lit with the fire of hundreds of candles and hundred-year-old chandeliers, all for a party for a girl who was never supposed to amount to anything.

The grandfather clock struck nine, and right on cue, a virtual army of white-gloved waiters appeared, moving silently through the crowd distributing champagne. Steve's parents made the formal announcement, which surprised no one but was a nice touch. She gave Steve a quick kiss, then touched the champagne to her lips. She never did any more than that. Some fears never went away.

Which had her thinking of her mother, first a simple *if only she could see me now,* followed quickly by relief that her mother wasn't there. She'd be drunk by now.

She and Steve made a round of the room, accepting congratulations. When he slipped away to deal with a business associate, Julie walked onto the terrace. The path through the extensive formal garden was discreetly lit and looked inviting. She needed a moment to herself, but hadn't gone five feet when she heard footsteps behind her. Sighing heavily, she braced herself for making nice to one more person.

Then she turned around and there was Zach.

"Julie." He smiled and took her by the arm, steering her deeper into the garden and away from the house.

She stopped on the other side of a six-foot hedge and snatched her arm away. "What are you doing here? If Steve sees you, he'll have a fit."

"Relax. I didn't even come in the front door. I came around the back and slipped onto the terrace. I figured you'd come outside sooner or later."

"Do you really want to ruin this for me?"

"Of course not. I just needed to talk to you, but you didn't give me your phone number. It's not listed in the book. I figured I could come by the store, but Steve works there, too, right? I knew he wouldn't appreciate seeing me. I called a few times, but couldn't catch you in your office, and I didn't want to leave a message, just in case. So here I am."

"Why?" she asked.

"I need to tell you something. One thing. You listen, and then if you still want to turn your back and walk away, I won't bother you again, okay?"

She looked at him warily. "Steve and I are engaged now. It's official."

"Good for you," he said. "One thing? Okay?"

"No." She could feel it all slipping through her fingers, felt everything she'd ever tried to run away from grabbing her, like a dozen unseen hands.

Let me go, she thought. *Finally. Once and for all. Just let me go.*

"Hey, nobody died or anything like that," Zach said, taking her hand between the two of his, his palm rubbing against hers.

"Then don't tell me." If she didn't know, she could forget, couldn't she? She'd managed to forget so many things. "Do you think anyone back there's wasted a moment worrying about whether I'm okay? If disaster struck tomorrow and I needed them, do you really think any of them would give a damn?"

"I don't know, but I think you're better than them."

Oh, God. Trust Zach to find just the thing to say. Surely she was better than them. "I'm done trying to fix their messes. I've been doing that since I was eight or nine years old."

She'd made excuses and apologies by the hundreds. Lied like a pro. When things were good she worried about keeping things running smoothly and her parents sober. When things were bad she tried to figure out how to make them good again. She never got a chance to catch her breath.

"I'm afraid your mother's been working at one of the local banks and some money turned up missing," he blurted out.

"She stole money from a bank?"

"Looks like it." Zach frowned, hands shoved deeply into his pockets.

"Sorry."

"Why? You didn't take the money."

"Force of habit, I guess." She had the drill down. Deny it happened. If she couldn't do that, dismiss it as practically nothing at all. *Never let 'em see you sweat.* "Besides, it doesn't matter. They can't hurt me anymore. That's the beauty of being a woman from St. Louis who has no family at all."

"Look, it's not just your mother. She had help. I'm hearing your stepfather was in on it, too. A friend of mine's the county attorney, and I . . . Well, let's just say I know things I shouldn't. I'm afraid they'll be arrested, and when that happens . . ."

"Oh." She got it now. Julie spotted a stone bench a few

feet away and went to it, sinking down on the cool, hard surface. "What's going to happen to Peter?"

"That's why I had to tell you. I didn't remember any other relatives who were close . . . and stealing from a bank . . . it's no small thing. They don't have much of a criminal record, just the DUIs and the domestic disturbances over the years. But still, getting 'em out of jail is going to be expensive, if they can even make bail. And in the meantime . . . Peter."

"Where will he go?"

"I don't know," Zach said. "Aren't there any other relatives?"

"There must be. On my stepfather's side somewhere."

"It'll be a hard time to pull him away from everyone and everything he knows, even if there were someone who'd take him. And if there are no relatives, he's looking at foster care. Who knows? Maybe he'll get lucky. I know social services would try, but . . ."

"But there aren't a whole lot of foster kids who end up as lucky as you."

"That's for damned sure," he said.

"Sorry." Julie buried her face in her hands for a moment. She'd equated luck with what he'd been through. "I didn't mean . . . I know that luck isn't quite the word."

"No, I was better off. I consider myself very lucky. But Peter . . ."

"What about your parents? Are they still taking in foster kids?"

"From time to time. Unfortunately, they have two little girls right now. Sisters. A sexual abuse case. It was a cousin of theirs not much older than Peter. Social services won't allow them to take a boy of his age into their home at the same time. It would be too hard on the girls."

"Well, there has to be someone. . . ."

She willed herself not to picture her brother's face when he was little and scared. When her parents had done something crazy or the house had been in an uproar. When he was crying and looking to her to make it better somehow. There'd been times when he'd clung to her, like she was the only solid thing in his world. She'd dried his tears and cuddled him close and lied to him, telling him everything would be okay.

And then she'd just left. Years of trying to hold everything together had worn her down. She couldn't do it anymore, and Peter . . .

Well, things had changed between them. By the time she left, he hadn't thought of her as his savior anymore, and she hadn't been capable of saving anyone but herself. Surely there came a time when she was allowed to do that. To save herself.

She looked around the garden, up toward the house, all the twinkling lights and soft voices. She'd made a place for herself here. It was the best place she'd ever known.

"There's nothing I can do, Zach."

"Sure there is," he shot right back. "You can go back there and see him through this."

"No, I can't."

"What's stopping you? That stuffed shirt you think you want to marry?"

"He's not like that," she claimed.

"Sure he is."

"He thinks I don't have any family," she tried.

"Well, tell him you do."

"And then what? Tell him they're embezzlers?" She could imagine how that would go over with Steve and her future in-laws.

"Tell him whatever you have to. But go home and see

that your brother's not alone right now, Julie. Oh, hell, lie if you have to. You're good at that."

She flinched, the words stinging against her bare arms and maybe what was left of her conscience and her heart. She wrapped her arms around her middle, holding herself as best she could and would not let herself cry.

"Shit, I'm sorry," Zach said. "I didn't come here to yell at you, and I know, Julie. I know this is everything you've tried to get away from all these years. I understand that. But Peter . . . Can you really turn your back on him now?"

"I wouldn't be any good for him," she said. What did she know about parenting anyone? She never really had parents. She just happened to live in the same house with two lousy adults who were related to her. "I might as well be a stranger to him. He probably hates me for leaving him all alone with them."

It was one of the things she feared most—that he'd hate her now. And there was Steve, who was already so upset, so suspicious. "He would never forgive me."

"He won't exactly be in a position to turn you away, Julie. He won't have anyone else."

Zach was talking about Peter. She'd been thinking of Steve, and she was ashamed of herself for that. Ashamed of what she'd come from and what she'd become.

"I'm sorry," she said.

He laughed, a humorless sound. "So am I."

They stood for a moment, staring at each other. When she couldn't take the disappointment in his eyes for one more moment, she turned and left, hoping Zach wouldn't follow, that he'd do what he promised and leave.

And then she ran right into Steve.

She stopped short, staring at him. Zach came around the corner, nearly running her over.

The two men glared at each other for a moment. Steve had her arm in a punishing grip, and she was practically sandwiched between the two men once again, as she had been in the restaurant.

"You're going now, I assume?" Steve said.

Zach hesitated, glancing pointedly at her arm. "You gonna be okay?"

"She'll be fine," Steve answered for her.

"I will," she reassured him. Steve would never intentionally hurt her. His hold was loosening already.

"All right," Zach said. "I guess that's it. Bye, Julie."

"Steve," Julie began as Zach disappeared into the night, "I can explain."

"I'm sure you'll try. But not now. We have guests who are leaving, and we are going to go up to the house and pretend nothing happened out here—"

"Nothing did."

"And when everyone's gone," he said, his voice turning harder and even more unforgiving, "you can say whatever you want, and I suppose I'll listen. But right now I don't want to hear a word about it."

"All right."

She pasted on a smile and pretended nothing was wrong, as she'd done so many times in her life. The party turned interminable. Her feet ached. So did her head. She'd have a bruise on her forearm, she feared, which wasn't a big deal. She doubted he was even aware of having done it, and it wasn't like she'd never had a bruise before. It had just been a while, and she'd forgotten how it felt. The way you carried the bruise around with you, seeing it long after the argument was over. The way it made you remember, when you wanted to forget. The way it made it harder to pretend, even with all the little lies.

Finally, the last of the guests were gone, the servants

moving silently through the house, cleaning up. She and Steve said good-bye to his parents, his mother watching them closely, obviously sensing something was wrong.

He walked down the front steps and onto the driveway beside her, opened the passenger-side door for her and, once she'd climbed in, shut it behind her, a display of courtesy she found ridiculous in the moment.

She sat there in the plush leather seat and hung her head, wondering how a civilized man like Steve handled disagreements. She was used to yelling, to tears, hysterics or throwing things, to someone reaching for alcohol to deaden the pain.

This kind of control scared her a bit. She wasn't sure what lurked beneath it. She and Steve had seldom disagreed about anything.

He climbed into the car and started the engine, not saying a word as he drove through the night. It took a scant fifteen minutes to reach her apartment. He parked by her building and cut the engine, then eased his seat back as far as it would go and turned to her.

"I'm sorry," she began.

"For what?" He stared straight ahead into the night.

"Everything." Every little thing. Every big one. All of it.

"You said you wouldn't see him."

"I didn't mean to. I mean, I didn't think I would. I just walked out into the garden and there he was."

"Waiting for you, right?"

"Yes," she admitted. "But it's really not what you think, Steve."

He laughed at that. "It never is, according to you. What exactly is it?"

"He just needed to tell me something."

"And he had to do that at our engagement party? He

had to hide in the garden, where no one would see you, just so he could talk to you at our party?"

"I didn't even give him my phone number, Steve. It's unlisted. He said he thought about coming by the store, but he knew that would upset you—"

"So he thought sneaking around in the dark at our party would be better?"

"He just wanted to talk to me," she repeated. "Something happened. To someone I used to know. And Zach thought I should know. That's all."

"Something?" he repeated. "To someone you can't tell me about?"

"Does it really matter? It's nothing to do with us. It's all in the past—"

"Right now it's very much in the present. It's our engagement party. I found you hiding in the dark with your hands all over another man."

"No. Just talking. That was it."

"You looked pretty close to be just talking."

"I . . ." She had to think. What had they done that he could have possibly misconstrued in this way? "He held my hand for a minute. I was upset. And he started to walk away, and I stopped him by putting my hand on his arm. That was it. Steve, I've told you. It's not at all what you think."

"Then what the hell is it?"

"Nothing. Those people . . . They're nothing to me. I haven't been back there in eight years, and I'm not going. Nothing could drag me back to Ohio again—"

"Ohio?" He zeroed in on that. "What the hell is in Ohio, Julie?"

She gaped back at him. This was beneath a liar of her caliber.

"I don't . . ." What could she say? No little lies sprang to mind.

"Wait a minute. Your friend Zach . . . He lives in Ohio now, right?"

Julie was practically struck dumb. It was the Zach curse. He seemed to short-circuit that instinctive skill she had at evasion and deception. All her wires got crossed, and it took a while before they got straightened out again. She should just hide after talking to him and give herself time to get back to normal.

"But he used to live in St. Louis, right?" Steve kept going, kept pushing.

Give it up, Julie.

Zach had said that to her so many times.

What was the use in fighting it now?

"He's never lived in St. Louis," Julie admitted. "And neither have I."

Steve laughed again. So many people were laughing tonight, who were clearly not amused in any way.

"I just . . . It's just a place where I lived. Not St. Louis. Ohio. That's where I knew Zach and his family. But it's just a place, Steve. I didn't want to have any ties to that place anymore, and I liked saying I was from somewhere else."

It had been false security, at best, but she'd take any sense of security she could find.

"I'm sorry," she said.

Steve nodded. "Me, too."

"Can I . . . Would you like to . . ."

"Get out of the car, Julie."

"But—"

"What I'd like is for you to get out of the car. Now."

*   *   *

He hadn't asked for his ring back. She thought about that later as she lay in bed, curled up into a miserable ball. Of course, he might ask tomorrow. Or the next day. Or the next. Any day at all. She didn't think he was going to give her a chance to explain, and even if he did, she hadn't figured out anything she could say.

The phone rang shortly after one o'clock. Startled, she nearly jumped off the bed, then took a breath and picked it up. "Steve?"

"No," a deep, soothing, familiar voice said. "Zach."

"Oh. Hi. I . . . I didn't think you had my number."

"I didn't, but I called in a favor from a guy I met on the local police force while I was looking into the Tony Williams case. Told him I was worried about a friend and needed to get in touch with her."

"Oh," she said again.

"Guess I should have done that in the first place, huh?"

"It's not your fault." All he'd done was try to help her, time after time.

"You okay?"

"Yes," she said, then ruined it by starting to cry.

"He didn't hurt you?"

"No." But she was crying so hard, she had trouble making him believe her.

"Julie, I'm going to come over there, okay?"

"No." That was the last thing she needed. Okay, maybe she would like it. He'd hold her while she cried, and she wouldn't be so alone. He'd done that before, when things were really bad. There was no place she knew of that felt as safe as Zach's arms. But she couldn't allow herself that comfort tonight. "With my luck, Steve would find you here, and all hell would break loose."

"Okay. If you're sure. But promise me he didn't hurt you."

"I promise. He didn't. He wouldn't. He's not like that, Zach."

"Okay. Sorry I messed things up for you."

"You didn't. I did that all on my own."

"Julie, you can't go on like this. You see that, don't you?"

"I don't know what else to do."

"Tell him the truth, and go home. Grace is there. She'll help you. Emma's there. My parents are there. I'm there every now and then, and all you ever have to do is call me, and I'll help you."

Which only made her cry harder.

"It doesn't have to be like this for you," he said. "You're better than this. Stronger. Tell the guy the truth, and if he can't handle it, to hell with him."

"He's the best thing that's ever happened to me," she claimed.

"Surely not. Surely there's something better for you than this."

If there was, she didn't think she'd ever find it. This was it, the mess she'd made of her life. No great surprise there. Deep inside, she'd always known that nothing good would ever last for her.

"Julie, please," Zach said. "Come clean about it all and go home."

She'd never do either one of those things, she decided as she hung up the phone.

Chapter 4

It was a tense two weeks.

A problem cropped up with one of the company stores in Birmingham. Steve decided to go himself. Julie got a few curious looks around the office. Gossip had it that either she and Steve had a fight or the problem in Birmingham was more serious than he'd let on.

She kept her head down and the makeup heavier than usual, to try to hide the dark circles under her eyes. There was a knot in her stomach and a permanent ache in her head. She jumped practically every time the phone rang, thinking it might be Steve finally ready to talk.

When her assistant buzzed her one afternoon and said there was someone on the line claiming to be an old friend, Julie braced herself, expecting Zach, or maybe her mother. If her mother did get arrested and managed to track Julie down, she would have called to try to get Julie to bail her out.

But the voice on the phone was Grace's.

"Hi, stranger," she said. "I couldn't believe it when Zach told me he'd found you. I want to hear everything that's going on with you. Zach said you're engaged?"

"Yes. To my boss." It was such a cliché. *Picked up the boss.* But she had.

She told Grace all about Steve, all those things she always said about him. Solid. Dependable. Steady. The most even-tempered man on earth.

"But . . . you love him, right? You said everything but that."

"I do," she said with only the slightest hesitation. "What about you? I meant to ask Zach, but we got to talking about other things—"

"About your parents?" Grace said gently. "I'm so sorry about that."

Julie shrugged. *Dismiss. Deny. Go on.* She had the drill down pat. "Par for the course with them. I wouldn't expect anything different, not at this late date."

She supposed in a normal conversation the next question should be whether they'd been arrested, but she really didn't want to know. Plus there were other things to take care of.

"Grace, I'm so sorry about the way I left and for not ever calling or writing. I . . . It's no excuse, and God knows you deserved better. You were always so nice to me. I just didn't know what else to do. One day I decided I couldn't stay another minute, and I left. But I should have at least said good-bye."

"I missed you," Grace said. "I thought about you so many times, wondering what happened to you and hoping you were okay."

"I am," Julie claimed. "I'm just fine. But tell me about you."

Grace said she'd been something of a perennial student, earning a master's in fine art in the states and then studying for years in Europe. Painting, sculpture, architecture, they all interested her. She'd come back to Ohio a few months ago and decided she wated to know more about her mother's work—stained glass.

"I'm glad you're so happy," Julie said. "And that things are going so well."

"I'm happy for you, too. And I'm afraid I have to go in just a minute. But I did want to ask one more thing. A favor."

"Anything," Julie said.

"Go see my big brother, okay?"

Julie took a breath, thinking, *Anything but that.* But how could she say no? Besides, there was something about the way Grace asked . . .

"Something's wrong, isn't it?"

"I just haven't been able to get him to talk to me lately. He calls when I swear he knows I'm not here and leaves messages about being busy and promising to get back to me later. And then he doesn't. None of us have been able to get him on the phone for a real conversation in weeks. I mean, he gets this way in trial sometimes, but . . . this is different."

"What's different?"

"The last six months have been tough. His . . . Well, our biological father got out of jail, and it's been . . ." Grace took a breath. "It's something I never really thought I'd have to deal with. I guess I should have known I would, at some point. But it kind of sneaked up on us all, and it's been hard on Zach."

"Oh." As Zach had reminded her that first night in the restaurant, he certainly hadn't had a perfect life. For so long it had just looked like he did. "I'm sorry. I didn't know."

"Oh, no way you would have, unless Zach told you, and I don't think he talks about it with anyone."

"He's always seemed so together, so invincible," Julie said. "I forget sometimes that he's human like the rest of us."

"Me, too. We went to see him . . . *That man.* I'll never call him my father. He wanted to see us, and we didn't want to go, but after a while it seemed like it would be better just to do it and make it clear that we didn't care what he had to say."

"What happened?"

"Not much, at least not that I saw. But Zach was alone with him for a few minutes, and when he came out he was so upset. He claimed it was all over, that that man would never bother us again, but . . . he just hasn't been himself ever since. He's avoiding our calls, and he won't come home. Which is why I'm asking you to go see him for me."

"Sure."

"Thanks, Julie. So . . . I guess I'll see you soon? I mean, with what's going on with your parents and everything?"

"I . . . Well . . ." Out of excuses and ashamed of wanting to make them, she buzzed her assistant, two short beeps, the signal to interrupt her, to save her, and sure enough, Maggie buzzed her right back. "Grace, I'm sorry. That's my secretary, and I really have to go. But I'll call you after I talk to Zach."

And with that, she escaped.

"Anything I can do?" her secretary asked through the intercom.

"No, thanks, Maggie. That's all I needed."

She sat there for a minute, thinking about Zach seeing a father who'd been in prison since Zach was just a little boy. How would that feel to him? She thought of what he might remember of the time he'd spent living in the same house with that man, what it would take to shake someone like the man Zach was today. She'd never even seen him break a sweat.

Julie glanced at the clock on her desk. It was almost

eleven. Not indecently early for lunch, and court had to break at some point, didn't it?

Five minutes in the courtroom, Julie told herself. She'd be done. Life could get back to normal. Steve would be back. She'd explain somehow. They'd get married, and Zach would leave town. Everything would be fine.

The courthouse was packed. She slipped into a seat in the back corner in time to catch the last ten minutes of Zach's closing argument.

He was calm, sincere, persuasive, painting a picture of a boy who'd never had a break in his whole life, one who'd been abused and neglected and tormented in ways that would make most people sick to even hear about them.

What would a child do under those circumstances? When he was pushed one step too far and there seemed to be no hope of escape, no way out?

She looked at Tony Williams sitting in a chair that seemed too big for him, wearing an ill fitting suit that swallowed his small frame, shoulders hunched forward, gaze glued to the surface of the polished table in front of him.

He looked like a little boy.

Sad, angry, possibly dangerous, and lost. Definitely lost.

She hadn't expected to get so caught up in his dilemma, but she had tears in her eyes by the time Zach was done.

The judge announced a break for lunch. The crowd got to its feet and began to drift out. Julie waited in the back of the room until Zach was done with his client and a few reporters, until the two of them were the only ones in the room.

Zach sat back down, one arm folded across his chest, the other going up so that his hand covered half his face, as if he couldn't bear to see, and he looked oddly vulnerable sitting there. He was tired, too. She could see it in every line in his body, see the tension and what looked like pain.

Obviously Grace was right to be worried.

Julie slowly rose from her seat and walked toward the aisle. She bumped her knee on one of the last seats in the row, and at the noise Zach turned around, startled and obviously not happy to find that he wasn't alone.

"Hi," Julie said, standing where she was, about ten feet away from him.

He got to his feet but didn't come any closer. "What are you doing here?"

She shrugged and played dumb, thinking she'd slowly get around to what his sister told her. "Bad day, huh?"

"Bad week. Did you hear any of the closing arguments?"

"About ten minutes of yours. You did well, had at least two of the jury members in tears."

"I'm afraid that won't be enough if we're going to win this thing. One or two people aren't going to be able to hold out against all the others," he said, giving her a look that said he obviously thought it was lost.

She tried to imagine Zach failing and feeling the way she did sometimes, but she just couldn't do it, tried to see him as a boy who grew up knowing his father was in prison, and a man with that father walking around on the streets free, seeing him face-to-face one day.

As Zach had talked about Tony Williams's life, she'd wondered if the emotion in his voice had come, not from listening to Tony talk about his childhood, but from Zach's memories of his own. If that's where the passion and the drive came from that made him so good at defending people like Tony Williams.

"You look tired," she said. And strung tight as a piano wire.

"Like you said, bad day."

He probably had a lot of those. How could he not, doing a job like this? She wondered who took care of him when he wasn't sleeping or eating the way he should. Who did he talk to late at night, when the world seemed like a big bad place and he just wasn't sure if he could make it through another day?

He must feel like that. Sometimes she thought she was the only one, but she saw the fallacy in that. And she was worried about him, too.

"Have you had lunch?" she asked.

"There's a canteen downstairs. I'll grab a sandwich."

"From a machine?" She made a face.

"Wouldn't be the first time," he said, turning to the stack of papers in front of him and trying to bring some order to them.

"But I thought you were done. That was your closing argument, right?"

"The judge still has to charge the jury."

"Charge the jury?" she asked, daring to come closer finally.

"We get to tell the judge what we want him to say about the points of law as they apply to this case." He stuffed papers in his briefcase. "What it takes to find Tony guilty. What applies to bring a finding of not guilty. But that won't take long. The jury will probably start deliberating this afternoon."

"And then you can rest?" she asked.

He shook his head. "Not while the jury's out."

"What do you do?" she asked. "While a jury's out?"

"Pace," he said, closing the briefcase and getting to his feet. "Run. Lift weights. Hit a punching bag, if I can find one. Go over my notes from the trial. Things I wish I'd done better. Things I might have tried but didn't. Things I might use on appeal, if it comes to that."

"You have to rest sometimes, Zach."

"Not in trial," he said. "Why are you here? Another fight with Stevie Boy?"

"No. He's out of town."

Zach nodded. "So you thought it was safe to see me, since he's gone?"

"No . . . Well . . . I guess. I really wasn't thinking about him. I was thinking you need a keeper almost as much as I do." She walked over to him and slipped her hand through his arm. "Come on. Let's get out of here have a decent lunch, at least. We'll let you breathe some air that doesn't come from a courtroom or your hotel room. Have you seen anyplace else since you've been here?"

He shrugged. "The jail?"

"Doesn't count."

He stared at her. "You still didn't tell me why you're here."

"I was worried about you." She stayed by his side, her arm linked with his.

"Me?" He found the energy to summon a grin at that. He really was a gorgeous man, even dead tired and drained.

"What? No one's allowed to worry about you?"

"I'm fine, Julie," he insisted.

Which was odd, because had she been in his position, exhausted and dreading the next minute, she would have smiled and lied through her teeth. Just like that.

She didn't expect anyone to take care of her, didn't let herself lean on anyone. Not really. She'd tried with Steve, but she'd never really shown him the deepest, darkest parts of herself. She wondered now if Zach did the same thing. If maybe they had this one thing in common.

"Humor me," she said. "I came all the way down here to see you. Come and have lunch with me."

"I can't. Really. I have to be ready for this afternoon."

"Well, how about you sit here and work, and I'll go get something. Something much better than vending-machine sandwiches, and we can sit outside and eat. There's a park half a block away. Great shade, lots of benches. It won't take fifteen minutes."

"Julie, really—"

"Let me do this one thing for you." Because she hadn't ever before, not that she could remember, not in all the time she'd known him.

"Okay. Fifteen minutes. That's it."

"I'll be right back. Any requests?"

"I'll eat anything," he claimed.

Julie smiled for what felt like the first time in a month. It wasn't much, but at least she could feed the man.

She was back too quickly, Zach claimed, and she practically had to drag him out of the courtroom and across the street.

"See." She pointed to an elm. "It's called a tree. See how green it is? And that blue stuff up there? That's the sky. Those puffy things—aren't those nice?—they're clouds."

"I think I have some vague memory of them," he said as they settled themselves on a bench and she presented him with two huge roast-beef sandwiches and some potato salad. "Thanks. How are things going with Steve?"

He said his name like he despised the man, which puzzled Julie. How could anyone find anything objectionable about Steve? He got along with everyone.

"They're not," she admitted. "We argued after the party, then hardly spoke until he left for Birmingham, and he hasn't come back yet."

"Sorry. I shouldn't have come there that night."

"It's not your fault. I made this mess all by myself."

"What are you going to do?"

"I don't know. Just try to make it through the day, I guess. Do you ever have times like that? When it's all you can do to make it through one more day?"

"Yeah, I do."

"That's the sum total of my plan right now."

"So you didn't come down here to ask me about your parents or Peter?"

"No." She'd picked up her own sandwich, turkey and avocado on a French roll, but now she put it back down without taking a bite. "Could we not argue about this, Zach? I know you think I'm . . . Well, I know what you think, and I'm sorry."

"For what?"

Disappointing him, mostly. The man had been like a conscience to her, the measure of what was right and wrong, and she knew he thought she was dead-wrong on this. She'd been waiting ever since the night of her engagement party for the phone call telling her that her parents were in jail, asking her to come take Peter. So far, the call hadn't come.

"It hasn't happened yet, has it?" she asked finally. "They haven't been arrested?"

"Not yet," he said.

But clearly it was coming.

She picked up her sandwich and ate, any pleasure there might have been in the day gone. He ate, too, and they didn't say a word for the longest time. Until he got up to throw the food containers away and then stood there, hands in his pockets, staring down at her.

"I have to get back," he said. "Want to give it one more try? Tell me why you're really here?"

Julie could read between the lines. He thought she wanted him to talk her into going home. He'd done that so many times—convinced her to do the right thing. It seemed he'd never give up on her, never lose hope that maybe someday she'd be a different person, a better person.

She shook her head. It just wasn't going to happen. "I came because you need to call your sister."

He frowned. "Grace?"

Julie nodded. "She told me about your father getting out of prison."

"He's not my father," Zach shot back, all the tension she'd seen in him before in the courtroom back with vengeance.

"I know. Sorry."

"No." He waved off her apology. "I'm sorry. I know you know who he is. I just . . ."

He wasn't handling it well. *Wow.* She didn't think she'd ever seen Zach *not* handle something well.

"Is he bothering you?" Julie asked.

"Everything about that man bothers me," Zach said.

Of course it would. The man had beaten his mother to death. Zach had lived in that house. The things he must have seen and heard . . . Julie knew about yelling and screaming, about what happened when people drank. Her stepfather had slapped her mother around, and sometimes Julie, too, but he hadn't . . . She was thinking that he hadn't really hurt them. But the truth was it had hurt.

Still, it seemed the things that had gone on in Zach's home when he was a little boy were much worse. She'd just never seen the scars before. Or maybe she hadn't been looking. She'd seen the facade of perfection that shined around him and taken that at face value, was ashamed now of not seeing it for what it was.

"So, that was it?" he asked. "Grace sent you?"

"Yes. Is there anything I can do for you? Now?"

He looked like he simply didn't understand the question. It would have been funny, if it hadn't been so sad. No one could be that strong all the time.

"I'll be fine," he claimed, again reminding her of herself.

"Okay." But no matter what he said, she was going to worry. "I'll tell Grace you'll call. This'll be over soon, and you'll be going home, right?"

"I don't know," he said. "We're down one attorney in the office, and I'm not sure what kind of juggling might have been done to the schedule."

"You need to go home, Zach." To the people who loved him and would take care of him. If she had a place like that to go to, she'd be there in a heartbeat.

"We'll see," he said.

"Call Grace." She frowned. "And if you need anything, I'm right here."

"What about Steve?"

"He'll just have to handle it." If he was here and speaking to her.

She had a hard time sleeping that night, finally dropping off around three A.M., slept right through the alarm, and got to the office late to find that Steve was due back that day.

It was time, even if she still didn't know what to say to him.

Somehow, she made it through the day. Steve had been in the building since two. She knew because the receptionist told her when she came back from lunch. But he hadn't come to see her yet.

She nervously drummed her fingers on her desk and waited.

Oddly, she wasn't thinking about what little lies she might tell him. Much as she'd always tried to control everything, she'd never really been able to. Bad things still happened, and she was tired of trying to manage everything. It just didn't work.

Six o'clock came and went. Still no Steve. Finally, at six-twenty, she tried his secretary, only to find he was stuck in a meeting that ran late.

"Could you tell him I'll be at home, please?" she asked.

"Certainly. I know he's anxious to see you."

Julie wasn't so sure about that.

She went home, ate a carton of yogurt and a banana, then stared at the clock some more. It was starting to rain. She heard thunder in the distance, shivered a bit as the temperature dropped.

Maybe he wasn't coming. Maybe he really was done with her. What would she do then? Learn to live without him, she supposed. It wouldn't be the first time she'd been all alone.

The phone finally rang shortly after nine. She was sitting in front of the TV, half watching a sitcom that just wasn't funny. She jumped as the phone rang, her heart pounding, then made herself pick it up and say, "Hello."

"Julie, it's me. It's taking me longer than I thought to get out of the office."

"All right." He was late. No big deal. Not like lying to the person he was supposed to marry.

"I'm afraid I'm still not done here."

"That's fine." She could wait to hear her fate. Another sleepless night didn't sound so bad at the moment.

"I guess I'm still trying to decide what it is I want to say to you."

"Well . . . I can understand that." My how tentative they'd become with each other.

"I may come by later tonight. I'm not sure."

"Whatever you want to do." She'd sit here, waiting, thinking, beating herself up, things like that.

"I've missed you," he said.

"I've missed you, too."

And then he was gone.

She sat there, the TV droning on in the background. Before she knew it, the local news was on. Was it really that late? Then Zach's face appeared on the screen.

Julie hit the volume button. Tony Williams had been convicted of murder.

Just the look on Zach's face was enough to bring tears to her eyes. Sometimes life was just too hard, and those were lousy times to be alone.

She knew. She'd been there herself.

She looked at the clock. Eleven-ten.

She didn't want him to be alone, not after the way he'd looked the day before. She didn't know what she'd say to him. But she couldn't leave him all alone.

Chapter 5

Fifteen minutes later, she knocked softly on his door.

"Go away," he called out.

"Zach? It's me."

"Not tonight, Julie. I'm not fit company for anyone. Go."

"I can't," she said. "I won't. Let me in."

He sounded just a little crazy, and there was a slight slur to his words. She felt a shiver of unease work its way up her back. He wouldn't be drunk, would he?

"Zach, please, just let me in. Let me know you're okay."

She banged on the door, deciding it felt pretty good to hit something now. He said he hit a punching bag if he could find one, when things got bad. She'd tell him to try the door next time.

Which made her think about her stepfather and Zach's birth father. They drank and they hit. Did it feel this good to them?

Zach flung open the door just as someone opened the one next door and scowled at them both. "Jesus, Julie, what are you doing?"

"Getting you to open the door," she said defiantly,

cradling one of her fists in her hand. It hurt now. But then everything did eventually, didn't it?

She pushed him aside and walked in. He'd knocked over the end table in the far corner and all the papers on it. There was a bar glass, half full of an amber-colored liquid, on the coffee table and a bottle beside it.

So he had decided to have a drink. Or two or three or five.

She turned back to look at him. His hair was mussed, like he'd run his hands through it too many times. He'd discarded his suit jacket. His feet were bare, tie gone, shirt unbuttoned, as if he'd given some thought to undressing and falling into bed. There were lines she'd never seen before in his face, at the corners of his eyes and his mouth, across his brow. His mouth stretched into a bleak line, and he wouldn't look at her.

"Grace send you here?" he asked.

"No. I was watching the news. . . . Zach, I'm so sorry."

"Me, too. Shitload of good it does Tony Williams."

"But . . . you can appeal, right?"

"Yeah." He laughed. "Maybe we could get it overturned. After he's sat in jail for ten or fifteen years. I'm just praying I made some kind of colossal mistake that gives us grounds. Or that somebody did, and I can find it."

"I'm sure you did everything you could," she said.

He finally looked at her. Defiantly. Angrily. "Well, it just wasn't good enough, now was it?"

"Well, sometimes, no matter what you do, it just isn't enough." She certainly knew that from her own miserable life.

He sighed and walked over to the table where he'd left his drink. His steps weren't quite steady and the words were definitely slurred. She'd never seen him drunk before. He picked up the glass and took a long draw on the liquor, then stood there staring at it in his hand.

"I know you don't think that's going to help," she said.

He gave her a disgusted look, then flung the glass against the opposite wall. She flinched at the sound as it shattered into pieces and at the smell of the booze.

He swiped a hand through his hair, took a deep, deep breath, and when he faced her once again, said, "I really think you should go."

"I can't do that. You . . . You've helped me so many times. I couldn't even count them all, and I've never done anything for you."

"Well, this isn't the time to start," he claimed.

"It's exactly the time."

She took a few tentative steps toward him. He put his back to her, his head falling forward, back bowed, as if he could hardly stay upright, the pain was so staggering.

She walked up to him and put her hand on his shoulder.

He stiffened at her touch and warned, "Stevie isn't going to like this. He'll find out you were here again and blow his top."

"I'll probably tell him," she said, rubbing his back a little with that one hand, thinking what she really needed to do was put her arms around him and hang on. She'd been hurt before, and she'd always wished for someone to hang on to. "I'll get my dose of Zach-truth-serum and . . . Did I ever tell you about that?"

"No," he said softly.

"You have the oddest effect on me. I can't seem to lie to you, no matter how hard I try. And the effect seems to linger after you're gone. My whole mess started that first night when I came here to talk to you. Steve had called before I got home, and what did I have to do? Tell him I was in the shower. That would have been it. No problem. I would have married him, and everything would have been fine."

"You're lying to yourself now, Julie."

She nodded, tears starting to fall for him and for her. "I guess I am."

She slid closer, resting her head against his back, encircling his waist with her arms, hanging on tightly to him. He was trembling and seemed every bit as miserable as she was.

"Sometimes it all just seems too hard, you know?"

"Yeah, I know," he agreed.

"Sometimes it seems like nothing will ever get any easier or any better. I know what it's like to feel that way, Zach. I'm thinking you probably don't have a lot of experience with those kinds of feelings, but . . . You can keep going, you know? Things are bound to get better eventually."

"They won't for Tony," he said.

"You don't know that. Anything could happen—"

Zach whirled around to face her, and she backed away from him, giving him some room, waiting to see what he'd do next.

"Oh, hell," he said finally, sitting down a bit unsteadily on the coffee table.

She sat across from him on the sofa, her knees pinned in by his. He drummed his fingers on the surface of the table for the longest time, playing a little percussion solo, his agitation painful to watch.

She finally took her hands in his to still them, liking having that connection to him, hoping to soothe him just a bit. "Tell me," she said. "Anything at all, and I'll listen."

"Nothing good has ever happened to Tony Williams," he said bitterly. "He lived a shitty life to this point, and now it's going to get worse. Day in, day out, he'll be with people who make his father look like a grade-school bully. He'll get even more scared, and then he'll get angry, and before long, he'll wish for the day they finally execute him. And there's probably nothing I can do to save him from that."

"Then you'll go and save someone else," she said, holding on to his hands when he would have pulled away. "I know it's not what you want to hear. I could see that he means a lot to you. But I know you did all you could. I bet tomorrow won't be quite as horrible as today. There are lots of people you can save. So much good that you do."

"It doesn't seem like enough," he said, shaking his head.

"I know. Sometimes nothing we do is enough, no matter how hard we try."

And some people didn't even try. Like her. Some people just walked away. It had all seemed so easy, so smart, before Zach came back. Maybe that's what she could give him. She could teach him to walk away. Maybe this job was just too hard and he couldn't do it anymore. Not if it did this to him every time he lost.

But he wouldn't give it up. He wasn't the kind to walk away from anything.

Suddenly she was so ashamed. She had no idea what she was doing here. She went to stand up at the same time Zach did. But the table was low to the floor and he was so tall. His knees bumped into hers. He tried to step around her and misjudged the placement of his foot, stepping on her toe instead.

"Ow."

"Sorry." He pulled up his foot, and then, off balance, slid around, fell to the floor, and sat there.

She waited for him to try to kick her out again, but he didn't, so she sat down on the table where he'd been a moment ago. He leaned against her side, slipped his hand along the back of her calf, and pressed his temple to her knee.

Oh, Zach. She put her hand over the side of his face, then bent her head until it lay against the top of his.

"I know I'm the last person who should ever be telling anyone how to deal with his problems, but . . . I'm the only one here. So I guess you're stuck with me."

"There's nothing you can do, Julie. Nothing anyone can do."

"Can I just stay here? Please? So you're not alone?"

"I've been alone before," he said bleakly.

"Like this?"

He took a breath. "I'm not sure if I've ever been in a place like this before."

"Which is a good reason not to go through it alone." She lifted her head and stroked a hand through his hair and down his neck, rubbed his shoulders. It was the oddest of embraces and the most intimate. She'd never felt this close to him, maybe to anyone. She'd never wanted more to take away someone else's pain.

"I haven't had that much to drink," he said finally.

She kept stroking his hair. "Okay."

"Sorry about the glass."

"It's all right."

"No, it's not. It scared you, and I'm sorry. With your family history, I know the last thing you want to deal with is a short-tempered drunk."

"You're not either of those things," she said.

"Maybe not now, but someday . . . who's to say? I've

got the genes of an alcoholic and murderer running through my veins. Oh, and a battered woman. Can't forget her. A woman who fell in love with a man like that and then let him use her like a punching bag for years, and then turn to their kids."

"He hit you?" Julie asked.

"No. Given the chance, I'm sure he would have. But he got Emma once, and my mother finally decided to leave him before it happened again."

"You remember that?"

"Yeah." He laughed bitterly as he finally raised his head. "My earliest memory. A loud, out-of-control drunk hurting my sister."

"You're nothing like him," Julie said.

"I kind of look like him tonight, don't I? Lose a case, drown my sorrows in a bottle, and then throw something across the room. Who knows what'll be next. Break some*one* instead of some*thing.*"

"You'd never hurt anyone," she said.

"Be nice to think I wouldn't."

"I know you wouldn't," she insisted.

He didn't say anything, just looked away.

"Zach, is that what this is all about? Him being out?"

"I hate having him out walking around. I wish I could erase every memory of him, every speck of his blood, his genes, everything. I try. And then I get a client like Tony."

"What does Tony Williams have to do with your father?"

Zach shifted on the floor until his back was against the sofa. He lay his head back against the cushion and stared up at the ceiling.

"Not my father. Me. Tony and I started out just alike. Drunken, abusive fathers, battered women for mothers.

The only difference between the two of us is that my mother managed to get me out of there, and I got lucky as hell with my next set of parents. The real ones. My life was completely different from Tony's from that point on. But what if my birth mother had never gotten me and Emma and Grace out of that house? What do you think would have happened?"

"I don't know," she said. "There's no way you could know."

"But it's not that hard to imagine, is it? Emma wouldn't have let him hurt me, not if there had been anything she could do to stop it. I wouldn't have let him hurt Emma or Grace, and if I could have gotten my hands on a loaded gun . . . who's to say who'd be in that cell convicted of murder?"

"You're not Tony Williams," she insisted.

"But I could have been. So easily, I could be right where he is today."

Oh. So there was some odd sense of guilt and obligation at work here. A debt he thought he had to repay for the blessings life had bestowed upon him. He thought he'd just defaulted on a major payment.

She could explain to him the flaws in that logic — that he no more deserved the terrible days of his early childhood than he should have to pay for the good days that followed. That he hadn't been rescued from that life only to leave Tony sentenced to it. She didn't know how the world worked, but not like that. He'd just gotten lucky, she supposed, except she'd always thought he deserved it, that he deserved the very best, because he was such a good person.

How could she explain that to him?

"You're just one person," she said. "You can't save everyone. I'm sorry it ended up like this for Tony. I guess you'll just have to feel lousy about it, and tomorrow you'll get up and start all over again, trying to help someone else. Don't you win more than you lose, Zach?"

"I don't keep score. They're not scores. They're kids. Kids' lives."

"I know, but . . . you do all you can. You can't ask any more than that of yourself." But the look he gave her said that he could and he did.

His lips were trembling, and there was a muscle twitching at the corner of his mouth as he fought for control. He blinked once, then again, and then his eyes filled with tears.

He was coming completely undone, right there in front of her.

A big, strong man falling apart.

She saw the muscles bunch in his shoulders, saw him choke back a breath, and then his brows settled into a flat, unhappy line.

"It's all right, Zach." She slid to the floor beside him, facing him, wrapping her arms around him tightly, and she was crying, too, probably even before he was.

Sometimes hope was just too far away, so that you simply couldn't see anything but the bad. She'd cried like this, too. The only difference was, she usually didn't have anyone to hold her.

So she did for him what no one had done for her. She hung on tight, trying to be his anchor in the middle of sheer misery. To hold him so he knew he wouldn't simply dissolve away into the agony of his emotions. Because sometimes it felt like the pain was so great it might literally consume her. She wouldn't let that happen to him.

Julie felt a fierce trembling rake through his body. He shuddered violently, all control gone.

"Don't let go," he said.

"I won't," she promised.

His arms clasped her around her waist, pulling her body flush against his, so that she was up on her knees, his face buried in her neck, his head cradled in her hands.

Oh, Zach.

She wiped her tears away with the back of her hand and then pressed the side of her face against his forehead, nuzzling the tip of her nose against his temple, finding dark, slightly curling hair that smelled so good. He always smelled so good, and his body was so warm to the touch. She noticed it every time she got close enough for a hug.

He held on tighter, his arms like steel bands wound tightly around her waist. Her ribs were crushed against his, her breasts, her hair falling around them. She felt him shudder once more, pushing his face against her neck.

"It's all right. I'm right here. I won't let you go."

His shoulders were heaving, his whole body, with every breath. It didn't seem to be slowing at all, this storm raking through him.

This was what happened when you cared too much. It ended badly, and you hurt like hell.

She didn't want anything to ever hurt him. She wanted him to have a perfect life, that illusion she'd believed for so long. If anyone deserved it, it was Zach.

She ran her hands up and down his back, pulling at the tension here and there, trying to work out the knots. His breathing finally slowed. He pressed his wet cheek against her neck and her collarbone for a moment, finally eased away, wet, weary eyes finding hers.

"Sorry," he said, staring at her.

His hand came out, brushing the moisture from her cheeks, the side of her jaw, his tears from her neck, her collarbone. Still, he looked like he was ready to shatter completely.

"It's all right," she said.

But it wasn't. He shuddered once more, took a gulping breath, and then hung his head. She pulled him back to her, nestled his head into that hollow below her chin at her neck. His breath was warm against the top of her breasts, and his cheeks were wet. She held him with both her hands against his head, and after a minute he lifted her off the floor to tuck her against him on his lap and held on tight, lashing them together like they were facing yet another brewing storm.

This is what it felt like, she supposed, when the world just came apart, even though people tried as hard as they could to hold it together.

"Don't leave me," he said in a harsh whisper she scarcely recognized. "Not yet."

"I won't. I promise."

She kissed his temple and then his cheekbone, wanting nothing more than to soothe him. His hands at her back were trembling, but they were soothing, as well, working their way up and down her back, as if she were in need of comfort, too. His breath was warm, hot even, and her thin blouse was damp with his tears, and she became aware of her body in a way . . .

She couldn't help it. It was a completely involuntary reaction, completely inappropriate. But she felt her nipple bunch up and tighten as he exhaled, his breath rushing across that damp spot.

She ignored it, thinking that he wasn't likely to notice at all, not in the shape he was in. A woman couldn't help what her body did in such close proximity to a man. It was nothing.

But it felt good. The side of his face was pressed against her chest, and all that warm air coming out of his lungs was funneling down her cleavage.

She must be hard up when a man breathing could do this to her.

Much as she tried to block the sensation, it was there. Her breasts felt heavy and swollen. It had been a long time since morning, since he'd shaved, and the stubble on his jaw was slightly abrasive against her sensitive skin, but in a nice way, in a way that makes a woman know a man is touching her.

He'd gotten very quiet, very still. The hands at her back were no longer moving. Hers had stilled, too. He still held her, but something had changed.

"Julie?" he whispered.

"Yes?"

She had no idea what he intended. Honestly, no idea. She just opened her mouth to answer him, and he lifted his head and pressed his mouth to hers.

She was so shocked she just sat there with her mouth open and let him do what he wanted. Which was to taste her in the most desperate way, a help-me-I'm-lost-and-about-to-drown kind of kiss, as needy as any she'd ever felt.

No one had ever really needed her. Not like this.

His mouth latched on to hers, and then he was devouring her, pushing deep down inside of her, with just a kiss. And it went on and on, like he had to know everything there was to know about her, just from this kiss.

She was still reeling from the insistence of his mouth when she realized his hands were on her breasts. She'd been aching for that touch. No way she could lie about that. Sometimes it felt so good to be touched.

There'd been a time when that kind of need had made her do things she later regretted, just because she'd been so desperate to have someone touch her, hold her, for just a little while. To escape from life as she knew it.

It had only made her feel lonelier and sadder in the end, but sometimes the only thing that mattered was making it through one more long, dark night, and maybe that's where he was.

And she was . . . Julie couldn't say exactly where she was.

He seemed to have scrambled her brain somehow, too many sensations piling on top of too many pleasurable sensations. She liked to be touched. What lonely, neglected girl didn't? It was something a woman never outgrew.

But this was so much more. Intense, the pleasure almost like pain. His hands were firm and sure, cupping, holding, rubbing at those nipples begging for his touch. Her blouse came undone and then her bra, and then they were skin to skin, those strong, sure hands of his on her flesh.

She'd never thought of herself as a terribly responsive woman. Her sense of reserve was too strong for that. Surely she could maintain some sort of detachment here, she thought, as his warm mouth slid down the side of her neck. He used his teeth, sending a thousand sensations shooting down her body. Involuntarily, she pressed herself even closer, shivering from head to toe.

He was too good at this. Some men just knew how to touch a woman, how to hold her, how to kiss her, when to linger and when to push onward. Or maybe sometimes two people were just in synch with each other, instead of being hopelessly awkward and out of tune.

Had she ever been with anyone like that? Anyone who seemed to know exactly what she needed?

His lips were at the base of her neck, his hands lifting her breasts, his mouth moving over the tops of them, and she knew where he was going. It was like she could already feel his mouth closing over her distended nipple, knew just how good that would be.

"Zach," she said, because she was still thinking on some level. She ought to tell him to think about whether he really wanted to do this.

Sad, lost people did this. Just reached out for the first person they could find, and she doubted he'd ever made a habit of it or that it was the smartest thing either of them could do at the moment. One more mistake to add to a long, long list of hers, and likely have him feeling even worse in the morning.

"Let me," he groaned, his mouth opening over her breast, taking it inside, sucking, using his teeth. "Let me do this."

She shuddered, sheer pleasure shooting through her, all the way to her toes. She bent her head, so that it rested on the top of his and let him hold her body up when she might have simply collapsed onto the floor.

His mouth . . . How could a man create such havoc in a woman's body with nothing but his mouth on her breast? She felt the pulling sensation deep down inside, heat, tightness, wetness, spiraling down inside of her from the point of contact with his greedy, multitalented mouth.

Oh, my.

She thought about just letting him go ahead and do whatever he wanted.

What did it matter anyway?

It was just sex, and not even that, really. It was a lost, desperate man reaching out for someone, drowning his sorrows in her body. Much better for him than a bottle. He could use her for that. She'd certainly let him.

Except it didn't feel like she was being used. It felt like he needed her. She blocked out all thoughts that any willing woman lying beneath him would do.

He stripped her body of her blouse and tugged off her bra. His mouth settled over her other breast, as greedy as ever. That wonderful tugging sensation started up again. It was like he'd hot-wired her body for electricity. Sensations were zipping along. She couldn't control herself anymore, couldn't pretend, no longer thought of protesting.

There was no kind of mental distance, no rationalization she could find. She wanted him to touch her, everywhere, all at once. She wanted his big, powerful body stretched out over hers, and wanted to open herself to him and welcome him inside. She wanted him straining and groaning and pushing her up and over the top, never letting up, showing no mercy at all in his quest to make her absolutely come apart in his arms.

That was pretty much the way it went.

It was awkward, there on the floor with the sofa on one side of them and the coffee table on the other, but there was no way they were going to take the time to find a more comfortable spot.

He stripped her bare and then half undressed himself, and she found herself beneath him, just where she'd wanted to be, found that the feel of that wonderful body of his on top of her was every bit as magnificent as she'd imagined.

She'd been aware of his erection, heavy and pulsing between them, for some time. How could she not be? And then he freed himself and she let her thighs fall apart, her hands on his hips urging him forward.

"Let me," he said again, his body poised over hers.

She felt him at the entrance to her body, felt the width and breadth of him pressed against her. There was heat and wetness and a scary kind of need.

"Yes," she said, and he slid inside.

It was a snug fit. She whimpered a bit, and he withdrew.

"No." She pulled him back. *There. There. There.* That's where she wanted him. *There.*

"You're not ready."

She could not imagine being any more ready for anything, and if she could have formed the words, she would have told him that. But all she knew was that he was suddenly pulling away from her. She grabbed at him, catching his arms, ready to beg him to come back. But he merely eased himself down her body and settled his mouth between her legs.

At the first touch, she gasped and raised up off the floor, her body curling into itself and onto her side, pleasure rolling through her. It was too much. She'd nearly died from the pleasure of his mouth on her breasts, but this . . .

There were sounds coming from deep in her throat that she scarcely recognized as ones she, herself, made. Part of her was scrambling to get closer to him, her hips rising up off the floor, her legs straining, closer and closer, and the other part of her just wanted to roll away. She tried that. He came with her, following her to the left and then pulling her back to center. Him, at her absolute center, pushing inside with his tongue.

She was coming apart, had no control left, no senses remaining. Except pleasure.

He pushed her on and on and on, and he wouldn't let her up, wouldn't let her get away, even when she begged him and told him she couldn't stand it anymore. He pushed her higher and higher and higher until she screamed. Her entire body was caught there, within the climax that rushed through her, wave after wave after wave.

Everything went black for a moment.

The world was nothing but sensation.

No limits. No doubts. No worries. Just sheer bliss.

What more did anyone need, anyway, except to feel?

Especially when the feelings were like this.

Slowly her senses began to function again. She thought she was falling and falling, afraid of what the landing would bring, then realized he held her tight, that between his body and the floor, she wasn't going anywhere.

And she could smell him, smell the warm, musky scent he wore, and sex, the scent of that, too, on him. She could feel his arms around her, his hard chest and abdomen pressed against her naked body, the muscles of his thighs once again sliding between hers.

He was there again, reading to push his way inside her ultrasensitive flesh, and this time, it was so good, impossibly good. She felt a deep throbbing in his body, one that echoed the remnants of the climax in hers. He was big, and she was so wet. He pushed in deep and then waited there, rocking just a bit, teasing or maybe giving her time.

She didn't know. She didn't much care, as long as he was here.

He touched her everywhere, held her so tenderly. All the pain was gone. All the feelings of being so alone, so lost, so hopeless. He'd taken all of it away.

And this was Zach.

She couldn't quite believe that.

Her and Zach.

She looked up into his eyes, dark and troubled and intense, but there was pleasure, too. She'd given him that, at least. He rocked against her once again, kicking the sensation up a notch higher.

And then it started again, him drawing her deeper and deeper into that web of sensation, and there were just no half measures with him. He wanted to make her scream. She wanted to tell him it was okay, that it didn't matter. That what he'd already given her had been so much more intense than she'd come to expect from anyone. But he kept right on, his gaze locked on hers, intent on that one thing—her pleasure.

She wanted to look away, didn't want to think about everything that had happened, and maybe wanted already to start trying to make excuses for it or make it into something it wasn't.

This seemed to have gone beyond comfort and loneliness and need. Way beyond, into territory she simply didn't understand. *It's been enough,* she wanted to tell him. *More than enough, and it's not about me, anyway, and it isn't supposed to mean anything at all.*

But he just kept right on going, pushing and pushing and pushing. Higher. Deeper. Darker. Until the world just shattered from within. She clung to him, probably leaving marks on his skin, and her body throbbed in time with his, over and over again.

He groaned and shuddered and finally went still, lying heavily on top of her, so that she could barely get breath into her lungs. Not that she really cared.

If the sun failed to rise in the morning, she wasn't sure she would care.

She lay beneath him, her body spent. Later, he slid onto his side, taking her with him, draping her body against his, her head against his shoulder.

His arms fastened around her. He told her to go to sleep, and she did.

Chapter 6

They slept on the floor, arms and legs entangled.

At some point later, he rolled away from her. She protested the loss of the warmth of his body, but then he stood up and gathered her in his arms, telling her to go back to sleep, that everything was fine.

She was vaguely aware of being carried, of being tucked into a bed between cold sheets. He settled himself behind her, pulling her up onto her side and back to him, spoon fashion. His arm was beneath her neck, her head back against his shoulder. His other arm came around her waist, anchoring her to him. Their legs intertwined, all that glorious skin pressed against warm, firm skin.

He kissed the tip of her ear. "Sleep with me."

A part of her mind was racing. What they'd done. That it was Zach. How it had felt. What in the world they'd do in the morning. And a part of her never wanted to move.

She couldn't. She'd promised to stay. No way would she leave him now.

So for whatever was left of the long dark night, she was his.

Julie relaxed against him. Let herself luxuriate in being held this way, in the strength of his arms and how safe she felt. Honestly, there was nothing like having a man's arms around her. Especially a good man's, like this one's. Even if it was for all the wrong reasons.

She looked down at his arm, stretched out flat on the bed beneath her head, reached out and fit her hand to his. His fingers closed over hers, squeezing her hand, and then she found she really needed to touch him. She had hardly gotten to do that at all. It had been all him before.

So she slid her palm from his and trailed her hand up his wrist, his forearm, to his elbow and the muscle in his upper arm, and then went back down his arm again.

"Are you all right?" she asked softly.

"Yeah. You?"

"Yes."

Maybe she wouldn't sleep. It was so nice to be with him, hidden in the dark. The night had an unreal quality to it, and this was probably all the pleasure she'd ever have from it. Come morning, they'd both be beating themselves up over it.

So why not stay awake and just lie here with him, soak up the sensation, the sexual lethargy that was pulsing through her body?

She groaned, unable to help herself, her body going boneless against his. It wasn't long before she felt his body start to react to hers. Against the fleshy part of her bottom, he was hard again.

They both went still.

She wanted him all over again, and what did it matter, anyway, after what they'd already done?

It was just the night, she told herself. One, black, black night.

"Let me?" he asked, leaning over her side and turning her face up to his.

"Yes," she said against his lips.

His hands went to work, holding her there on her side against him, he stroked his way up and down her body, light, maddening strokes, leaving her ready to beg. She would, if that was what it took.

But neither of them had the patience for that. Not anymore.

He kept her right where she was, his mouth locked on hers, and then with one subtle shift of his body, found his way between her thighs and deep inside of her. He rolled her then, onto her belly, his body pressing her down into the bed, her legs closing around him, squeezing him deep inside, his legs tight around hers.

Her hands clutched at the sheets, trying to hold on, and her body rocked up and back with each powerful stroke of his body. His hand pushed her hair aside, and then held on to it, tugging with his fists until she turned her head to give him the access he wanted to the back of her neck, her nape, the top of her right shoulder, and then her mouth. She shivered and tried to grasp him more tightly with all the muscles deep inside her body, and then she was coming apart again.

The sensations were just too intense, the feel of him too big, so far up inside of her. There was no place left to go, she wanted to tell him. He was as far inside as he could possibly get. They were joined as tightly as two people could be.

He got an arm beneath her chest and then another, holding her breasts in his hands and searching out her mouth, kissing her and kissing her and kissing her until she felt a shudder run clear through him. He groaned and held her tightly until the throbbing finally slowed, her body seeming to milk his of every bit of pleasure.

As she lay flat on the bed, his body pressed on top of hers, she realized absently that her skin was damp. His was. His chest. He'd worked up a sweat, and his chest was pressed to her back. That's where the dampness had come from. And he was kissing her right shoulder, very, very softly.

His arms pulled her back against him and he rolled them once again, until they were back on their sides, facing the other way. She looked across the tangled mess of sheets on the bed and shivered at the idea of the two of them and what they'd done in this bed.

He loosened his hold long enough to grab a blanket from the end of the bed and cover them both, then settled her back against him once again.

He wasn't letting go.

She wasn't sure if she could have stood it if he had.

She was facing the window now and looked at the edges of the curtains, glad to see not even the faintest traces of dawn, not ready to face the morning light. Just wanting to hide here in the darkness with him and what they'd done. It was almost like she could still hear it, the sounds they'd made echoing around the room, like the sensations that still echoed through her body.

She turned her face into his shoulder, hiding in him.

"Go to sleep," he said.

And she did.

It was something like a dream, he thought. Waking up in an unfamiliar bed in the deepest part of the night with her. Images of the day before started running through his brain. The trial, the verdict, how crazy he'd been afterward. Buying the bottle, taking a drink, throwing the glass against the wall and scaring Julie.

Julie . . .

He peered through the darkness to the shadowy shape of her lying on her stomach, the smooth expanse of skin at her back bare for him to see. Her hair was everywhere, long and luxurious and completely covering her face.

But it was Julie.

He'd reached for her, been inside of her.

More than once.

There on the floor and again in this bed.

He could feel his body stirring even now as he reached out to run his hands through her hair and down her back, into that little indention at the base of her spine and up over the soft curve of her hips.

She made a gentle sound of pleasure. He stroked her back again and let the palm of his hand linger at the swell of her bottom, remembered being pressed up tight against it, in so deep he thought he might honestly get lost inside of her. That was such a nice place to be, lost inside of her.

How the night had gotten so bad and he'd done this, he would likely never understand. There was a part of him that was as rational as could be, and as careful, that was shocked through and through, and another part that just didn't want morning to come. Maybe didn't want another day. Just this night.

"Julie," he said, and she turned to him.

She was warm and sleepy and practically boneless in his arms. Without a word, she pressed her mouth to his. Her arms came around him, and it was the easiest thing in the world to roll over onto his back and pull her to him.

He liked the way she felt on top of him. Her hair fell around them like a shield, and he could almost think that the things they did here were hidden away from the rest of the world and somehow just didn't count in the light of day. Although he knew they would, come morning.

But he didn't want the morning. He'd stay in this night with her, willingly, and leave every problem he had behind.

Live in the moment, Zach. Whole new concept for him.

People got in trouble doing this, he thought. Not thinking. Just reacting. Feeling. Taking what they wanted.

Julie's arms came around his neck, and her breasts rubbed against his chest as she shifted against him. His hands went to her bottom, curved just right to fit into his hands, the skin soft and smooth.

It was the easiest thing in the world to draw her knees to either side of his body and ease himself inside of her. Again.

She whimpered, and her breath came out in a rush. Her body pulsed around him, like she was coming apart already, and he wasn't far from it. His mouth latched on to hers, and he eased her into as slow and steady a rhythm as he could stand.

Take it, he thought. *All of me. Take it all away.*

It was slipping away from him. Not just everything that was wrong, but any sense of control he had. He held her tighter, urging her to be still, rocking his body ever so softly against hers. She lifted her head, opened her eyes. He could barely see her face through the darkness, but he took it into his hands, holding her so that her mouth was just a fraction of an inch away from his.

He thought about saying, *Tell me. Tell me what this is. Make sense of it for me. Don't let it end. Don't make me wake up and go on in the morning, when everything feels so wrong.*

"Shhh," she said softly, taking his face in her hands, her thumb brushing across his lips. "It's all right."

It wasn't.

But he could forget that, with her kissing him ever so softly, her body moving in what should have been a thoroughly frustrating rhythm against his. Soft and slow, rocking gently, maddeningly. The pressure was exquisite.

He felt himself swell inside her, the climax shuddering through him as he grabbed her and ground his body up into hers.

She was right behind him, those inner muscles of hers squeezing and squeezing and squeezing. He felt the sensation work its way through her entire body. He held on tight, not letting her go anywhere when it was done, thinking they could just stay there. Stay in the night, in the darkness.

Where he could lose himself in her, and nothing seemed as bad as it had the day before.

It never failed. No matter how much she dreaded it, morning always came, invariably much too soon. Invariably with regrets.

The ones she had that morning were larger than most.

She'd slept like the dead, not the merest sliver of consciousness piercing the deepest kind of sleep, the ultimate in relaxation.

Waking was as harsh as the beam of light pouring through the slight gap in the heavy curtains and hitting her squarely between the eyes. She winced and covered them, went to roll out of the way and encountered a broad, decidedly male chest that was pressed against her back. She wasn't going anywhere, not with the arm locked around her waist.

The fact that she wasn't wearing a stitch hit next. Then, that neither was he.

Then, that it was Zach.

She was in bed with Zach

She almost laughed because it struck her as absolutely ludicrous.

Her in bed with Zach McRae.

He didn't even like her.

Oh, he could be kind, but then he was kind to everyone. He'd looked out for her because that's just what he did, and maybe he felt sorry for her, but he didn't respect her. He knew exactly what she was. A liar. A woman who ran away from her troubles rather than ever facing up to them. Someone who was about to marry a man who didn't really know her.

And then she thought about Steve.

Julie groaned and buried her face in the sheet covering the pillow beneath her head. Which was a mistake. It smelled like Zach. Like whatever kind of cologne he wore.

It made her think of the way his skin smelled pressed so intimately to hers. It made her think of the fact that she was lying naked in bed with him and of what it had felt like when he'd been inside of her, of the way her body had come alive under the brush of his lips and the touch of his hands.

Me and Zach McRae. Never in a million years would she have believed that.

She took stock of her predicament. She was lying against his side, while he was on his back, still sleeping. Their legs were tangled together, but she thought she could get hers free without disturbing him. The only real problem was the arm hooked around her waist.

She took a chance and rolled away from him and onto her belly. His grip eased. She held her breath, thinking he might follow her, but she rolled again, off his arm, off him completely. He remained sprawled on his back, the sheet bunched precariously low on his abdomen, a veritable wealth of skin revealed in the morning light.

She didn't give herself more than a moment to admire it. The clean lines, the broad muscles, the rush of hair along his chest, arcing down into a single thin line toward the center of that narrow waist,

She remembered a little more than she should about that altogether impressive body of his and the skill of his hands. She was afraid she'd remember this for a long, long time.

Julie slid to the edge of the bed and stood, naked and cold, feeling thoroughly exposed. Where were her clothes?

He'd carried her in here. She remembered that. He'd stripped her bare before they even made it to the bed.

She tiptoed into the living room, her cheeks burning at the disarray of the room. The table he'd turned over before she'd gotten there and all the papers she knew he must have worked so hard over, in a tangled mess on the floor. The smell of liquor in the room and the shattered glass in the corner. The coffee table he'd shoved out of the way as he'd lowered her to the floor by the sofa.

There were her clothes.

Skirt, panties, stockings, at least one shoe. Bra. Blouse. She picked up the blouse, minus the three buttons that tumbled back to the floor. She was going to look great making her early-morning escape.

Tears filled her eyes, but she refused to let them fall.

She couldn't quite believe she'd done this.

She put the blouse aside on the sofa, scrambled into her panties, and pulled up her skirt, not worrying with the zipper at the moment. Her trembling hands couldn't have managed it. Next she grabbed the bra, fitting the cups to her breasts. She was reaching for the blouse when she more sensed than heard someone else in the room.

Oh, please.

When she turned around, there he was, bare feet, weary, bloodshot eyes, razor stubble all over that stubborn chin, hair all mussed, a towel knotted hastily around his waist. Regrets like none she'd ever seen stamped across his face.

"I was . . . I'm going to go," she said. That was the answer. *Go*. Without another word. What was there to say anyway?

He nodded toward her skirt barely hanging over her hips, the bra barely covering her breasts, the ruined blouse in her hand. "Like that?"

"No" she admitted as he came closer.

He went to her back and carefully, skillfully raised the zipper and slipped the little button at the top of her skirt through the buttonhole. She tried to stay perfectly still, to not so much as breathe at the slight touch of his fingers against her bare skin.

The bra posed no challenge at all. It seemed he dressed women as easily as he undressed them.

He took the blouse from her trembling hand, frowning at the state it was in. Running a hand through his hair, he looked down at that spot on the floor where they'd been and said softly, gravely, "Did I hurt you?"

"No," she whispered.

He came to stand in front of her, took her chin in his hand, making her look at him. "Are you sure? Because I think I was rough with you."

She held his gaze just long enough to say, "I'm sure. You didn't hurt me." Then she went back to staring at the same spot on the floor that seemed to fascinate him as well.

Her skin tingled in places she didn't care to admit, a bit abraded by the roughness of his jaw and probably the carpet. There was a slight soreness between her legs and maybe in the muscles of her thighs. He'd held her, probably tightly enough in moments that there was a little bruise here and there, but it had been sheer desperation driving him on, and she understood that There was nothing to forgive.

He took the blouse from her hand and held it out for her. She slipped her arms through the sleeves, and then he began buttoning those tiny buttons with the kind of dexterity she couldn't help but admire.

He got to the gaping hole in the middle where the buttons were gone, her lavender-colored bra showing through, and frowned.

"Not gonna do much good, is it?"

She clutched the ends together. "I'll be fine. I just have to get home."

"Not like that." He bent over and grabbed his own shirt, which was lying in a pool of stark white on the sofa. He reached out to her and slipped it on her.

She stepped back before he could go to work dressing her again. It seemed he never stopped taking care of a woman. She hastily buttoned the shirt and rolled up the sleeves, pushed a hand impatiently through her hair to try to get it to lie down and not look so mussed, then stepped into her shoes, all the while he just stood there staring at her.

"I don't know what to say," he began.

"Nothing." She gave him an out. "There's nothing to say."

"I'm sure there must be something. I just don't know what it is."

"Look, it was a bad night," she said as blandly as possible, trying to look very much like it was nothing to her. "You were upset. You didn't need to be alone."

"And that's supposed to make it okay?" he asked.

"It's just one of those things, Zach. It happens."

"Not to me."

She stared at him, a thousand questions running through her mind. He'd never once felt that bad? Been that lost? Never once reached for a woman just because she was there and he needed to lose himself in her? His life had never been this bad? Well, hers had.

"Oh, hell, I didn't even use a condom," he said, his eyes going even bleaker.

"It's okay. I'm not going to get pregnant—"

"You're on the pill?"

"Yes."

"Thank God for that." He was still upset. "Sorry."

"It's all right." Stupid, but no harm done, right?

He frowned at her. "That's it? I got drunk and poured out my troubles to you and then we end up in bed, and all you say is that it's all right?"

"What else is there to say?" she asked.

"I don't know."

"Yeah, I know. Because you don't do this."

"And you do?"

Her cheeks burned at that. It really wasn't any of his business what she'd done over the years or how badly she'd felt about any of it.

"I'm just saying that I know what this was. I understand. You needed someone, and I was there. It's awkward, and I'm sure we both regret it and find it a little embarrassing, but there are worse things in the world people have done. We'll just put it behind us and go right on."

"Go right on?" he repeated.

"What else would we do? Beat ourselves up over it? You really don't need to do that, Zach. It was one night, and in the grand scheme of things, it really doesn't matter all that much, does it?"

"I don't know," he said.

"Well, I do. I know what it was. Two people helping each other make it through the night. That's it. Now it's morning, and the thing is, problems never look quite so bad in the morning. You go put your life back together, and I'll go do the same to mine."

He frowned once again. "What about Steve?"

She winced. Zach might not believe her about this, but it was one thing she could not lie about. She found her other shoe, grabbed her purse and her keys. "I have to go."

He stopped her with a hand on her arm. "Julie, I'm sorry."

"It's all right," she said.

Then, unable to help herself, she turned to face him. Which was a mistake. She needed to forget him and this sad, lost look on his face. The sight of all that bare skin and him all rumpled and uncertain. She'd never seen Zach uncertain, and it made her want to try to take care of him some more. Look where that innocent little impulse had gotten them both.

She rose up on her tiptoes and gave him a quick, soft kiss on the cheek. "Take care of yourself, okay?"

He nodded bleakly.

"And go home." Jesus, he had people who loved him, people who would take care of him. He didn't have to live like this.

"The trial isn't over." He looked defeated all over again. "We still have the sentencing phase to get through."

She didn't want to know that, to think of him still being here, to worry about him and want to come see him. She wouldn't. She couldn't.

"But after that," she said, thinking he just had to go.

He frowned, still looking uncertain and so damned

lost. "Houston. I heard yesterday. I have a case starting soon in Houston. They love killing people in Texas."

Which was the last thing he needed to do. Go rushing off to save someone else when he was feeling so bad himself. She was going to worry about him, even if he wasn't hers to worry about. He would never be. Just that little piece of him she had last night. That was it.

"I have to go," she said, and slipped out the door, refusing to look back and think of things she could never have.

After she left, Zach stood in the middle of the room, smelling the whiskey he'd hurled into the opposite wall at one point.

He'd kicked over the table, too. He remembered that. He'd called Gwen.

Jesus, Gwen.

He sank down onto the sofa, leaning back against the cushion, head pounding. He absolutely could not believe he'd done this. He didn't go off on trips and get drunk, pick up strangers and take them to bed with him. He didn't fall apart. He didn't cheat. He didn't lie. He and Gwen were engaged, and that meant something to him. One thing it meant was that he didn't sleep with other women.

"Shit," he muttered.

He still wasn't quite sure how it had happened. He'd heard other guys say that exact thing, and he'd thought, *Bullshit. You know exactly how it happened.*

Yet here he sat, his feet on that spot on the floor where he'd had *her.*

Julie Morrison.

It was even worse that it was a friend of his little sister's. Someone who had enough troubles of her own without him adding to them.

And then there was Gwen. God, what was he going to say to Gwen?

Zach covered his face with his hands, rubbing at the ache in his head. He'd called her last night when things got bad, before he'd gone out to buy the bottle. How he could have let himself do that . . . ?

But before, he'd called Gwen, feeling lousier than he ever had in his life and trying to work his way around to telling her just how bad it was. Lately, there was just no distance between him and his clients. Feelings seemed to be multiplying inside him, like a virus gone out of control. Last night, he just hadn't known what to do with them. And Gwen had been too distracted to listen.

So he'd drank too much and had ended up in bed with Julie. She'd been kind and close, kissed him very softly on the cheek, and then it was like a neon sign started flashing on and off in his muddled brain that said, *Get inside her. Now.* That he wouldn't feel so horribly alone, so lost, if he could just be inside of her.

So he did it. Didn't think at all beyond that. *Just make it through the night somehow.* She'd said that this morning, hadn't seemed mad or sad or outraged or anything. Had men used her like this before? Or had she sometimes felt as bad as he had last night and found someone to help her through a night like the one that just passed?

He wasn't sure if he wanted to know.

But there was one thing he absolutely had to do, and it wasn't going to get any easier. He picked up the phone and dialed. Gwen answered, brisk and efficient as ever. He found out where she was, Cleveland, and told her he was coming up there. Today. It was Saturday morning, and nothing would happen with Tony's trial until Monday. Zach wouldn't be able to do anything until he took care of Gwen, and how long could his confession possibly take? Once she calmed down and figured out what she wanted to do about it . . . Well, he'd get through this and worry about the rest later.

"I'll be there as soon as I can," he said. "I need to talk to you."

"All right. Is everything okay?"

"No."

Julie cried a little on the drive to her apartment although she wasn't sure why. What was there to cry about? What's done was done. Her life . . . Well, it always ended up like this, one way or another.

She'd just held it together longer than usual here.

She parked in front of her apartment and quickly let herself inside before anyone saw her with a man's dress shirt thrown over her torn blouse. Inside the apartment, she dropped purse, keys, and shoes as she went, heading directly for the shower. She stripped off her clothes, not nearly as efficiently as Zach had because her hands were shaking—her whole body actually.

A glance at the big mirror over the sink told her she did indeed have a few bruises and scuff marks, but nothing bad, nothing that would really show. He hadn't hurt her. He'd just been . . .

What word could possibly apply? Insistent? A little desperate? Needy? All of that, and she had tried to provide him what comfort she could. That's all it had been.

So why was every nerve ending in her body alive and tingling this morning?

She quickly turned away from the image in the mirror and made the water in the shower as hot as she could stand it. She could still smell him on her. There was that distinctive musky odor of sex that clung to her body. She needed to wash it all away, and if she could, wash all memory of this night from her mind.

Honestly, it was no big deal.

He was a kind man, and if she'd needed him in that same, desperate way, he probably would have done the same for her. He'd have felt guilty about it, but if that's what she really needed, he'd have done it. And he'd done so much for her over the years.

So this was nothing.

She owed him. Most people probably wouldn't think of paying off a debt like that with sex, but what the hell? She understood. So what if nobody else would? It didn't really matter, did it? And it wasn't like she'd hated it. Not at all. She just felt . . . She couldn't put it into words, so she gave up on even trying. It was over, and she'd once again screwed up her life. Nothing new there.

Julie scrubbed her skin raw and cried a bit more, then shut off the shower, toweled off, and dressed in the first thing she found. Jeans and a sweater. She tied her hair back, grabbed another pair of shoes, and left.

The town house she and Steve were to share after their marriage was only fifteen minutes away, and one might think she'd use the time wisely by trying to figure out what she was going to say. But her mind was a total and complete blank.

She climbed out of her car and rang the bell. This was not the morning to use the key she had.

Steve stiffened at the sight of her. "Sorry I didn't make it last night."

"It's all right. As it turns out, I wasn't there."

"You weren't?" He let her in, then closed the door, looking a little unsure of what to do next.

"Well, actually, I waited for a long time—"

"Sorry. I know it's been two weeks. I just don't know what to say, Julie."

"I can help you with that. I spent last night with Zach."

All the color drained from his face, his gaze narrowing on hers. "What?"

"Zach. He lost the murder case. He was upset. I was worried about him, and went to check on him, and I ended up spending the night."

"You had sex with him?" he asked incredulously.

"Yes," she admitted, then, too late, had new doubts about just how easygoing Steve might be. If ever there were a time for a man to lose his temper and take it out on a woman, this was it.

He barely blinked, didn't seem to move a muscle until a bitter smile came across his face. "I knew it. First minute I saw the guy, I knew it. There was something between the two of you."

"Well, you're wrong."

"Shit, Julie, you just told me you slept with the guy."

"Yes, but it wasn't like that."

"Oh?" Steve started to laugh in the ugliest way. "What was it like?"

"I told you. He was upset. I was worried about him, and . . . It was just one of those things. One of those stupid, meaningless things."

"Meaningless? I'm afraid I don't see it as meaningless."

"I never thought you would," she agreed.

"But that's the way you see it? It doesn't mean anything to you?"

"No. I know it means something to you and me. I know it has to hurt you, and I'm sorry for that. I really didn't want to hurt you."

"Oh, well. There you go." He shrugged. "You didn't mean to hurt me."

"No, I didn't. You're one of the nicest men I've ever known."

"And this is what being a nice guy gets me, huh?"

"It should get you someone much nicer than me," she said.

He folded his arms across his chest and took a breath. "Let me guess. This is the part where you apologize again and tell me you lied about one more little thing, but that—"

"I didn't lie. I wouldn't. Not about something like this."

"Oh, well. How stupid of me. But then, how would I know? I don't know what you lie about and what you tell the truth about. Maybe you could give me a list. Things you're willing to lie about and things you aren't. Maybe you could explain it to me, because I just don't understand."

"I don't expect you to understand," she said.

"But you expect me to marry you?"

"No, I don't expect you to do that, either," she said. "And I'm sorry. I thought I was finally going to get something right. Be the kind of woman I'd always wanted to be, that together we'd have everything I ever wanted."

"What did you want, Julie?" he asked.

"Something that would last." Anything that would last.

"You never loved me?" he asked.

She did start to cry a little then. "I was so sure that I did, but I never quite believed you loved me."

"And I had a lot of trouble believing you loved me, too," he admitted, being more generous than she had a right for him to be this morning.

"I guess we both tried hard to make something work

that just wasn't meant to be. I'm really sorry, Steve." She pulled the engagement ring off her finger and handed it to him.

"So what are you going to do?"

"I don't think I can keep working for you now." One too many mistakes staring her in the face every day — she didn't need that. "I'll clear out my stuff. Everything's planned out for the next quarter. Maggie's up to speed on all of it. She's more than qualified to do the job. And I'd like to just go, if that's all right with you."

No horrible two weeks to work through.

"What are you going to do? Go back home? Back to him?"

"Zach? No. Besides, he's hardly ever in Ohio." Thank goodness for that. She didn't want to have to face him. "There's uh . . . Well . . . my mother and stepfather are in Ohio."

"So you do have family?"

"I guess you could call them that. They're in trouble, and Peter . . . He's my half brother. He's only thirteen, and . . ."

If he was feeling half as lost and confused as Zach had felt last night . . . That's what she kept thinking about. What if Peter was feeling the same way, with no one to help him through it?

God, she didn't want to go.

"I don't know where I'm going," she said honestly. "Maybe I'll go get Peter and see if he wants to run away with me. It's all I ever wanted to do when I was growing up there."

That wouldn't be so bad. She'd grab him and run. How bad could that be?

Steve said, "I'll miss you."

She cried a bit more, let him pull her into a quick embrace. "There's someone out there for you, Steve."

Surely he was too nice a man to end up alone.

"I wish things had been different," she said. "I never intended to lie to you. It just . . . happened. When I got here and rented an apartment, my landlady was hard of hearing. I don't know what I said, but she thought I was from St. Louis, and as I was sitting there trying to correct her, I thought, what does it matter? No one would know differently unless I told them, and I just loved that idea. It was a chance to reinvent myself, be anyone I wanted to be, and it felt so good. Just me and whatever I could make of my life here."

And look where it had gotten her.

"I never meant to hurt you," she said.

"I'll be all right." He kissed her forehead. "Take care of yourself, Julie."

Chapter 7

Zach found Gwen in her element, strolling through a banquet room at a fancy hotel, checking all the arrangements. She could keep a thousand details straight in her head, she never forgot anything, never seemed to rush, and never, ever broke a sweat.

She was absolutely unrattleable, hardworking, ambitious, brilliant, and beautiful. He'd met her five years ago, when she'd been doing grunt work in the district attorney's office because it would look good on her résumé later, should she follow her father into politics. She'd seemed as out of place prosecuting petty thieves and drunks as she would have been in a third-world country. Zach had been in court that day, doing a favor for a friend whose son had gotten out of hand. He and Gwen had thoroughly enjoyed matching wits with each other and had gone to dinner that night.

They'd been together ever since, as often as their schedules allowed. Both young and ambitious, they'd been fine with the way things were and saw no reason to rush into the wedding and family thing. They had plenty of time for that.

Zach hated that he was going to hurt her this way.

He walked across the ballroom, where black-coated waiters were setting up serving stations for finger food and drinks. Gwen turned around and saw him. A slow, satisfied smile came across her face. He went to her and took her in his arms.

"Hello, stranger." She gave him a long, slow kiss. "You look terrible."

He nodded. "Bad day."

"Well, we'll just have to make this a better one. We're starting in an hour. I hope you brought your tux."

"I can't stay, Gwen. I'm heading back to Memphis in three hours."

"Not even one night?" she asked.

He shook his head. "Sorry."

She wouldn't want to spend the night with him after what he had to say.

"Well . . ." She held out the clipboard in her hand, a neat line of checks running down the page. "I still have a half-dozen things to do before the party."

"It's important," he said. "I know the timing's bad, but . . . I wouldn't have come all this way, except it's not the kind of thing to say over the phone."

She frowned. "You're scaring me, Zach." And she wasn't a woman who frightened easily.

"Is there someplace we can go?" he asked.

"Sure." She passed the clipboard to her assistant. They took the elevator to the penthouse suite. Hotel employees were setting up for a precocktail party gathering there. Gwen glanced over the arrangements, then led him into her bedroom and closed the door.

She walked to the window, which held a stunning view of the lake, the lights of the city below just starting to come on, then turned to face him, the length of the room between them. Coolly, she said, "You met someone?"

"No."

She frowned again, studying his face. "You didn't come to tell me you're in love with someone else?"

"No."

"Then what?"

"I was upset last night."

"I know. You and I talked about it."

No, they hadn't. Not as far as he was concerned. He'd needed her and tried to tell her so much, but ended up feeling like she just didn't care. Which didn't excuse what he'd done. He got that. But he'd needed her.

"Zach, what is it?"

There was no easy way. No real excuse. He blurted it out. "I was upset last night, about Tony Williams, and I had a little too much to drink, and I slept with someone else."

She stood there, staring at him, her lips parting slightly. He could see the words sinking in slowly, her bottom lip starting to tremble. "I don't think . . . Uhhh. I don't think I heard you correctly."

He approached her slowly, putting his hands on her arms. "I'm sorry. I did."

She shivered and backed away from him, a tear falling down her cheek that she hastily brushed away. She took a breath, raising her chin. "Why?"

He threw out his arms in a sign of frustration. "I don't have an excuse. No good one, anyway. Hell, I don't think there is any good excuse. It happened, and I'm sorry."

She nodded, her hand covering her mouth. He wondered if she was going to yell, if she was going to throw something or get hysterical. He couldn't imagine Gwen hysterical, couldn't imagine where they went from here.

"So, you just . . . What? Thought this would make you feel better? Having sex with someone else?"

"I wasn't thinking at all," he said. "I just . . . felt so bad."

"Having sex with this woman? It felt bad?"

"No—"

"So it felt good?"

"No."

"One or the other, Zach. There aren't that many possibilities. It either felt good or it felt bad."

"It felt . . ." Necessary. That was the most appropriate word he could come up with, but that one would require a lot more of an explanation than he thought he was capable of giving. He tried Julie's own words. "It wasn't about sex."

"Oh. Okay." Gwen jumped on that. "It wasn't about sex. But that's just what you did have. Sex. So what was it about, exactly?"

Zach told himself to suck it up and take it. He'd screwed up royally, and whatever she dished out, he deserved.

"I'm sorry," he tried again. "There's nothing that excuses what I've done. I know that, Gwen. I just . . ." *Come on. Spit it out.*

"I trusted you. All those long trips, the trials. I never doubted you," she said. "Was this the first time? The first time you've been unfaithful to me?"

"Yes," he said.

She kept her head up, fury mingling with tears she just barely held back. "And I'm supposed to believe that?"

"If you can. It's the truth."

"I don't know if I can believe anything you say right now. And the fact that you're sorry doesn't seem to help, Zach. Not a bit."

He nodded, accepting that.

"So? What now?" she asked.

He wasn't going to say anything else about what had driven him to this point. He couldn't. Maybe he never would. Maybe things would get better. Maybe he hadn't just screwed up his whole life. Maybe she'd forgive him, and they'd go right on.

"Whatever you want," he said. "Whatever you say."

"I don't know what I want."

"Okay. Think about it. I'll . . ."

He went to her, tried to draw her into his arms, but she shoved him away. Then, taking a minute to think about it, she slapped him across the face.

The sound echoed around the room. She was furiously brushing away the tears that had finally escaped.

"Do you want me to go?" he offered. "I'll go."

She nodded. "I have two parties tonight, and half a dozen events tomorrow."

"I'm sorry. I felt like I owed it to you to tell you right away, and there's just no break for either of us anytime soon."

"I'll handle it," she claimed, head held high. "I always handle everything."

He nodded. He hoped she could.

He was halfway to the door when she called to him, "Who was she, Zach?"

He turned back around. "No one you know."

"You picked up a total stranger?"

"No. Someone I ran into in Memphis. An old friend."

"Old girlfriend?"

"No. Nothing like that."

"But you'd been seeing her while you were there?"

"I ran into her and her fiancé at a restaurant one night and had dinner with them and her future in-laws."

"She's engaged, too?"

Zach nodded. "I went to her engagement party. We had lunch one day during a break from the trial. That's it."

"And when you got upset and a little drunk, you knew right where to go?"

"Actually, she came to find me."

"Oh, I see," Gwen said.

"No, you don't. There's a lot going on that you just don't understand, Gwen, and that's my fault, because I really haven't told you. But I was trying last night. I was trying to tell you." He'd actually been reaching out for help, the first time he'd let himself, and it had been like she hadn't even heard him.

"About your case?"

"More than that," he said.

"The kid killed his own father. What's he going to do the next time he gets mad? Pull out a gun again?" she argued. "And what's he to you, anyway, Zach? Other than an excuse to screw around with another woman?"

"He's me, dammit." He just blurted it out. "How can you not see that? That so easily, he could have been me."

She shook her head. "What are you talking about?"

"My life. You know what my life was like in the beginning. You know my old man just got out of jail for murder."

"What is this? Some kind of psycho crap that's supposed to keep me from focusing on the real issue? That you've been seeing someone in Memphis and you ended up in bed with her while you were engaged to me?"

"No. It's how I feel, Gwen."

How lousy and lost he felt.

Like he'd just laid his soul bare to her, and she'd dismissed it as nothing at all. Which he knew wasn't fair. He'd just told her he'd cheated on her. She thought he was trying to make excuses. Hell, he supposed he was.

I feel like shit, Gwen. I need help. It's bad, and I don't know what to do.

If he said that, would she help him? Could anyone?

He started again to try to explain it all, but a knock sounded on the door. A moment later, without waiting for an invitation, her assistant, Tina, walked in. "It's a quarter till. People are starting to arrive."

"I'll be right there," Gwen said.

Tina backed out and shut the door with one hasty glance between the two of them. Gwen sat down at her dressing table and started working feverishly to repair the damage their little argument had done to her makeup.

Zach stood back and watched her. She composed herself and covered all traces of her tears, pulled herself together beautifully. Then she squared her shoulders, did one last check in the mirror, and faced him.

"I have to go," she said.

"Don't," he said. "There's more. Things I haven't even begun to tell you. Let's go somewhere. Talk this out."

She shook her head. "Everyone's waiting."

"I need this, Gwen. Surely your father can get through one damned cocktail party without you."

"Oh, stop it, Zach. I'm furious, and I'm hurt, and I'd really like to smack you again. Maybe I will. But not now. Right now, I have to go out there and make sure this evening runs smoothly," she said. "And you're going back to finish your precious trial, right? We both knew going in what it was going to be like, so I guess it can't come as any great surprise that something like this would happen."

"What?" he asked.

"Men do these things, right? They just do, and women get hurt and then . . . I don't know. I guess they just learn to put up with it or walk away. God knows, my mother's put up with enough of my father's little flings. I don't know why I ever expected things to be different with us."

"I don't expect it to be like that. I don't expect to have little flings and for you to understand. That is not who I am, Gwen."

"Isn't that exactly who you are right now?"

To which he could say nothing.

"I have to go," she said.

"Should I call you? Or would that just make it harder?"

"I don't know, Zach. I don't know of anything that's going to make it easier."

And with that, she squared her shoulders and walked into the other room.

Julie wrote notes for her assistant and then packed up her office, planning never to go back. She drove home in a cold, dreary rain, dropped the boxes just inside the door, and collapsed on the sofa, water dripping off her hair and her coat, her shoes. Cold, she thought of getting up and turning on the heat, but that seemed like too much trouble. So she pulled the afghan off the back of the sofa and wrapped herself up in it instead.

Here she was, no more fiancé, no job, no idea what she was going to do next. She sat there for a long time, floundering in her misery, and then the phone rang. She stared at it, like it was a roaring monster come to attack her in her own living room. It couldn't possibly be good news.

Zach? There was nothing to say to him.

Steve? Nothing left there, either.

Steve's mother, gloating? That wouldn't surprise her.

Someone from Ohio? Julie shuddered at the thought.

The phone finally stopped ringing, the answering machine picking up. She braced herself for whatever came, the machine broadcasting the message as it recorded.

It was Grace, asking her if she'd talked to Zach because she'd heard about the verdict in his trial, and no one had been able to get in touch with him since then. Julie was sure he was fine, probably hard at work on the rest of the trial.

"Oh, and. . . . Well, I guess you heard," Grace said. "But just in case . . . your parents were arrested today. I'm sorry, Julie."

Perfect. What a twenty-four hours. Sleep with an old friend. Lose a fiancé. Quit a job. And now her parents were in jail.

There was only one more thing that could make it complete.

Peter.

Where was Peter?

Ask the question, Julie.

It was the only one left.

Coward, the voice inside taunted her.

Lousy sister.

Lousy excuse for a human being.

Maybe this was when she found out just how horrid a person she was.

Grace was still there, talking to her machine, telling her if there was anything she could do to just give her a call.

Julie drew her feet up onto the couch, hugging her legs to her chest, hunkering down into a little ball, like she'd done when she was little and trying to make herself as tiny as possible. Wondering if people could just disappear. She used to want to do that so badly.

Grace finally hung up.

Julie cried a bit more. Wanting Zach. She wanted him

to hold her. She remembered drifting off to sleep all curled up against him, as relaxed as she could be and every inch of her body touching a part of his. She remembered when her body was still tingling and throbbing, the glut of satisfaction that followed pushing every other thought out of her head.

It hadn't felt wrong in the darkest part of the night. It had felt . . .

She didn't even have the words, and it really didn't matter.

She wondered what he'd say if she called him up and said, *Come and hold me, Zach. It's an absolutely awful night, and I don't know how I'll make it through without you.*

She remembered that first night she'd seen him in Memphis when he'd said he was worried about her, and she'd teased him about coming to her rescue again.

I would have, he'd said. Just like that. No questions asked. No hesitation.

Well, it wouldn't be like that. Not anymore. Sex changed things. Any kind of sex. Including the desperate, get-me-through-the-night kind of sex.

She groaned and pressed her face down onto the tops of her drawn-up knees. Tears fell yet again. There had to be a bottom point to her life, she kept thinking. Time and time again, she'd thought surely she'd found it. So far, she hadn't. Today? Or maybe she could still go lower.

The phone rang just as she got to that thought. *Things could get worse.*

She wanted to shove the phone across the room, shatter it against the wall as Zach had shattered the glass, and maybe she wanted a drink. She'd always thought someday . . . So far, she hadn't. But someday . . .

She hated herself sometimes. Just absolutely hated

herself. All her weaknesses. All her little vices. All her tears. All the mistakes. All the lies.

She hated her life.

The answering machine clicked on. She put her hands over her ears in a childish gesture to block out the sound. This was what she'd been reduced to today.

"Ms. Morrison? This is JoAnne Reed with Child and Family Services in Baxter, Ohio."

There it was. The bottom. The worst.

"I'm trying to reach Peter Morrison's sister," the woman continued.

Julie swallowed back a groan as something that felt like a physical pain moved through her body.

And then another voice came into her living room, courtesy of that awful answering machine. Peter's voice? Was that him? He sounded so big. So different. So angry. No surprise there.

He was yelling. The same words over and over again. *She won't come. I told you, she won't come.*

Her mind turned blank. The words kept coming, but she just couldn't take them in. It was too awful. Peter's voice became more and more agitated. The social worker was trying to console him. Finally, it was over. The machine clicked off, but Peter's voice echoed throughout the room.

She won't come. She won't come. She won't come.

He sounded like he hated her, and his words shamed her as nothing ever had. It was too late for so many things in her life. For her and her mother. Her and her real father, who'd died ages ago. Her and Steve. Her and Zach. It sounded like it was too late for her and Peter, too, but he was desperate.

Maybe, as bad as things were, she still had a chance with him. Julie hadn't gotten too many second chances.

What could she do for him, anyway? Teach him to lie and run away? Those were her most accomplished traits.

She could teach him to laugh when there was nothing funny at all about the situation. Maybe she could teach him just to keep going, because somehow she'd always managed to do that.

The phone call she made was brief and businesslike. Ms. Reed offered her condolences on her parents' arrest, explained that her office had taken custody of Peter. If at all possible, they'd prefer to see him in the care of a blood relative. Otherwise, he'd be sent to a foster home, if one was available, and if not, a group home.

Kiddie jail, Julie thought. Just like Mom and Dad. How was it that she'd never ended up there?

She told Ms. Reed that she'd be in Baxter the next day and turned down an offer to talk to Peter herself. He was making it clear that he didn't want to talk to her. Julie could hear him through the phone.

She threw things into a suitcase and then stared at her bed, not at all sleepy. It was a seven- or eight-hour drive to Baxter, depending on traffic. She thought about taking a plane, but she was without a job and wasn't sure how long she'd have to stay. It would be easier and much more economical to take the car.

Finally, she dug through her medicine cabinet until she found two pain pills left in a bottle her doctor had given her last year when she'd wrenched her knee. She hadn't taken that many of them because they left her woozy and put her to sleep, but she'd kept them around for when her headaches got so bad and days of trying to get rid of them hadn't worked.

Her head definitely hurt, and she had to have some sleep.

Julie took one pill and climbed into bed.

The drug started to kick in soon. Her lids got heavy and the thoughts weren't rushing through her brain so frantically. Everything was slowing down quite nicely. She wondered if booze could feel this good.

No wonder her mother and stepfather drank. She'd always worried she might start drinking and like it too much. These pills . . . Well, she was thankful the doctor had only given her ten. It wasn't the feeling she got from being in Zach's arms, but it was the best she could do tonight.

Chapter 8

In what she'd always believed to be the cruelest of ironies, the town Julie had grown up in was a picture-postcard-perfect image of small-town America. *Literally.*

Not just perfect, but *Christmas perfect.*

Gently twinkling lights, ribbons, and wreaths, warm fires burning in the fireplaces, Christmas trees in the front windows. White clapboard churches, bells ringing in the bell towers. Carolers singing in the streets. Snow gently falling, creating the perfect image. Kindness. Happiness. Joy.

It was the "Christmas town."

Zach, in fact, had grown up in the "Christmas house."

She'd been in something of a daze the first time she realized it. She'd made friends with a little girl in the Christmas house, and she played there all the time.

It was all Zach and Grace's grandfather's fault. He was a man who'd turned snow globes into an art form, and the images he created of Baxter, Ohio, were known around the world.

When Julie and her parents had moved here, she'd had a book of *The Night Before Christmas* featuring his images from this town, and she'd always thought it must be the perfect place to live. She hadn't quite believed it when she'd found herself living there, playing in that house on the cover of the book.

And she'd probably thought it was going to change her life magically. That her mother and stepfather would stop yelling and stop drinking. That they'd love her. That Christmas would look like the way it did in the book. That life would.

She quickly realized how foolish those dreams were. Life here went on mostly the way it had always been, except she escaped to Grace's house as often as she could manage.

Driving down that same street now, she had hopes that the town had gotten bigger and more impersonal. That she might be left to handle her family's problems with some degree of anonymity. But it still reeked of small-town, picture-perfect images on this quiet day in October. Trees towered overhead, the leaves seemingly set aflame with color. A hint of wind came and the leaves rained gently down and skittered along the street, pooling in the wide yards of the big Victorians that lined the streets.

They all looked so pretty, so painstakingly restored and maintained.

All of them except her parents'.

They'd never had the money or the inclination, would never have had the house if not for a great-aunt who died childless and left it to Julie's mother. It was a miracle they'd managed to hang on to it all these years.

Julie kept her eyes resolutely on the road, passing mailbox after mailbox and counting them down until she was there, pulling into the driveway.

There was a dark blue Ford Explorer and a little red convertible in the driveway, a plain, beige sedan parked on the street out front. She'd called Mrs. Reed as she'd gotten to the edge of town and the woman had offered to meet her here.

Julie turned off the engine and made herself look up at the house, a flush of heat and shame coming into her cheeks.

She'd wondered if the sadness and the neglect had been as easy to see on her as a child as it had been on the house. As it still was. The house was a dull and fading yellow with what had once been white trim and a white porch stretching along the front and down one side. Three stories, tons of windows, three fireplaces. The yard needed mowing. Someone should rake the leaves. The pipes probably still labored and rattled with each use.

For a moment she thought of what it must cost to keep this place going. She'd be shocked if it wasn't mortgaged to within an inch of its life, and the heating bill alone . . . Her without a job, and all the savings she'd spent on a suitable wedding dress, the shoes, the veil . . . the former bride-to-be.

Not the time, Julie.

She got out of the car, the wind whipping around her, leaves fluttering softly to the ground, as she headed for the door.

Something, a feeling, maybe a sound, had her looking up just before she got to the porch steps, and there in one of the second-floor windows, she saw a face in shadows. The shadow jerked back, the curtains falling once more into place.

Peter? Watching for her, even though he'd claimed to know she'd never come?

Just a little bit of faith, she thought. One little bit. In her. If he had that . . .

The door opened, a kind-looking woman in her mid-

fifties with graying hair and a charming pink suit standing in the doorway smiling back at her.

"Ms. Morrison?" she asked. "You must have left before the sun came up."

"I did."

"Well, come in." She stepped back from the doorway.
"It's your parents' home, after all."

Julie reluctantly walked inside. She lowered her purse
to the little table by the door and slipped off her sweater,
holding it to her chest and making herself look around.
The house was dark and worn, cold and somehow op-
pressive. Same old beige carpet that sorely needed re-
placing. Dull, scuffed wood floors. Beige walls.

What had her parents done with all that money they'd
stolen? Maybe used it on the little red sports car in the
driveway?

"I'm so glad you could come," the social worker said.
"Peter was . . . Well . . ."

"He didn't think I would." Julie said the words for the
woman. Might as well get things out in the open. "No
great surprise. I haven't seen him in eight years."

A million regrets seemed to overtake her, like a rogue
wave rising up with no warning and coming crashing
down upon her. She was so stupid to ever think she could
do this.

"There's really no one else to take him?" she blurted
out.

Mrs. Reed gaped at Julie as if she thought everything
had been settled. "A cousin of your stepfather in Iowa
who's never seen Peter at all. She said she hated the idea
of him going into foster care. There's an aunt of your
stepfather in Kansas, but she's seventy-two and hasn't
seen him since he was a baby. If we had to, we could pur-
sue a placement with the cousin, I suppose, but . . ."

"No. I suspected as much." Julie pulled herself together. She'd come. Peter had seen her. There was no backing out now. She went to the front window and looked outside. "I suppose if Peter needs someone to look after him, this mess with our parents isn't going to be resolved anytime soon?"

"That's for the attorneys and the courts to decide, but . . . Well, I asked the same question. They told me the judge set a fairly high bail and didn't feel your parents had the assets to cover it. So, it could be a while."

Julie nodded, already dying to be anywhere but here. "Peter's upstairs?"

"Yes." The woman hesitated. "You don't have children?"

"No."

"He's going to be a handful, I'm afraid."

Julie nodded. "Runs in the family."

Her mother had always claimed that one day Julie would pay for the hell she'd put her mother through when she was an adolescent. By then, she'd given up on them ever caring about her and decided if she was going to be miserable, everyone around her might as well be miserable, too. The three of them had awful fights, yelling and screaming and stomping out of the house. Slamming doors. Roaring off in cars, her staying gone for days at a time.

Peter was thirteen now.

Just how bad had Julie been at thirteen?

"You should know, there's been some trouble at school," Mrs. Reed said. "A few fistfights. A couple of suspensions. Problems with schoolwork and grades. Attendance. He needs to be in school. Every day."

Julie barely managed not to laugh. She would be responsible for a barely teenage boy getting to school every day? But then she was well qualified. She knew all the good places to go when skipping school. Experience seemed to be a plus in this situation.

"I'll see that he's in school," Julie promised rashly.

"Whoever has him will have to," she said. "Adolescence is hard enough when a child doesn't have to cope with something like this. It's only been a day, and I haven't finished my evaluation of him yet, but I suspect it would be a good idea for Peter to talk to someone—someone outside the family—"

"You mean . . . a psychologist?"

"Yes. I believe you know the McRaes? They probably would have taken him themselves, but—"

"Zach explained about the girls they have now."

"You know Zach, too?"

"Yes," she admitted.

"He's a wonderful man." The woman looked relaxed and almost happy for a moment. So Julie got brownie points just for knowing Zach. "He's marrying a good friend of mine's daughter, in fact."

"What?" Julie had only half been paying attention until she heard the word "marrying" in connection with Zach.

"Zach. He's engaged to Senator Baker's daughter, Gwen. I went to school with her mother a long, long time ago. They're wonderful people. I couldn't be happier for all of them."

"I didn't know Zach was engaged," Julie said. "He didn't mention that."

Not at dinner with her ex-fiancé or at her engagement party. Not on the floor or in his bed.

Julie nearly groaned aloud.

"Are you all right?" Mrs. Reed asked, coming a step closer.

"Yes. I'm sorry. I just . . . I was just surprised. I've known Zach a long time. I used to be good friends with his sister Grace."

"And you knew Emma, too?"

"Yes."

"That's the reason I brought up the family. I suppose you know Emma's a child psychologist. She has a private practice here in town and does some work for social services from time to time. If you wanted someone to talk to Peter, she's wonderful."

"I'm sure she is." And there was that firsthand experience—alcoholic father who beat on their mother on a regular basis. "If we need a shrink, she'd be the one we'd call."

Mrs. Reed didn't seem to know how to take that.

"Sorry. This house brings out the sarcastic streak in me, I'm afraid. But I meant what I said. I'm sure Emma's very good at her job. If Peter needs to see someone, she's the one I'd want to help him."

And then, because no other stalling tactics came to mind, she turned to the stairs and looked up. "I guess I should go up and say hello to him."

"Go ahead. I'll wait here."

Julie wondered what that meant. Was there some sort of test she had to pass? The fit-parent test? If she did, where in the hell were these people when she was growing up or for the first thirteen years of Peter's life?

She went to the stairs and slowly started to climb. From above, she heard someone scrambling away. So he'd been listening at the top of the stairs. *Great.* She thought back over what she'd said. *There's really no one else to take him?* That should win her some points right off the bat.

She made it to the top of the steps and into the hall.

What used to be her room was off to the right. Briefly, she wondered what was there now. She'd taken practically nothing but the clothes on her back when she'd left.

Her mother and stepfather's room was to the immediate left and Peter's was at the other end of the hall, door closed. She forced herself to knock. "Peter? It's me. I need to come in."

No answer.

"Peter? Come on. Just let me in."

Still nothing.

She tried the door. It was locked.

She had vague memories of locking herself in her room, her mother on the other side of the door screaming at her, her stepfather shoving the door open. She wasn't going to do that.

"Fine." Julie sat down on the floor instead, right on the other side of the door. "We can talk this way, if you want."

Utter silence came from the room.

"I'm sorry for leaving the way I did, Peter. I just . . . I couldn't stand it here anymore. I had to get away. I thought it was the only thing I could do. For me." She couldn't have saved him then. "I missed you."

He wrenched open the door and glared down at her. "You did not."

"I did," she said, thinking, *He's so big. So grown up.*

What had happened to the little boy she'd left behind?

Julie got to her feet, dismayed to find that they stood nearly eye to eye. If anything, once she was shoeless he'd probably be a bit taller than she was. His bare feet were huge and somehow manlike. Wide and long and bony, like a man's. There was what seemed to be an impossible bulk to his chest, his shoulders and arms, a sprinkling of dark hair on his upper lip, dark eyes brimming with anger, dark, thick brows, and an unruly head of hair in sad need of a trim.

It seemed at first there was nothing left of the boy. But after a moment, he got tired of glaring at her and looked away. From that angle his face still looked a bit boyish. Like it just didn't fit on his body. Like all of his parts were growing at a different rate, his face one of the last things to turn manlike.

"I did miss you," she said.

"Yeah. I could tell." He shrugged and stared at the opposite wall. "All the phone calls. The letters. Birthday presents. Christmas stuff. You were really thinking about me, weren't you?"

"I'm here now," she said. "Doesn't that count for anything?"

"You don't want to be here," he shot back.

"No, I don't." No lying about that. "But I don't want you here alone, either, and that meant more to me than how much I hated the idea of coming back here."

"You didn't have to," he said, shrugging again. "I can take care of myself."

"No one's going to let you do that, Peter. You're only thirteen."

"I'll be fine till Mom and Dad get out of jail. It's not like they take care of me when they're here."

True, but . . . "The lady downstairs won't let you stay here by yourself. I don't want you to be here by yourself with no parents and no one to take care of you."

"Look, I don't need them," he growled. "And I sure as shit don't need you."

Julie took a breath, not liking arguments like this any more than when she'd been a teenager herself. She should probably give him hell about his language. That seemed like the motherly thing to do. But there were more important issues to settle. Like the fact that he was stuck with having someone taking care of him. Like the fact that she truly did care, even if she'd done a lousy job of showing it.

"Well, I'm here now," she said. She could be as stubborn as anybody. "And I'm going to do my best to take care of you."

"I told you, I don't need anybody to take care of me."

"Then there shouldn't be much for me to do," she said, switching tactics midstream. "Maybe I'll just consider this a little vacation. I haven't had one in a long time."

He seemed taken aback by that. Was this the way? Agreeing with him and just staying? God, she didn't want to stay.

"You could come back to Memphis with me," she offered.

He made a face. "What's in Memphis?"

"Not much," she admitted. No job. No fiancé. A few friends, but no one she was close to. "I live there. They have good barbecue. Nice music. The Mississippi . . ."

Peter shook his head and snarled, "I'm not going anywhere with you."

"Fine. We'll stay here," she bluffed. Surely he wouldn't really want to do that. Surely he'd always wanted a chance to get away, just like she had.

He seemed at a total loss then. Like he'd expected a good fight. Like he might enjoy it. She took perverse pleasure in denying him the opportunity. Maybe that was the way to get through this. Agree with whatever he said and go right on doing what she thought she should.

Peter's bottom lip started to tremble and a telltale glistening came into his eyes as he stood there, as defiant as ever on the outside and crumbling inside.

She felt tears gathering in her eyes as well, as she reached for him. "I'm sorry, Peter. I'm so sorry."

He backed up a step, his chin jutted up, and his tears never fell. "I hate you," he said. "I hate you almost as much as I hate them."

Then he slammed the door in her face.

The social worker had obviously heard every word. She was standing halfway up the stairs as Julie came back down. They walked into the living room. Neither of them sat down. *Might as well get this over with,* Julie decided.

"So, what now? Do we have to fill out some paperwork? Sign something? It's been a long day already, and . . ."

"We have forms to fill out, and there will be things to sign. But I wanted you to have some idea of what you'll be dealing with with Peter, first. If you're sure . . ."

"I'm sure," Julie claimed.

"All right. Why don't I take Peter back to the shelter, and I'll come back. Then we can get started."

"Shelter?" Julie said. "What's he doing in a shelter?"

"It's the best we could do at the moment. I'm sorry. We didn't have any open slots with foster parents at the moment."

Kiddie jail. To think she'd joked about it. In that moment she was glad she'd come. Peter must have been so scared, thinking that she wouldn't.

"I'll go see if he's gotten his things together, and we'll go," Mrs. Reed said.

"Go where?" Julie still didn't understand.

"Back to the shelter," Mrs. Reed said. "I'm sorry. Obviously I didn't make myself clear. Yesterday, when both his parents were arrested, Peter was taken into the custody of the Division of Child and Family Services. Once we do that, he's our responsibility. Mine and the judge's and a whole host of other people's, and our job is to make sure he's in a safe place."

"He'll be safe with me," Julie said. "I'm his sister."

"But you're not his legal guardian or his parent. Which means we have some work to do. References, court records, criminal background check, work history, medical history, credit history. All sorts of things."

Julie wondered if she'd pass. "And how long does all that take?"

"If everything checks out—quickly—we might be able to get you temporary custody in forty-eight hours or so."

"Oh."

"It's for his protection. To make sure he's placed with a responsible adult."

Responsible? That would be me?

"I just broke up with my fiancé and quit my job. Yesterday," she said. "Is that a problem?"

"It depends . . . You and your fiancé . . . Was it . . . an abusive relationship?"

"No."

"Do you drink? Use illegal drugs?"

"No."

"Ever been arrested?"

"No."

"We'll check," she added.

"Fine. Check."

"What about stability? How long had you been in that job?"

"Just two years, but I'd been with the company for seven. I started working there while I was in school."

"That's good. Your employment record won't show any problems?"

"No." Somehow she'd managed to be a model employee.

"We'll need to speak with your former employer."

"That would be my former fiancé," she said, wondering if Steve would tell her Julie was sleeping with Zach, the fiancé of Mrs. Reed's good friend's daughter. "Working there didn't seem like a good idea after breaking our engagement."

"I can understand that."

"So . . ." Julie took a breath and dared to ask, "how do I look, from the safe, responsible adult standpoint?"

"We're not asking that you be a saint, or someone who's never made a mistake. Just responsible, law-abiding, reasonably stable. If everything you've told me checks out, we should be fine. Provided you can handle your brother."

Julie laughed yet again.

"You did fine up there. He's angry at the whole world right now, with good reason. It's better to have it come out than for him to be bottling it up inside. And it's going to be hard for him to trust that you're going to stay, because he must feel like his parents just abandoned him. You can work past that, in time, if that's what you really want. If you don't, it would be better for him if you left right now than to let him come to depend on you and then lose you, too."

"I—"

"Think about it," Mrs. Reed said. "I'm going upstairs. It was late when we gave up on finding a foster home to take him last night, and he didn't pack any more than he needed for one night. I don't think he believed me when I told him he wouldn't be here for a while. If he's finished packing, I'll take him back to the shelter and then come back here so you and I can get started."

"Thank you."

Julie sat down on the sofa. This was going to be more difficult than she'd feared. From upstairs, she heard shouting, Peter mainly, going "Why?" and "I don't understand." Did he want to stay with her after all? Maybe she was better than a shelter, at least.

He came downstairs a few moments later, a scuffed-up duffel bag in one hand and a basketball in the other, Mrs. Reed following closely behind. He paused for a moment by the front door and glared at her before stalking outside.

Mrs. Reed handed her a key. "To the house. It's Peter's."

Julie took it and went to the door, calling after him, "I'll be right here, Peter, and you will be, too. Just give us a couple of days."

He didn't acknowledge her words in any way, just walked across the overgrown grass of the front yard and stood rigidly, his back to her, by the social worker's car.

"Try not to worry so much. He's far from the first scared, angry teenager we've dealt with," Mrs. Reed said. "We'll be in touch."

And then Julie found herself in the last place she wanted to be. With no job, no fiancé, and a brother who claimed to hate her. Oh, and a social worker who was good friends with the mother of the fiancée of the man she'd slept with two nights ago. As she saw it, she didn't have a chance in hell of making this work.

She also needed to talk to Zach. She could say she was sorry again, and then maybe beg him not tell his fiancée about the two of them, for Peter's sake.

Julie looked at the clock. Almost one o'clock. Thirty-six hours after they'd done the deed. If she knew Zach, he'd already confessed.

She picked up the phone, relieved to find the service hadn't been cut off. She dialed the number he'd given her that first night in the restaurant and ended up getting his voice mail.

"Zach, it's Julie." *Damn.* Her voice was shaky. She cleared her throat and tried to steady it, to not sound quite so needy. "You'll never guess where I am. Never in a million years. I'm home, and I saw Peter today, just for a minute." Okay, she couldn't hide it. She was needy as hell. "Peter can't stand me. He's in an emergency shelter, because they didn't have space in a foster home for him, and they're going to do some big investigation into my background before they'll even let him live with me temporarily. If they let him live with me. And . . ."

And I'm scared again, Zach. I'm so scared.

Not that he needed her to tell him that. It would be painfully obvious from the message she'd left so far.

Julie tried to think of something to say to save herself from sounding so dismal and from looking so pathetic.

"Oh, and the social worker said she knows your fiancée's mother—" She got that much out before the voice-mail system cut her off.

Chapter 9

Zach got to Memphis late Saturday night, spent Sunday feeling guilty about everything and reading over files, then went to visit his client.

Returning to his room Sunday night, he found the phone ringing, but he wasn't about to answer it. Once the ringing ceased, he dialed into the hotel's voice-mail system and played the messages. Mother, father, sister, sister, mother. He listened to a few words of each one and then hit the erase button.

Until a sad, shaky voice said, "Zach, it's Julie. . . ."

He played the message three times, and each time she sounded worse than before. And what a bad break with the social worker. A friend of Gwen's mother? Life just got better and better, didn't it? And Peter was in an emergency shelter while the social worker picked Julie's life apart. She must be loving that.

Zach sat down, kicked off his shoes, put his briefcase on the sofa, and called directory assistance to get her parents' phone number. She hadn't left it, hadn't even asked him to call. Asking him to keep quiet about a secret of hers or to just leave her alone was as close as she'd ever come to asking him for help.

Which was why he didn't wait for her to ask. Which might be why he'd found himself charging in to try to save her, time and time again. Because she needed help and wouldn't ask for it.

She hadn't asked anything of him this time, except for him to go away. And what had he done? Butted into her life, pissed off her fiancé, tried to play conscience for her, then just grabbed on to her like she was the only solid thing in the universe, drawing her down to the floor beneath him, pulling off her clothes, pushing inside of her, and—

Zach put down the phone and got to his feet, needing to get out of that room. Just looking at that spot on the floor could make him practically break out into a sweat. The bedroom wasn't any easier.

He grabbed his cell phone and the slip of paper where he'd scrawled down her number and went outside, welcoming the slight chill to the breeze.

No use in going back to that night again. There was no changing it. But she was in a mess that was at least partly his fault, and he owed her. So he called. That's what he told himself—that this was an obligation.

She had him lying to himself now. He just needed to hear her voice.

She answered, sounding sleepy and very, very vulnerable. None of that Julie-the-tough-girl evident tonight. He glanced at his watch, checking the time. It wasn't that late.

"Hi," he said softly.

"Hi."

She'd barely breathed into the phone, and already, the sound of her voice was doing funny things to his insides. There was a little kick of heat in the region of his groin, which he was determined to ignore, and something seemed to ease in his chest, as if with one or two little words, he could gauge her mood and be reassured that she was okay. He thought she sounded tired, but not bad, all things considered.

And he felt better, something he chose not to examine too closely. He'd felt like shit for three days straight. If the sound of her voice from hundreds of miles away could bring him some measure of comfort, surely he could have it.

"So you're really there, huh?" he began. Because there was an odd kind of need floating around inside of him that he didn't understand but had no intention of fighting. Not when he just wanted to talk, and she was so far away.

"Yes, I'm here," she whispered. He imagined her there to say it in person, say it softly with so much understanding. *I'm here.*

He wanted to talk to Julie Morrison more than he wanted his next breath.

"I can't believe it," he said. "I had to call the number and hear you say it again before I believed you were there."

She laughed. He heard the faint creak of a chair. As she sighed, he imagined her settling deeper into the corner of a big, comfy chair, her feet curled up underneath her, the phone tucked against her shoulder. *That's it,* he was thinking. *Get comfortable. Let me see what I can do for you tonight.*

"Surprised you, didn't I?"

"Yeah, you did. I know how hard that was for you, Julie. I'm proud of you for going and trying to help," he said, because some people never, ever heard that, not at any time in their entire lives, and because he *was* proud of her. She'd been running for so long.

"Imagine that. Zach McRae, proud of me."

He grinned. She was probably aiming for sarcasm—she often did—but the emotion in her voice ruined the effect.

"I am," he insisted.

"I kind of thought you might be. Even though, to be perfectly honest—how's that coming from me?—I really didn't want to come here, Zach. You know that. Peter shamed me into it."

"Hey, it doesn't really matter why you're there. You still went. That's what counts. You don't think people do the right things because they want to, do you? Of course not. The right thing is usually the hardest thing of all to do."

"You do the right thing."

"Not always." The words came out too fast to take them back.

"Oh, yeah . . . *That*. So . . . you were engaged, too?" she asked softly. "You didn't tell me, Zach."

"Yeah. It just never came up," he said. *What a lame-ass excuse.* He could just hear himself telling Gwen, if she ever asked, *Did that woman you slept with know you were engaged? No, darling. It just never came up.*

"I guess it's too late to ask you not to tell her?" Julie asked.

"Yeah. I flew up to Cleveland Saturday morning to talk to her in person."

"She lives in Cleveland?"

"No. Cincinnati. Her father's a U.S. Senator, running for reelection, and she works on his campaign, so she moves around a lot lately."

"Oh. How did she take it?"

"I'm not sure. It's probably going to take a few days

for it to sink in, and then . . . I don't know what's going to happen, Julie."

Zach, the man with the plan. He had no clue what was coming.

"I'm sorry," she said again.

"And I told you, you don't have anything to apologize for."

It had been all him. If he was really up for some of that legendary honesty she credited him with, he'd admit that he wouldn't mind hanging on to her right now.

"What about you?" he asked, pulling the oldest argument tactic in the book. When floundering, change the subject. "What did you tell Steve to get away long enough to go to Baxter?"

"The truth."

"You didn't," he shot back.

"I did," she insisted. "Surprised you again, huh?"

"Yeah."

"I couldn't marry him. Not after . . . you know."

"You said it didn't mean anything," he reminded her, in dangerous territory he couldn't seem to avoid.

"Not to you and me. It's not like . . . you know."

Don't go down that road, Zach. But he couldn't quite help himself. "No, I don't think I do know. Why don't you explain it to me?"

Maybe then he could explain it to Gwen. And to himself.

"I meant that it wasn't like there was anything between us. Not really. It was just—"

"Sex?" he said. What did it mean when people said that? Sex, to him, didn't seem to be one of those words you could put a "just" in front of. It was always something. Memorable. Forgettable. Mind-blowing. Awkward. Comforting. Nice. Really nice.

They hadn't had forgettable sex, which was a real problem, since he was supposed to forget about it. And it hadn't been awkward, although it should have been, there in that little slice of space on the floor between the table and the couch.

It had been wild and desperate.

He didn't think he'd done desperate since he'd lost his virginity back in high school.

"Yes," Julie claimed. *Just sex.* "A mistake."

"Bad night," he said, using her own term.

"Yes."

Then why did the images of it, the sounds, the taste of her, the feel, remain stubbornly in his mind, coming back to him at the most inappropriate times, like now, crowding out nearly every intelligent thought? Could she explain that to him?

"Why are we talking about this, Zach? There's nothing to say, is there?"

If there was, he sure didn't know what it was. "I'm just . . ." He tried. "I'm sorry about you and Steve."

Liar. No way he was sorry she couldn't marry old Steve.

"I know how much you wanted that," he said, trying to mollify his conscience.

"It would have been a mistake. You knew that all along."

"It's not for me to say, Julie. You told me, and I didn't listen. I never do."

"You just never gave up on me. That's all."

She said it like it wasn't a bad thing, when he was starting to think it was, the way he always thought he could fix anything. He couldn't.

"I'm really sorry the marriage thing didn't work out," he said again.

"It wouldn't have, with or without you. Come on, Zach. I was lying to the guy, and you know how well that's always worked for me."

"Hey, you didn't lie to the social worker, did you?" he said, remembering then that he was supposed to be helping her.

"No, but I was planning on asking you not to tell your fiancée about you and me. For Peter's sake. But that wouldn't have been fair, either. So . . ." she said, "please tell me my social worker hasn't heard from your fiancée's mother that the engagement's off because you slept with me. I didn't think that would do my petition for custody any good. I can just see me trying to explain to Mrs. Reed about a bad night that didn't mean anything. That's not going to work with her."

"Gwen's not the type to run crying to her mother." She'd pull herself together and handle it. "I could be wrong, but I'll check and see what I can do."

"Could you?"

"Sure. I'll ask Gwen if we can keep this between the two of us for now. At least until we decide what to do."

"Zach, the hero," she said. "Charging in to save the day."

"No."

"Yes," she insisted, "you do. I . . . I am so sorry about how this turned out. Do you really love her, Zach?"

What could he say? He knew he sure as hell shouldn't be so eager to spill his guts to Julie when he was supposed to be in love with Gwen. Not when their relationship was hanging by a thread and he might still be able to save it.

He still wanted that, didn't he?

"I mean, I thought I loved Steve," she jumped in. "And that he loved me, but how could he? I hid so much from him, so much more than where I was from or what my family was like."

"I think we all do that to some degree," he said, the words hitting way too close to home.

"I can't hide anything from you. It used to drive me crazy. I always felt like you could see right through me and that you must—"She laughed softly. "Never mind."

"No. Tell me."

"I thought you must hate me."

"Never." He'd never come close to feeling that way about her.

"You know, this honesty stuff is a lot easier late at night, in the dark, when you're hundreds of miles apart. Maybe I could manage it that way. Long-distance honesty. Start there and work my way up to being honest with people closer and closer to where I actually am."

"Sounds like a plan." He and Gwen did the long-distance thing really well, but they were seldom in the same town for more than a day or so at a time.

He knew her, didn't he? He still wanted her.

"I'm really scared," Julie said.

Gwen went right out of his head. Except to think that she never would have said that to him. He doubted she would ever have felt it. She'd probably be shocked to hear that he'd ever been afraid in his life, that he was scared right now.

"I know, Julie." He knew all about it.

"That's why I called. Not so much to ask you to lie, but because I'm scared."

"I know." She never had to say the words for him to figure that out.

"I hate it here."

"I know that, too." He didn't want to be there now, either, and it was tearing him up inside.

The place was his anchor, the safest place in the world. A place where people understood him and loved him and stood by him, no matter what, and he wouldn't let himself be there. Because he didn't have the skill or the energy to cover up how awful he was feeling. It took a tremendous amount of effort, holding something like this inside, especially to hide it from the people who knew him best.

"What if they won't give Peter to me?" Julie said.

"They will," he promised her.

"How can you know that?"

It got really quiet. Her voice trailed off abruptly on the last word. He was afraid she was crying, and he wasn't there. He wished he was.

Zach did the next-best thing, putting on his most persuasive, know-it-all-lawyer-voice and telling her, "This is what I do. I know the system inside and out. They'll give you Peter."

"He hates me," she said. "He told me so today."

"He's scared, and he's angry," Zach said. Like Julie had always been. If anyone was going to understand Peter, it was her. "He might think he hates you right now, but he won't for long. Just don't give up on him."

And don't run away. Please, Julie, don't run this time.

He might just have to chase her down and drag her back, if she did.

You can't run forever, he'd tell her.

But shit . . . That's what Zach'd been doing ever since his old man got out of prison and moved to that little town two hours away from the place he would always think of as home.

It had only been six months, and he was exhausted from the effort already. Julie had been running her whole life. Maybe she was just tougher than he was, and if she was, who the hell was he to be telling her anything?

"It'll be okay," he told her, despite all that.

"Promise?"

"Promise."

"Okay." She sniffled, and he could just picture her trying to pull herself together, that little determined look coming over her face. "And you must believe that, because you don't lie, and you're always right, so they have to give Peter to me."

"I'm not always right," he admitted. "But I am about this."

"I believe you," she said, in a way that had the power to make him feel about ten feet tall, at least temporarily.

Until the reality of what had happened the last few days, all his faults, came rushing like a slide show through his mind. Mistakes. Like the ones he'd made with Tony Williams's trial. The way he'd hurt her and Gwen. All the things he wished he could fix and couldn't.

"Things are going to get better, right?" Julie asked.

"I sure hope so."

"You don't sound so good, Zach. Anything you want to tell me?"

"Just another bad day," he said, afraid it was going to be a bad week. Bad month. Maybe a bad year.

How was he going to get through all that? Where was he going to go, when he couldn't run anymore and nobody understood?

"Did something happen?" she asked. "With Tony?"

"No. Not yet." But he was expecting it to be bad. Where would he go with all that if it got even worse? If she wasn't here, if he couldn't face the idea of going home, and if Gwen didn't care?

"You can tell me about it," she offered. "You can tell me anything."

"I know," he said, testing that idea, even as he said it.

He thought about how she never asked for help, never expected it, and realized he didn't either, didn't often accept it when it was offered. Maybe he just didn't know how.

That night . . . Maybe Gwen didn't expect him to ask, so she wasn't really listening. It wasn't like she ever asked him for anything, either. Maybe she didn't know how, herself. Maybe they were just two screwed-up people fumbling through as best they could, okay until things got tough.

And maybe he was trying to somehow justify what he'd done, to assuage his guilt over sleeping with Julie. Somehow everything came back to him sleeping with Julie.

She sure was easy to talk to.

He had to stop this.

"Listen," he said, turning his mind back to her problems and not her in bed with him. "I'm going to call my mom. She knows all about the social services system, too. She'll talk you through it, and you'll feel better."

"Thanks, Zach."

"You're welcome."

Time to hang up the phone, Zach. There was a woman in Cleveland who was supposed to be his wife one day. But he couldn't say these things to Gwen. He couldn't go dumping his problems on her when he'd just slept with another woman and wanted to be with Julie tonight instead.

Not for *that,* right? He didn't want *that.* He couldn't. But he could talk, and she would listen. She would care.

"I'm worried about you, too," she said.

"Well, don't." Everyone was worried about him, and he didn't like it. He'd always taken care of himself just fine. He'd find a way to do that again, to put everything behind him and go on. He'd be fine. No one would ever have to know how bad it had gotten.

"Zach," she began.

"Take care of yourself, Julie," he said. Then couldn't resist adding, "Call me, if you need me."

Because if she needed him, he'd be there.

The next morning Julie lay in an old bed in a room in the farthest corner of the house — not the one where she'd slept as a child. There was nothing left of her room except the four walls. It was a storage area now, crammed full of boxes she hadn't bothered to open.

She'd found this bed covered with clothes and coats and linens no one had ever bothered to put away. Probably things her mother had bought, but couldn't afford. Her mother had an odd habit of buying things with money she didn't have, and eventually it ended up in a heap like this one. Julie used to sneak out of the house with her mother's things and sell them at the consignment shop to get money for things like lunch at school and clothes for herself.

Last night she'd simply swept everything off onto the floor and fallen into bed, had been lying here nearly asleep when Zach called. The house had seemed enormous and dark and full of unfamiliar noises, and she'd been so lonely. She was awake for a long time after hanging up the phone with Zach, most of the time just missing him, and there'd been a moment when she'd let herself replay that night.

Not the sexual part. The other. Holding him. Him

holding her. Drifting off to sleep with her head against his bare chest, his heartbeat thrumming along reassuringly beneath her right ear. The heat of his skin, the little ripple of muscles along his stomach, the little hitch in his breath every now and then as he slept, and the way he smelled.

It had been nice, him holding her all the night through, and she still had the shirt he'd put on her that morning. It smelled of him, and foolishly, she'd brought it with her. One day, she might let herself sleep in it. It was likely the only comfort she'd have here, and ill advised as it would be to climb into bed with his shirt, she'd learned long ago to take whatever obscure comfort life offered her.

Julie sat up and leaned toward the window just to her left, pushed the drab yellow curtains aside and looked out at the wet, dreary world. The sky was bluish gray with a low cloud cover, the street glistening and wet, matching her mood exactly. She thought about climbing back into bed, but was afraid that memories of the night she'd spent with Zach were just too close this morning. She really had to forget him. She could keep the shirt. That was it.

She pulled on her sweats and drew her hair back into a loose braid. She went into the kitchen, grimacing at the mess she hadn't had the energy to tackle the night before. She'd begun riffling through practically bare cabinets when she heard a knock on the back door. There was Zach's mother, looking beautifully serene and welcoming, holding a small white bag that smelled of coffee.

"Good morning. I hope I'm not too early," Rachel said.

"Of course not," Julie said, wishing very much that

she had cleaned up the kitchen, but still happy to see a familiar face. "Do I smell coffee and doughnuts?"

"A half dozen," Rachel said, giving her a quick hug as they stood in the doorway. "You liked the jelly ones, right? I thought so, but I wasn't sure if I was remembering correctly, and there's always the chance that your tastes might have changed. Or that it might be a really bad day. So I got six, all different kinds."

"That's perfect. Come on in," Julie said, thinking Zach was practically a saint. He'd called his mother to take care of her.

"Look at you," Rachel said, unbuttoning her coat, which was wet from the rain. "You're all grown up. So tall and so pretty."

Julie smiled in spite of herself, thinking that surely every bit of the last few days showed in her face. She took Rachel's coat and hung it on a peg by the door, took the paper bag and made room among a few newspapers, days' worth of mail, three old coffee cups, and a bag of chips.

"Give me just a minute."

Julie started clearing the table, pushing things back to make room on the counter. Housekeeping had never been her parents' strong suit, just as upkeep of the house or parenting hadn't. Her face burned once again, reminded of the way they'd lived. Haphazardly. Clumsily. Loudly. Irresponsibly. Chaotically. Fearfully.

And Zach's family had been kind.

She made herself stop what she was doing. The table was clear enough that they could sit and drink their coffee and have a doughnut, and this wasn't anything Zach's mother hadn't seen before.

"You look great," Julie said, meaning it sincerely.

She'd always believed Zach's mother was kindness personified. "I'm so glad you're all still here."

Rachel smiled. "Now, don't you dare cry. Zach will call and ask how you were, and I can't lie to him."

"Okay. I won't." Julie forgot the state of the house and thought of Zach checking up on her. She remembered his voice as he'd said *Call me, if you need me.* Something she had no right to do. But she liked knowing he'd offered. "Zach's been . . . Well, he's wonderful, but I'm sure I don't have to tell you that."

"No, you don't."

"He's always been so kind to me. All of you were. I don't think I could possibly tell you how much that meant to me when I was living here."

"I'm glad you could come to us. I wish we could have done more. Grace wanted us to just keep you so she could have you for a sister. Did you know that?"

"She told me." Julie had been eight and a half at the time, Grace nine. Julie had gone straight home and packed her bags. She'd waited for a week, thinking they'd come to take her away. But it never happened. She was too embarrassed to tell their mother she'd actually thought it might come true. She'd been sure no one at her house would have minded if she'd gone to live with Grace's family.

"It's going to be all right, Julie," Rachel said.

She nodded, working hard to hold back those tears, not wanting Zach to hear about her crying this morning, after she'd cried to him last night.

"Drink some of this, while it's still hot." Rachel opened the bag and pulled out napkins, a stirring stick, artificial creamer and sugar, then a steaming cup.

Julie grabbed a napkin and quickly blotted the moisture from the corners of her eyes, and then busied herself pouring sugar and cream into her coffee. Rachel tactfully did the same, and once Julie had had a few sips and thought she might live through the morning, she reached for a doughnut. After all, sugar was one of the finest comforts known to mankind.

Which made her think of Zach's shirt, of smelling it.

Which made her think of Zach without the shirt, in bed with her.

"Zach told me everything," his mother said.

Julie's jelly doughnut got stuck in her throat. She coughed once, then again, and Rachel looked concerned.

"I'm fine," she managed to squeak out. No way he'd tell his mother about that. They'd talked about it last night. She'd asked him to make sure Gwen's mother didn't find out. No way he'd tell his own mother. She was probably friends with Julie's social worker, too.

"Sorry," Rachel said. "He wanted me to know so that I could help."

"Of course," Julie said.

It was about Peter. She should be thinking about him. He was the reason Julie was here. Not because she was running away from all her problems in Memphis. That little thought was nagging at her. That she wasn't being noble at all. She was running again, doing what she did best.

"So, what can I tell you?" Rachel asked. "I really do want to help."

Tell me how to stop running, she thought. Rachel didn't run. Her husband, Sam, didn't run. Zach didn't. They should teach that in school. Life 101: How Not to Screw Up.

"I don't even know what I need to know," Julie admitted, and then it occurred to her that Rachel had been just down the block all these years, while Peter had been right here. She must know so much more about him than Julie did. All she had to do was ask. . . .

"Has it been really bad for him here?" she began.

Rachel didn't say anything right away. She seemed to be sorting through her thoughts, picking her words carefully. "Well, he didn't . . . come by the house as often as you did. And with our kids grown . . . Sam and I aren't as plugged into what's going on with the neighborhood kids as we used to be. But we saw him from time to time. I don't think much has changed in this house, Julie. I think it's probably been a lot like it was when you were growing up."

"But Peter's their son," she said.

She had only been her mother's daughter, and she'd always known where that left her. Outside the loop. A nuisance, at best, always underfoot. Peter was her mother and stepfather's son.

Rachel's compassionate look told Julie that it hadn't mattered.

"I thought . . . I mean, it was tough for me, but with him . . . They always treated him differently." *Better. Not quite as bad.* "I mean, I know it wasn't the perfect home, but they didn't come down on Peter, the way they did . . ." *With me.*

Rachel nodded, reminding her of Zach, way too much understanding in those eyes.

"I thought it would be better for him than it was for me," Julie said.

"I don't know for sure," Rachel said. "Peter doesn't really talk to me. It's just . . . from what I've seen, I'm guessing that he felt kind of . . . lost and lonely. I wish I'd done more for him—"

"No. That's not what I meant. He's not . . ." Rachel's

child. Or Rachel's brother. He wasn't her responsibility in any way.

"Still," Rachel said, "I wish I had."

Julie nodded. What could you say to people like that? The ones who tried to take care of kids who weren't even theirs? Of friends of their little sister, who they hadn't seen in years or a woman their son had slept with on a really, really bad night? This was something she just didn't understand.

"I know you must have tried to help him," Julie said. "And I'm so glad you're here now. Now that I'm back."

"I'm glad you were in Memphis for Zach."

Julie went still, trying to gauge the look on Rachel's face.

Finally Rachel said, "When the verdict in his trial came down against him."

Julie nodded. Carefully, she said, "Zach took it hard."

"He always does."

"It happens a lot?" she asked, because she just couldn't see Zach losing often.

"Any case he loses is one too many to him, and he takes the toughest ones he can find. He claims he does it for the sheer challenge in it, but—"

"I don't believe that," Julie said.

"Neither do I," Rachel agreed. "His birth father got out of prison six months ago. Did he tell you that?"

"Grace did."

"They went to see him. Emma and Grace are okay, I think. Upset for a few days afterward, but okay. Zach insisted that he wasn't upset at all, but everything about the way he looked and the way he sounded told me he was. And he's hardly been home since."

"What did the man say to him?" Julie asked.

"I don't know. Did he talk to you about it?"

"A little," Julie admitted.

"I'm not going to ask you what he said. I'm just glad he talked to someone about it. I'm glad you were there when he needed someone."

"I'm glad, too."

To hell with everything else. He'd needed her, and she didn't want to think of what he might have done had he been alone. *There.* She'd almost managed to make it sound noble — sleeping with this other woman's fiancé.

"I know how he seems to the world," Rachel said. "So strong, so self-sufficient and together . . . He doesn't let me take care of him very often, which I suppose is normal now that he's all grown up, but we all need someone at times."

"I know." Julie needed more than most.

"I want someone to be there for him, even when he doesn't know how much he needs someone."

Julie nodded, ready to agree, and then remembered it wasn't her place. He had a fiancée. Maybe. Julie was supposed to stay away from him and not mess that up any more than they already had.

"He's always been a good friend to me," she said, beginning with the vaguest thing she could think of that applied. "And I'd do anything for him."

Okay, that definitely wasn't vague or noncommittal, but it was true. That counted for something, didn't it? She tried to backtrack quickly. "I mean . . . I'm sure he has a lot of friends who feel the same way. That if he ever needed anything . . ."

"He won't ask, Julie. That's what I was trying to say. He won't ask for help."

"Oh. Okay." So what was she supposed to do? If the situation were reversed, Zach wouldn't wait for her to ask for help. He'd just show up. Except she couldn't now. "He's in Memphis, and I have to be here. For Peter."

"I know. But the penalty phase of the trial shouldn't last long. A few days, maybe. And after that, I want him home. I've told him that myself, when I can get him on the phone, but it's not doing any good. But he called me last night, after weeks of ducking my calls, because he was worried about you. I was just thinking . . . He's a lot more comfortable taking care of others than having anyone take care of him. If he thought you needed him here . . ."

"Oh." She got it now. She was supposed to play the helpless female to Zach's hero. She should be perfect for this role. She'd been practicing her whole life. No acting abilities required and no lies. All she had to do was tell him how she really felt. If she could get him here, his family could take care of him.

What was she supposed to do? Resist something she wanted very badly because she was afraid of what else might happen between them if he was here?

It would not happen again. He didn't really want her. He'd just needed someone, and she'd been there. She firmly shut her ears to the little voice inside that insisted it had sure felt like he'd wanted her, despite the fact that he was supposed to be in love with someone else.

Julie blurted out, "He's engaged, isn't he?"

"Yes," Rachel said.

"I just thought . . ." Julie began. "If he was in trouble, she'd be here."

"She's busy with her father's campaign. And I'm being an interfering mother, which I try not to be. I just thought, if you asked, he might come home."

"Well, I was just pitiful on the phone with him last night, if that helps."

Rachel grinned. "There you go."

"I guess if he gave me a chance, I could pour out my troubles to him again."

Julie couldn't be happy that Rachel was so worried about him, but if this was where he needed to be . . .

She'd never deny Zach anything when he was in need, and yet . . .

They couldn't do it again. That one night—that was all she'd ever have of him.

Chapter 10

It took exactly forty-eight minutes for the jury to decide the fate of Tony Williams. Zach timed it, pissed that they'd taken so little time.

Tony stood beside him, trembling and crying, scared to death. It was all Zach could do to stand still. He'd have liked to be pacing the floor, but instead concentrated on trying to breathe slowly and deeply. After all, he was supposed to be the calm one here. He wasn't facing a death sentence.

Toward the end, Zach put his arm around Tony, who huddled like the child he was against Zach's side. He stood like a statue, stared at the judicial seal on the wall above the jury box, and clamped his mouth shut.

Through the fog of his anger, his frustration, and his fear, the verdict finally registered: life in prison. Tony sagged against him, the boy's legs giving out. Relief was a hard emotion to let in, given that the verdict was a life spent in a cage. But it was life, and Zach wouldn't stop fighting once a verdict was in.

They finished with the formalities. The guards were waiting to take Tony to prison for a long, long time. Zach should really say something. *It's not over yet. Don't give up. Just try to stay alive in there.* He would choke on the words.

"Mr. McRae?" The bailiff was at his side. "Judge would like to see you in chambers. Now." That was odd.

He looked back at Tony. The guards were hustling him away already. "I'll be back," Zach called out, then headed for the judge's chambers. It didn't take long.

The judge didn't want him back in his courtroom anytime soon. That little tussle at the end, as they were arguing over how the judge would charge the jury had been a bit ugly, and he probably had been out of line. He probably deserved this dressing down.

Zach took it as best he could, nodding and trying to hold his tongue. But in the end, he just couldn't. He yelled, "You think that boy deserves to be in prison for the rest of his life?"

"That's not for me to say, son, and you know it. That's for the jury."

"He shouldn't have been charged with the crime in the first place."

"Enough," the judge said. "You're lucky I didn't throw you in jail for contempt. If I hadn't known your boss for years, I may well have done it. I settled for calling him instead. Adam wants to see you in his office, first thing tomorrow. Which means you should be going, Mr. McRae."

"Kicking me out of the state, judge?"

"I could. You've got to step back, son, or you're not going to be any good to any of your clients, and you're sure not going to get anywhere pissing off judges."

Zach opened his mouth to argue, but the judge cut in. "Enough. Go." Zach turned and went.

He drove a bit recklessly and too fast to his hotel, threw his clothes into his suitcase and crammed his papers into boxes. He called the airline from his cell phone on the way to the airport and barely managed to catch the last flight to Cincinnati that night. He took a taxi to the apartment on the river he and Gwen shared on rare occasions when they happened to be in the city at the same time, collapsed in his own unfamiliar bed, and was in Adam's office first thing the next morning.

Bleary-eyed and still pissed, he just lost it with Adam, yelling at one point and slamming his fist down onto Adam's desk. Twenty minutes later, he was back on the street, his chest heaving, having been ordered not to show his face inside his own office for thirty days. When he'd argued about that, Mark made it sixty.

It was ludicrous. What the hell was he supposed to do for sixty days?

He took to the streets, walking fast, trying to burn off some restless energy, some tension, something that felt like despair. He didn't screw up like this. He didn't fall apart. He wasn't stupid or reckless. Yet within the space of a few days, he'd taken an old friend to bed while he was engaged to someone else, drank way too much and thrown things against a wall, lost a case that sent a young boy to prison for life, been kicked out of a courtroom, and now was suspended from his job.

He had a hard time believing it all himself.

Zach walked until he'd calmed down a little. He found it hard to be still these days, to make his mind be quiet. He didn't want time to think, didn't like the direction his thoughts took, the tightness that came into his chest or the funny things that happened to his breathing when things got bad. Usually he could walk it out. If that didn't work . . . Well, there was always his so-called father's tried-and-true methods. A bottle of something. That had worked really well last time.

His next impulse—which he completely denied him-self—was to call Julie. It was right there. *Call Julie.* Like a neon sign flashing on and off in his brain.

No, he would not do that. He could call his father, but if his family knew he was this close to home, they'd de-scend en masse, and he just couldn't handle that now. He supposed he should call Gwen, just to see if she was at all interested in the fact that his life was falling apart.

He glanced at his watch. Close to noon on a Wednes-day.

She is probably getting ready for a cocktail party. The idea moved through his head in a nasty little voice, a mean, petty one. Like he had a right to complain about the woman he'd thoroughly wronged so very recently?

He searched his heart for what he felt for her. Where had it gone? They'd slid into a satisfying relationship, comfortable, compatible. He admired her body as much as her brain, her determination as much as her wit. They had made sense together.

Why didn't they, anymore?

He pulled out his Palm Pilot. Gwen, one of the best-organized women on earth, did a linkup and fed her schedule into his, his into hers, once a week or so, so they could always find each other. He checked it now. She might actually be in town. If he dumped his problems on anyone, it should be her. He called campaign headquar-ters. They were expecting her today.

Fine. Maybe he could just hide at the apartment and see her tonight. Maybe he'd have calmed down by then. He took a cab back to his office to get his car, then drove back to the high-rise on the river they called home. When he unlocked the apartment door, he saw Gwen's raincoat draped over the back of the sofa, her purse and her keys on the table beside the door.

Well, hell. No hiding here.

He called out her name, but heard no response.

Maybe she was asleep. She just crashed sometimes, after coming in from a long trip.

He thought he heard something in the bedroom, which was at the end of the hall, next to their his-and-hers offices. They'd gotten a three-bedroom so they'd both have space to work.

Zach pushed open the bedroom door. It was dark in the room, and Gwen was in bed, leaning back against the pillows, a sheet wrapped around her, barely covering her breasts. Her hair looked mussed, and she seemed a little dazed.

"Sorry," he said. "Didn't mean to wake you."

"Zach? I didn't . . . I saw your things, but . . . What happened?"

"I lost the case," he said. "It's over."

"Oh." She just sat there for a minute, staring at him, and then glanced quickly toward the bathroom. "I thought you'd be at work. . . ."

"No, I . . ." He didn't want to explain. Not yet. And he was starting to get a funny feeling about this.

Slowly, he turned toward the bathroom door. There in the pool of light spilling from the opening stood a guy he'd known for the better part of ten years. He was shoving his shirttails into the waistband of his slacks and looking like he expected to be knocked flat on his ass any minute.

"Zach . . . I'm sorry," the guy began.

Zach laughed. What could he do? It was so . . . cliché. The perfect ending to the perfect day.

"I didn't . . ." Dan tried. "It didn't . . ."

"Never mind." Zach knew what came next. *I don't*

know how it happened. Or, *It didn't mean a thing.* Yeah, right.

Gwen didn't say a word. She would have seen his luggage by the front door and known he was back in town. And she'd done this anyway. So she wanted him to find them together. Maybe she just didn't care anymore. He'd slept with someone else, and apparently, so had she.

"You mind leaving us alone?" Zach asked, his voice dead even as he stared at Gwen.

"What?" Dan asked.

Zach took a breath and said, "We have some things to talk about. Gwen and I. Privately, if you don't mind."

"If I don't mind?" Dan repeated.

He supposed civility seemed out of place at the moment, unless one was in on all the little nuances of the situation. Maybe Dan didn't know about Zach's little fling.

"Yeah, if you don't mind," Zach said.

Dan laughed nervously. "I thought you'd break my jaw or something."

Zach shook his head. This was between him and Gwen.

"I'm really sorry." Dan gathered up his socks and shoes, belt and keys, and hovered by the door. "You're not going to go off or something as soon as I walk out the door, are you?"

"Nope," Zach said.

"He doesn't care that much," Gwen added helpfully.

Dan looked baffled. Apparently, he was in the dark here. Finally, he gave up and left.

Zach sat down in the chair by the antique dresser that had been in Gwen's family for about a hundred and fifty years, the dainty, lace-covered thing he'd nicked when they'd moved in, laughing and happy and thinking this was forever. Where had those feelings gone?

He drummed his fingers on the arm of the chair for a minute and then stopped when the motion seemed too measured, too tense.

"So, this was about getting even?" he asked.

"I'm not sure," Gwen said. "I think I just wanted to know what it felt like."

"To have sex with Dan?"

"To have sex with someone other than you," she said.

"He just came to mind first?" Zach asked.

She shrugged. "He always seemed . . . agreeable. I'd just never done anything about it before. Because I was engaged to you."

As digs went, that certainly hit home. "So . . . how did it feel?"

"Different. It felt . . . good. And exciting. And then it got kind of awkward and wrong, and then it was just . . . sad," she said at last, anger and remorse mingling on her face. "It made me sad. Sad for us, and sad for Dan, for me using him that way. And pretty soon I didn't feel much of anything. I didn't really like it, but I was the one who started the whole thing. So I just laid here and let it happen, hoping it would feel better at some point. But it didn't. Isn't that stupid? I didn't even like it, but I'll be damned if I'll be sorry for it. Not that I did it or that you caught us."

"Okay." He could accept that. He could understand all of that. He couldn't argue a thing. It was his mess, first and foremost, not hers. She never would have done this if he hadn't done it first. So it didn't seem there was much to say except, "What now?"

"I don't know, Zach. What do you want to happen? You don't even seem angry."

"I don't have the right, do I?"

"I don't know," she said, her voice rising slightly. "It's

crazy, but I think I'm mad at you for not being angry. I mean, you find another guy coming out of our bathroom half dressed, and me sitting here naked in our bed. . . . Our bed, Zach. It was ours. And it looks like you don't even feel a thing."

"I could ask him to come back so I could knock him down, if that would help," he said, finally getting mildly irritated, at least.

"You don't care, do you? You don't care that I slept with him."

"Yeah, I care." It irritated him that they were here, playing out this scene. But he knew exactly where this was coming from, and he'd started it, dammit. "What do you want me to say?"

"I want to know how you feel."

He shook his head. "Stupid. I feel really stupid, and I don't like it." Gwen would understand. Her IQ was nearly a perfect match to his.

"That's it?" she asked, anger winning out over regret.

"That's all I've got," he said. "All I can come close to identifying. I feel stupid and frustrated beyond belief. I'm sorry. Sorry we've come to this. I didn't want to hurt you."

"Well, I wanted to hurt you."

"Yeah, I got that part."

"Well, I don't want you to understand. I think I wish you had hit him, and that you'd yelled at us both, and that you'd cared. But I don't think you do."

He threw up his hands and shook his head some more. What was a man supposed to do when it was his own actions that had brought them here?

"I think you should leave now," she said.

"Okay." He was more than happy to leave.

"You could stay in a hotel, couldn't you?"

"I'll find someplace," he said, as she sat there naked in their bed after having sex with someone else. But then, this was him and Gwen, logical, calm, practical, reasonable. How could that possibly be bad?

"Well, I'll be here a while," she said. "Someone conveniently found a little problem for me to fix here in town at campaign headquarters, thinking you might be here and we'd have some time together. That worked out really well, didn't it?"

"Yeah," he said.

"Where will you go?" she asked.

"I'm not sure."

That was a lie. The first one he could remember telling her. He was going to see Julie, if he could make himself go to Baxter.

"Is this it, Gwen? Are we over?" he asked, because maybe she was thinking more clearly than he was, and he always told clients to try not to make decisions while they were just crazy. "Just tell me what you want."

"Why?" she asked. "If I tell you, are you going to give it to me?"

"I don't know," he admitted.

"Well, that's just perfect." She glared at him. "I don't know what I want, and you don't know if you want to give me what I want, either."

He went into the other room, picked up his bags, and left.

Zach still didn't want to go home.

No, that was too mild a description of his feelings. He dreaded it. He was breaking into a cold sweat just thinking about it.

A part of him said it was time to deal. That there comes a time when running is no longer an option, lying a luxury a man can no longer afford. He lectured clients on this, and it was good advice. He didn't think he could run anymore.

Julie was back there, and he really wanted to see her.

But going to Baxter . . . There was something really pathetic about a grown man who was scared to go home, scared to face up to what was inside of him. It wasn't like anyone back there was going to crucify him or anything like that. They'd do anything they could to help him. The thing was, he didn't know if anyone *could* help.

Maybe that's why he still wanted to run. Right now, he had the luxury of lying and thinking things might get better, that this whole mess might go away. That maybe he'd find the strength to handle it. But if he went back and spilled his guts to his family, they wouldn't let him run. They'd make him face it all, and then he'd know how bad it really was.

He felt his breathing going shallow and fast, started counting as he inhaled and exhaled, trying to take deeper, slower breaths. Sometimes he could make that happen. Sometimes it helped.

It took less than an hour to get to Baxter, Ohio.

The road took him past his sister Emma's, first. He could go there. If he asked, she'd let him stay and not tell anyone he was there. But her kids would blab or someone would see him or his car, and his secret would be out. Plus, she had this nasty habit of trying to play shrink with him lately, something she never used to do.

She'd probably see through him faster than anybody.

He kept driving.

Grace had a tiny apartment on the wrong side of town, but she was probably working in the studio with his mother today. Plus, Grace wouldn't hide him.

And then there was home, the only one he'd ever really known. His sanctuary. His saving grace. An old Victorian, lovingly restored and cared for over the years by the only man he'd ever think of as his father, with gray siding and a high pitched roof and the most beautiful stained-glass windows, which his kind, generous mother made.

He loved them so much it hurt, and it was hard as hell to think about facing them now.

Zach pulled over to the curb four houses away, a spot that might buy him five minutes if the two little old ladies across the street weren't home at the moment. Damned if he hadn't ended up nearly in front of Julie's old house.

Way to go, Zach.

He stared at it like a man going down for the count, hurting and his head spinning, his heart just aching.

He wanted to be there with her.

He wanted her arms around him, wanted to be able to press his face against the sweet, warm skin of her neck and get drunk on the feel and the smell of her. He wanted to get lost in her, and he knew she'd let him. She'd listen and understand and give him anything he asked for.

Because she thought she owed him? That thought sure didn't sit well with him.

Because it was nothing to her? Just sex? He didn't like that idea any better, and he didn't really think it was true. Sex always meant something. He wouldn't listen anymore when she told him it didn't. Even when it was just understanding and caring and let-me-take-away-the-hurt sex, it meant something.

But did it mean she cared about him? Or that she thought she owed him? Back to that.

He didn't want her rolling around on the floor with him to pay him back for something, no matter how lousy he happened to feel, and he'd be damned if he'd let himself use her that way. Again.

So he couldn't let himself go inside, but he had to talk to her.

One thing about coming back, hideously hard as it was, was that he could be as close to her as he dared let himself be. Zach picked up his cell phone and dialed. She answered on the first ring, sounding breathless and a little sad herself.

"Hi," he said.

"Hi," she said, more cautious now. Then, "What's wrong?"

The tension inside him eased just a bit. He hadn't said more than one little word, but she knew. And it was nice to have someone who listened to the nuances of each little word and who worried about him. He hadn't quite known what to do with that until this point, but maybe it was okay. That she worried and she cared.

"Bad day," he said, trying really hard to hold it together there in the car.

"Another one?"

"Yeah. Tony got life. Not as bad as it could have been, but . . ."

"Still bad," she answered. "I'm sorry, Zach."

"Me, too. How are you?"

"I'm a coward. How are you?"

"A coward," he agreed readily. After all, he was sitting in the car outside her house, not about to let himself go inside and having a hard time admitting what it meant that he'd come here, to her, or that he had to quit hiding things from everyone.

"You've never been a coward in your life," she claimed.

"Oh, yes, I have." It had taken him this long to get

here, after all, and hell, he still hadn't said anything he really needed to say.

If he said, *Run away with me, Julie* . . .

But he wouldn't say that. Any more than he'd say, *Let me in.*

He was afraid of what he'd do if he got too close.

He had some work to do, truths to face, things to make clear, quickly, because once he did, he could let himself inside her house with something of a clear conscience. She'd open up her arms and help him forget everything for a while. Nothing would seem so bad anymore or so overwhelming with her by his side.

"Why do you think you're a coward?" he asked, all too happy to let her explanation come first.

"Because I should have talked to Peter today, and I didn't. Or . . . I did. Kind of. He yelled at me through a locked door. Does that count?"

"I think it does."

She made a little choking sound that was probably the beginning of a sob she wouldn't let out. "I went to see him and promised myself I was going to get somewhere with him today, and all we did was yell through a locked door at the group home. He hates me."

"No, he's just mad at the whole world, and you're the most convenient target. Give it some time."

"I'm trying. You said to come back, that it was the right thing to do—"

"But I never said it would be easy," he added.

She laughed a little bit. Kind of. Kind of sobbed. He really wished he could hold her.

"Well, you could have told me that part, Zach."

"Not while I was trying to get you back here."

"Thanks a lot. It does me a lot of good now that I'm here and miserable. I don't know what to do."

"Just keep talking to him. Keep showing up. Things will get better. Maybe tomorrow won't be as horrible as today," he said. "Somebody told me that recently when I had a really lousy day."

"And was I right? Was today any better?"

"It seems a lot better to me now," he said.

She caught her breath. He thought maybe he'd said too much, but, hell, he was always the one who was telling her to stick with the truth. What exactly was the truth here?

"What's going on, Zach?"

"I'm not sure," he said. It wasn't completely a lie.

"Why do you think you're a coward today?"

Good question. "Go to the front door."

"What?"

"The front door, Julie. Open it."

"I'm not sure that's a good idea," she said.

"It's fine. I'm not there."

"Oh."

Was she disappointed? He wanted her to be.

He looked back to see her fling open the door and look all around.

"I'm in the car in front of the Wilson sisters' house," he said.

Her gaze locked on his. He was close enough to see her mouth fall open, no words coming out. He could see her tighten her grip on the phone and take that first step toward him.

"Don't," he said.

"Why?"

"Because I can't let myself come inside." And dammit, he was a little uneasy about what he might do in the dark on the street in front of her house if he got within arm's length of her.

"Why?" she whispered.

"Because it's been a really bad day, and there's only one place I want to be, and I can't let myself be there. It wouldn't be fair to you or to . . . well . . ."

"Gwen?" she asked. "I know her name. Gwen."

"It wouldn't be fair to either one of you." He could tell Julie he was going to end it with Gwen, but didn't every guy who'd made a commitment to one woman and want another one say those things?

He'd handled this badly enough already. Time to try to do this right—if there was a right way to go from one woman to the next. He couldn't just latch on to Julie because he needed her so badly. That wouldn't be fair.

"So . . . what are you doing here, Zach?"

"Trying to clarify some things in my mind."

If he hadn't known before he'd pulled up in front of her house, he sure did now. This was where he wanted to be.

Now he just had to know why, and he had to know what she thought of the whole thing, and just how it was going to progress. When all he really wanted was to lock his arms around her and hold her tight.

"So . . . did you figure out anything?" she asked.

"Yeah. I miss you."

Her breath caught and held. He could feel her gaze on him, searching his face from the distance, could almost feel her body pulling him closer.

"I miss you, too," she said.

"Well, that's something." Something very, very good.

"I'd let you come inside," she said.

"Julie, don't—"

"I mean . . . I know I shouldn't. But I would."

Shit.

"Gonna be noble, Zach?"

"Tryin' my damnedest."

"Okay. So . . . you're going to be at home for a while?"

"Yeah," he said.

"Five doors down?"

"Uh-huh."

"But you're not coming into my house?"

"That's right."

"How long do you think that's going to last?"

"Not long," he admitted, seeing the absolute lunacy to his whole plan.

To hell with everything else. He could drive back to Cincinnati tonight and talk to Gwen. *If she isn't in bed with another friend of mine.* Which really, really wasn't fair, and damned if he hadn't always prided himself on being a fair man. Any woman he happened to be involved with deserved better than this. Especially Julie. Way-too-vulnerable Julie. Life had been screwing her over for way too long.

"I just have to figure some things out," he said.

"Okay."

Just like that. No demands. No harsh words. Pure acceptance. That sure felt good. "I'll try to hurry."

"That would be good," she said.

"But I have to be sure."

Sure of what, Zach? That you want to be with me? He waited. The question never came.

Instead, she leaned back against the wall of the house and slowly sank down until she was sitting on the porch, staring at him. *Okay, she got it.*

"Nothing to say, Julie?"

She shook her head, not uttering a sound, barely breathing.

"Don't run away," he added, because she looked scared.

Way to go slow and be careful, Zach.

"Wouldn't matter if you did run," he said. "I'd just find you and drag you back here." She made a little distressed sound. A groan or a sigh or something, and she was still sitting on the porch. Zach felt better.

To his right, a screen door banged shut. One of the Wilson sisters showed up on the porch, peering at him through the darkness and frowning. "Zach McRae?"

"Yes, ma'am."

"Forget your way home, boy?"

"No, ma'am."

"It's just down that way." She pointed to the right. She was about eighty now.

"I'm going," he said.

"Good thing. I was about to call the cops on you."

"Yes, ma'am."

He took one last look at Julie on the porch, telling himself it was time. He had to face this. He couldn't be with her until he did.

Chapter 11

It was still hard as hell. He sat in the driveway for a long time, remembering the day he'd first seen this house. He'd been sitting in the back of a complete stranger's car, a social worker who turned out to be Rachel's aunt. Grace hadn't even been walking yet. Emma had been trying her best to take care of them all for days when the police had come. Zach had thought they were going to jail.

He remembered telling them over and over again that his mother was coming back. But it had already been so long, and the nice lady from social services had taken them away from the motel where they were supposed to wait. Zach was worried that their mother wouldn't be able to find them.

It had been a terrible day.

And then they'd ended up here.

Walking up to the door and going inside couldn't be any harder now than it had been then, could it? He sat stubbornly in the car, fighting the urge to get out and pace, counting as he inhaled and exhaled. Two, three, four, five. *Shit.*

He thought about all the clients he'd seen over the

years, scared to death, imagining all sorts of horrible possible outcomes to their legal troubles, and him telling them to tell him the truth and trust him to help. He'd been a complete stranger. Why the hell would they trust him when they were scared to death? And here he was, having a hard time telling his own family about his problems, when he knew them and knew he could trust them.

No place else to go, he told himself. *Nothing left to do. No more running.*

He groaned and took as deep a breath as he could manage. He opened up the car door to let in some air, because he was sweating when it wasn't more than forty degrees out.

Come on, Zach. Walk into the house.

He felt like he was coming apart at the seams. People didn't really do that, did they? Except maybe in bad science-fiction movies.

He was terrified, something that seemed a terrible kind of weakness to have to admit to the people he loved. His earliest memories were of feeling like this. Of that man who now claimed to be Zach's father taking his fists to the woman who'd once been his mother. His mother sobbing, blood coming from her nose, eyes swollen, lips busted. He remembered. It had become easier since he'd seen "that man" six months ago.

Zach got out of the car, grabbed his hastily packed bag.

That first time he'd come here, there'd been snow on the ground. It had been cold, and he'd been hungry. It had felt like he'd been hungry his whole life. He remembered his first good look at Sam, who'd seemed like a giant, with a gruff voice and a stern manner that had scared Zach right off the bat. Sam who'd turned out to be nothing at all like the animal of a man whose blood ran through Zach's veins.

He and his sisters had found a home here and as much love and understanding as any child could want. He'd never complained about the life he'd led, had always been grateful for all the things he'd been given.

Then his old man had gotten out of jail. Zach's nice, neat little life had gone into a tailspin. *Time to deal, Zach.*

He heard the front door open, looked up to find his mother there, a knowing smile on her face. "Hi, stranger. You coming in, or are you going to stand outside all night?"

"I'm coming in," he said, thinking it was a good thing she'd caught him. He couldn't turn around and run now. She'd come after him.

"It's about time." She caught him in the doorway and hugged him tight. He kissed her on the cheek, and for a minute, he didn't think he could let her go. He was shaking, he realized. Did she know?

"Where's Dad?" he asked, pulling away. The mask he'd worn for months wouldn't quite go on tonight.

"Still on a job site. He should be home soon. He'll be so glad you're here." She glanced at the bag in his hand. "Can you stay a while?"

"If you'll have me."

"I guess we could put you up for a few days," she said, then turned serious on him. "You should know I was this far away"—she held up two fingers, a centimeter of space between them—"from getting on a plane to Memphis and dragging you back here."

"Sorry. Things got a little crazy down there."

"No, Zach. It didn't happen there."

He stopped just inside the door, slipping off his coat

and hanging it up in the closet with more care than the act required, then finally faced her. "You're right."

She always was, and she'd been more than patient waiting for him to come clean on this. He still didn't know if he could do it.

"I'm starving," he lied, deciding he couldn't quite launch into it a couple of feet inside the door. He headed for the kitchen, and his mother followed. He opened up the refrigerator and might as well have inventoried the contents by the time another delaying tactic occurred to him. "And I was thinking you might be able to help me sort out my love life while I'm here."

His mother reached around him to grab a foil-covered pan. "Lasagna?"

"That'll work." He'd choke down a few bites somehow.

"I didn't think you had a love life," his mother said, her back to him as she reached for a microwaveable plate.

He was digging through the silverware drawer for a fork and something to scoop out the lasagna, and he didn't look up. "You didn't?"

"No."

Okay, he couldn't hide with his head in the silverware drawer forever. He turned back around and handed her a spatula, because she was closest to the stove and the pan she'd pulled from the refrigerator. "But . . . Gwen . . ."

"No," she said emphatically, staring at him.

"We're engaged," he said, then added, "Kind of."

His mother put a mound of lasagna on the plate and put it in the microwave. "There's no such thing as being 'kind of' engaged."

True, he supposed, and when he couldn't find anything

else to do, looked down at the floor as if he'd never seen it before and said, "I thought I loved her."

"No, Zach."

"Never?" he asked, because maybe she knew so much better than he did.

"You two have known each other for . . . what? Five years?"

Zach nodded, head still down. He'd somehow thought this would be easier to talk about. That was why he'd brought it up after the food thing hadn't bought him any time at all.

"And you couldn't find time to get married? Not once in five years?"

"We were busy," he explained.

"No, you didn't care enough about each other to find the time. You never even see each other. What do you think that says about the two of you?"

He frowned, finally looked at her. "Is this a trick question?"

"No."

"Then, I guess . . . I didn't really love her?"

"There you go."

"You knew that?" he asked.

"Of course." The microwave dinged as the cooking cycle ended. She made no move to turn around, just kept staring at him.

"You could have told me."

"You're a smart guy. I was sure you'd figure it out sooner or later."

Zach scratched his head and wondered how he could have been so wrong. "I thought she was perfect for me."

"Maybe if you were looking for a business partner, but not a woman to spend the rest of your life with."

He could have talked about this a bit more, because he

was really surprised she'd seen it when he hadn't. But then, he'd just found Gwen naked in their bed, which she'd just shared with one of their friends, and he was more irritated than jealous. He supposed that said just about everything about his feelings for her.

"We're not really engaged anymore," he offered.

"Which is what? One step down from being 'kind of' engaged?"

He tried to laugh then. It came out sounding more like he was choking.

"Zach?"

"Yeah, that's where we are. I've got to go talk to her. I'm afraid I haven't handled this well. I uhhh . . ." He stopped and took a breath. "I messed it all up."

"Well, we all do that from time to time."

He stood there, waiting for her to be surprised or disappointed or shocked. She wasn't. There was more of that really nice acceptance that came so abundantly with Julie, along with understanding and kindness, as there'd always been when he was growing up. He still felt like he was about to disappoint them terribly, and probably scare them. He hated to do either one.

Time to deal, Zach. He'd started with this part of it, which seemed easiest to explain. "I hurt her."

"Gwen?"

"Not just Gwen. Her and Julie. I was engaged to Gwen. There was no 'kind of' to it at that point, and I slept with Julie." There. That was part of it.

He looked down at his mother. It still took him by surprise sometimes, even now, looking down at her. It had been a seemingly endless source of amusement at first when he'd gotten taller than she was, and it had seemed like something had gone haywire with the world. He was bigger than she was, when it seemed like forever that he'd looked up to her. He still looked up to her, in every way but this one.

"What do you want me to say, Zach?" She brushed her hand over his shoulder, smoothing out a wrinkle in his shirt and then giving up on that pretense and just taking him by the shoulders and hanging on. "You screwed up, and you know it. Do you want me to bawl you out for that? I could, but I really don't think it would do any good. Looks like you're doing a great job of it yourself."

He nodded. Damn, this hurt. "It's not just that."

"I know."

She knows? Okay.

"Do I need to say the rest of it?" he asked. "Or do you know it all?"

"I think I know," she said. "But I think you still need to say it."

"I really hated seeing George Greene," Zach told his father later that night.

"I know, Zach."

He'd stumbled through a little of what was going on with his mother that afternoon. She hadn't pushed, had just listened and understood and hung on to him. Which had been nice. He wasn't quite so wound up once he'd talked to her, and he was thinking he had a plan.

It was great to have a plan again. He'd never in his whole life been completely without a plan for how he was going to handle something. Which was why this was so terrifying for him. He hadn't known what to do.

Now he had a plan. He'd tell them what was going on. A little at a time. See how they handled that much, and if that was okay, he'd tell them a little bit more. Maybe, in time, he'd get the whole thing out.

He and his father were in Sam's office, an old carriage house Sam had converted into work space years ago. Zach had spent so many nights and summers out here, learning patience and how to be careful. He'd seen his father take things that looked hopelessly broken and put them back together. He wished his father could pick up one of his tools and put *him* back together again.

They were talking about that other man who wanted to claim the title of father.

"I hated that man's voice. I hated the way he looked, the things he said, the things he made me remember. I hate letting him matter at all to me," Zach admitted. "I feel like I'm being disloyal to you and Mom by letting him mean anything to me, even just being someone I despise."

"Don't worry about me and Rachel. We're fine. We're just worried about you." Sam finished locking up his office and they headed through the backyard toward the house.

"And what's with that? Everybody worrying about me all of a sudden. Did everybody suddenly decide I can't take care of myself?"

"Everybody needs a little help sometimes, Zach." This from Sam, who always seemed invincible. "What happened? Other than with you and Gwen?"

Zach stopped on the back porch. "I lost my case in Memphis," he began. "There's a boy who's going to spend his life in prison—"

"Not because of you," Sam insisted.

Zach shrugged, thinking about arguing that point and deciding not to. "I kind of lost it in court and yelled at the judge, who told me to get the hell out of his state and stay out."

"Not too smart, but definitely not the end of the world."

"The judge called my boss, and I kind of yelled at him when I got back into town, and now I'm not supposed to show my face in the office for two months."

"Well, you could use the time off."

"I can't say I did much better handling my last case or the one before it."

"Nobody wins all the time. You know that."

"And I don't know what's going on inside of me." He finally just spit it out as he leaned against the porch railing like it was the only solid thing in the world. "It's like there's all this stuff inside that my skin can't hold in anymore. Like there's a force of some kind zipping around inside, causing everything to go haywire. My heart. My head. My lungs. My bones, even. And the harder I try to hold it together, the worse things get. I'm afraid my skin's going to split open, and all this stuff is going to come spilling out of my body, and I don't know what's going to happen then. Will I walk around leaving little pieces of me scattered behind everywhere I go? Will I keep losing pieces until there's nothing left of me?"

He risked a glance at his father, who through the dim light looked worried but not shocked, which gave him the courage to go on. Once he started, it just kind of spilled out.

"I'm afraid I could screw up my entire life right now. . . . Everything I've cared about. Everything I have. I could lose it all, because of the way I'm feeling inside, and it all started with that damned man who just had to see me. That man who's supposed to be my father."

"I'm your father," Sam said, grabbing him by the arms

and hanging on, looking him right in the eye. "Listen to me. I'm your father. And you're my son. You always will be. No matter what."

"I know that." Zach had never doubted that. "I told myself there was nothing that man could do or say that would change anything. That he didn't matter at all."

"He doesn't," Sam said. "But these feelings he's stirred up inside of you do."

Okay. That worked. It was a helluva lot easier than trying to tell himself George Greene didn't matter at all. He sure hadn't gotten anywhere with that.

"I just feel like shit, Dad," he said.

"I know." His father still hung on to him. "But it's going to be all right."

"You don't know that."

"Yeah, I do."

Zach stepped back. "How could you possibly know that for certain?"

"Because I've been there. I've been right where you are, and I know it can feel like the end of the world, but it's not."

Zach wasn't sure he believed that. Not that he thought his father would ever lie to him. It was just so unlike the Sam he knew. Sam who could do anything.

"What happened to make you feel like this?" he asked.

"Everything. Everything I was feeling and never wanted anyone to know."

Zach knew Sam had been through all kinds of shit himself, losing his own parents at a young age, separated from his only brother for years, tossed around from relative to relative, finally ending up with a grandfather who hadn't wanted him. He and Rachel had married young and lost a baby. Their scars ran deep, but Sam had always seemed like a rock. As solid and steady as a man could be.

"What happened?" Zach asked instead. "When you felt like this, what did you do?"

Sam took a breath, looked Zach in the eye again, and said, "I decided to leave Rachel."

"No way," Zach shot back. His parents' marriage was the kind no one believed existed anymore, as strong as anything in this world.

"I did. And that's not all. When Rachel's aunt showed up at the door with you and your sisters, wanting us to take you in, I told her no, Zach. I would have turned you all away, if it hadn't been for Rachel." Sam's gaze was unwavering. "How's that for screwing up?"

"You wouldn't do those things."

"I did." Sam nodded. "Would have been the biggest mistakes of my life."

"But you love Mom. You always have."

Sam nodded. "Always."

"And you didn't leave, did you?"

"No. I never did."

"And Emma and Grace and I ended up here. So what happened?"

"The three of you happened. Rachel happened. Zach, that feeling like you can't hold all those things inside of you anymore?"

"Yeah."

"That's part of the problem, but just a part. The rest is about what you let in. Who gets to help you. Who gets to love you."

"I know you all love me."

"But you couldn't come to us, and you couldn't go to Gwen. Why was that?"

"I don't know."

"Yeah, you do."

"Going to Gwen wouldn't have helped. And the rest of you . . . I knew you were worried. I knew you cared, and I knew you'd try to help. . . ."

"But?" Sam asked.

"I guess I didn't want you to know how crazy I feel. How the feelings just keep building up inside of me until I don't know what's going to happen."

"This is all that happens. Eventually you can't hold it in anymore, and it comes out. Like this."

"Yeah, I really hate this. What the hell do I do with this?"

"Just what you're doing now."

Feel like shit? Like he was coming apart? He was tempted to look down at his body and check for cracks at the seams, stuff oozing out. But as far as he could tell, he was still whole. Still standing. Still breathing, even if it hurt.

"And then what?" he asked.

"Let it go. Put it behind you. Move on."

"I don't know how to do that," he admitted, feeling utterly defeated and plain exhausted. "I just don't know."

"It's all right. We do. This is the part where you let the people who love you help you."

Oh. *That.* The other thing he really wasn't good at. He couldn't even bring himself to tell them everything.

"We're right here," Sam said. "Always will be. You don't even have to ask."

But he did. He finally said the words. "Help me." And much as he expected it, the world didn't fall apart.

Julie stood awkwardly beside the social worker at the group home the next day, waiting as Peter reluctantly gathered his things. Apparently, Zach knew the local family-court judge and had made a phone call late yesterday afternoon. The few details standing between her and temporary custody of Peter had been dealt with. Here she was, taking him home.

He was less than thrilled by the idea.

Julie glanced around her at the group home and thought she must be really low in his estimation if he thought he'd rather be here. It wasn't . . . grim, exactly. Just old and crowded and utterly lacking in any kind of cheer. Like entering a gray, crowded, noisy world. She was sure the people running it tried their best, but she just wanted out of there as quickly as possible.

Of course, that meant being alone with Peter, which made her nervous and more than a little intimidated. But she couldn't back out now. She'd stopped running and stopped lying, and look what it had gotten her—scared to death.

But Zach was here, and he was proud of her and . . . She glanced nervously at Mrs. Reed, a friend of his fiancée's mother. What was she supposed to do about Zach?

In the next room, Peter snapped at someone. Julie and the social worker both headed for the door, seeing Peter glaring up at a big, intimidating-looking boy who had to be close to six feet tall.

"Is there a problem?" Mrs. Reed asked in her best don't-mess-with-me voice.

They both glared at her for a moment and then looked away, the older boy backing up. "No problem," he mumbled.

"Good. Peter? Are you ready?"

He said something under his breath, maybe something vile. Julie was glad she hadn't quite heard it. She didn't have to do anything about it if she hadn't really heard it, right? Oh she could dare him to repeat it to her face. A snappy *What did you say?* uttered about five seconds ago would have done it. She remembered playing that game with her mother and stepfather too many times to count. There'd come a time when she'd given up on pleasing them and taken great satisfaction in irritating them as much as possible. So if anyone said something like, *What did you say?,* she'd turn around and repeat it, daring them to do something about it. She was bigger and faster by then, and she didn't drink, so she wasn't as clumsy as they were. She could usually get away.

She wondered if Peter was anything like her, wondered what those words—*What did you say?*—would sound like coming out of her mouth.

Julie sighed heavily. She just wanted to go back to last night on the phone with Zach. She could sit on the porch, scared as could be, and stare at him in the car, willing him to come inside. She'd woken up thinking it must have been some kind of bizarre dream. Zach sounding like he was honestly interested in her. Poor little Julie Morrison, the lost girl, the liar.

Guys like him didn't fall for girls like her. Good things didn't really happen to her. They never had. And having Zach would be a very, very good thing. She must have dreamed the whole thing.

Her life was her parents in jail, accused of taking money from the bank. Peter grumbling and wishing he could stay in this gray kiddie jail, rather than be in the same house with her.

He finally bundled up his things in a ratty-looking duffel bag and a backpack and they left. He sat in the backseat of the car, sulking silently the whole way.

At the house, Peter headed for the stairs without a

word to either of them, but Mrs. Reed stopped him and ordered him into the living room, where she proceeded to lay down the law. This was a temporary arrangement, and if it worked out, he might be allowed to stay here with Julie. But any reports of trouble — missing school, fighting, drinking, drugs — and they'd have to rethink this arrangement. She'd be checking up on them both.

Peter looked utterly disinterested. Mrs. Reed dismissed him, and he left. She got to her feet and held out a hand to Julie. "He's all yours now."

It was all Julie could do to keep from wincing, to keep from saying, "You're going? Already?" It suddenly struck her as sheer lunacy that anyone would ever entrust a child to her care.

"Want some advice?" Mrs. Reed offered.

"Yes, please."

"Don't sweat the little things, especially at first. See that he eats, that he puts on clean clothes and takes a shower every now and then. That he goes to school, does his work, keeps his appointments with his therapist, and stays sober. Count that as a victory."

"Okay." Julie nodded. That didn't seem like so much to ask.

"He's really angry, and that's going to come out, probably directed at you. It won't be pleasant, but it's not the end of the world, either. Let him get it out. Talk to him whenever you have the chance, even when it doesn't seem like he's listening, and hopefully, once he figures out he's not going to drive you away, he'll open up to you."

"That's it?" Julie asked.

Mrs. Reed broke into a grin. "Easier said than done.

I'll be back on Friday." Julie was afraid she'd be counting the minutes.

She managed not to beg the social worker to come
back inside and stay, to not leave her with this sullen
stranger.

The social worker's car pulled away as the mailman
made his way down the street. Julie stayed outside and
took the mail from him herself, and he made her sign for
one of them—a large, ominous-looking manila envelope
from the bank. Not the one where her mother had
worked.

Julie, always up for avoidance as a first measure,
flipped through the other envelopes, cringing at what
looked like utility bills and credit-card statements, lots of
them. She was finally left with nothing but the registered
letter. It had to be important. She could always drop it by
the jail for her parents, but she doubted they'd be taking
care of problems anytime soon. This definitely had the
look of a problem. Inside, she found legal-looking docu-
ments referencing a mortgage number. She winced at the
amount owed, the payments missed.

The red stamp in the corner said FORECLOSURE NO-
TICE. *Lovely.* Nothing like a good swift kick when you
were already on the ground.

From upstairs, music blared, loud enough to make her
wince even while standing on the front porch. Was she really going to have to resort to that well-worn motherly
threat of *If you don't turn down that music, I'll . . .*

She couldn't remember what came afterward. Maybe
the electricity would be cut off soon, and the music would
go with it, and she'd never have to fight this particular
battle. Plus, she wasn't supposed to sweat the little
things. The social worker said so. Music was little, she
decided, until she got a headache from it. Foreclosure

was a big one. That one, she'd have to try to do something about.

She sat down on the front steps, not far from the spot where her knees had gone weak last night when she'd thought she knew what Zach had meant even though he hadn't said the words. That he wanted to be with her.

She was fighting the urge to run away, and he'd known that and claimed it wouldn't do any good because he'd just come after her and drag her back. Julie sighed and picked up the foreclosure papers once again. No one had ever cared enough to come after her before and bring her back.

Chapter 12

Contrary to what Zach had feared, his world didn't end. The sun came up the next morning, just like it always did. He slept late, having stayed up late talking to his parents, carefully measuring their reactions to the things he'd managed to get out. They were worried, but they hadn't freaked out. At least, not in front of him.

He dragged himself out of bed the next day at ten-thirty, showered quickly and dressed, padding downstairs in bare feet, his hair still damp. He heard his mother in the kitchen talking to someone, and he waited in the hall-way, not really wanting to see anyone. Then he realized she was on the phone.

"He's okay. Shaken, but okay, and we've got him now. We just won't let him go."

He smiled, imagining his mother barring the front door if he tried to get out before she was willing to let him go. She was the gentlest soul imaginable until some-one threatened someone she loved, and then she was fierce. She really would have dragged him back from Memphis if he'd stayed away much longer.

"Okay," she said. "I'll call you when he gets up."

She hung up the phone. Zach took the last three steps into the kitchen. "Grace or Emma?"

"Emma. Grace called earlier. She said to tell you she loves you and that you'd better still be here when she gets back into town." His mother came up to him and put her arms around him, squeezing him tight. "Sleep well?"

He nodded, amazed he'd slept at all. He'd actually wondered at some point last night if they'd call one of Emma's colleagues to come stick a needle into his arm and give him something to calm him down, then cart him off to a nice, soothing, psychiatric hospital. He'd felt that out of control.

Of course, it could still happen. He should have brushed up on the laws involving involuntary commitment, just in case. He didn't fear so much that they'd try it, as he feared that he might actually need that kind of help.

"What are you planning to do today?" his mother asked.

"I have to go talk to Gwen."

"She's home?"

Zach nodded. Would they let him go that far by himself? "I promise to come straight home, Mom."

She grinned. The tightness in his chest started to ease. Maybe he'd make it through the day.

"Well, maybe not straight home," he decided.

He could see Julie, couldn't he? Once he'd talked to Gwen. Seemed a bit crass, running straight from one woman to the next with such indecent haste, but not nearly as crass as making love to one while engaged to the other. Besides, crassness was not his major problem right now. He'd come back, made it this far. His reward was getting to see Julie.

"You're not going to run away anymore, right?" his mother asked.

"Not anymore," he promised, then took both her hands in his and brought them to his lips. "I still can't believe you and dad almost separated."

"Life gets really hard sometimes," she said. "You can't be expected to handle everything life throws at you well, Zach. It's not like a test you either pass or fail. It's a series of endless tests and rewards. Sometimes surviving alone is a victory."

He nodded. It still felt like a test, still felt like he was flunking, and he couldn't remember ever failing a test.

"You're being too hard on yourself," she said. "But we'll work on that."

He could just imagine what that entailed. Some nice, understanding colleague of Emma's? He couldn't quite see himself with a shrink, lying on the couch, spilling out childhood traumas. He didn't think he had any, save for those vague, scattered memories of his early years. If he barely remembered them, how could they be screwing him up so much now? He was a grown man, for God's sake.

Over the years he'd seen so many kids in his practice who'd had horrible things done to them, and he'd always felt like their lives were so much more screwed up than his. So why was he falling apart this way? It seemed weak, and he would have sworn he wasn't a weak man.

"It's going to be all right, Zach," his mother said.

He nodded, trying to believe that.

He kissed her on the cheek, still had hold of her hands. "I'm going to see Gwen, and then . . ."

"I know where you're going then."

"Going to tell me to be careful? To make sure I'm doing this for the right reasons and to not hurt her?"

"No. I know you've already asked yourself those same questions."

"You're good," he told her, shaking his head, feeling better.

"I was going to tell you that when life gets hard, you want someone by your side who understands and who really cares about you. Someone you can depend on."

Zach frowned. He could see wanting a woman he could trust, wanting one he understood, wanting one who was loyal and kind, but to depend on one? He was certain Gwen had never depended on him, and that he hadn't depended on her. But he understood her. And Julie? He understood her, almost always knew what she was going to do. She'd certainly been understanding and kind.

He hoped that little thing on the floor and in his bed hadn't really been about kindness, and that he wasn't being unkind or unfair by running to her now, when he was such a mess.

"All I really know is that I have to see her," he said finally. Maybe if they stayed outside on the porch they'd be okay.

"Well, that should tell you something," his mother said.

Yeah. Life seemed really bad. And he wanted Julie.

Gwen answered the door wearing an old bathrobe of his and probably nothing else. Her hair was all mussed and her eyes were puffy and slightly red, her face pale and bare of anything resembling makeup. He didn't think he'd seen her in anything except a power suit, perfectly groomed, in longer than he could remember.

She looked almost vulnerable this afternoon.

"Rough night?" he asked casually.

"I got drunk," she said with a hint of defiance.

"You don't drink," he reminded her.

"Which apparently makes it very easy to get drunk, when one decides to do it."

"Can I come in? Just for a few minutes." She hesitated. He supposed it was worth asking, "If I'm not interrupting anything?"

"What about you?" she shot back. "Did you sleep alone last night, Zach?"

"Yes. If I say I'm sorry for that little crack, can I come in?"

She stepped back and allowed him inside.

"I am sorry," he said. "I didn't mean to come here and accuse you of anything. I know I started this."

She crossed her arms in front of her, her battle-mode position. It lost something when executed wearing his faded terry-cloth robe, with her eyes puffy and her hair mussed. "And you came to finish it, didn't you?" she asked.

"Is there really anything left, Gwen? We hardly saw each other. It took downloading each others' schedules into our Palm Pilots for us to be able to find each other on any given day." The absurdity of it was just starting to catch up to him.

"We were busy. We had priorities—"

"Which never involved each other. I'm not blaming you. I'm just saying we never seemed to be that important to each other. You know that."

"I thought we were building something, that you wanted it this way, and that one day . . ." Her chin came up. Mouth quivering, eyes glistening, she changed tactics. "Dan says you had to be deaf, dumb, and blind not to appreciate me."

"Well . . . good. You deserve someone who feels that way about you."

"So you're just turning me over to him? Like a used piece of furniture or something? You're done with me, and if he wants me, he can have me?"

"No, I mean it. I think you really do need someone who appreciates you much more than I have, and I'm sorry it took me so long to figure things out. We're a lot alike, you know. And we're comfortable together. We're just not in love with each other."

"And you think you're in love with this woman who used to live down the street from you? Whose parents are embezzlers?"

"I'm not sure," he said slowly, telling himself not to get his back up over what she said about Julie or that Gwen had been asking someone questions about Julie. He just needed to end this. Trying to take the heat out of the words, he said as gently as possible, "I really don't want to hurt you, but the relevant thing here is that I know I'm not in love with you."

Some women would have crumpled to the floor and wept. Some would have likely slapped him. Gwen stood her ground, all the more furious. She hated any show of vulnerability or weakness, which meant she must really hate him today.

"I'm sorry," he said. "But it's true, and I think once you think about it, you'll realize you're not in love with me, either."

"Well, that would be convenient, now, wouldn't it? Especially since you're done with me." She glared at him. "Fine."

She went to the tiny desk in the hallway, took something from a drawer, and held it out to him. It was the ring he'd given her two and a half years ago.

He held up a hand and said, "Keep it."

"You don't get to be noble, Zach. It's not your place.

Not in this breakup." She shoved the ring at him, and he took it.

The doorbell rang, and they both stared at the door as if they might see right through it, to who was on the other side.

"Expecting someone?" Zach asked.

"Maybe."

He walked over to the door and peered through the peephole, then straightened and gave her a speculative look. "Dan."

"He's persistent," she said.

"I'll entertain him while you get dressed, if you like."

"No, thank you." She pulled open the door.

Dan looked quite pleased with himself until he saw Zach.

"Don't mind him. He was just leaving," Gwen said.

"She's right. I'm leaving," Zach said.

It wasn't the prettiest end to a relationship, but it was done.

Surprisingly, the closer he got to Julie's house, the more he doubted what he was about to do. Not about seeing her, but about the things he had to tell her.

Help me.

Did he really have to say that?

He was afraid he did.

I'm falling apart.

There was probably no avoiding that little gem, either.

He didn't think she'd run. Not when he needed her, and he'd pretty much accepted without reservations that he did. He needed everyone who really cared about him now. It was just the process of admitting it. Being vulnerable. Being weak.

Zach remembered his father telling him about those

painful days when he almost walked away from his marriage. His parents had almost lost everything because, in a time of crisis, instead of working through it together, they'd turned away from each other, each locked in their own misery and guilt.

So this was the really hard part. The who-can-you-turn-to-when-life-turns-to-shit part. The stuff that really matters. And it probably wasn't right coming now, at the beginning of their relationship. If you could call a life-long friendship, a couple of heartfelt conversations, and one night together a relationship.

So no, this wasn't fair — at least, not to her — and he kept reminding himself that life had never been fair to her. *But I need her.*

Still not fair, he argued. *But I need her.*

So, he'd at least have to tell her exactly what she'd be getting into with him right now. It wouldn't kill him, would it? Forcing out a few words?

He got out of the car and approached the house. Music emanated from it in waves. Really horrid-sounding music, played abominably loud. He frowned and rang the bell on the off chance that she would hear it.

Nothing happened.

The door wasn't locked, so he let himself inside.

"Julie?" he called out as he walked around the ground floor. No luck. He glanced out a window to the backyard, and there she was, raking leaves. He felt better just at the sight of her. Nervous, but inexplicably better.

Zach stood there drawing in her presence like a calming drug, the kind he'd feared someone would inject him with last night. This was much, much better. He could breathe. No more counting in and out. The band across his chest eased. His feet moved of their own accord, out the back door, across the yard, to her.

She caught sight of him when he was about ten feet away and stopped dead still, the rake in her hands, leaves dancing on the wind around her feet, resisting all efforts she made to tame them into submission.

Her hair was loose and danced, too, in its own way. He remembered it from that night on the floor. Once it had come loose, he'd filled his hands with it, using it to anchor her to him. The way she'd leaned over him at one point, her hair falling like a curtain around them, closing them both inside their own little world.

He'd thought that night that he'd lost himself completely in her, but looking back on it now, it seemed like something else. Like he'd given up that damnable control of his, just for a few moments, and let the feelings take him completely. He'd reached for her, and she'd saved him.

That sounded a little better to him than *Help me*. Maybe he could say that to her. *Save me. I'm drowning, and there's just no strength left inside of me*. He was weary, but hopeful.

She stood there, leaning on the handle of the rake. He thought abruptly of how pretty all the colors were. The lazy blue of the sky and the puffed-up whiteness of the clouds. The fire of the light caught in her hair and the paleness of her skin, the wisps of colors in the leaves in a pile at her feet and the ones dotting the trees behind her.

A gust of wind came up, setting her pile of leaves to rustling and skittering away, and he felt like all those pieces of himself he'd fought so long to hold together might be a lot like these leaves. Rustling and shifting constantly, fighting all efforts to contain them, the restless energy inside him like a howling wind trying to scatter them.

He was so glad she'd been there when everything

started pouring out, and now he had to tell her everything. "You know that thing you said about the night we spent together not meaning anything?" He grinned, deciding to start there. "You were flat-out wrong, and you know it, Julie."

He thought she'd smile in return, maybe say something smart or try to play it off as nothing. But she didn't do any of those things. It looked like she might cry.

He took one of her hands in his, leaned down, and nudged the tip of her nose with his, his forehead pressed against hers. He closed his eyes and just took in the scent of her for a moment and listened to the wind and the leaves.

The sun was warm on his skin, the breeze gentle. With his other hand, he cupped her cheek, his thumb playing at the corners of her mouth, which he really wanted to taste.

They didn't have to talk right away, did they?

"I'm not engaged anymore," he said, his lips a breath away from hers.

"Really?" She kept her head down, so he had to bend his to touch her. Her voice was low and a little shaky, her breath uneven, body humming with energy, like she might bolt at any second.

"You don't believe me?"

"I don't think you'd lie to me. Not ever. I just . . ."

"You don't think I know what I want?" he suggested.

"Maybe. It's fast, Zach. Really fast."

"I know. And so we're absolutely clear about this, I'm not talking about just wanting you back in bed with me. I wouldn't treat you that way."

"See, that's what I was talking about. . . ." She stepped back, one hand on his chest, holding him away when he would have come after her. "I was thinking that maybe you wanted more than that, and . . . I . . . Zach—"

"You have a lot more to give a man than a night or two in bed," he insisted.

She wrinkled her brows and looked all put out. "And this thing you do when you read my mind . . . Dammit, I don't like that. I really don't want anyone seeing inside me that way."

"I let you see inside me," he said. "That night . . . I was more honest with you that night than I'd been with anyone in years."

"Don't," she said, all choked up and frowning. "Don't do this, Zach. Not unless you mean it."

"I mean it," he said.

She swore and let her head fall back so she could stare up into the sky.

"I need you, Julie."

"You need me? Because it's never been that way for us. It's always been me needing you, and that worked really well, but if you need me, I'm worried you're going to come out on the short end of this deal, and that I'll . . . well, that I won't measure up."

Her chin came up defiantly on the last words, as if she were proud of herself for getting them out and the honesty had cost her a great deal, and she was daring him to disagree with her on this point.

"And I don't want to hurt you," she said. "Or disappoint you. I really don't think I could handle that, Zach."

"Well, I've already hurt you," he began.

"No. I told you. It was—"

"Don't say it was nothing. You know it wasn't, and I know I hurt you. I'm sorry for that. But I can't bring myself to be sorry it happened, because it opened my eyes, and it made me stop running," he said. "All those years, I was after you to stop running away from everything, and here I was, running myself. I finally owned up to it, Julie. Because of you."

She had tears in her eyes. They spilled over from the corners, and he took the pads of his thumbs and the sides of his hands and wiped them away.

"I needed you then, and I need you now," he said. "And that's something I've never said to a woman before."

It was as if the words moved through her like a wave, rocking her back where she stood, and then she slowly gathered her strength and opened her mouth, surely to object some more.

"And I have to warn you that I'm a mess right now," he rushed on. "You saw some of it, but not all of it, and it's not pretty, and I just hate it. I don't know what's going to happen, and I've got to be the worst kind of risk in a relationship right now, but I'm still asking you to take me on. And one more thing. One big thing. I don't want you here because you think you owe me. Got that?"

"I do owe you. I owe you so much."

"No. No guilt. No paybacks. No sympathy."

"Then what am I going to give you?" she asked.

"Anything else you've got, I'll take," he promised her.

"Zach, I'm the worst when it comes to relationships, to making things last. I'm the last person in the world you want to be involved with."

"Well, that's just too bad, because you're the only person I want."

Every shred of self-preservation she had was telling her to run as fast as she could. That this couldn't be happening, that these feelings were too intense, too scary.

She wanted so damned much for all of this to be true. She wanted to believe love really did exist. That Zach meant every word he was saying, and that he was thinking with an absolutely clear head. That everything she'd ever believed about her future might have been flat-out wrong. That she could trust like this, love just like this. With him.

She'd probably loved him since that night when she was seven, the first night Zach had ever noticed her, when she had stayed at Grace's long after all the other kids had gone home and Grace had gone to bed, because Julie just knew her parents didn't care where she was. Zach had seen her, had walked her home from his parents' house late that night, wrapped his jacket around her to keep her from getting cold, and insisted on coming inside. Where he'd seen that, contrary to the way things worked in his world, no one was waiting for her. No one was worried. No one there cared that she hadn't been home for hours. That in her world, no one even noticed.

It seemed he'd always cared. She'd never thought it would turn into love.

Of course, he hadn't said anything about love, and she wouldn't let him if he tried. But the look in his beautiful dark eyes and the way he held her, the way his body seemed to be calling to her, drawing her closer with a kind of force she'd never felt before . . . When he'd said he needed her . . . It was so much, and she couldn't imagine what she might have to give him in return.

"Hold me, Julie," he said. "Wrap your arms around me and just hang on to me for a minute. I've been needing that ever since I let you leave my hotel room that morning, and I just can't wait any longer for it."

So she held him. What else could she do? She wanted to be in his arms every bit as much as he wanted to be in hers.

She dipped her head down low so that maybe he wouldn't see her tears. Her hand that had once pushed him away grabbed on to the sleeve of his sweater and tugged him closer. Her arms slid around his waist and then burrowed up under his sweater, finding warm, smooth skin and the strength she had reveled in that night.

She eased her face against his chest, burrowing into the soft wool, looking for the smell she remembered as his. His arms came just as slowly to her, as if he were carefully fitting together the pieces of a puzzle, separated into two halves that would now be made whole. His hands slid around her, working their way up and down her back, tucking her just a bit closer here and there and then locking around her.

"Don't let go," she said, as he'd done that night.

"I won't," he promised.

This was a place a woman could stay, where she could feel safe. There'd never been any place where she'd felt as safe as she had with him.

She wondered if he knew that. That there was a little girl inside of her she'd never truly acknowledged who'd always been in love with him and always would be, and this little girl was practically dancing, sure that she was finally getting what she'd waited for all these years.

He couldn't know that. She didn't want him to. The idea of being that vulnerable in front of another human being was enough to nearly make her sick, and she knew it was long past time to start throwing up all those walls of hers. Funny, but it seemed she'd forgotten how to build them, and she was too tired to do it, anyway.

Did he know what it would do to her to catch a glimpse of something like this and then lose it? She tried to ease herself away from Zach, just the least little bit, but his hold was unyielding. She leaned back in his arms and gazed up at him.

There was the barest hint of a smile on his face, and his gaze was as steady as ever. "You told me not to let go, and I'm not going to."

"I don't know how to do this," she protested.

"Neither do I. I was thinking we could make it up as we go along."

She frowned up at him. Of course he thought that. He could do anything.

"You don't believe me about that, either?" he asked. "Julie, you already told me you don't think I'd ever lie to you. I'm sure not going to start now."

Which meant what? That he was serious? That he really wanted her? In some way other than sexually? Which had the mistaken effect of making her think about sex. With him. Which she wasn't supposed to think about at all and had not managed to stop doing ever since she'd left his hotel room.

It was still there, a slow, sexual heat simmering between them. They were close enough that her breasts were pressed against his chest. They felt tight and heavy. Her skin was tingling, practically calling out, *Touch me, touch me, touch me,* and she could swear she could already taste his lips on hers. He leaned in to her ever so slightly, just enough to let her know the way his body was responding to hers. He was hard and ready, despite claiming he wanted more than to have her in his bed again.

Everything inside of her seemed to go soft at the feel of him pressed against her this way. It was like he'd fine-tuned her body to pick up the rhythm emanating from his, and he'd been broadcasting a signal to her ever since. And now he was finally here, touching her, wanting her. Claiming he needed her.

How much resistance could one starved-for-love woman be expected to muster? She groaned and stood on her tiptoes, wrapped her arms around his neck, and pulled him to her, as close as they could get. Her mouth locked on his, and her knees went weak at the first touch of their lips.

"Mmmm." The part of her mind that said they really hadn't settled anything seemed to be wiped clean as he claimed possession of her mouth, taking the initiative for the kiss when she'd barely gotten started taking what she wanted from him. But this was okay. This was just fine.

She groaned again, and so did he, and then their bodies started throbbing, one in time with the other. She felt like she was coming alive in a way she'd never been before.

It reminded her of one time when she'd been outside in the snow for way too long and gotten too far from home, thinking she might well freeze before she made it back. Her whole body had nearly gone numb. She'd stripped off her wet clothes, and in the heat of the house the feeling slowly came back to her limbs. It was like someone was setting off sparklers inside of her, sputtering and spitting out sparks, little flames dancing along just beneath the surface of her skin.

It was like that now. Thousands of little sparklers. She could almost hear the hissing, burning sound they made, and she could feel the heat, the magic.

Hold me tighter, she thought. *Don't ever let me go.*

One of Zach's hands pushed its way up her shirt in the back, skin finding skin, and then his other hand joined the first. More skin on skin. Then it slid lower, cupping her bottom, and pulling her up against him more tightly.

She had a wicked flash of them, zippers undone, pants shoved down, everything just far enough out of the way so she could have him inside of her, right out here in the backyard on the fall leaves and the grass.

"Good God," he said, breaking off the kiss and backing away, breathing heavily but not letting her go.

"I know," she said, laughing from pure joy, her fears forgotten for the moment. Even then, he hadn't let her go. He was a man of his word.

She watched his shoulders rise and fall, breath by breath, as he struggled to find some control. "I didn't come here for that," he said.

"You didn't?"

"Not just that," he clarified.

And Julie laughed again, thinking it really was a shame that they lived in town, where the houses were so close together and everyone could see everything. The pile of leaves and the autumn grass sounded so inviting at the moment, and sex with Zach was much easier to think about than love.

"We'll work it out," he said.

"Okay," she said, reaching way down deep inside of her for some kind of faith, maybe even enough to see this through. She'd always believed in him. If she could do this with anyone at all, it would be him.

"Don't get scared," he all but commanded.

"Easy for you to say."

"No, it's not. I'm scared, too."

"What about this scares you, Zach?"

"Everything," he claimed. "Oh hell, just about everything in my life scares me right now."

He frowned down at her, nervous energy radiating from him, mixing with the sexual heat. She put her hand to his face, reveling in the ability to just reach up and touch him, to pull him to her and kiss him again, if she dared let herself. But as inviting as that was, she sensed this wasn't the time.

"What's wrong?" she asked.

"Just some things I have to tell you. So that you know what you're getting into. I'm at least half crazy right now."

"Zach, you're the sanest person I know."

"Then you need some new friends," he said.

She stopped teasing, stopped smiling. "You're serious?"

He nodded, and that insane sexual heat was finally dissipating. He waited a long time before he said, "We really do have to talk about this. Can we go inside?"

"We could, but I doubt we could stand the noise. Peter's home. It was your phone call to the judge that got him here this quickly."

"Nobody to blame but me, huh?"

Julie nodded. "You're changing the subject."

"Trying to."

He was nervous, and she was amazed. "It's me, Zach. You can tell me anything."

"I'm counting on that."

"I need you, too," she said. "Just in case there's any way you don't know that already, and in case it makes whatever you need to say easier."

"It does."

"You need some kind of help?" she guessed when he said nothing.

He nodded.

"And it's that hard to ask me?"

"You don't ask me," he pointed out.

"I never had to. You always just jumped in and started taking care of me."

"You wouldn't ask. You never do. And I don't, either. That's one thing you'll probably need to remember, if we're going to make something of this. I have a hard time asking, a hard time admitting I ever come up against anything I can't handle on my own."

"Okay. I'll make a note of that. Don't wait for Zach to ask for help. What else?"

"I really hate that . . . that man . . . George Greene, is out of prison."

"I know."

"And I'm not handling it well."

She nodded, then gave him a tentative smile. "Well, you don't handle everything well, do you?"

"Usually," he insisted.

"Well, most people don't."

"That's what my mother said." He took a breath and looked even more nervous, more serious. "Sometimes I think . . . I'm just going to fall apart, Julie. Like I can't handle this, and it's going to get too hard for me to deal with, and then . . . I don't know what's going to happen then."

He said it as if it were some terrible sin. She just didn't understand.

"Well . . . doesn't everybody feel that way at one time or another?"

He stared down at her. After a long moment, she caught the faintest upturn of his lips at one corner. The barest hint of a dimple appeared in his right cheek, and then he started laughing. It rose ever so slowly from deep inside and trickled out.

"What?" she asked.

He put his arms around her, picked her up at the waist, and swung her around in a circle.

"Zach!" she screamed.

He laughed even harder, hoisting her up onto his shoulder in something resembling a fireman's hold and spinning around in a circle some more. She shrieked and

clung to him as best she could, getting dizzier by the
minute, until he slowly began to lower her to the ground.
Either he was dizzy or they hadn't completely stopped re-
volving when he did it, because she felt herself slipping
out of his hold, and him struggling to hang on to her and
keep them both upright.

It didn't work that well. They finally collapsed together on the ground in her pile of leaves. He ended up
flat on his back with her sprawled on top of him. She
managed to rise to her hands and knees, straddling him,
laughing herself. Late-afternoon sunshine came streaming through the trees, a beam of it settling like a spotlight
on him. It was like being anointed by the gods, she decided, and felt so amazed to be here like this with him
that she just had to kiss him.

Which was probably a bad idea, since he'd finally
managed to tell her some of what was wrong. But she just
couldn't help herself. Besides, she wasn't supposed to
wait for him to ask for anything, which she supposed
meant she'd have to try her best to figure out what he
needed and give it to him.

Kissing seemed like a good idea at the moment.

She leaned over him, the weight of her upper body on
her hands. Her hair draped around her and him, and she
thought about what she could do to him with it another
time, when it wasn't broad daylight and they weren't in
her backyard.

He liked her hair. She remembered that from the night
they'd been together, him playing with it with his hands,
fingers stroking through it so soothingly just before she'd
fallen asleep in his bed, the way he'd grabbed it at one
point and held her to him. Not that she'd been trying to
get away. But she'd liked the idea of him grabbing on to
her and keeping her close.

For now, it simply hung there around them, giving them the illusion of being alone. She fit her mouth to his, the sweetness of it bringing more tears to her eyes. She was going to cry more over this man than any she ever had in her life, she feared, but hopefully have more happiness with him, as well.

The kiss was soft, full of yearning and with a measure of patience they hadn't shown each other before. Almost like a promise. Like saying, *Let me take care of you. Let me give this to you, any kind of comfort you can find in my touch and in my heart.* She'd always known she'd give him anything.

"Here." The pressure of his hands urged her down to lie fully on top of him.

She did, and he rolled her over until she was on her back on a bed of leaves and he was on his side, leaning over her. His hand brushed her hair off her face and then his palm curved around her cheek and the side of her face. His thumb traced the crease of her lips in a touch that felt almost like a kiss, and she closed her eyes and pulled his mouth back to hers, because it was one thing she knew to give him.

It seemed the ultimate in luxuries and joy, lying in the grass with Zach in the late-autumn sunshine, kissing like two people who had all the time in the world.

She thought about telling him she loved him, just because she wasn't sure she could hold in the words, and because it seemed to be a day for crazy kinds of risk taking. There he went, being that irresistible truth serum to her.

One more minute and the words would come spilling out of her, no taking them back, no more fighting the feelings. She did love this man and opened her mouth to tell him so when he glanced up and turned abruptly to the right.

"What?" Julie turned her head in that direction, and there was Peter standing about five feet away from them and glaring at them.

"So this is why you came back," Peter growled.

Chapter 13

Zach sat up. She did, too. There were leaves all over her, and she quickly checked to make sure her sweater covered everything that needed covering.

"I knew you sure as hell didn't come back for me," Peter said furiously. "You came for him."

"He was down there with you in Memphis. That's the only way anybody even knew how to find you. And I knew—" His voice broke, lips quivering. He was going to cry. "I knew you didn't give a shit about me, but some guy to fuck around with—"

He didn't get out another word. Zach got to his feet and grabbed Peter by the arms, hauling him up until they were nearly nose to nose.

"Don't say another word," Zach said slowly, enunciating every syllable.

"You don't tell me what to do—" Peter began.

"Don't." Zach could growl, too, apparently very well.

This was probably the look he saved for people like Tony Williams's father and maybe that man who claimed to be *his* father. She envied the don't-mess-with-me quality, because it silenced her brother and left him looking a bit scared, which probably wasn't a bad thing at the moment. Peter certainly scared her at times.

"You're upset. That's understandable," Zach said, backing down a bit. "But you've got some of the facts wrong, and now you're jumping to conclusions and using the kind of language a man does not use in front of a woman. Particularly a woman who happens to be his sister and who is trying to take care of him at the moment. So you need to calm down and be quiet, and if you want to talk we can. But not like this."

Peter tried his best don't-mess-with-me look on Zach, but at thirteen, he was far from mastering it. He finally backed off.

Zach let go of him, but ordered, "Tell her you're sorry."

"Sorry," Peter said, as sarcastic as could be.

Zach arched a brow at that and continued to stare.

"I'm sorry," Peter repeated.

"Okay. Now that the music's not threatening to bring down the house, why don't we go inside?" Zach said.

Peter looked from one to the other, then said, "I'll talk to her. But I don't have anything to say to you."

Zach started to say something, but Julie put her hand on his arm to stop him. "It's okay. Go inside, Peter. I'll be there in a minute."

He stalked off, wrenching open the door and slamming it behind him.

"Sorry," she told Zach.

"You didn't do anything."

"Not for him," she said. "Not for the longest time, and he knows it."

Zach took her into his arms, comforting her now. "You couldn't have taken him with you, Julie. You were eighteen. He was what? Five?"

"I know," she admitted, her face tucked into the hollow between his shoulder and his neck.

"So you did all you could then. You saved yourself. And now that you can do more, you are."

"That's a pretty generous portrayal of the situation." She eased away from him. "I don't deserve you."

"Then I'll just have to convince you that you do."

"God, this is so scary," she said.

"Yeah. Life's like that sometimes."

"I have to go inside and talk to him."

"I know." He kissed her forehead. "You be careful. You can't know for certain what he's capable of."

"You think he'd hurt me? Physically?"

"He gets into fights at school, and you don't know what might have happened to him in this house. He had some nasty bruises on him when social services took him into custody. They took X rays. Found a couple of old fractures."

Every bit of pleasure she'd found in the day slipped away. Reality was back with a vengeance. Her mother and stepfather were in jail. She was a woman who'd run away from these problems ages ago and come back to find them still here waiting for her. She had a brother who'd likely been abused and had learned to hate her, and Zach, a man she couldn't imagine ever deserving, but wanted so badly.

"Did they hit you when you were here?" Zach asked.

She shrugged it off, as she always did. "It wasn't that bad."

Zach's look told her he feared that it had been.

"You saw it," she said. "You know. It was chaos. It was like falling into a hole. You keep thinking surely you'd hit bottom already, and damned if things didn't keep getting worse. My mother fell in love with this jerk.

If I'd just disappeared, he would have been happy. As it was, the best I could do was try to make myself invisible. When I grew up and got sick of that, I decided to try to make them as miserable as I was. You know how well that worked."

She made the mistake of stopping to take a breath and looking up at him.

"Don't look at me like that," she cried. "Don't feel sorry for me."

"I don't, I think I lov—"

"And don't you dare say that."

"Okay," he said softly.

"He didn't really hurt me. He'd get mad and drunk, or my mom would, and if things got bad enough, they'd hit, but . . . You were there. There were no broken bones, no marks on me. I just tried to stay away and hoped the world wouldn't fall apart on me, you know?"

"Yeah, I know."

She wondered how much he really did know of living like that. And was he talking about his life before he came to Sam and Rachel's? Or about something else? He was definitely upset about something. He'd tried to tell her, but she'd made him laugh, and she couldn't help but be a little suspicious about how easy it had been to get him to laugh. Laughter was her first response when she didn't want anyone to know how really lousy she felt, how afraid she was.

Would Zach try to cover up his feelings that way?

"So . . . it was just kind of crazy here?" he asked.

She nodded. Distraction was another of her favorite tricks. "You had things you wanted to talk about?"

"They'll keep," he said, trying to smile. "Maybe even come out a little easier another time. You should get in there and talk to Peter. And be careful. You've got my cell-phone number, if you need me?"

"Yes, I do."

His hand was hanging by his side, and she slipped hers into his and leaned up to kiss him softly on the lips, wanting to say so much and not able to find a place to begin.

I love you would sum it all up nicely.

She couldn't quite manage the words at the moment.

"Go on," he said, squeezing her hand before he let her go.

"You'll be all right?"

He nodded, then turned and walked away.

Peter was again locked in his room, his hideous music blaring through the house. Julie stood on the other side of the door, thinking about the social worker's advice. Big thing or little?

It felt big. Which meant she had to do something.

Her stepfather would have broken the lock or the door. She didn't want to do either. She turned off the electricity instead. Silence reigned throughout the house. Peter came out of his room, not realizing he'd been tricked.

That's one point for me.

He went to go back inside, but she barred the door, not letting him, and thankfully it didn't come down to a shoving match, because probably, she would have lost. Zach was right. Peter was a lot bigger and stronger than she realized.

He also looked like he was in no mood for a prolonged or civil discussion, so she boiled it down to as few words as possible.

"I didn't come here for Zach, although I am very grateful he's here, because he's just about the best thing that ever happened to me. And not just now, Peter. When

I was your age and even when I was smaller, he was one of the few people in the world who cared about me. Can you understand that? Is there anybody who cares about what happens to you now? Anybody who helps you when things get really bad and really scary?"

"I don't need any help," he insisted.

"Well, I did, and Zach helped me. Back then and in Memphis. I was scared to come back here—"

"You didn't want to. I know you didn't."

"Would you, if you ever managed to get away?" she asked.

He said nothing. She thought she'd just scored Point No. 2.

"I was every bit as miserable here as you were," she said. "I know what you're going through. I know how angry you are, how hurt."

"They don't hurt me," he insisted.

"That's strange, because they sure hurt me."

"I'm fine," he insisted. "And I don't need you. I don't need anybody. I take care of myself most of the time anyway, so why don't you just go?"

"If I did, you'd go back to the group home."

"I told you, I don't need anybody—"

"You can try arguing that with social services, if you like, but you won't win. They don't leave thirteen-year-olds alone to take care of themselves. So I guess you're stuck with me."

"You won't stay," he said. "Unless you stay for him."

"I didn't even know he was going to be here. When I saw him in Memphis, he was working on a case, and he was supposed to have another one to go to in Texas right after that. I don't know what happened with that one. He may be leaving tomorrow." It was a terrible thought. She desperately wanted him close, no matter how much he scared her. "But I didn't come for him. There wasn't . . . Zach and I have never been anything but friends."

"Sure didn't look like that," Peter snapped.

"Until today. Or the last two or three days. It's never been like that between us, but things change, Peter. All the time. Sometimes they even change for the better."

He glared at her.

Fine. "I came for you, and because I was angry at myself and ashamed for leaving you here all those years."

"I was fine," he claimed.

She ignored that and went right on. "I should have found a way to help you. To stay in touch with you."

"Why?" He snarled at her. "I didn't miss you."

"Well, I missed you."

Peter tried hard to hide it, but his face took on that hurt look once again. Julie figured she'd pushed it as far as she could today. She let him return to the sanctuary of his room. Thankfully, the music didn't come back on when she turned the electricity on. She ended up outside again, raking the leaves, just because she wanted something to do and she really didn't like being in the house.

She supposed she should ask Zach about the foreclosure process. She'd probably have to face her mother to find out about the criminal charges and if there was any money to keep them from losing the house.

She needed to ask Zach why he was here and how long he could stay. Try to figure out what had him so uneasy, and then . . . Lord, she had no idea what would happen then. Her head was still spinning from all that he'd said and the look he'd had in his eyes when he'd told her he wanted her, that he needed her. They were going to have some kind of relationship, it seemed, and she knew what she wanted from it. *Everything.* She wanted everything with Zach.

* * *

Okay, so he hadn't said much of anything he really needed to say to Julie. He'd gotten distracted by how good it had been to see her, to touch her. But he would tell her. He'd pick his time and force it out. For the moment, he settled for facing his older sister instead. Emma, the pro. The shrink.

He closed his car door and stared up at her house, wondering why his sister had to go and do that with her life. It was proving damned inconvenient to him. Not that he would ever deny her one bit of happiness. But surely he could at least be mildly irritated with her at the moment.

He got out of his car, slammed the door shut, and then leaned against the right fender, stalling for a moment.

The house looked great. He was happy to think of his sister living here now and so happy. In an odd little twist that still had people talking, Emma had taken one look at Sam's long-lost brother and not only figured out who Rye was but had somehow fallen in love with him and finally convinced him to marry her. What did it really matter if she was the adopted daughter of the brother Rye hadn't seen in thirty years? Most everyone had learned to overlook that little detail.

Zach didn't think there'd ever been a single day when either his sister or her husband had regretted their decision, despite the family connection and the difference in their ages. It had simply worked. Sixteen years of marriage and three children later — with a fourth on the way — it was obvious that they belonged together.

Standing outside their house, with children's toys littering the lawn and the driveway, the sound of laughter drifting from the backyard, Zach found himself wondering how they'd known they'd end up like this, still so obviously in love after all these years.

And he wondered what Emma had taken with her from those chaos-filled years with their other mother. There had to be scars. Emma had been twelve when they escaped for good.

Zach heard a shout. His nephew, Jamie, the four-year-old, came barreling around the corner, howling with laughter as he ran down the sidewalk. He got halfway there when he spotted Zach, then ran to him, short stubby legs pumping wildly as he plowed through the flowers that edged the driveway.

He launched himself into Zach's arms, yelling something that sounded like, "Unka Dack."

"Close enough, short stuff." Zach grabbed him and wiped a bit of dirt from the boy's cheek. "Where's your mom?"

"Back dair." He pointed to the backyard.

"And probably looking for you," Zach said, heading that way. "I might as well haul you back to her."

The kid chattered the whole way, a string of gibberish about his new red truck, the cookies he'd had for a snack, and his best friend, whose name might be Jeremy or Jimmy or even Jennifer. Zach couldn't tell. He just kept smiling and nodding and let the kid talk, happy that his sister had so many good things in her life. Hoping she could help him.

They ran into his niece Tricia, who was seven, heading toward the front yard as they were heading for the back.

"Looking for this?" Zach asked, pointing to the little boy.

"Uncle Zach!"

She threw herself into his arms just as he rounded the

back corner of the house and spotted Emma. She was sitting on the ground under a giant oak tree, planting purple and yellow pansies. Her twelve-year-old, Dana, was lying in a hammock on the other side of the yard, talking on the phone. Soon he found himself mobbed by females, the girls first and then Emma.

She must have been worried, because she grabbed on to him and didn't let go for a long time, then talked the girls into taking their brother inside and attempting to get him down for his afternoon nap. Emma took Zach by the hand and dragged him back to her tree, where a whole flat of bedding plants waited to be transplanted into the soil.

"You put 'em all in today?" he asked, as he sat down on the ground beside her.

"Yes, why?"

"Jamie might have taken out a few by the mailbox when he spotted me."

Emma shook her head. "He moves so fast he doesn't take time to even look where he's going. Last week, he ran into a tree and scraped the whole side of his face. He said he was chasing a butterfly and it turned faster than he could."

"Sounds reasonable." Zach glanced across the yard, like he needed to inventory the kids' toys and the landscaping, anything rather than look his sister in the eye. "How are you feeling?"

"Still a little queasy, and I swear, I sleep all the time, but I just can't seem to get enough rest."

"Cut back at work?"

She nodded and went back to work on her plants. "I've gone from three days a week to two. Thank goodness we just took on a new partner a few months ago. Otherwise, I don't know how I'd be able to make that work."

"Just kids, or grown-ups, too?" Zach asked, checking

the distance between plants and clearing a little rock, then another, from the spot where she'd want the next purple flower to go.

"What?" Emma asked.

"The new person—does she just do kids? Or grown-ups, too?"

"Oh." She dug into the soil with her tiny shovel. "Jane Atwood. She's great. Part of a big practice in Philadelphia for twenty years. She has an aunt here who's getting on in years, and needed someone with her, and Jane was ready to escape the big city. She sees adults and children. Why?"

Zach tried to tip a tiny plant out of its plastic container, roots, dirt, and all, not very successfully. "How do these work?"

"Turn it upside down and squeeze it a little. The whole thing should pop out in one piece."

"Oh." He managed, kind of. "She any good?"

"Jane?"

"Yeah."

"We wouldn't have brought her into the practice if we hadn't thought so. What are you really asking me, Zach?"

"You know what I'm asking you," he said, taking the tiny hand shovel from her and starting to dig in the dirt by his side, suddenly feeling antsy and ready to grumble. Anything but this. "Is that a shrink thing or something? To never answer a question, just ask another one?"

"I answered a lot of your questions, and you know it," she said, forgetting the plants altogether. "And you might not have noticed, but I've been really good. You've been in town for nearly twenty-four hours. It wasn't easy, but I've been waiting for you to come to me."

"You wouldn't have lasted another fifteen minutes," he claimed, more than happy to bat words around with her rather than talk about what was wrong. "That little boy wouldn't have been asleep for a minute before you were in the car, headed for Mom and Dad's house."

"I would not have," she insisted, then admitted, "Okay, I was going to wait until tonight, once the kids were asleep. I thought this would take more time than I'd have with Jamie napping. Wouldn't want to rush you, once I finally got you talking."

He frowned at her, practically mauling a flower as he tried to place it correctly in the hole he'd dug into the ground. Only problem was, the hole was about three times too big.

"I think I showed admirable restraint to this point. And don't kill my flowers. It's not their fault." She put her hand on his, trying to save the next bloom from being manhandled. "You have to let me help now, Zach."

He laughed then, emotions rising inside of him, clogging his throat and making saying anything difficult.

"What?" she asked gently, her hand on his arm now.

"You," he said, dropping the flower and just sitting there with her. "Just saying it that way. That I had to let you help me. Not making me ask. I really wasn't looking forward to asking."

"We've been trying to help for months. You just weren't ready to let us."

"I know." He finally looked at her, saw the worry in her eyes. "I'm sorry."

"It's okay."

"So . . ." What were they talking about? Oh, yeah. Him and his little issues. "It didn't bother you when George got out of jail?"

She didn't balk at the abrupt leap in conversation. Just sat there and looked at him and finally said, "Of course it did."

"But it didn't do this to you?" he asked.

"Do what?"

He took a breath that wasn't at all steady. No way he could make it steady. "Make you feel like . . . like you were choking? Like you were coming apart at the seams, and all these things about the past you could have sworn you'd put behind you were suddenly right there. Right beneath the surface fighting to get out?"

"No. George didn't do that to me. Mark, that guy I was seeing freshman year in college, did."

"Oh." Zach remembered. That guy had hit her. Left bruises on her. Broken into their parents' home to get her. Thank goodness Rye had been there to save her.

"That guy made you think of George?" Zach asked.

"Worse than that, he made me think about Mom."

She meant Annie Greene. She called Sam and Rachel by their first names, although she definitely considered them her mother and father, but she'd always referred to Annie Greene as Mom.

"Sorry." Zach suddenly felt guilty for escaping so much more of the past than Emma. "I didn't even think about that, Em. That guy must have brought back so many bad memories for you."

"Not just the memories," she said. "The feelings. They're the important part. I was so angry at Mom for the way we lived, for letting him hit her and hit me and scare us to death. I thought she must have been the weakest woman on earth and the stupidest, and I was so angry at her. But at the same time, she was our mother, and I loved her, too."

That would be difficult—loving and still being so angry.

"I didn't think I'd ever understand her," Emma said.

"Then there I was, living her life for just a little while and scared to death, just like she must have been."

"Oh." He saw what she was getting at, kind of. "I thought . . . You and that guy. It was just the one time that he hurt you, right?"

"No. There was one other time. That's what made me come home from college in the first place. And the whole thing from start to finish only lasted a few days, which is nothing like what she lived through, but . . . Well, let's just say I had a whole new understanding of how scared she must have been."

"I'm sorry," he said, struck by how many times he'd said that lately and to so many different people. It seemed totally inadequate in comparison to the pain suffered by so many people who were close to him. "I should have known—"

"Why?"

"Because you're my sister. I just didn't . . . I didn't think."

"I didn't want you to think about it. Or to remember it or have it screw up your life the way it is now."

"You knew?" he asked. "All this time, you knew what my little problem was all about?"

"I knew the memories and the feelings had to be inside of you somewhere, and if they were ever going to come out, ending up face-to-face with George Greene seemed like a likely time for it to happen."

"Oh, hell, I didn't even know I had anything of those times left in me. I didn't see how they could possibly be this strong, this awful, when I remember so little about that time."

"But the impressions were so deeply planted, and even things you don't consciously remember from your early years can still have an effect on you. Think about Jamie.

He probably won't remember much at all from his life to this point, but do you honestly believe he could have lived with a violent drunk, scared and neglected, maybe beat up until he was four, and have it not affect him later, even if he had a perfectly wonderful home from now on?"

"I guess not," Zach said, picturing that laughing, happy, completely secure little boy ever being in a place like the one he and Emma had lived in. "I didn't think about it that way."

"It all gets inside of us somewhere. We carry it all around, whether we realize it or not. We can build defenses against it, like building a well inside of us and dropping it to the bottom and sealing it tight. But it's still there, and one day something happens to bring those issues back to the surface."

"And then what?"

"It all comes out. It's like poison. You don't want it inside of you."

He nodded, working really hard to breathe right now. He'd been kind of hoping she could tell him how to stuff it back inside of him. *Poison,* she'd said. "It feels like that, and I don't know what to do with it, Em."

"That's all right. I do."

She sounded so calm, so accepting, he found the courage to confess, "I feel like I'm falling apart."

"I know. It's just the walls coming down, letting you feel all those feelings you've been trying to hide from. And it's scary, but you'll get past it."

He felt like all his protection was gone, and he wasn't sure he could cope with all the ugliness inside of him.

Next question. Big, scary question. "So you don't think I'm crazy?"

"No. You're just so smart and so sure of yourself and

so capable, that coming up against something you don't know how to handle makes you feel a little crazy."

"But you can fix that?" he asked, needing to hear her say those words.

"You can. With some help. It's what shrinks do, Zach."

He nodded, both comforted and dismayed. Like a man who's been told the disease isn't fatal but the cure is really atrocious. "I was afraid it would come down to that." How about it? He'd admitted that, too.

"There's nothing wrong with needing help," Emma said.

He couldn't argue that point with her. She'd made it her life's work, after all. "It's just not a place I ever thought I'd end up."

"Me, either," she said.

He looked up at that and could not have been more surprised. "You, too?"

She nodded. "After all that mess with that guy."

"I never knew," he said.

"Well, most people don't exactly take out an ad in the paper when they go into therapy." She sighed. "I probably should have told you, but I guess I was scared about the whole thing, and it made me feel stupid and vulnerable, thinking I couldn't handle it on my own. I'd handled so many other things."

"Yeah. Exactly. I feel like I've handled things that were so much harder than this."

"It just means it's time to deal with it. That's all."

"So, this doesn't surprise you at all? I come over here and tell you I'm falling apart and I need a shrink, and . . . it's no big deal to you?"

"Did you think I'd be shocked?" she asked, grinning.

"There you go," he complained, trying desperately to

make light of this, "with that damned question-to-answer-a-question again."

"Sorry. I'm not shocked, and I'm not nearly as worried as I was before you came home. It would be a big deal if you were determined to try to run from it. That's when people get into trouble—when they need help and for some reason don't get it, either because they're scared or ashamed or just don't know there are people who can help."

Okay. One more step that he'd taken. One more piece out into the open. He got to go spill his guts in therapy. If he didn't go, Emma would keep at him until he did. What the hell? Maybe he could bring himself to tell the shrink everything he still hadn't said to anyone else.

"I really hate this, Em."

"You'll hate it even more before you're through, but you can do it."

He shook his head and managed to smile just a bit. "I don't even want to tell you what I thought might happen. . . ."

"When you finally said those things out loud?" She smiled back at him. "It'll be all right."

And then he really wanted to be done with this conversation. He had the perfect diversion. "Mom mention that Gwen and I are calling it quits?"

"Finally." His sister grinned broadly, no surprise there, either.

"What is this?" he said, louder than he normally would have, feigning outrage. "Everyone knows more than I do about my own life?"

She just grinned some more.

"Women," he muttered. "What's a guy supposed to do with them?"

"You could probably address that in therapy, too, if you needed to," she deadpanned.

He sat there, absolutely still for a moment, then realized she'd made a joke of him going into therapy. Which could only mean she truly wasn't that worried about him. She wouldn't be able to joke about it if she was.

A split second later, Zach laughed, and then he lunged at her, shoving her sideways in the grass, careful to grab on to her and roll her so that he hit the ground instead of her.

She landed on top of him and shrieked, "You rat!"

Emma grabbed a handful of leaves and threw them at him. He threw some right back, manhandling her some more until she was flat on her back on the ground and they ended up wrestling, him trying to get at her ribs, because she was ticklish as hell.

She was giggling and still shrieking on occasion when he got her in a particularly tender spot, and it was after one of those shrieks that her husband came barreling around the house and into the backyard, yelling her name.

Zach saw Rye coming and held up his hands in surrender as Rye stopped short, a foot and a half away. "Sorry. It's just me."

Zach took his sister by the hand and tugged until she was sitting up on the ground beside him. They both laughed again, until they caught the thunderous look on Rye's face.

"Jesus, Zach. You took ten years off my life, and I really can't afford to lose time like that, now that we're having another baby." Emphasis being on "another" baby. "What the hell were you doing?" Rye demanded, still breathing hard and glaring at Zach.

"It's all right," Emma said, brushing her hair out of her

face and finding leaves tangled up in it. She started pulling them out.

"God, I thought someone had jumped you in the backyard or that something had happened with the baby."

"Nothing's going to happen to me or this baby," she said. "Zach tickled me, and you know what happens when someone does that. You do it, too."

Rye took another breath, calming down a bit. Zach knew nobody messed with Emma. Rye made sure of it. He came to stand beside his wife, gently moving her hands out of the way and freeing the last of the leaves from her hair.

The gentleness of his touch, the way he let his hand linger there, as if he'd stroked it through her hair a million times and might well do that very thing a million times more, suddenly seemed so intimate, Zach had to look away.

She was just fine, he reminded himself. No matter what she remembered of her time with George and Annie Greene and what emotional wounds had been inflicted, his sister was whole and surrounded by love.

Rye finished with her hair and then sat down on the ground beside her, pulling her against his side and glaring at Zach. "This is how you treat pregnant women?"

"Only ones who happen to be my sister," Zach said. "Sorry. I forget how loud she can be when she's riled." He leaned over and kissed her, trying to get back into her husband's good graces.

Rye shook his head and took a breath, then looked over at Emma. "And you couldn't wait for him to get home?"

"He'll behave now," she said, kissing her husband. "And if you really want to hurt him, you and Sam can gang up at him on the basketball court tomorrow. Rachel called earlier, and she said it's supposed to be nice and warm. She wants to get everybody together there for a cookout."

"Whipping him on the court might make me feel better," Rye admitted.

"Oh, right. Like the two of you are going to hurt me?" Zach boasted. They shouldn't be able to. Even though they were both in great shape, he had more than twenty years on Rye and even more on Sam.

"You sit in a courtroom all day in a fancy suit, Zach. Makes a man soft and slow. Didn't you know that?"

"We'll see who's getting soft," he bragged.

Rye's cell phone rang a moment later, and with a warning to Zach to behave, he got up and took the call, walking toward the front of the house.

Zach got to his feet and then helped his sister up, taking a minute to fuss over the little bulge of her tummy. "I didn't hurt the little guy, did I?"

"No, and my little guy's a girl," she insisted.

"You know that for sure?"

She nodded. "Genetic testing. I'm thirty-seven now."

"Everything okay?"

"She's perfect."

"I meant with you. Rye sounded worried."

Emma sighed. "Well . . . this was something of a surprise. Things happen, you know?"

"Emma—"

"I did not make this happen on my own," she said, feigning outrage over a question he never had a chance to ask. "I had help from my husband, and I assured him that if he's up to making babies at his advanced age, I'm pretty sure he'll be around to help me raise them."

"Oh," he said.

"You know how he gets. Every time I get pregnant, he

starts running timelines in his head and grumbling about how old he'll be when the baby does this or that. And then once they arrive he forgets all about that and just turns into a great dad."

"You don't worry?" Zach asked.

"He's my husband, and we're going to have a new baby together," she said. "And we'll raise this baby together, the way we're raising all our children."

She looked serene when she said it, and triumphant, he thought. He wished he could borrow just a little bit of her faith and tuck it away inside of him.

She gave him a giant hug, and said, "I'm so glad you're home. Don't you dare go ducking my phone calls like that again."

"I won't," he promised.

"Mom?" Dana opened up the screen door and yelled. "Amy called to remind you of your three o'clock appointment. It's quarter till, now."

"Thanks, sweetheart. I'm coming." She turned back to Zach. "I have a patient. Walk me to the office?"

"Sure." He took that to mean she wasn't done with him. Or maybe she'd introduce him to her colleague Jane.

Time for Zach's adventure into therapy. *Great.*

Chapter 14

Emma got herself together and made sure the kids were settled; then she and Zach took off.

"I would have followed through and made the appointment with your friend, Em," he said as they walked. "I'm not looking forward to it, but I know I have to do something."

"That's not why I asked you to come today," she claimed.

"Then why?"

"You'll see."

They were still a block away from her office when he looked down the street and spotted Peter and Julie getting out of Julie's car, which was parked on the street in front of Emma's office.

Zach stopped in the middle of the sidewalk and grumbled, "Do you and Mom tell each other everything about me?"

"Gotcha." Emma grinned. "Rachel didn't say a word about you and Julie. I guessed."

"Shit," he said. They drove him crazy, just knowing stuff like this about him. "What gave me away?"

"You wouldn't call us at all, Zach, no matter what we

did or said. But when Julie needed help, you were on the phone to us right away."

"That's it? A couple of phone calls, and you've got me and Julie—" He broke off abruptly.

"You and Julie, what?"

"Never mind," he said.

"You knew they were coming, right? I mean, I wouldn't have had you come down here . . ."

"Yeah, I knew, and I hope you can do something with this kid," Zach said, thinking this was just great. He and Peter could both be in therapy together. Then Zach realized something else he really should tell his sister, for Peter's sake. "Listen, the kid saw us together earlier today, and he was pretty upset."

Emma stopped where she was, still half a block away from her office. "What were you and Julie doing?"

If he remembered correctly, he was thinking about stripping Julie naked under that big old tree and having her right there, no alcoholic haze, no anger, no despair to get in the way, and he was thinking it would be the closest thing to heaven he'd ever experienced.

"We were kissing," he said. Technically, it was true. Which sounded like something Julie would say. Zach started grinning.

"Must have been some kiss," Emma said.

"It was." And then he had to add, "Peter thinks we were involved in Memphis and that Julie came here to be with me, not because Peter needed her."

His sister, surely through sheer force of will alone, managed not to ask exactly what had gone on in Memphis. So he didn't have to try out Julie's sex-is-nothing line on her, which Emma wouldn't have bought anyway.

He settled for saying, "It didn't happen that way. She

came for Peter. I told her I wasn't even going to be here.
I had that trial starting in Texas, and . . ." *Shit.*

"I remember. You're not heading for Texas anytime
soon, are you?"

"No." Nothing else. Just no. She'd find out sooner or
later. "Anyway, Peter was upset. I just thought you
should know."

"Okay."

"I don't want him to hurt her. I mean, I know he's already hurt her—emotionally. But I'm worried." He hated
even thinking this way. He defended kids who did things
like this, but the thought of someone hurting Julie . . .
"Should I be worried that he might hurt her physically?"

"If I saw anything that made me worry he might, I'd
warn her and social services—"

"Emma?" That wasn't going to be good enough for
him.

"I know how to do my job, Zach. I'm really good at
it."

"Okay, but . . ." He couldn't let it go. Not with Julie. "I
don't want her hurt."

"I understand. Now get out of here. If you're trying to
convince Peter there was nothing going on between the
two of you until you came back to town—"

"Okay. I'll wait around the corner."

"I'll tell Julie."

"Thanks, Em."

Peter was nervous and complaining bitterly about having to see a shrink. The nice lady at the reception desk
gave Julie a mountain of forms to fill out. She followed
Peter into the darkest corner of the room, where he
seemed to be hiding out, hoping no one he knew saw him
here.

Julie was just starting to worry about what this was going to cost and whether her parents had any insurance when Emma walked in. She came straight over to the two of them and gave Julie a big hug.

"It's so good to see you again," Emma said. "You look great."

"So do you. And . . . someone told me you're having another baby."

Emma's hand went to her slightly rounded tummy. "Yes. Number four. Another girl."

"Congratulations," Julie said.

"And you must be Peter," Emma said, turning to him.

Peter didn't say anything at first. Julie supposed this was where the parent type would prompt him to remember his manners, but before she could get them out, the funniest look came over Peter's face.

"Are you Dana's mother?" he asked.

"Yes," Emma said.

Peter looked horrified.

"My oldest," Emma told Julie. "She's twelve. The two of you go to the same middle school, don't you, Peter?"

He nodded.

"I won't tell her you're seeing me, if that's what you're worried about."

He shrugged, as if he didn't care at all, and looked down at his feet.

"Well, why don't we go back to my office and get started?" Emma said, pointing Peter toward a door. He went into her office, and Emma turned to Julie. "Rough day?"

"Day? I've only had him for a few hours," Julie admitted.

Emma laughed. "Yes, days can go on forever with

kids, especially when they're unhappy. I'm sorry about all of this. I know it must be hard on you."

"Harder on him," Julie said. How about that? Here she was, putting someone else's welfare above her own. "I don't know what to do for him."

"You know how it felt to be him, and you know what you wish you'd had when you were living here," Emma said. "Just try to give him what you needed."

Julie frowned. Stability? Predictability? A sense of safety? She couldn't give him what she'd never had, could she? What she'd never been able to find herself.

"Margaret told me you have temporary guardianship. Any idea how long your parents will be gone?"

Gone? Nice euphemism. "No," Julie admitted, then felt like the worst kind of a coward as she admitted, "I haven't talked to them."

"Oh," Emma said.

"I have to talk to them? Is that what you're saying? Peter needs to know?"

"I'm sure he'd feel better if he had some idea of what was going on."

"Of course." Julie groaned. "I should have thought of that. I just . . . I really don't want to see them, and I wasn't thinking of him. I was thinking of me."

"It's all right. You've only had him a few hours. I'm sure you haven't managed to scar him for life in that amount of time."

Julie nodded, feeling like a screwup, but determined to do better. "If I have to see them, I'll see them." It wasn't like it was going to kill her. "I want to do anything I can to help Peter."

"Good," Emma said. "Stability is always a big concern. He's going to want to know how long this living arrangement's going to last. It may be that no one has a hard-and-fast answer right now, but it would be better if we could tell him what to expect of the legal process. That sort of thing."

"Okay. I'll find out. Anything else?"

"We'll talk more when I'm done with him. Give us until four-thirty, okay?"

"Sure. Thanks for coming in today to see him."

"No problem. And Julie?"

"Hmm?"

"Zach's waiting for you around the corner. He was at my house when I left to walk over here, and he didn't think it was a good idea for Peter to see him."

"Oh." Had Zach told her Peter found them rolling around in the grass?

Emma smiled kindly. "Thanks for helping us get Zach home."

"Oh, I didn't. I mean . . ." She was going to say he hadn't come home for her, any more than she'd come here for her. But if he meant what he'd said once he got here . . .

Maybe he had come for her. At least, he might believe that now. When he was thinking more clearly, he might feel differently, and she'd have to hold her head up and try to smile and let him go, and it would be horrible.

Emma put her hand on Julie's arm. "Go on. He's waiting."

"Okay. Thanks."

Julie left the office in a daze.

Me and Zach? Get real, Julie.

She turned the corner, walked into the parking lot, and there he was. He came to her, stopped inches away, and cupped her elbows in the barest hint of an embrace. "What's wrong?"

"Nothing."

"Come on, Julie. It's me."

And then, just like that, she almost started to cry.

"Hey." He drew out the word, almost like a caress. He slipped one arm around her waist, led her deeper into the small, secluded parking lot, backed her up against the brick of the building, standing between her and the rest of the world. His head bent down to hers, and he said, "Tell me."

She shook her head, stubbornly trying to hold back her tears and the words.

"I don't know how relationships have worked for you in the past, Julie—"

"They haven't worked at all."

"Well, that's about to change," he claimed. "And we need to set up some ground rules. One of which is that when you feel so bad you're about to cry, you have to tell me what's wrong, so I can help."

"That's a rule?" she asked, sniffling a bit and feeling miserable.

"Yes. Start talking or else."

"Or else what?"

"I'll kiss you, and you know what happens when I do that. We probably shouldn't risk it in a parking lot in the middle of downtown."

She closed her eyes, dipped her head lower. He was being extremely kind, and she didn't think she deserved it. She never thought she deserved good things.

"You scare me to death," she whispered.

"Okay, now I have to kiss you."

She gave up then. The tears in her eyes overflowed and ran down her cheeks. He gently brushed them away, brushed his lips ever so softly across hers.

She made herself push him away. "Zach, someone will see us."

"Who cares? As long as it's not Peter. Is that what this is about?"

"No," she admitted, then berated herself for that. That's all she would have had to say. That they had to slow down, so Peter wouldn't be so angry or so suspicious. She could have held Zach off until he came to his senses. And maybe if it never went any further, it wouldn't hurt so badly to give him up. That one stupid night didn't really count.

"This will never work out," she said miserably.

"Why the hell not?"

"It just won't."

"Scared, Julie?" he asked, calm as you please and maddening as hell in his dead-on assessment of the situation. "Sorry. You'll just have to get over it."

"I don't want to get hurt, Zach."

"Neither do I. How can you be so sure I'll hurt you?"

"Everyone hurts me," she said.

"Well, that's going to have to change, too."

He looked downright arrogant then and irritatingly calm about this. Lawyer training, she supposed. State your position and stick with it. Overcome all objections. Win. How was she supposed to fight him when she wanted him to win this one? Which made her think of his trial.

"Do you have to go to Texas soon?" she asked.

"No."

"What happened?"

He actually looked embarrassed. "I've been ordered not to show my face in my office or in any courtroom for two months. That's what happened."

"Why?"

"I kind of . . . yelled at the judge in Memphis," he admitted.

236   *Teresa Hill*

"Zach—"

"I tried to tell you this morning, Julie. I'm a mess right now, and if you don't want to be with me because of that, I'll understand—"

"Oh, hell. I could never *not* want to be with you," she blurted out.

He grinned wide enough that those absolutely adorable dimples showed up in his cheeks.

"Shit," she muttered.

"No, really . . ." he began, looking ridiculously pleased, then more serious. "When you know the whole of it, you might have second thoughts. I'd understand."

Julie looked at him. Really looked at him. He kept saying that—that there were things he had to tell her, but he hadn't said much yet. Not that they'd had that much time. They seemed to keep getting distracted. It was too easy when he was this close.

He seemed a little tense, but not too bad. Julie studied him more closely. She would have said she was the world's best at covering, but maybe he was better. After all, he was so worried he thought that once she knew what was wrong she might change her mind about wanting to be with him. He was dead serious. And scared. Zach full of confidence was a hard man to resist, but Zach vulnerable in the least little way, slayed her through and through.

"I'm not going to change my mind," she said, resigned to the fact that she simply had no defenses against him. "Not about you."

It was scary as hell, but it felt good, too. How something could be both at the same time, she would never understand. But there it was. She'd come out here determined to push him away and ended up in his arms telling him everything he needed to know about her.

"Well, you don't have to look so miserable about it," he said. "Is it that bad? Feeling this way about me?"

"It will be," she said, raising her chin defiantly. "This will never work."

"Why?"

"Oh, Zach. Look at me."

"There's absolutely nothing wrong with the way you look."

"Think about who I am," she cried. "I'm a screwed-up woman. I had a lousy childhood. I don't trust anybody—"

"You can trust me."

"I haven't ever been able to make a relationship work. My parents are in jail, and my brother's in therapy. I probably should be in therapy myself. I have no job and hardly anything in the bank, because I spent so much on a wedding I called off at the last minute. The bank's re-possessing my parents' house. Jesus, I'm a mess, and you're . . you're . . ."

"I'm the one who understands all of that," he claimed.

"Don't say that," she yelled.

"You think I'm going to condemn you for your parents' mistakes? My old man's a murderer and a drunk, and my mother let him beat her until he put her into an early grave."

"I know, but that's not who you are."

"And you're not your parents."

She raised her chin and proclaimed, "I'm a liar."

"Well, you're just going to have to give that up, Julie."

As if it were that easy. Will herself to change, and what? She'd just be different?

"What else?" he asked. "Might as well get it all out up front. Tell me. What else about you is so bad?"

"I always run away when things get hard," she said,

laying one of her trump cards on the table. "If I can't lie, I run."

"You'll have to give that up, too," he said, maddeningly calm and so sure of himself.

"What if I can't?"

"What do you have to lie about?" he reasoned. "The only thing you ever really lie about is your childhood, your parents, and I already know everything about them. And you ran away because you thought there was nothing left for you here. I understand that."

"I ran away from Memphis after I screwed up everything there."

"No, you came here for Peter."

"Oh, Zach. I'd love to believe that. I'd love for you to believe it. But if my life had been going really well there, I probably would have stayed."

"You could have. All you had to do was never tell Steve about you and me or about Peter, but you couldn't lie to him about either of those things."

"I could have."

"You didn't," he countered. "Face it, Julie. You have a conscience, and you care about your brother and me. And right now, you're just scared. But it's going to be okay. I'm going to be here, and when you get scared, you just run to me, and I'll hang on to you so tight you won't be able to get away."

She blinked up at him through her tears, the promise of his words too much for her to take in. She found it in her to make one more tiny protest.

"That doesn't seem very fair to you."

"Well, I'm counting on you holding on to me, too, when I get scared."

"You don't get scared," she insisted.

He looked a little uncomfortable then, and for a moment she had the idea that he was going to give in, that he'd finally listen to what she had to say and be convinced that this would just never work. That he'd turn around and walk away, and Julie didn't think she could stand that.

It looked like she was going to be one of those awful women who said one thing and then did the opposite. Who wanted a man to talk her into what she really wanted in the first place. She felt mildly guilty about that, even as she threw her arms around him and just held on, not breathing any easier until his arms locked around her in return.

He slowly brought her fully against his body, doing that interlocking thing he did, until she just fit, as if she were made to be the other half of him, and to hell with the idea that there was surely someone else in this world who'd be so much better for him than she would. She needed him. She'd worry about the fairness of that later.

Julie snuggled against him, reassured by the sheer solid mass of him. That wicked little zing of awareness was heating her blood, humming along her veins, and then she was kissing him, as wildly as she had that morning on the grass.

She remembered then. . . . He wasn't engaged anymore. They didn't have to feel guilty about this. They could do something she understood, something that just plain felt great.

"Forget about this." She dragged her mouth from his. "About all the talking and all the rules. We're ten minutes from my house—my empty house—and we have an hour and a half before Peter's done. Take me home, Zach. I need you."

He groaned and gave her an absolute scorcher of a kiss. It was going to be okay, she decided. For the imme-

diate future, it would be okay. They'd have this. She'd
make it through the next few days or weeks, maybe even
months, and she wouldn't worry about what happened
after that. She'd make the most of what they could have
now, during this otherwise awful time, and whatever happened later would just happen.

"Come on. Let's go," she said.

Zach pulled back and nearly growled in frustration.

"What?" She could strip him right here, the way she
felt right now. It seemed it had been decades since they'd
been together.

"No," he said.

She frowned up at him. "What do you mean, no?"

"I mean, no. I mean, there are things you have a right
to know before this goes any further. And much as I'd
love to be back at your house, in bed with you, I'm not
going to do that. I'm not going to sneak off to bed with
you when no one's looking, just because the sex part of
this doesn't scare you when the rest does."

Julie's mouth hung open. She didn't make a habit of
trying to drag them off to her bed, and she sure didn't like
the idea of him turning her down.

"You're not going to make this about sex and nothing
else," he said, looking as stubborn as her thirteen-year-
old brother had this afternoon when she'd tried to drag
him off to the therapist.

"You . . . you don't want to?"

"Hell, yes, I want to," he roared. "But I'm not."

"Zach," she protested.

"I'm just not that kind of guy," he said, a "take that"
grin on his face.

"I don't believe you," she roared.

"I know. That's part of the problem. You don't believe
this could possibly last. You don't believe I really want

you, and you're trying to make this into something that wouldn't absolutely terrify you. Sorry. If that's what I do to you, you're just going to have to get over it. You can't have me until you do."

"I can't *have* you?"

He nodded, looking supremely satisfied with himself.

She wanted to smack him, but she'd been on the wrong side of an exchange like that too many times to ever hit anyone, even in a playful kind of way, and damned if her body wasn't still humming along on pure sexual energy. Like every nerve ending knew he was right here, and was going, "Gimme, gimme, gimme." And she wasn't going to get him?

"Don't hurt me," he protested. "This is the way, you'll see."

"The way to what?"

"You and me. We did it all wrong in the beginning and ended up in bed together way too soon, and now we have to back up, take it easy. You have to know you can trust me, and I really do have some things I have to explain to you."

"Something else along the lines of 'I'm not having sex with you'? Because I really don't want to hear it."

"No, it's not about sex," he said, then frowned. "You know, this isn't going to be any easier for me than it is for you. I can't close my eyes without having some image pop into my head of you and me rolling around together on the floor or in that bed in my hotel room. I couldn't sleep there anymore, for thinking of you. I nearly jumped down the maid's throat one morning, because she stripped the bed and took the sheets that smelled like you."

"Don't tell me this," she said.

"It's true. All of it. It's been four days, and I feel like

it's been four years. We're going to have to get this right, and fast."

No way. Julie thought. She didn't think it would ever be right. She'd just have to seduce him. How hard could it be? They practically set the world on fire when they touched.

"I don't think I like that gleam in your eye," he said.

It was her turn to grin. She took a step closer, her hands pressed flat against his chest. "There's nothing for you to worry about. This won't hurt a bit."

"It hurts already." He grabbed her by the wrists and pulled her hands off him. "And I'm worried."

She grinned. "You can't fight me forever."

"You can't fight me forever, either," he said. "I'm counting on that."

Julie fumed. *Stalemate. Fine.* She'd take that for now.

It was a ridiculous argument to have, him wanting her for . . . What? *Forever?* That was crazy. And her wanting him in her bed, instead? Did he think he was going to win this argument? He didn't have a chance.

Except he didn't look like a man who didn't have a chance. He looked like a man who argued for a living and won. Like someone who studied his opponent and the case before him and plotted and planned and outwitted people until he got his way. She suspected he was a master at it.

But she was fighting for her emotional life, which made her more desperate than he was. "You're crazy," she said.

"Maybe," he admitted, calm as you please now. "What are you and Peter planning to do tomorrow night?"

Julie frowned at the change of subject. What was wrong with the man? "Probably grumble at each other some more, with more of the stuff he calls music played at ear-splitting volume, so that the whole house shakes." She couldn't wait for tomorrow night.

"My parents are having a cookout. You two should come."

"To your parents'?"

He nodded. "You know, like a date, Julie. I'm inviting you out, and you can even bring the grumpy kid. This way you won't have to be alone with him."

"He went nuts when he saw us together this afternoon."

"When he saw us about to rip each other's clothes off. I can't have him thinking I'm only after you for your luscious body."

"That's all I want you for, Zach," she claimed.

"Liar."

"How is it that I've never seen this snippy side of you?"

He grinned some more. They really had to do something about this arrogant streak of his.

"Come to my parents', Julie."

"Why?"

"Because I want to see you."

She practically shivered at the words. He was getting to her. He knew how much she wanted to be with him. *Be.* In every way possible. And how much she wanted everything with him. It seemed ridiculous to even think of saying, *Couldn't you just sneak into my bed late at night when no one's looking?* Was she really crazy enough to throw away this chance? Even if the chance of it ever working out was infinitesimal, how could she throw it away?

"I don't know what to do with you," she complained.

"Keep at it. You'll figure it out."

"Zach—"

He kissed her once more, just long enough to set her heart to pounding once again, and before she could get a decent grip on his shoulders and just hang on, he was pulling away.

"Six-thirty," he said. "Don't be late."

"I never even said I'd come."

He dismissed that as a minor detail and went right on. "Now, what else can I do for you today? I feel better when I'm actually solving problems, and I could have sworn there was something in the middle of that little tirade of yours that I could help with. . . . The house. Did you say someone's trying to take your parents' house?"

"I don't know," she said miserably.

"You don't know if someone's trying to take the house?"

"No, I don't know half of what I said to you. I was upset."

"But someone's trying to take the house?" he repeated.

"Yes," she admitted.

He took a breath. "Well, they teach us about those things in law school, you know. You remember that I went to law school?"

She nodded.

"Somebody send you some threatening-looking papers?"

"Yes."

"Want to show 'em to me?"

"You're too good to me," she said, willing herself not to cry again.

"I haven't been to this point," he said offhandedly. "But I'd like to work on moving in that direction. Now, what else can I do for you?"

Julie shook her head. He said that, and the oddest feelings welled up inside of her, ones that left her wanting to lay all her troubles at his feet. She couldn't do that to him or to herself. No one carried her burdens for her.

"Tell me," he said. "If I can't fix my own problems, maybe I can fix yours."

"Emma says I have to talk to my parents," she blurted out.

"Oh."

"I know. I know. How could I come back here to take care of things and not even talk to them? I don't want to talk to them, Zach, and I sound like a six-year-old when I say that, but that's how I feel."

"Hey, I've been avoiding a few people myself lately. I know the feeling. Is this about Peter? You need to talk to them because of Peter?"

Julie nodded.

"I could go with you," he offered. "And you don't have to talk to them about anything but Peter. Not if you don't want to."

"Emma said Peter needs to know as much as we can tell him about what's ahead for them legally. The arrest. Bond. Court hearings. Anything."

Zach took her face in his hands and waited until she looked at him. He was grinning in the kindest sort of way. "Hello? Law degree. Remember?"

"I can't ask you to go help them."

"You didn't ask, Julie. Remember our deal? You never have to ask, not as long as I can figure out what you need."

"Still . . ." she said. "I can't stand them. They're horrible."

"I have clients who kill people. I can defend a couple of small-town embezzlers. Especially if they're related to you."

She couldn't help but smile a bit then. "So all my relatives get a break on the best legal services available?"

"Bring 'em on," he said. "I don't have anything else to do for the next fifty-nine days."

"Oh, Zach, I . . ."

"What?" he asked.

It would have been so easy.

I love you, Zach.

She wanted to say it. God help her, she very nearly did say it.

"Nothing." She closed the distance between them, pulling his mouth down to hers. His wonderful mouth. Reveling in the taste of him, the heat coming off his body. God, she missed him. "Couldn't we just go home and go to bed?"

"No. The jail or the bank. You pick."

"Let's see . . . Jail. Bank. Or my bed? How many men would pick anything but the bed?"

"I told you, I'm not easy."

No, he was not going to make this easy. But then nothing in her life had ever been easy. And nothing had ever been this good. Terrifying, but very, very good. She wondered briefly if that's what love was. Terrifying and so good.

She put her hand in his. His fingers closed over hers, reassuring and comforting and real. He was here, and it didn't look like he was going away or giving up. Everything was changing, and it was possible it might actually change for the better. Peter might forgive her some day, and she might actually do him some good by being here. She didn't care what happened with her parents, as long as she didn't have to deal with them, and Zach . . .

She couldn't help loving the man, but maybe she could keep herself from telling him so. But what if he figured out that what she really wanted was his love? If he just offered that to her, without her ever having to ask, and he made her trust in that love and in the idea that it could last? She'd be lost then. Or maybe she'd be found.

Chapter 15

Maybe she was weak, because she just let him take over and try to fix everything. She had the threatening bank papers in her car, which he glanced at and frowned and decided to take them with him to study more closely. Then they headed for the town's new jail.

"Want me to go in with you?" Zach offered at the door to the visiting area.

"No. Thanks. But . . . no." No need for him to see how ugly things could be between her and her mother. He'd seen enough of that when they were younger.

"Okay. I want to call the prosecutor who's handling their case, see what I can find out, while you're in there."

Julie managed a nod. She wanted to turn around and run, but a vague sense of pride kept her where she was. She wasn't really scared of her mother, was she?

A guard led her inside to a row of cubicles with chairs and phones at each space, a heavy glass wall separating her from an identical space on the other side. Julie sat down as a woman entered from the other side. An old, gray-haired woman in a bright orange jumpsuit, with wrinkles on her face and a mildly irritated look in her eyes.

Julie thought at first they'd made a mistake, that her mother couldn't be this old woman, and then the woman looked her right in the face, and Julie barely held back a gasp. It looked like her mother had aged twenty years in the past eight.

The guard closed the door, leaving them alone, and that sound was the last one she heard for what seemed like the longest time. Neither she nor her mother said a word. They didn't even look at each other.

Finally, Julie picked up the phone, waited until her mother did the same, then looked away again. "Peter's with me," she said. "I have temporary custody, and I hope social services will let me keep him until . . . I don't even know when. We need to know what's going on with you. He needs to know. How long are you going to be here?"

"I don't know," her mother said. "The judge set bail high enough to cover the money that's missing. We don't get out until the case comes to trial or we pay the money back."

"Do you still have it?" Julie asked. She'd thought of searching the house for it, that it might prove that simple. Find it. Give it back. Be done with this thing.

Her mother said nothing.

"But you took it?" Julie tried. Still nothing. Julie took her silence as an admission of guilt. "Do you have an attorney?"

"The court appointed one. A kid who looks about your age, maybe younger."

"Do you like him? Does he seem like he knows what he's doing?"

"Not really," her mother said.

"Okay. Zach McRae offered to help, as a favor to me and to Peter. But it has to be your decision, and you have to fire the other attorney first, for Zach to be able to step in. I left his business card with the guard for you. But whatever you do, I need to be able to tell Peter something. Social services needs to know. We can't all live in limbo like this."

"You're really going to stick around?" her mother asked.

"I don't know," she said, anger pouring in past the numbness that had gotten her through to this point. "Somebody has to take care of Peter. He was in a group home until I got here, Mom. That's what happens when your parents go to jail and there's no one left to take care of you. Did you ever even think about that? Did you ever think of anyone but yourself and your husband?"

Julie turned her head away as far as the phone cord would allow, shifting in her chair to turn her body away from her mother's, too. She really didn't want to be here, and she didn't want to talk about this.

"Look, I have to go," she said, then remembered one last thing. "The bank's foreclosing on the house, but I guess you already know that. Looks like it's been in the works for a while. I don't suppose . . . No, I'm sure there's no money to fix that. If there were, I guess the cops would have seized it by now to cover what's missing."

Her mother stared blankly at her.

"You know, there was a time when I would have sat here arguing with you until I figured something out or I fixed it. But I'm done. I'd rather bang my head against that wall. It would be just as productive. You made this mess. You get yourself out of it, and I'll take care of Peter as best I can."

Julie got to her feet and knocked on the door. The guard came to let her out.

Oddly enough, it didn't feel like running this time. It

felt like a choice she'd made. A smart one. *How about that? Julie makes a good decision.* She felt like shit, but she thought she was doing the right thing. It was more than she could say for most decisions in her life.

Julie still felt really lousy once she was done with her mother, and she had an idea that maybe if she looked really pitiful and asked nicely, Zach might change his mind and take her home to bed. But he was one determined man, and he just wouldn't take her home for fix-every-thing-sex.

"What's a woman supposed to do with a man who withholds his wicked body from her in times of need?" she asked.

He laughed at her. "Save it. You're not getting that kind of sympathy from me. But I will get you ice cream."

"Ice cream?" she complained.

"It worked when you were seven."

"I'm not seven years old anymore, Zach."

"Does that mean you don't want ice cream?"

"No, that is not what it means."

"Thought so." He laughed as he parked her car near the town square.

She hadn't wanted to drive when she'd come out of the jail. He'd driven, and at first he'd held her hand, and then as she'd gotten even more miserable, he'd tugged until she was leaning across the console in the middle of the seats until her head was in his lap, her cheek against his right thigh, his hand toying with her hair.

So she had that and ice cream. It wasn't the kind of comfort she'd find in being in bed with him, but it wasn't bad.

He parked the car. She went to raise her head, but before she could get too far away, he drew her face to his and kissed her slowly, sweetly. She made a pitiful sound that might have been a whimper. She was a pathetic woman at the moment. He grinned and nuzzled his nose against hers and kissed her cheek.

"I'm telling you, my sympathy doesn't extend that far."

"Rat," she complained.

"You haven't tasted this ice cream."

He got out of the car and was coming around to open the door for her, but she did it herself and was waiting for him when he got to her side of the car.

"You're telling me this ice cream is somehow comparable to a night in bed with you?"

Zach just grinned. It took her a minute to realize that he wasn't just grinning at her, but at someone behind her. Groaning, Julie turned around to find his sister Grace standing there grinning like the devil herself.

"I don't know, Zach. I have trouble thinking you're *that* good," Grace said, then burst out laughing.

Julie thought she must have turned six different shades of red. Zach came closer, slipping his arm around her and not letting her move away from him.

"They all know, anyway," he said softly, his mouth close to her ear. "They know everything. Always. It's the most annoying thing."

Julie frowned at Grace, and the only thing she could think to say in her own defense was, "He's not engaged anymore."

"I know," Grace said, proving Zach's theory.

Julie groaned once again, and Grace gave her a big hug, then pulled Zach into it, too. Zach gave her a kiss, and said, "'Bout time you got back here."

"Me?" Grace frowned at him. "I'm not the one who's been gone for the better part of four months."

"I had some things to take care of," he said.

"Sure you did." She turned to Julie. "I can't believe you're back! I feel like it's been forever. And look at you. You look great. How are you?"

"I'm . . . handling things. Kind of," Julie said, then looked at Zach. "He's making me crazy."

"He's good at that."

"You look wonderful, too," Julie said. Grace had always been a beauty. A delicate, blond angel. "Your mother said you were off on a job?"

"Yes. Finalizing some details about one. The glass is amazing. I can't wait to get my hands on it."

"When do you start?" Zach asked.

"As soon as they can order all my equipment and it comes in. Maybe a month, so I'll be here, and you'd better be here, too." She glared at him. "You have to talk to me."

"I will. Promise."

"And you have to talk to me, too," she said, looking at Julie. "Are you two coming to Mom and Dad's tomorrow night?"

"Yes," Zach said.

"Good." She looked from one of them to the other, seeming thoroughly pleased with what she saw and what she'd heard. "I guess I'll see you there, then. I hate to rush off, but I have to take care of a couple of things and I wouldn't want to interrupt anything. Sounds like you have important things to settle about how good this ice cream is. I wouldn't want to get in the way of that." She grinned, kissed her brother on the cheek and then gave Julie a quick hug and ran off.

"She does look great," Julie said. "And happy."

"Grace is always happy," he said. "So . . . ice cream?" Julie glared at him, embarrassed to the core. "Your whole family thinks we're sleeping together. That I broke up your engagement."

"No. They know the engagement's off, but I never told anybody it was because of you. It wasn't. I mean, I probably finally figured it out now because of you. But it's not like you . . . You know what it was like," he said. "And I didn't admit to anything about sex. Except to my mother—"

"You talk about your sex life with your mother?" she cried.

"Not usually, but . . . I felt bad about everything, and it kind of slipped out."

Julie groaned.

"She's not going to say anything to anybody. Except maybe my dad—"

Julie winced and covered her face with her hands. Zach pried them away. He sighed as he stood there holding her close, right in the middle of town on a sunny afternoon. "It's going to be okay."

"They must think I'm awful."

"No, they don't. They think I'm a mess right now— that's what I told them—and that this was my fault, and they're glad you're here to help me through it."

"The great big sex cure?"

"No, Julie. It wasn't that. It was a lot more than that, and you know it."

"But . . . I . . ." She would have protested long and loud. But then he kissed her again. It wasn't such a terribly inappropriate kiss. It was sweet and soft and kind, and he held her lightly, his hands on the sides of her face. But he touched her, and she just melted and clung to him.

It was so good, having just this much of him. If only she could keep him. . . .

Julie broke the kiss and backed away.

"What?" he asked, mild irritation coloring the word.

"I don't know," she said miserably. "It's just . . . We're standing in the town square, for God's sake. Half the town's probably seen us by now."

"And that's a problem?"

"I don't know. Everything seems to be a problem right now."

"I was just trying to make it a little better," he said.

She frowned yet again and would have sworn there was just no making this day better, but he always seemed to find a way. Kissing was a good start. Even if it did make her a little uncomfortable in such a public place, thinking everyone would be talking about them.

"All right," she said, sounding like she was still complaining, when she knew he had been trying to make everything better. "Can I have my ice cream now?"

"Sure."

His arm came around her, and he steered her down the block and into the store. It was brand-new, and it smelled heavenly inside. They saw a half-dozen people they knew in the time they were inside waiting their turn, another half dozen on the way from the store to the town park across the street. Julie sat on top of a picnic table eating her ice cream, and Zach stood beside her, leaning against the tabletop, looking out over the river.

"Well?" he asked when she was done with her cup of chocolate swirl.

"Not bad," she said.

"Not bad?" He came to stand in front of her, easing her thighs apart and settling between them.

"Zach, there's no food in the world that's better than good sex."

"None?" he asked, leaning down and taking the merest taste of her lips.

"None. I feel sorry for women who think there's a food that can come close. But this is really good. And it was sweet of you to take such good care of me this afternoon."

"I'm not feeling very sweet at the moment."

She took a handful of his shirt in each of her hands and tugged until he came closer, wondering if anyone ever had sex on these tables in the park when it was pitch-black out here. He wanted her. Right now. There was no mistaking that when his hands slid down to her hips and pulled her against him.

"You're not making this easy for me," he complained.

"I don't plan to. What do I have to do exactly to get you back in bed with me?"

"I can't remember," he said, kissing her once more.

They might get arrested in the park, she thought. Somebody might have to pry her hands off him, hopefully before she ripped his clothes off. She was easing closer, her body opening up to his, her bottom leaning off the edge of the table and into that wonderful hardness of his.

"Want to have a picnic?" she asked.

He broke the kiss and stepped away, breathing hard and swearing. "You are a wicked woman."

"I know." She finally grinned. "Tell me again. What exactly do I have to do to have you?"

He was standing about a foot away, standing straight and tall and looking like a man in the absolute prime of his life, his body strong and lean, a determined look on his face. The wind was blowing through his hair, and he never took his eyes off her. She reached out and took one of his hands, which was hanging by his side, and tugged him back to her.

"What? Tell me. I'll do it."

"You have to let me love you," he said.

"Zach—" She couldn't believe he'd just thrown it out into the open that way. Didn't the man know anything about self-protection and evasion? She'd have to teach him. It was much easier than this.

"No trying to talk me out of it or to change my mind. No pushing me away or making excuses. You just have to let me, Julie. It's as easy as that."

She shook her head. "There's nothing easy about it."

"Let me in," he said. "Believe in me—"

"I do believe in you," she complained. "It's just—"

"Us, then. Believe in us. And find a way to believe in yourself. If you did, just a fraction as much as I believe in you—"

"You have always been such a fool that way," she insisted.

"No, I'm not. I'm the most reasonable man you know. Think about that."

"But why?" she asked, near to tears again. "Why would you want me?"

He put his hand on her knee and then eased it up onto her thigh. "I like your legs in those little bitty skirts you wear."

"I don't wear little bitty skirts."

"Then I like your legs in those not-so-little-bitty skirts of yours, and I like your hair, especially when it's loose and I've got a handful of it, holding you close to me with it, or it's falling around my face. Or my body."

"That's sex, Zach. The thing we're not having."

"And I like the way the hardest things in the world can be happening and you try to laugh it off or make a joke of it and keep right on going. I like how stubborn you are and how hard you try to make things work and how nothing seems to break you, and I see how kind you can be and how generous—"

"By sleeping with you?"

"And worrying about me, and wanting to take care of me. By listening to me and understanding so many things about me that I didn't even see myself. I like taking care of you, and I want to protect you and make you happy. I always have. I want to make everything in your life easier, and I want to see you smile day after day after day. I want you to believe in every good thing in the world and know you can have them all. I want you to see yourself the way I see you. I want you to see me as exactly who I am and still love me."

She glared at him through her tears.

"Nothing to say to that?"

"Oh, hell, how could anyone not love you?"

He grinned. "You know, as declarations of love go, that needs some work, Julie."

"I didn't say—" Oh, hell, she had. Which didn't mean she couldn't try to save herself now. "I'm not . . . Zach!"

"Okay." He finally came back to her, his hand at the back of her head, inviting her to rest it against his shoulder.

"I'm still scared," she said miserably.

"Okay. And I'm pushing. Sorry."

"Couldn't this be some midlife crisis of yours or something?"

He laughed, still holding her. "I'm only thirty-one. I don't think so."

"Well, you've always been ahead of the curve. Maybe it just hit early."

"And you think I just don't know what I want? Or

what's good for me? That I'm just a little bit crazy now, and I'll come to my senses one day and . . . What?"

"You won't want me anymore," she whispered.

"I will," he said.

"Well, I have trouble believing that right now."

"Okay."

"Please don't be mad at me."

"I'm not. I'm the most reasonable man on earth, remember?"

She nodded as best she could, considering she was still in his arms, her head tucked under his chin. "Can't we just go on like this? With you not sleeping with me and making me crazy and trying to fix everything for me?"

"Yeah, we can do that."

"I do love you, Zach," she confessed.

His arms tightened around her. She felt him take a big long breath and let it out slowly, felt a slight tremor work its way through his body.

"I tried not to, but I just couldn't help myself," she said.

He backed up, kissed her forehead, and then her right cheek, and then found her mouth, working over it like a man with all the time in the world for just one kiss. She wanted to crawl inside of him and never come out, and at the same time, she wanted to turn around and run as hard and as fast as she could.

"It'll be all right," he said. "We have plenty of time to get this right."

She nodded, and he brushed away her tears.

What could she have possibly done to deserve him?

"It's almost four-thirty," he said. "Peter'll be done soon."

"Okay." Peter, who hated her and thought she'd only come back here for Zach, whom she loved. *God, help me.*

"Try not to worry so much," Zach said.

She'd try. Try not to be terrified. Try not to screw this up or get her hopes up too much. Try to protect herself and not hurt him or Peter or anyone else.

Try to be a woman he could love.

Peter was agitated and fidgety and grumpy. So was Julie.

She'd taken Zach home before she went back to pick up Peter, so he didn't see Zach. He complained bitterly about having to see a shrink, about how his feelings were none of her business, none of anyone's business, and how he was perfectly fine.

"Yeah, me, too," Julie said. "So what if Mom and Dad are in jail? I'm fine."

Peter glared at her from the passenger seat.

"I went to see Mom this afternoon."

He watched her even more closely, but said nothing. He wouldn't even let himself ask. Maybe she'd have to treat him like Zach, try to figure out what he wanted and just give it to him.

"I told her that you and I needed to know how long she's going to be there, that we had to make plans."

"What kind of plans?"

"For us," she said. "How we're going to live."

He shrugged as carelessly as he could manage. "I told you already, you don't have to stay here. They're always in some kind of trouble, and they always manage to get out. They will this time."

"I don't think so, Peter. The judge wants them to give back the money they took or go to jail, and Mom said they don't have it to give back. Do you know anything about that?"

"Dad's been betting ball games. I guess he hasn't been

doing too well. And he got laid off about a year ago and hasn't had luck finding anything else. Things kind of went from bad to worse. I guess they needed the money."

"I guess so, but they can't just take it like that."

"They did it for sure?" he asked quietly.

"She didn't say exactly. But . . . it seemed like they did."

"They'll get out of it," he insisted. "Don't worry. They always do. Go back home. I'll be fine."

"I'm not leaving you. I guess I'll have to keep saying it until you believe it."

She was irritated at first. How many ways could she say it? What would it take for him to believe that she wanted to be with him. That just because the world had screwed him over royally for the first thirteen years of his life, didn't mean the rest of it would just suck.

And then she realized he was just like she was. Just as suspicious. Just as scared. Just as stubborn.

And she was using the same arguments on him that Zach was using on her, neither one of them having much luck. Except she wasn't sure she had Zach's patience or his wisdom.

She started to laugh, just a little. "What?" Peter asked, irritated.

"Nothing. I was just thinking . . . Life is so strange sometimes."

Peter looked at her like she'd absolutely lost her mind, and maybe she had. She'd told Zach she loved him, and he claimed he loved her, which terrified her, and here she was with Peter, fumbling this horribly. But she felt better all of a sudden.

She'd had ice cream and kisses, had faced her mother without falling apart, and survived all of five hours with

Peter without ruining him for life, and Zach thought he
loved her.

It was more than she'd had in a long, long time.

She didn't tell Peter where they were going the next
evening, except to dinner. He got suspicious when they
didn't get in the car, but started walking down the block
instead.

"There aren't any restaurants down here."

"Did I say we were going to a restaurant?"

"Where else would we go?" he grumbled. "You said
we were going to eat."

"You'll see."

He got more and more suspicious the closer they came
to the McRae house, and he probably would have turned
around and run once he realized what was going on. But
there was a car out front, and a girl got out of the backseat just as they arrived. She looked like she might be
Peter's age, maybe a little younger, and either she hadn't
hit that awful awkward age of adolescence yet, or she
was going to sail right through it beautifully. She was
long limbed and willowy, with dark hair and dark eyes
and a big smile on her face.

"Peter? Hi."

"Hi," he mumbled, stopping a full five feet away.

Emma got out of the car a moment later, and Peter
turned absolutely red. She headed toward Julie, but whispered to Peter as she passed him, "Don't worry. I promised I wouldn't tell anyone, and I won't."

Peter looked suspicious but torn. The girl was gorgeous and seemed happy to see him. The grill was obviously already going in the backyard, and the meat
smelled wonderful.

"You're coming to my grandparents' for dinner?" the girl asked.

He shrugged and mumbled, "Guess so."

"Great," she said.

Emma held out a hand to the girl and drew her to her side. "Julie, this is my oldest daughter, Dana. Dana, this is Peter's sister, Julie. She and your aunt Grace used to play together when they were little."

"Hi," the girl said.

"Why don't you take Peter to the backyard and introduce him around?" Emma suggested.

Julie sighed as she watched the two of them head for the backyard. "Thank goodness. I was afraid that once he figured out where we were going, he'd walk home and sulk all night. I'm not handling this well, Emma."

Emma laughed. "It hasn't even been two full days."

"You're right." Julie managed to laugh herself. "It just feels like it's been a decade or so."

"Come on." Emma linked her arm with Julie's. "Dana can keep Peter occupied for a while. We'll all eat way too much fattening food and laugh and talk and forget about everything else for a while."

It proved to be a dead-on prediction for the evening. Zach's family had always welcomed her like a long-lost and much-loved relative rather than the neglected little girl from down the street. And it was wonderful to be back in the midst of them, despite speculation about her relationship with Zach and the fact that her parents were in jail right now. They were just nice people.

The children ran around in the backyard. The men manned the grill, while the women gathered in the kitchen, preparing side dishes and dessert, nibbling and laughing the evening away. It was a relaxed, happy place, and she felt at home here.

"Julie, didn't Grace say you were in PR?" Zach's mother asked as Julie was tearing apart a head of lettuce for the salad.

"Yes. For a department-store chain."

"But you're not going back there, right?" Grace asked, giving her an expectant look.

"I guess not. I mean . . . I quit my job when I came here."

"So you'll need something here?" Grace grinned. "Perfect. Tell her, Mom."

"Brandon Lowery just got transferred to Seattle, immediately, and his wife, Patricia, works for the Chamber of Commerce. She's in charge of the Christmas festival, and this is the worst possible time we could lose her. We need someone ASAP, and I told her boss you were free. . . ."

"Oh." They'd practically found her a job? Here? She tried to laugh it off. "Did you tell him I could be trusted not to run off with all the Chamber's money?"

"No, she did not tell him that," Grace said.

"He's got to wonder," Julie reasoned.

"When have you ever been like your parents?" Emma asked.

Julie frowned, thinking this had to be a trick question. A shrink thing. It seemed so deceptively simple on its surface, but it was making her think and think and think.

"You're not." It was Zach's voice, coming from behind her. He slid an arm around her waist and pulled her back against him, right there in his parents' kitchen. His other arm came around her, too, and he just held her. "That's the right answer, in case you're still wondering."

And then he kissed her on the cheek and grinned up at all the women in his life, who were beaming at them both.

"They think they've found me a job," Julie said.

"Good," he said, as if it were the most natural thing in the world for her to take a job here and stay here.

"I gave Brandon your number. He'll call you," Zach's mother said. As if it were all settled. No problem that her parents were embezzlers or that she was still trying to find the courage to stay.

"And Sam had some ideas about your house," Zach said casually. He let go of her, only to take her hand in his and tug her along with him, calling over his shoulder. "Think the three of you could give us a minute?"

His mother and his sisters laughed, as if they couldn't be happier.

"What did you tell them about us?" she asked as he tugged her through the family room and toward the front of the house.

"That I was in love with you, and that you didn't want me to be."

"Zach—"

He laughed. "I'm kidding. I really don't tell them everything. They just figure out most things for themselves. It's really annoying, but they mean well. They like you, and they're crazy about me. So there's no problem, right?"

He caught her in his arms, in a tiny alcovelike area below the stairs where they had some semblance of privacy.

"Relax, Julie. Everyone's in the backyard or the kitchen," he said, that wonderful mouth of his coming down to hers.

The kiss was all too brief, too sweet, and it made her want too many things they seemed intent on denying themselves. She'd never understand why. She wanted to wrap her arms around him and just never let go.

"Having a good time?" he asked as he slowly drew away.

"Yes. You know I've always loved being at your parents' home. How's Peter?"

"Following my niece around like a lovesick puppy. Rye's about to kill him."

"Why? What did Peter do?"

"Nothing. Rye's not happy about any guy looking at his little girl like that."

"She's not so little anymore," Julie said.

"Don't tell Rye that. He's living in denial for as long as he can, and my dad's enjoying the hell out of this."

"Oh."

"He wasn't very happy when Emma decided she was in love with Rye, so it's payback time. Rye gets to suffer, and my dad gets to watch and enjoy it."

"Oh."

And then Zach kissed her again. Longer, this time. She pressed her entire body against his and moaned, clinging to him.

"Couldn't we go upstairs?" she asked, just to make him even more frustrated than he already was.

"No, we could not."

"You never sneaked girls into this house? Into your room?"

"Hey, a guy doesn't kiss and tell. It's bad manners."

"So you did," she teased.

He groaned and gave up on kissing her, but still held her close. "What were we talking about?"

"Sneaking upstairs."

"No, before that."

"Peter and Dana."

"Before that . . . The house," he remembered.

"I don't want to talk about the house. I'm happy now, and I'd like to hang on to the feeling as long as I can."

"No, it's good. Or . . . it's not great, but it'll work short-term and maybe make things a little easier for you. I talked to someone at the bank, and . . . Well, it's not good. I thought you'd have some time, because a foreclosure isn't something that can happen overnight. But the process got underway months ago."

"What exactly is the good part in this?" she asked.

"I'm guessing your parents don't have any money anywhere. Otherwise, they wouldn't be borrowing it illegally from the bank. So they're probably going to lose the house anyway."

"Great." Where were she and Peter going to live?

"But banks really don't like to foreclose. It's a hassle, and they usually lose money on the deal, and it makes them look like the bad guys. If you could sell the house, you could get out from under the loan and walk away. Not a bad thing."

"I thought you didn't want me going anywhere," she said, getting a little scared.

"I'm not letting you go anywhere," he insisted. "I'm fixing it so you can stay. I told Sam what was going on. . . . Not that it was a big secret. Foreclosure proceedings are a public process. And he and Rye want your house. We'll pull the bank into the deal, try to stop the foreclosure proceedings, try to make sure the amount your parents owe is covered. You're done. Out of it."

"And out of the house," Julie said.

"No. That's the best part. It'll take months to fix up the place the way Sam wants to. He said you and Peter are welcome to stay while they're doing the work. It won't be the most pleasant place, but it's a big house. They can start on one end, and you can stay on the other. You can make it work, buy yourself some time, see what's going to happen with your parents. It's a good plan, Julie."

"Still fixing all my problems for me?" she asked.

"You said I could, remember? You said we could go back to not sleeping together and me making you crazy and fixing all your problems."

"I can't ask you to do that, Zach."

"You didn't ask," he reminded her.

No, she didn't. Their deal . . . He was too good at figuring out what she wanted, what she needed. "It's too much."

"No, it's not."

"We're talking about your father buying a house. That's a bit much."

"He's happy about it. He's been dying to get his hands on the place for years." He frowned. "Julie, the place is a dump."

Okay, she knew that. Property values all over the neighborhood would likely go up once someone did something about her parents' house.

"It's probably mortgaged to the hilt. I wouldn't be surprised if the mortgage was more than the house is worth," she said, and by the look on his face, she knew. "It is, isn't it?"

"No. There's probably no equity, but . . ."

"You are not going to have your father bail me and my parents out financially. Or you . . . Are you a part of this deal? Because I won't take your money, Zach." It was humiliating to think of doing so.

"You're not taking anything from anybody. This is what my father does—he fixes up old houses, and he makes a good living doing it. He wants to come look inside and look around, just to be sure of what he's getting into, but he swears he'll make money on this deal. Ask him, if you don't believe me."

"I will." It would be absolutely humiliating, but she'd ask. "It's too much."

"It makes perfect sense," he argued.

"Have you ever noticed that any idea you come up with supposedly makes perfect sense?"

"That's because I'm the most reasonable and logical man in the universe," he claimed, grinning again.

"You embellish that idea more every time you mention it to me."

"Everyone I've ever known has thought that about me," he claimed.

"Including the judge who kicked you out of the state of Tennessee?"

"Okay, maybe not him. Give this a chance, Julie. It's a good idea. And . . . Well, I might be convinced to reward you for how reasonable you were being in agreeing to this deal."

"Reward me? How?"

"I don't know." He eased his lower body against hers. He still wanted her. Badly. "I'm sure I could think of something."

She laughed out loud. "You're saying I can have you back in bed if I agree to this house plan of yours?"

He flashed his dimples at her. "Well . . . there must be something I've got that you want."

"You're going to bribe me with sex now?" she said incredulously. "I thought you weren't that kind of guy."

He shook his head, looking serious and a little scared for a moment. "I didn't like the look in your eyes when I told you I loved you this afternoon. Don't run away from me, Julie." *Damn.*

"I'm not," she claimed.

"I mean, if I have to put out to keep you . . ."

She laughed even harder, and when she stopped, he looked all serious again and said, "So you're not going to run?"

"I'd like to. You know I would. But I won't. Promise."

Chapter 16

The evening went well. Dana didn't let Peter out of her sight, and Peter behaved like an angel in front of her. Never grumbled once and ate like he hadn't been fed in a week. Zach managed to make Julie laugh a little, and he sneaked off into the corner with her a second time and kissed her until he couldn't stand it anymore.

This celibacy idea was nuts, but he was afraid he was too far into it to back down now. Besides, he was right. She would make this about nothing but sex if he let her, and he wasn't going to allow that. And he still hadn't told her the hardest things. Until he did . . .

"Hi, Zach." Grace was at the front door putting on her jacket. "You didn't even know I was here, did you?"

"Just thinking about something," he said. "Where are you going?"

"Home. I went down into the basement to work for just a few minutes and got caught up in something, lost track of time."

He frowned. She was doing the whole starving-artist thing rather well, and she lived in a dump, in a neighborhood that wasn't the greatest. He didn't remember seeing her car here earlier. "You were going to walk?"

She nodded. "It's a nice night. And I spend too much time sitting on a stool working. I can use the exercise."

"It's two miles. How about I drive you?"

"How about you walk with me?" she suggested.

"Okay." He grabbed a jacket himself, knowing he was being manipulated big time. He hadn't confessed his little problem yet to her, although he was sure she had the gist of it by now. Still, she'd want to hear it from him. Might as well do it while walking her home. He found it hard to be still while he discussed it.

They set off into the darkness and the quiet of the pleasant, cool night. She didn't say anything at first, giving him some time, which he appreciated.

"I'm going to see a friend of Emma's," he said finally.

"A friend?"

"Colleague," he clarified.

"Oh. Well . . . good. I mean, I guess it's good. If it helps."

"Emma thinks it will. She thinks this is something that can be dealt with."

"Well, sure. I mean, I was just worried. We all were." She went quiet for a minute. "What did he say to you? When you made me and Emma leave you alone with him—what did he say?"

"It wasn't anything he said, Grace."

"Then . . . what?"

"It was me. The things I said. The things I felt." The things he'd done. "I'm just . . . having a little trouble dealing with it."

"But that's it, right? Just him? Because for a while I thought you might be sick with something dreadful you wouldn't tell us about or . . . I don't know."

"I'm not sick," he said. He'd had all sorts of tests to

make sure. "And I'm sorry I worried you all. I just . . . I thought I could handle it on my own."

"I never thought you couldn't. It's just that you help all of us all the time. I wanted to be able to help you for a change. And I was worried."

"Well, try not to worry so much," he told her.

"I won't. Not now that you're here. And I'm really glad about you and Julie."

"Me, too."

"She won't make it easy. I know her well enough to know that."

"She hasn't."

"But you don't care, right? You won't give up on her?"

"No, I won't give up."

"Good."

They walked in silence after that. Grace was smiling as they arrived at her apartment, a cavernous, second-floor space above what had once been a warehouse.

"Don't frown at my apartment," she said.

"It's a dump," Zach grumbled, wishing he could just give her some money and that she'd take it, so she didn't have to live this way. Some problems were so easy to fix. Why didn't she just let him fix this?

"No, it's not a dump. It's cheap, and big, and mine." She fit her key into the lock and turned around. "Want to come up?"

"So you can grill me some more?"

She nodded.

"That's all right. I think I can do without it tonight." He kissed her on the cheek and gave her a hug. "Please tell me you don't walk home alone at this hour on a regular basis?"

"No, Mom makes me take her car when I stay too late.

I was just waiting to ambush you tonight." She grinned. "Which I did."

"Night, Grace," he said.

"Night."

He waited, watching from the street until the light came on in the front window on the second floor, then headed home. Walking wasn't a bad idea at all. He'd gone three blocks when he heard someone behind him, not really worried. It wasn't the greatest neighborhood, but this was a fairly quiet, peaceful town.

But when he turned around, there was a man in the shadows about twenty feet back. Something in the set of his shoulder or the shape of his body, maybe the way he walked, had Zach on edge. Did he know this guy?

Zach studied the man. He looked older than Zach first thought, and surprised. The man stopped walking and stayed where he was in the shadows, on alert, too, now. *What the hell?*

Zach's heart started pounding, adrenaline and anger spurring it on. He took a step toward the man, then another. The man behind him backed up, too, landing in a shallow pool of light, his face illuminated for just a moment.

Zach took off after him. The man stumbled backward, and Zach was on him in an instant, grabbing him by the collar of his coat and shoving him up hard against the wall, cracking the man's head against the brick.

"You bastard," he said, one hand on the guy's throat, cutting off his air. "What the hell do you think you're—"

And then he broke off abruptly, not sure anymore what he was seeing. The guy was gasping and trying to shout something.

Zach let go and backed away. "George? George Greene?"

"What?" The guy shoved Zach backward.

It wasn't him. They were about the same height and weight, same kind of hair, but it wasn't George.

"Shit," Zach muttered.

"What the hell is this?" the guy growled, obviously not so frightened now and very upset.

"Sorry." Zach backed up and held up his hands, to show he was done. "I thought you were somebody else."

The guy started cussing a blue streak, and Zach just stood there and took it, feeling stupid and crazy and just wanting to get the hell out of there.

"I'm sorry," he said. "I didn't . . ."

The guy nearly spit on him, cussing still as he turned and walked away.

Zach couldn't seem to move at first. He was still breathing hard, adrenaline still surging through him. He kept thinking that one day he was going to turn around and there would be George, come back to haunt him. The feelings just kept getting worse, chasing him, like the memory of the time he'd spent living with that man.

He stood on the street, shaking and swearing and sweating in the cold night air. He had an appointment with the shrink tomorrow, and he wasn't sure that would be soon enough. The night seemed endless, and he felt like he was the only person in the world who'd ever felt this bad, this out of control. If no one could help him, what would he do? Where would he end up? A mean drunk like George? That was his greatest fear. That he was going down that road, and no one could stop him.

He walked for a long time that night, nervous energy pushing him on. He thought at some point it would ease and he'd be able to sleep, and he wouldn't do anything else. *Like take a drink.*

He wanted a drink, and he wanted Julie. Before, she'd

made it all go away. Maybe she could get him through this one more awful night, and then he could go spill his guts to the shrink. After all, there were only so many times a man could count his breaths in and out. He was afraid if he got drunk he might never stop. That the feelings might never stop. He'd keep trying to drown them, and then where would he end up?

Just like Daddy. Assaulting people on the street, maybe? Did his jerk of a father do that? Or did he just hit women? How bad could it get? How low could he go? Maybe this was the night he found out.

Zach looked up and found himself at Julie's, as if maybe somebody was looking out for him and had steered him to the place he needed to be. All he had to do was go inside and open the door to the cellar of his soul. *Shit.*

He saw no lights upstairs, but there seemed to be one downstairs. Maybe the kitchen? He went around to the back door and tapped softly. Julie came walking into the kitchen and snapped the back porch light on, then opened the door.

"Hi. What are you doing here?"

He shrugged, thinking, *deny, delay, anything.* How long could he last? "I walked Grace home, and then I . . . I need to talk to you. Is Peter still up?"

"I don't think so. The music stopped fifteen minutes ago. I threatened to turn off the electricity again if he didn't go to bed, and I think he finally did." She paused, watching him. "Come on in, Zach."

He looked out onto the porch, seeing the old-fashioned glider sitting in what was mostly dark. He liked the dark. Maybe this would be easier in the dark. "Why don't you come out?"

"Sure." She came outside and took a seat.

He frowned at the idea of sitting. She was looking at him like she was already worried. Maybe if he had her close, it would be okay. Zach sat down, put his arm around her shoulders, drew her to his side. She snuggled against him, her head against his side, arms wrapped around his waist. Yeah, that was better.

He closed his eyes for a moment, thinking maybe some of the peace of her might soak into him. She'd been in the shower. Her hair was still damp. She was wearing her pajamas and probably nothing else, and she smelled good, like soap and woman and something else he couldn't quite identify. They could sit just like this for a while, couldn't they?

He put his other arm around her and turned her in his arms until she was sprawled across the cushions of the glider and facing him, practically lying in his arms, and he realized he didn't have to say a thing if he was kissing her. He could forget everything then, and he really didn't want to talk.

He groaned, and his head bent down to hers, taking her mouth like the lifeline it was. He remembered from that one night in his hotel room, thinking there was life inside of her when at the moment there had seemed to be none inside of him, and that she'd been the one person who could keep him going for one more night.

Maybe that's how it was tonight. He kissed her and kissed her and kissed her, got his hand under her top and found nothing but soft, creamy, warm skin, and maybe if he could get inside of her again the bad feelings would just go away and there would be peace in her arms.

She came willingly into his arms at first, but when his hand went to the buttons on her top, she put a hand on his to stop him. "Zach, we're on the back porch."

"I know, but . . ."

"Come on. Let's go inside."

And in the time it took to grab a breath, he saw his hand on the buttons of her top, her hand on his, that soft, sexy anything-you-need look in her eyes. *Go inside,* he thought. *Get inside her. Don't tell her a thing. Hold it all in.* He couldn't anymore, had promised himself he wouldn't use her this way. She needed to know what she was getting into with him, what a mess he truly was.

Julie leaned down to kiss him again.

"No." He pushed her back and abruptly slid off the seat. She'd been leaning against him, and he saw her put out a hand to catch herself so she didn't fall. *Damn.*

He stood not five feet away, breathing heavily and trying not to panic, the feelings rushing back over him, as they had on the street when he'd slammed that man against the brick wall and thought about strangling him.

Julie didn't say anything, and for that he was grateful, because he was having trouble getting enough oxygen right now and that made conversation difficult. He didn't think she'd moved at all. *Shit.*

"I'm sorry," he managed to force out.

Still, she said nothing. He had his back to her and couldn't tell what was going on, was honestly afraid of what he'd see in her eyes. She might well think he was crazy.

He started trying to fight off the emotions through sheer force of will. For so long, he would have sworn he was stronger than anything, could overcome anything, but this stuff inside of him—inside his own body— made him feel puny. It made him feel weak. And scared. Like a little kid, dammit.

Zach groaned and sank down to the floor of the porch, bracing himself on the column to his right to keep from falling completely.

Julie was beside him in a second, sitting there on the floor with him, one arm around him, her face down close to his. "What is it?" she asked. "Did you hurt yourself tonight playing ball?"

"No."

"Are you sure? I saw you go down so hard that one time. You and your family play like idiots. It looked like you were trying to kill each other."

"It was just guy stuff, Julie. I was giving 'em hell earlier about getting old, and it was payback time." He was huffing and puffing as he said it, just as he'd been on the basketball court that evening.

"Then what's wrong?" she asked. "I'd do anything for you, Zach, but I don't know what to do right now."

"Sit here with me," he said, his breathing getting more and more shallow, more labored. He remembered that night in his hotel room. Once he'd gotten his hands on her, hers on him. *Don't let go. I won't,* she'd promised. And she hadn't.

"Don't . . ." he began, then stopped, gasping now. It was too much like before, like that night, and he wasn't going to do that to her twice, wasn't going to treat her like that. "Hang on to me, Julie."

"Do you need a doctor? Is it—"

"No. It's not like that." But he might need Emma. Was it that bad? Could he breathe? Could Emma help him if he couldn't? Could she get him to calm down? Could Julie?

"Zach, you're scaring me," she said.

"Scarin' myself. I have been for a while."

"Let me call a doctor."

"It's not . . . physical, Julie."

"What?" She clearly had no idea what he was talking about.

"I saw a doctor when this all started, had a complete physical. The problem's not there. It's in my head."

"You hurt your head?" She put her hand on his head, checking for a bump or a cut. "What does your head have to do with you being unable to breathe?"

"No. Inside," he said. "It's what's going on inside my head."

"What's going on inside your head?"

"It's my father," he said, his throat threatening to close down completely rather than let the word slip past. "All this stuff with that fucking bastard who claims to be my father . . ."

"What about him?" she asked.

"I can't get him out of my head. . . . The way he looks. The way he sounds. The way he walks. All the shit he's done."

"Zach, you can't breathe," she said.

He shook his head. "I know, but that's not the problem. It's that I hate him. Do you understand? I hate him."

"Okay," she said, still holding him. "You hate him. But Zach, you have to be able to breathe."

"And I can't get away from him, because I came from him. Part of who I am is him, and he's shit, Julie. He's a coward and a drunk, and he beats up women for fun, and he's my father."

"In some ways, he's your father," she said, her grip tight on his shoulder. "Some little, insignificant ways."

"And I hate that. . . ." He huffed and puffed and got it out. "I hate it so much. That there's anything of him in me. I want to get every little bit of him out of me. I want to rip it out, except I can't find the pieces. I don't know where he stops and I begin. I don't know what would be left of me once I got every bit of him out of me. And that's crazy. I know it's crazy. All of it . . . Shit."

He leaned weakly against the column of the porch, his shoulders heaving. He could hear his heart racing, like someone was beating a drum inside of him, and his whole body pounded with each thrum. He wanted to run as far as he could go, so he'd never have to say this. Couldn't he outrun it? Wasn't there some way he could keep from taking it with him?

Except running was what Julie did, and he'd given her hell about it. He should tell her that he understood now, that he'd been wrong all along. Staying and facing stuff was hell.

Zach made himself face her for the briefest of moments. She was pale. Or that might just be the light, what little there was of the moon. And it was cold out here. He was just realizing that. She was probably cold.

He was hot, like there was a fever burning him from the inside out. But he'd gotten this much out, this many words. *Poison.* He was supposed to feel better, wasn't he? He sure as hell didn't. And he was afraid Julie was going to get up and run, lock her doors against him, call the police or a doctor. Call someone.

"I think I'm going crazy," he said, the words spilling from him before he could stop them.

"Because of this? Because of the way you feel about your father?"

He nodded. "And because of what's going on with my body."

"It's happened before? You've felt like you couldn't breathe before?"

"Yes."

"And you saw a doctor?"

"Yes."

"And he said there was nothing physically wrong?"

"Yeah."

She was quiet for a long moment. "Have you talked to anyone else about it?"

"Emma," he said. "It comes in handy sometimes, having a shrink for a sister."

"And what did she say?"

"She doesn't think I'm crazy," he said, because he really didn't want to scare her any more than he already had. "She doesn't think I'm so far gone that . . . She says it's something they can deal with. Her friends. A shrink. She wasn't even shocked that I needed one, but then, I didn't show her as much as I did you. Now. I've been trying hard not to show anybody. But I just can't keep it inside any longer."

"Then don't," she said. "Tell me. I'm right here. Just tell me."

Zach closed his eyes and said, "I wanted to kill him."

He let the words just sit there. They echoed inside his head. Or maybe this was him cracking up. He'd always wondered exactly what would happen when he did. Would he be able to pull himself back? Did people go to the other side and make it back to this one?

"Okay, so you wanted to kill him."

Julie didn't sound that shocked. He wondered, again, if he'd made everything clear. Because it sounded scary as hell to him.

"I really wanted to kill him," he said. "I haven't told anyone that, but I thought if I'd had enough to drink, maybe I could have done it. With my bare hands. That's how I wanted to do it. Nice and slow. As painfully as possible. I wanted him to have to look in my eyes and know I was going to kill him. That he'd never again be able to hurt anyone or scare anyone I love."

"But you didn't," Julie pointed out.

"I threatened to. I made Emma and Grace leave the

room, and I put my hands around his neck and squeezed. I probably left bruises on him. If he'd tried to tell anyone, I would have been disbarred. Hell, I could go to jail, right where he's been all this time. Of course, I didn't think that was much of a risk — somebody taking the word of a murdering drunk over mine. But a part of me wished he'd given me a reason, so I could have killed him, and we'd never have to worry about him again."

Zach closed his eyes to the horror of it. The feel of that man's throat between his hands, the satisfaction that came from hurting him, scaring him, and all the time he'd spent wondering how close he'd come to actually doing it.

"I finally let go, and he collapsed in a heap on the floor, gasping and coughing, and I wasn't even sorry," he confessed, finally coming to the bottom line. "Do you know what that makes me, Julie?"

He laughed in a way that scared himself even more. "It makes me just like him," Zach said. That was the worst of it. Finding out he could be just like dear old Dad.

"No, it doesn't," Julie said.

"I had my hands around his neck, squeezing, Julie. I asked him how it felt to be at the mercy of someone else. To know I could do anything I wanted to with him. He could call here tomorrow and say something to Grace or to Emma, and who knows what I might do."

"Once you calmed down, you'd call his parole officer and have him thrown back in jail, Zach."

"You don't know that," he yelled. "You don't know how I felt that day. He just had to see us. He wouldn't fucking go away. He wouldn't shut up. I wanted to slap a restraining order on the bastard, but shit, everybody knows how well those damned things work. My sisters didn't want to see him, but they didn't want it hanging over their heads, either. As if that bastard deserved to have any say about anything the three of us did.

"But they wanted to see him and be done with it. So I went with them. Grace was almost sick in the car. I had to pull over on the side of the road so she could throw up, and Emma was so pale it was like she didn't have any blood left in her body. And I hated that he could do that to them. I didn't think it was possible to hate someone that much, but I did. I saw him, and . . ."

"What, Zach? What happened?"

"I look like him," he confessed. "I looked into his face, and I could see me thirty years from now. He had a picture of me and him, claimed he'd had it all these years he spent behind bars, and once he got his act together and straightened up, he looked at this fucking picture and missed me so fucking much and was so fucking sorry. . . . He's just full of it. He's full of shit, and he's a drunk and a murderer, and he looks just like me. I've got his blood running through my veins. His genes. Maybe how much he loves to drink.What about that?"

"What about it?" she asked softly.

"It's the damnedest thing. All this stuff that's going on . . . How crazy I feel? How out of control? Having a drink helps. Talk about scaring the shit out of me."

"You've been drinking?" she asked.

"A little, now and then. When it gets bad and I can't calm down. When I can't breathe, and I can't be still, and it seems to get worse and worse, and I just don't know what else to do."

"You know it's not the answer, Zach."

"Logically, yeah. I know it. But I get like this, and the choice is either feeling like this some more or having a drink, and that's when drinking doesn't look so bad. I did that night with you. You saw how crazy I was. But drinking let me forget for a little while that he's a monster, and he's inside of me, and I can't get him out."

Zach closed his eyes, and the words seemed to echo through the stillness and the dark. For the longest time, neither one of them moved. There was no sound anywhere. Nothing. Just the blackness of the night.

Slowly, other things started to creep in. He could hear himself breathing heavily still, could feel the chill of the cold air on his hot skin, and he knew where he was—sitting on Julie's back porch.

His lungs were still working. His heart hadn't exploded inside of him. That bastard's blood was still running through his veins. He'd told Julie the worst of it, and she hadn't run away. He'd asked her not to let go of him, and she hadn't.

Thank God.

Still, he'd probably terrified her. "It's crazy," he said, his voice raw with despair. "There's a part of me that can step back from it and see how illogical it is— me falling apart because this man I hardly remember at all is out of jail and just had to see us. I mean, I've known my whole life exactly what I came from, and I didn't give a shit. It didn't have anything to do with who I was. Logically, I know that. But I can't stop feeling this way."

"Okay." She squeezed him more tightly for a second and then let go.

He thought that was it, that she was done. He couldn't blame her, any more than he could stop himself from trying to grab her and make her stay. *God, Julie. Don't. Don't leave me now.*

"It's all right," she said. She eased down off the porch, never taking her hand off his right knee. Slipping around in front of him, she stood on the ground by the edge of the porch, which put her face level with his. She slid her arms around him and pressed in close between his thighs, holding him. His head fell to her shoulder, and his arms locked around her. If he could just never, ever let her go . . .

"That's it? That's what's been going on this whole time?" she asked.

"Isn't that enough?"

"I just wanted to make sure there was nothing else you wanted to tell me."

"Well, I kind of attacked this guy on the street tonight. I was walking Grace home, and I heard somebody following me and thought it was George. Grabbed him and shoved him up against the wall. I'm damned lucky I didn't really hurt him, and that he just cussed me out and walked away. Of course, he could be calling the police right now. They could be looking for me."

"Zach—"

"I just saw the guy and freaked out, thinking he was George, and then I couldn't hold all this in any longer. I had to get it out. Everybody said it would be better if I could just get it out."

"Okay. I'll help you. I will."

And then she just held him some more. He groaned it felt so good, and then he started shaking. It really had gotten cold out here. He was worried about her now and thought he should be trying to warm her, but he wasn't sure he could move.

So he stayed there with his head on her shoulder. He could breathe again, the air going into his lungs effortlessly. His heart was slowing down. He no longer feared he'd go running off into the night, trying to escape the thoughts running through his own head.

"I tried to tell you," he said finally. "So many times, I tried. I just couldn't do it. I couldn't tell anybody. I . . . I don't think I've ever really been scared in my life. Except when I was still living with that man, I guess."

"Everybody gets scared, Zach."

"Like this? This out of control? This crazy?"

"I don't know. You said Emma didn't think you were nuts. Do you think she'd lie to you?"

"No. I just . . . I didn't . . . She didn't see me like this. I didn't let her. I didn't want anybody to ever see this. Especially not you."

"Well, it only seems fair that it would be me, doesn't it? You've seen me at my absolute worst. My most reckless. My angriest. My saddest times—"

"I hate it," he said. "I hate having you see me like this."

"Well, I sure wasn't happy about having you witness all my finer moments, but there you were. One thing about you, I knew you'd try to understand and help me, and that's a lot, Zach. It's a whole lot. You can't think I wouldn't do the same thing for you. Do you?"

"I don't know. I don't let people take care of me."

"Well, you're going to have to start," she said. "How did you think this relationship was going to work? That I'd be screwed up forever, and you'd just keep fixing things for me?"

"I know how to do that," he said. "But this . . . I don't know how to do this."

"Well, you'll just have to figure it out, Zach. And I think the first thing I want to do with you is get you inside and warm you up. It's cold out here."

That was it? She was worried about the cold? "Okay," he said.

She eased away from him, never completely letting go, and he loved her for never letting go. She did a little circular move around the porch beam and up the steps, one hand staying on his knee until the other landed on his shoulder. It didn't even seem ridiculously awkward when she did it. It seemed exceedingly kind and comforting to him, half crazy as he was.

"Come on," she said.

He got to his feet, moving like a man in a stupor or like one who'd been beaten to within an inch of his life. He felt like he had. They went inside, through the kitchen, down the hall, pausing at the foot of the stairs.

"I think you should come upstairs with me," she said.

He hesitated. He could think, kind of, and he didn't like what she was doing. "We did this once before, Julie. It wasn't fair to you then, and it wouldn't be fair now."

"Oh, hell, when has life ever been fair to me?"

"It should be," he said. "Better than fair."

"And it's not exactly a hardship, having you in my bed, Zach, you know?"

"Yeah?" He managed to make his voice almost sound normal, like he hadn't thought he might die a few minutes ago. "Trying to make me think you'd do anything to have me?"

She frowned. "I'm worried about you, and I don't think you should be alone tonight."

"Afraid of what I might do, if I were?" he asked.

"No—"

"Liar. I thought we weren't going to do that anymore, Julie."

"I don't see any reason why you should be alone, not when I'm right here, and I'm worried about you, dammit. You scared me. I've never seen anybody who just couldn't breathe like that and claimed the problem was all in his head, and I get to worry about you and take care of you. That's the deal. You set down all the rules, and you can't back out of them now."

Which brought them squarely back into the territory of the serious stuff. He had to say this. He owed her. "You can back out. I give you permission to completely and totally ignore any rules we agreed to."

That seemed to make her angrier than anything he'd ever said to her. She got a furious look on her face. "Well, I'm not giving you that permission. I'm worried about you, and you owe it to me to stay with me tonight. Otherwise, I'll worry even more."

"So . . . it's like I'd be doing you a favor by staying here?"

"Yes, dammit. You said we'd take care of each other. You promised. You're not going to back out on me the first time it gets hard for you to let me help you."

He turned away and swore softly. "I really don't want your pity, okay?"

"Did you pity me?" she asked. "All those times I was out screwing things up again and again, and there you were, always so ready to drag me out of one mess or another and make me see how stupid I'd been or how reckless or how foolish—was that pity?"

"No, dammit. That was me wishing you'd finally get your shit together and straighten up. That you'd get past all that crap your parents dealt you and realize there were things about you that were special. That you could do anything you wanted. That you deserved so much better than the life you were living back then."

"So, when you're helping me, it's all of those things coming into play, and when I try to help you, it's pity? Explain that to me, Zach. Because I just don't see the difference."

"It's . . . I . . . Shit."

"What? That was you, and this is me? And you're the

strong one, the one who always has to be right, and I'm the screwed-up one—"

"That's not what I'm saying."

"You're the man? Is that it? And I'm the woman? And the big, strong man always has to take care of the woman?"

"No," he growled. "Okay . . . maybe that's a little bit of it. I . . . It's not exactly the kind of thing women want to hear these days or that men are supposed to think, but Sam—"

"Don't blame this on your father."

"A man takes care of the women in his life. It's just what he does."

"And you don't think Rachel takes care of Sam in return?"

"I don't know—"

"Oh, hell. Of course you do."

"He's always seemed so strong to me, like he could handle anything. Like he'd stand between us and the whole world and the world would lose."

"He is strong. That doesn't mean he doesn't need someone else sometimes. The way I need you, and you need me."

"I do need you," he confessed.

"Then come upstairs. It's late. Peter's asleep. I'm right here, and you feel like shit. There's no reason on earth for you to be alone tonight. Except some idiotic kind of pride."

"So I'm an idiot and entirely politically incorrect when it comes to some of my views on men and women, and at least half crazy. But you still want me?"

"Yes."

She tugged on his hand and turned toward the stairs. He stood there, eyes closed, telling himself not to go.

He'd been so sure before he came over here that there was something wrong in taking her to bed with him now.

"This is getting old, Zach," she said.

He frowned. "I was going to try to tell you sex never really solved anything, but I think you may have saved my life the first time. Honest to God, Julie, I don't know what I would have done that night."

"And you're having another bad night, Zach. And you're right where you're supposed to be. With me."

"I meant what I said earlier. I love you."

"Only when things are good for you and bad for me?" she asked. "God knows I'm no expert on love, but I'm pretty sure it's supposed to be an all-or-nothing thing. You can't just love me when it's convenient for you. When you're feeling strong and sure of yourself and can take care of me."

She stared down at him from the first step, confounding his every argument with what he was afraid was sound logic, leaving him with a big case of badly wounded pride, fatigue that was bone deep, and desire that just wouldn't let up.

He must be crazy not to let her just take him off to bed.

"You know the biggest doubts I have about you and me?" she asked. "About this ever working?"

"I'm not sure I want to know." Not tonight. Tonight was bad enough already.

"I wonder what in the world I have to give you, Zach. You're so generous with me, so supportive. And you're almost always right, which is the most annoying thing, especially since I keep screwing up my life, and you always seemed so together—"

"Not now," he said.

"I know, and I would never wish anything like this on you. But you're not that perfect boy I fell in love with years ago. You're a grown man, and you've actually made some mistakes lately. You have doubts and fears and regrets."

"And you find this attractive?"

"I find it human. I find it not so intimidating. I see myself as not so lacking, not such a screwup. And I see that maybe you do need me."

"I do," he said.

"Maybe you do." She smiled beautifully, kindness radiating from her. "Because nobody knows crazy like I do. And the world-falling-apart stuff? God. I've been there so many times, I practically wrote the book on that."

"So that does it. We were meant for each other?"

"Only if you let me help you, too. You have to get this part, Zach. It's got to work both ways."

He took her other hand, ran his thumb over the back of it, and tried to consider what they both needed. He felt like complete and total shit, and here she was, this strong, incredibly generous woman ready to hang on to him, even when he was being foolish and filled with pride.

He loved her more than he'd thought it was possible to love anyone.

"Take me upstairs, Julie. Please."

Chapter 17

She led him to the door at the end of the hall and tugged him inside. "Peter's at the other end," she said.

He pushed the door shut behind him and locked it, just in case. To the right was an old-fashioned bed made of iron, piled high with covers now in disarray.

So this was where she slept. The idea warmed him through and through. Not like his little spells with insanity did, leaving him thinking maybe his blood would start to boil in his veins. This was smooth and gentle heat, the easiest thing in the world. Like lying in the grass on an early-summer day, a little breeze blowing, the sky a hazy blue, when all was absolutely right with the world.

As if anything could be right now . . .

She made him feel like it was. The idea that she was here, just a few houses down the street from him. She climbed into this little iron bed every night and went boneless with sleep, and if he was here, he could sleep with her body draped over his, limbs entangled, her hair spread out over him. He wanted to sleep like that, with her, in this bed.

"What are you thinking now?" she asked, slipping her hand into his.

"About you and me in this bed."

She smiled sweetly as she clicked off the overhead light and sent the room into a maze of shadows, undressing him slowly, her hands slipping the buttons of his shirt free and pulling it off of him. He put himself into her soft, willing hands, the ones that skimmed lightly across his chest, as if she were learning his body by touch alone. She rubbed at the tops of his shoulders, his arms, hands running down the line of hair that extended from his chest to below the waistband of his jeans.

She found the snap, grinning as she worked the zipper down very, very slowly, his body stirring at her touch. "I thought you'd be exhausted after the day you've had."

"Exhausted, maybe, but I'm not dead yet, Julie."

She laughed, hooked her thumbs into the waistband of his pants and his briefs, and pulled them down in one move. Pushed him down on the bed, took off his socks and shoes, pulled his pants and briefs the rest of the way off and tossed them over a chair in the corner.

He'd been a model of complacency to this point, but he wanted her naked, too. He pulled her to a stand between his knees. "My turn?"

She nodded. He moved just as slowly, starting at the bottom button on her pajama top and working his way up, leaving the top two buttons fastened, enjoying the softness of her skin as he went. He pulled the ends open into a triangle, and then held her with his hands at her side and slowly kissed all the skin he'd uncovered, teasing her with his tongue, taking little bites of her bottom ribs.

She made a little squeaking, gasping sound and tried

to squirm away from him. He wrapped his hands around her hips to hold her still and then anchored her to him with one arm, continued unbuttoning buttons with the other, finding more soft skin, the tender undersides of her breasts. He nudged them with his nose, followed the line of the bottom of them, opened his mouth and placed warm, wet kisses from the inside curve to the outside, pushing at the material with his nose, working his way back toward the center again, toward her nipples.

Her hands caught in his hair as his mouth settled over one, then the other.

"Are you going to regret this in the morning?" she asked. "Because of that stupid no-sex thing of yours?"

"I regretted that five seconds after it came out of my mouth," he admitted, and she laughed again, then sucked in a breath as he used his teeth on her nipple, taking little bitty bites, his breath fanning over them.

He wished he could see her more clearly. Next time, he promised himself. Broad daylight. Maybe outside in the sunlight that felt so much like her.

He felt much, much better. Almost normal. The panic was receding, pleasure moving in. His hands went to the last button on her top, fumbling around with it until it gave and then tugging it off of her and throwing it onto the floor. He put his hands on her breasts, now that they were completely free. He held them in his palms, wanting to know the weight and the shape of them, and buried his nose between them and slowly kissed his way back down.

Her belly quivered as his mouth moved over it, and her hips moved restlessly against his. It was the most amazing thing. He'd felt half dead not ten minutes ago, and now he felt deliciously, gloriously alive. If this was a way of running from his problems, he simply didn't care.

He tugged one side of her pajama bottoms down, uncovering her hipbone and nibbling on that, palming her hips, pulling her to him. She had her hands on his shoulders now, holding on tight, like the weight of her own body might be too much for her legs to manage. No problem. He'd gladly hold her up.

He tugged the other side of her pajamas down, revealing more skin. He kissed that and moved lower, kissing her through her clothes, going for the heat at the center of her, teasing her.

Her hand grabbed on to a fistful of his hair, tugging him to her. He kneaded the flesh of her bottom, and she started swaying to him and back, ever so slightly, need taking over.

She wouldn't be able to hold back at all soon, and he wanted her that way. Mindless. His. His hands slipped beneath the fabric of her pajamas and onto the bare skin of her hips.

"If you don't take those off . . ." she began.

"What?" he asked. "What are you going to do to me?"

"There are other things you could be doing with that wicked mouth of yours besides talking, Zachariah."

He laughed and finally tugged down her pajamas. If the lady thought it was time to stop fooling around, he was willing to accommodate her. He pushed her backward one step, went down on his knees in front of her, held her with a hand on either side of her hips, and there was no teasing now. He spread his hands wide, using his thumbs to open her to his mouth, and pushed deep into her with his tongue, thrusting back and forth, another part of his body wanting to do that very badly. And he would. Soon.

She shuddered and collapsed on top of him, her body folding over his head and onto the bed behind him. He heard her give another little squeak, a sound she muffled quickly. Another time, another place, he'd have her screaming for real. He wouldn't let up until he did. But he didn't have it in him to do that now, and they weren't alone, and he had to be inside of her.

He rolled her off of him and onto the bed and then followed her down. He was kissing her before she landed flat on her back on the mattress, and he landed on top of her, forgetting to go slow. He feared it was going to be like that first night all over again, the frenzy, the need. Right now she felt like life given back to him, like sanity. Her arms came around him, holding him close, and her body opened up to his, and he hadn't so much as settled on top of her before he was inside of her.

She groaned and moved instantly to take him deeper, her hips rolling against his and her fingernails digging into his hips. Her knees came up around him, and he got his hands beneath her hips, palming them, pulling her to him even tighter.

The heat of her, the way she clasped him to her and moved against him left little doubt that this would last more than a few minutes, and he wanted more. Going against every need in his body, he wrenched himself back and out of that welcoming heat, holding himself up on his elbows and his knees, groaning as he lowered his head and kissed her.

"What?" she demanded. "What's wrong?"

"Nothing. You're just killing me. That's all. And I really would like this if I could make it last a little while."

He took a breath and let himself move back inside of her, shuddering as he did. As her body gripped him in a way that left him groaning once again.

"Give it up, Zach. You're the man who announced yesterday that you weren't going to sleep with me at all."

"Only until you knew this was about love and not sex," he said, rocking slowly back and forth inside of her in cadence with the words. "What did you tell me, Julie? You said you couldn't stop yourself from loving me. And I probably should give you time to reconsider after that little scene on your back porch tonight—"

"Have a little faith, Zach. Isn't that what you said I needed? A little faith? You don't have any in me."

"I do," he said. "I told you everything. Every blessed thing."

And now he needed her to tell him some things. He made himself pull out again and wait there, knowing this had to be insanity.

"Tell me you need me," he said.

"I need you."

He rewarded her by entering her again, only to pull back out.

"Tell me you still love me."

"I do."

Back in, one more time. It was heaven, right there. And then back out again.

"What if . . . What if I wanted to marry you?"

"I . . ."

"Don't get scared now," he said, teasing at her opening, rocking just a bit against her, just the blunt tip of him going in, sliding back out, little by little going deeper and deeper with every thrust, until there was nowhere else to go, nothing else he could do. Just need her.

She lay beneath him, breathing hard, her arms locked around him, and she felt like seven different kinds of heaven. He lay still inside of her, her body throbbing around his, him throbbing inside of her, a fine sheen of perspiration running down his chest, a fine trembling working its way through his entire body.

She hadn't run away, not when he'd told her he loved her, not when he'd explained his little problem in detail. She'd just opened up her arms and loved him.

There were tears in her eyes now. Her bottom lip was trembling. His body was begging. "This is what I want," he said. "You and me. Like this. Forever."

She looked like each and every word hurt her, and she started to say something, but he wouldn't let her. He didn't want to know what she'd say. So he took her mouth with his, and he started to move, harder and faster and so deeply inside of her, until she cried out, sinking her teeth into his shoulder in an effort to hold in the sounds that she made. Her body convulsed around him, and he closed his eyes, and for a minute everything just fell away. Every worry. Every fear. Every need. She took it all away.

For a long blessed moment there was nothing wrong in his whole world. Nothing to give him nightmares. Nothing to regret. Nothing to fear. Nothing, except her and all the beauty she brought to his world.

He came in a long hard rush, shuddering and shuddering and shuddering, his body wrapped around hers, his face buried in her shoulder, her hands trying to soothe him, running through his hair, down his back, her lips brushing a kiss along his cheek.

He felt like he could die on this very spot and be happy about it, as long as he could take her with him. He wanted to hold on to this feeling—this peace he'd found with her, wanted to pretend there were no more doubts in either one of them, no obstacles standing in their way, no problems to work through.

He just wanted her like this, her soft breasts pressed

against his chest, and her glorious legs wrapped around him, her hands holding him to her, her mouth on his in long, soothing kisses that left him weak and wanting more. He kissed her again and again and again, then realized she was breathing heavily, too, and he surely wasn't helping the effort by lying on top of her like this.

"Sorry," he said, putting his weight on his hands and off of her.

She stopped him, grabbing him by the shoulders. "Where do you think you're going?"

"I'm crushing you."

"I like it," she claimed, pushing him off to the left, just a bit, and then pulling him back down to her. "I like how big you are, how solid, how heavy."

He leaned on that left elbow, but otherwise stayed where he was, certainly in no hurry to leave. She touched his face, her fingertips tracing the line of his mouth, his jaw, his chin.

"Better?" she asked.

"Much. I meant what I said."

"About what?"

"Everything."

The words fell into the same kind of silence that came after he'd announced that he feared he was going crazy. He couldn't miss the irony of that or the idiocy of his timing.

"Just what you want to hear, right? The crazy guy wants to marry you."

"That's not what I was thinking," she claimed.

"What were you thinking?"

"That this whole relationship has progressed at a bizarre pace."

"We've known each other forever," he argued. And

then, because he feared what her answer would be if she gave him one in this moment, he said, "Do me a favor. Don't answer me now. Take some time. You deserve it. Think about you and me. Think about everything."

"Zach—"

"No. It's okay. I shouldn't have hit you with this now, not when I just laid all the other stuff on you. And we need to see . . . You know. If this works out for me. If I'm really not crazy."

He'd gotten to where he really didn't like using that word, to where he wasn't quite sure how anyone would respond to it in casual conversation, if they had a clue how he felt lately.

"I don't think you're crazy," she said.

"Half?"

"Maybe. But . . . most people are, wouldn't you say?"

He forgot about laughing, about trying to avoid this. He'd proposed to the woman for God's sake. "I'm sorry I scared you."

"It's all right. I'm sure I've scared you at times."

"Oh yeah."

"Are you okay?" she asked, the pain and the worry in her voice cutting right through him.

"Yeah, I'm okay." He kissed her softly on her mouth, his forehead pressed against hers, and then he kissed her again and again. "Better than that, in fact."

She put her hands on either side of his face, holding it between her palms and then gently drawing away. He stayed there, his nose half an inch from hers, and stared at her.

"I was just going to bring you up here and hang on to you for a while," she said.

"I know." He hadn't wanted her thinking he was so much of a mess he needed to lie in this bed with her and have her do nothing but hold him all night long. He'd wanted to feel normal and needed and whole, and he'd wanted them both to forget everything he'd said to her, at least for a while.

He kissed her one more time and then rolled to the side, pulling her along with him, so that they were facing each other in the narrow confines of the bed. He worried that she'd get cold again, so he fished around on the floor until he found the bedding and pulled it back to the bed, spreading it on top of them.

"Warm enough?"

She nodded, looking worried again. "Zach, did you really think I'd turn around and run away, once you told me what was going on?"

"Oh, hell, Julie, I wanted to turn around and run myself. I guess we're more alike than I thought. I couldn't get the words out. I kept hoping it would go away or that it would get better, that you'd never have to know."

They lay there for a moment, safe in each other's arms, and then he thought of one more thing he had to ask. "You're not scared of me, are you?"

"Why?"

"Because of what I almost did to that man, what I wanted to do."

"That's the difference between you and him, Zach. He killed someone, and all you did was think about it."

"Still, it made me wonder what I'm capable of."

"The drinking thing worries me. I won't tell you it doesn't." She held him tighter, kissed his jaw once, then his chin, all she could reach. "But I grew up in a house full of mean drunks, Zach. I really don't think you are one. Is it . . . Do you really think you are?"

"I know I never felt like I needed a drink before. I didn't really know what people were talking about when they said that. Needing one. Sam is . . . He drinks beer all the time. I never worried about it. I never looked at him and thought, 'What if he has too much? What if he gets mad and starts to hit us?' But when I start to think too much, and it gets hard to be still, hard to breathe . . . I just want anything that helps stop it, and it seems like alcohol does."

"Well, it acts like a sedative. I mean . . ."

"Maybe I need drugs instead?" He laughed. "Makes you think, doesn't it? Why do people drink? To get away from their problems? To numb themselves?"

"I don't know, Zach. But I'm not going to run away. I'm glad you finally told me everything. I want to help. You'll let me do that? Let me help you?"

"Yes."

And then she just held on to him, her face pressed against his chest, her legs tangled up with his.

Just before she drifted off to sleep, he said, "Can I stay?" Because it was a long time until morning, and it seemed it had taken him forever to get back to her, where he belonged. "I'll get out before Peter gets up. Promise," he said.

"Yes," she whispered sleepily. "Stay."

He was gone when she woke up.

Either she heard him downstairs as he left or Peter was up. She glanced at the clock at her bedside, saw that it was just a little after five. It wasn't even light outside yet. She slid out of bed, taking the comforter with her and wrapping it around her, and went to the window that had a view of the street and watched him walk home. He was okay.

All those things he'd told her . . . God, he'd scared her.

And the way he'd worked so hard just to breathe, the tension in his body, the bleakness in his eyes.

She'd felt a little like that before. Panicky and so scared she had a physical reaction to it. With her, it was her stomach. It could get tied into knots so easily. But she'd never been gasping for breath, the way she'd seen him.

He needed help. She wondered how much trouble he was going to give her about getting it. He was so stubborn, so sure he could handle things on his own. Well, that just wasn't going to work. Not with this. Not given his extremely physical reaction to his efforts to keep from telling her what was going on.

How tentative he'd been with her afterward—going ahead and giving her permission just to walk away from him. No expectations. No recriminations. It was what she'd always done best, after all.

She started to cry as she watched him walk down the street, cry tears she hadn't allowed herself the night before. Tears for him and for her. He'd asked her to marry him. How could he do that? How dare he—when he didn't trust her to stand by him when things got tough? Of course, she didn't quite trust him, did she? Not over the long haul. She had trouble imagining him wanting to be with her forever. It would just be great if all of her misgivings somehow canceled out all of his. They'd be even. Sort of.

She wouldn't let herself think of his proposal. Of him saying he loved her. Of the pleasure that came from simply sleeping in his arms.

She got back into the bed and straightened out the covers. He was hell on bedclothes. She thought enough to find her pajamas on the floor and put them back on, just in case Peter came to find her for some reason once the sun came up.

And then she rolled around in the bed until she found a spot that smelled like him, that was still slightly warm from his body, and pressed her face to that spot and went back to sleep, imagining he was with her once again.

Julie woke up two and a half hours later, groaning as she remembered this was a school day and that Peter had to be in school. She was doing so well with this mother thing.

She climbed out of bed, raced down the hall to his room to find the door firmly shut. She knocked on it, louder and louder as she got no response.

"What?" The voice came from behind her, low and gravely. *Not Zach's.*

She whirled around and there was Peter, up and dressed, not looking happy at all about it. Julie brushed her hair back out of her face and down, hoping she didn't look like a woman who'd spent the night in a man's arms.

"It's a school day, and I overslept," she said. "I was just trying to wake you up. Ms. Reed said you had to be in school."

"I'm ready for school," he said.

"Yeah. I can see that. Your door's locked?"

He nodded. "I always keep it locked."

Which meant what? That he had something in there he didn't want her to see? Did they have to fight about this now? Was she supposed to insist he let her in and then search? She used to hate it when her stepfather searched her room. It felt like the worst violation of her privacy.

She was trying to figure out whether or not she had to do the big bad mother thing when he said, "They steal things from me."

"What?" Julie asked.

"Money. If I have money, they take it, and I got tired of it. It's no big deal. I'm just trying to keep what's mine."

"Mom and Dad steal your money?"

He shrugged. "It's happened."

"Oh. Okay." And then she worried about something else. "You have a lot of money?"

"No. And I'm not doing what you're thinking. I just . . . You know . . . mow lawns, rake leaves, that kind of stuff. I don't have that much, but they haven't had much of anything lately, and you know how they get when they think they've just got to have a drink."

"Yeah. I know." He locked his door to keep his own parents from stealing from him. She'd had her things stolen more than once.

"I gotta go to school," he said.

"Okay." Then she remembered—the mom thing. How did that go? "Did you have something to eat? Do you need some money for lunch? Or a ride to school?"

He looked at her like she was nuts. She supposed he took care of his own breakfast and that if he wanted to eat, he found his own money, and if he didn't want to walk, he found his own ride.

Did he need anything from her? Because it would feel really good just to do one thing to help him.

"I'm going to school." He left, muttering under his breath as he went. Probably curses. Thankfully, she hadn't quite heard them.

Okay, Peter was off to school. Zach had gotten out of the house without being caught, and she'd gotten to spend the night in his arms. With Zach, who wanted to marry her.

Julie closed her eyes and told herself not to think about

that, not to hope, not to get scared. To just let it be. She didn't have to tell him anything right now, and by the time it came up again . . . Well, it might never come up again.

She might never have to force herself to tell him no. It would be one of the hardest things she'd ever had to do.

She had just shut off the shower and wrapped herself in a towel when the phone rang. She ran for it.

"Hi," the most gorgeous, sexy voice in the world proclaimed.

"Hi." He sounded like he might still be in bed. She wished he was in hers.

"Sleep well?"

"Yes. You?"

"Until I dragged myself out in the cold to come home."

"Sorry about that."

"Me, too. I wanted to stay. I mean, I know I couldn't. But I wanted to."

"I wanted you to, too."

"I see Peter's gone."

Julie laughed. "Are you watching my house?"

"Maybe. Are you going to see that guy at the Chamber of Commerce today about the job?"

"Yes. At ten. Why? Are you thinking about coming back over here?"

"I'd love to, but I don't think we have time. My dad and Rye want to come by and see the house, and the only time they can do it is early. Like in thirty minutes? Is that okay? I don't want to push, but . . . You really need to move on this if you're going to stop the foreclosure."

"That's fine. Whatever you say. You're my chief legal adviser and bed warmer, after all."

"Bed warmer, huh?"

"Think you're up to it?"

"Yeah, I think I can handle it." His voice got deeper, quieter. "Julie?"

"Hmm?"

"Thank you. For last night."

"You're welcome. I'll see you soon."

Chapter 18

She hurried and dressed—white blouse, skirt, matching jacket, stockings—hurried through her makeup, and was at the door when the three of them rang the bell. Sam and Rye, clipboards in hand, smiled at her and came inside. Zach winked and made a show of checking out her legs behind the two men's backs. She patted his bottom as he walked inside, and told him to behave.

Julie offered them all coffee, which Sam and Rye both said they'd happily take once they walked through the house and made some notes. She offered to give them the nickel tour, but they declined, and so she simply gave them a vague explanation of Peter's locked door, which had them grinning again. They both had experience with kids his age. Soon she was alone in the kitchen with Zach.

"Nice suit." His hands settled at her waist, fingertips flirting with the curve of her hips. "I thought you said you didn't own any little bitty skirts."

"This is not a little bitty skirt," she claimed.

He whistled. "Works for me."

"Is it too much? Really? I'll change."

"Don't you dare," he said. "A man can't help but admire your legs, no matter what kind of skirt you wear, and I'm telling you, it's a shame to cover up any more of them than you have to."

"It's a job interview. Not a date."

"Yeah, but a guy can't help but look."

"So you're okay with other men admiring my legs?"

"Well . . . like I said . . . a guy can't help looking. They're the first thing I noticed about you from across the restaurant that night."

"You haven't seen me in eight years, and the first thing you notice are my legs?"

"I didn't know it was you at first. You had your back to me. All I saw were gorgeous long legs and hair that I wanted to see loose and hanging down your back."

She frowned up at him. "You were standing there admiring me before I turned around and you figured out who I was?"

He nodded. "That can't be a big surprise. You're gorgeous."

He seemed absolutely sincere about that, and what could she say? Anything that resembled a protest would look like she was fishing for compliments, and he'd already given her some very nice ones. She might have to go shopping for some truly little bitty skirts. Might as well give the man something to look at.

"Don't tell me you're one of those women who hates her body?" he asked.

"I don't hate it."

"I can tell you don't truly appreciate it, but I do."

"You're feeling good this morning," she said.

"I'll feel better after I do this."

He leaned down and kissed her. It was all she could do not to sink into his arms. As it was, she took his face in her hands and held on to him. He was so precious to her, and she'd been so scared last night.

He sighed over her mouth, made a little sound low in his throat that sounded like he was a man enjoying a really delicious meal. "Good morning."

"Good morning." He smelled wonderful, and he'd obviously come straight from the shower. His hair was still a little damp, and he had on his lawyer clothes. She toyed with a button on his crisp white shirt, trying not to think about what it would be like to wake up to this every day. To him. "How are you this morning?"

"Not too crazy. Not so far, at least."

She could feel him watching her, waiting. . . . For her to say something about last night? She didn't know where to start.

The silence dragged on.

Was he going to talk about marrying her again? Because he'd promised her some time. She'd counted on having it, on figuring some things out before she had to tell him something. On finding the strength to say no to him.

Finally, he said, "If this guy offers you a job, he's going to want to know if you're going to stay awhile. What are you going to tell him?"

"Well, Emma thought his first worry was about finding someone quickly who knew the town and could get them through the festival. That's only two and a half months' work."

"And that's okay with you? Being here that long?"

Honestly, she hadn't been sure until this very moment.

"You're here," she said. "And Peter's here. That seems to outweigh anything else, like the fact that my parents are here or that they're in jail."

He nodded, putting on his lawyer face, which tended to hide everything. "Good."

"I'm not going to run away, Zach. Promise."

The lawyer nodded once more.

"Are you okay?" she asked. "Did something happen?"

"I freaked out on your back porch last night and scared you half to death, Julie. I'm trying to figure out how you feel about that. About me." And he was nervous about that, despite the reassurances of the night before.

She found herself falling even more for him. Zach, the man so sure of himself and capable of handling anything she threw at him, was something to behold. But this man, the one who honestly needed her . . . He'd tapped right into her heart from the very first moment.

She put her hand over the lapels of the expensive suit he wore with such ease and grace, running through the possible responses she could make. It had to be honest. He'd demand that. He deserved it. And she wanted to reassure him. But her feelings were an awful jumble.

"It surprised me," she admitted.

"Shocked you is more like it."

"Okay, yes. That you could—"

"Wrap my hands around a man's neck and squeeze?"

"A little. But given who it was . . . Zach, there were times I wished something would happen to my stepfather. Even to my mother. Times when I was so sick of the yelling and of being scared . . . I'm not going to condemn you for wanting to hurt him."

"And the other?"

She sighed and put her hand against his chest, thinking about him struggling to breathe and being afraid he was going to fall apart, wanting a drink. "I'm worried about you. I never really did before. I always thought you were invincible."

"Well, I'm not," he said, and she knew what it cost him to admit that.

Julie nodded, pressing a little kiss to his chest, through his shirt. "But . . . nobody really is invincible, right? I mean, it's not such a shock, is it?"

He shook his head. "Was to me."

And she laughed a bit, lifted her head and kissed his mouth ever so lightly. "But Emma said she could fix you, right?"

"We'll see. I have an appointment with a colleague of hers this morning."

The lawyer was still here, poker-faced. Was that supposed to shock her? That he was seeing someone for help? "I'm glad."

"Glad?"

"That there's someone who can help you. That you're going to let them. You are going to let them, aren't you?"

"I don't think I have a choice," he said.

"It's not that bad, is it?"

He shook his head. "It's sure not anyplace I ever thought I'd be. Sitting there with a shrink, whining about my life."

"It's not whining when it can keep you from breathing, Zach. It's serious, and you have to let them help you. You have to promise me that."

"All right. I'll give it my best shot."

She frowned. "I don't know what I'm seeing here. Is this your ego that's been dented a bit?"

"Maybe," he admitted.

"Are you embarrassed?"

"Could be."

"You think you're not allowed to need help?" she suggested.

"You told me I was, so it must be true, right?"

But she still didn't think she'd gotten to the bottom of it, and there wasn't a whole lot left. Prejudices people had about those who needed this kind of help. Skeptics who didn't think therapy did anything for anybody. People who thought therapy was for whiners and those interested in blaming others for their problems.

"Nervous?" she tried.

"Yeah."

Or maybe he was just scared. Maybe all those things. She ought to be able to help him with that one. She knew all about being scared.

Julie was trying to figure out a way to broach that subject when his father and Rye came back into the kitchen. She stepped away from Zach, but not before the two of them saw her in his arms. Julie blushed as she turned her back to them and found coffee mugs and poured two cups for them.

They sat at the kitchen table giving her a quick rundown of everything that was wrong, telling her what they thought the property was worth—enough to cover all the outstanding mortgages with a little bit of extra left over, which she found too much of a coincidence to believe.

"We'll have to talk to your parents. It's really their decision," Zach said.

"Sure. But I want you to promise me one thing. I want the house appraised, and I want you to swear not to pay them a dime more than it's worth."

The three of them frowned at her. No one said anything.

"What? Is that so unreasonable?" she asked.

"No. That's fine," Sam said, holding out his hand to her.

She shook hands with both of them, thanked them for coming, and then was left alone with Zach once again, eyeing him suspiciously.

"What?" he asked.

"What is this place really worth?"

"You heard them. They made you an offer."

"A generous one, I suspect."

"Hey, you want the place appraised, we'll get it appraised."

"Not that I don't appreciate what you're trying to do. But I'm not taking your money, Zach. Or theirs. It's sweet of you to try, but it's too much."

"They want the house, Julie. Sam knew about the foreclosure proceedings already. He was interested before I said anything."

"If you say so."

"And I don't lie, remember?"

"Not even to help me?"

He frowned at that, weighing his options carefully.

"Never mind," she said. "What time is your appointment?"

"Soon."

Then, because he looked so alone and because she didn't know what else to do, she said, "I have some time. I'm going that way. It's a nice day. Want to walk?"

"You're going to walk me to the office? The way my mother walked me into the elementary school on the first day of kindergarten?"

"I'm nervous about my appointment, and I thought you'd walk with me," she said, managing to make him laugh with the blatant lie.

"We could always skip both of 'em and go back to bed," he suggested.

"True. Or we could each go to our appointments and still have time to go back to bed before Peter gets home."

"All right. Deal."

She grabbed her purse and her keys, locked the door, and they took off together. It was a nice day. They walked without saying anything, and at some point, she slipped her hand into his, relaxing a bit as his fingers closed over hers.

They got to the office and stopped outside on the sidewalk. He did seem nervous. Peter had been, too, and he hadn't let her do anything for him.

"Come on," she said, opening the door with one hand, keeping hold of Zach with the other. "I'm going to be early, and you are, too. I'll sit with you."

His look said he saw right through her and really didn't appreciate how well she was seeing through him at the moment. But he didn't let go of her hand.

They got the requisite abundance of forms from the receptionist, and then she led him to the corner Peter had picked out when he was intent on hiding.

"I should have asked Peter for pointers," Zach whispered, pulling a pen out of his jacket pocket. "Did you get anything out of him about it?"

"He hated it," she admitted. "But then, he hates most everything these days, so I'm not sure if you should consider his opinion on the matter."

Zach filled out all the forms and returned them to the receptionist, then came back and sat down beside her. She took his hand once more, hoping she wasn't being too silly, wishing she could absorb some of his nervousness and help him relax a bit. She didn't know what else to do, except this.

Because there had been times in her life when she'd longed to have someone beside her, someone who cared, and times when it seemed like no one touched her, and she craved touch the way some women longed for chocolate or a new pair of shoes. So she held on to him.

"Afraid I'm going to get up and run away before I get in there?" he asked.

"No. Zach McRae doesn't run from anything."

"But he needs somebody to walk him to the doctor's and hold his hand?"

"I told you, I'm nervous about my appointment."

"Really want the job, do you?"

"Oh, yeah. Anything to keep me right here in beautiful Baxter, Ohio, for the rest of my life."

"It's not so bad," he said.

"What would you know about it? You're hardly ever here."

Which made her wonder just what his idea of settling down might entail. Living here? Not that it looked like she was going anywhere fast. She had Peter to consider and parents who seemed to be heading for some serious jail time. So many things were up in the air. Sometimes it seemed like her whole life was one big question mark. No answers, only uncertainties.

"I am glad you came," he said softly. "Not just back home, but here with me, today." Okay, maybe her life was not entirely made up of uncertainties.

"I do love you," she said, because that was the bottom line, the thing she couldn't escape.

He frowned. "Is this like that thing where people give the doomed man what he wants most in the world before they lock him away?"

"You're not doomed or about to be locked away. They're going to fix you, remember?" she said.

When what she really wanted to do was believe she was the thing he wanted most in the world. It wasn't so hard at the moment, with him sitting close beside her, needing her in a way that she'd always needed him.

"How long is this going to take?" she asked.

"Hour and a half. Why?"

She shrugged. "I could come back. Maybe you could walk me home afterward?"

"You'll be nervous *after* your appointment, too?"

She nodded. "Or . . . I guess I could always go home, take off all my clothes, climb back into bed, and wait for you there."

He gave her an honest, full-fledged grin, the first of the day. It had been the right thing to say.

"I guess that's even better than saying I love you. Or walking you down here and holding your hand," she said.

"What can I say? I'm a guy. A naked woman waiting for me in bed . . . that works for me."

He was still grinning when the doctor came out a moment later and introduced herself to him and to Julie.

Right before Zach left to follow the doctor into her office, he leaned over and kissed Julie on the cheek and told her it would be just fine if she was waiting here when he was done. He could take her clothes off himself, once they got back to her house.

She sat there for a long time after he disappeared into the office, wishing she could be back there with him, thinking that surely there was something else she could do. She didn't want to go to her appointment. She wanted to stay right here. But the Chamber of Commerce was only a block and a half away, and she figured the interview would at least kill a little time and keep her from being so nervous.

She really was worried about Zach.

So she went to the interview. The guy happened to be someone she knew from before, somebody a little rough around the edges whom she never expected to see in such a nice suit, sitting behind a lovely desk, doing something as conservative and respectable as running the Chamber of Commerce.

They laughed over that a bit, the things they'd left behind as they'd grown up. He told her he was in a real bind, that most of the plans for the festival were already made, but, as she knew from putting together events for the store, there were always things that went wrong, always dozens of last-minute details somebody had to handle.

"It would help a lot if that person knew the town, knew the people, knew the festival. In fact, I don't see how anyone could step into this job at this time of year and ever make it work without knowing all those things. Do I need to beg?" he asked finally.

"No. It's not that. It's just . . . I never thought I'd come back here, much less stay," she admitted.

"Hey, it's October already. I'm not asking you to promise me anything except that you'll get us through the festival. And then, if we both want to talk about you staying . . . great. If not, no strings. Okay?"

"That's it?" she asked. "You don't want to see a résumé or references?"

He shrugged. "Five years at Land's Department Store? My wife could practically support the whole chain, single-handedly. She's dragged me in there from time to time. And my daughter was part of the teen modeling board. . . . That was your project, wasn't it?"

"Yes," Julie said. One of her best. "The chain was losing the youth market, and we just couldn't afford to do
that. They have so much discretionary income. They're
our future."

"That was a great promotion. And I know Land's is a
first-class operation. This job's yours, if you want it."

He named a salary she thought was generous, told her
he didn't mind at all if she needed to take work home in
the afternoons if she needed to be around for Peter when
he got out of school, as long as the work got done. She
couldn't ask for anything more than that.

Everything seemed to be falling into place in ways that
life simply never had for her. It was terrifying in a way
and oddly comforting in another.

She took the job.

Julie was waiting right there where he'd left her when
he came back to the reception area. Without a word, she
got to her feet and came to his side, taking his hand in
hers and walking out into the sunshine with him.

He took a long, slow breath of the fresh, fall air, let
the sunshine and her warm him through and through, and
just kept walking. The urge to rush her off to her house,
to her bed, was strong, and he knew she wouldn't offer
up a word of protest, giving herself to him as willingly
as ever.

Anything he needed right now. Her hand. Her love.
Her understanding. Her faith. Her body, his for the asking. She hadn't gone anywhere.

Could he convince her to stay? Always? To stop running?

They walked on, and he took an ambling path in the
general direction of her house. It wasn't even noon.
They had a few precious hours to themselves before

Peter got out of school, and he knew what he'd find in her arms.

He settled for pulling her into the shadows on the side of the ice-cream store, behind a huge, sprawling oak, backed her up against the wall, and kissed her long and hard, pinning her to the wall with his body, lingering there over her lips, working over them with a patience he feared he'd seldom shown her before.

"That bad?" she asked, when he rested his forehead against hers and sighed.

"Well, they didn't try to lock me up on the spot," he said. "There's a plus."

She laughed. "Did you think they would?"

"I don't know, Julie. Like I said, it's a place I've never been before. Emotionally, I mean."

She just stood there, letting him rest against her, wanting to kiss her again and knowing they really needed to talk, that it was up to him to make that happen. But it was hard when her bed was waiting.

"She thinks we can work through this. That I'll be fine."

"There you go. Told you so."

"How the hell did I end up in therapy?" he asked.

"Classic case of a dysfunctional family. You were probably doomed from the start."

He laughed then. "It never sounds so bad when I talk about it with you."

"That's because it's not, Zach. I mean, it's no fun, but it's something people know how to handle."

He hadn't seen it that way—as simply something that someone knew how to fix.

"You told her everything?" Julie asked.

"Yeah, I told her everything. She didn't even seem to be shocked."

"So, you're not the first person to ever feel this way?"

He took a breath, thinking it would take some getting used to, the way she saw inside of him. Because that's exactly what he'd thought.

"No, apparently I'm not the first person to ever feel this way," he said, then grimaced, still getting used to the diagnosis. "She said it's a classic case of panic attacks."

Julie nodded, waiting, accepting. He really needed the acceptance right now.

"You'd think I would have figured it out, huh?" he said as easily as he could. "I had all the symptoms. One of the doctors I saw mentioned it, and I didn't even give it a second thought. I thought he was nuts. Me? Have something like that?"

"I guess it's not so easy when it's your own problem."

"Yeah."

He was still getting used to the idea that someone could truly fix the problem. There had been times when he thought he was dying, that it seemed too drastic a physical reaction to attach it to any problem normally addressed by a psychiatrist or a psychologist.

"She doesn't think I'm a drunk, either," he said. "Just that I was using that, trying to avoid the problem. She thinks if we deal with the problem, we'll stop the panic. Stop the panic, and I won't be tempted to drink. I never really wanted to drink before. I mean, it was okay, but not . . . I don't know. It just wasn't a big deal. People have a drink every now and then and don't go crazy. I didn't, and it's not like I've been drinking all that much, just wanting to. So, one problem down. Hopefully."

"Good. So, you'll go talk to this nice lady for a while,

and she'll do . . . whatever it is she does, and then you'll find a way to put this behind you and move on."

He nodded.

"Still having trouble believing it?" she asked.

"It shows?"

"Just a little. Give it some time. Sometimes things just work out, you know?"

He did grin then. "And you and me? What about you and me?"

"What about us? I have a job, by the way. I took it. Just until after Christmas. No promises either way after that. I probably won't have a house for long."

"Your parents have a preliminary hearing next week."

"Oh, goodie. Peter actually spoke to me voluntarily this morning, without a door between us."

"That's a step."

She nodded. "And this man who's at least half crazy proposed to me last night when we were in bed."

"Only half crazy?"

"Yeah. Of course, you know men. They'll say anything when they're in bed with a woman. Anything they think she wants to hear."

"You definitely did not want to hear it."

"No . . ." She smiled up at him, and he'd been so close to this point, nuzzling her cheek, kissing her lips, that he hadn't really looked at her. But there were tears in her eyes, which she was valiantly trying not to allow to fall, and she looked troubled and happy at the same time. "It wasn't that. I just . . ."

"Need some time?" he offered.

"Yes. It's not about you or what you're going through. It's me. Can I have some time?"

"You can have anything you want, Julie," he prom-

ised, smoothing the pad of his thumbs across her closed
eyes, brushing away the moisture there.

"Thank you."

"You're welcome. Now, about time . . . We're burning
daylight, darlin'. I had planned to have you naked by
now."

She and Zach spent the day in bed, making love in a
frenzy at first. Afterward, he slept like a man who was
exhausted. He probably was. She held him, thinking this
was going to take some getting used to.

Making love to him was like being stripped bare emotionally. Like peeling back several layers of skin along
with her clothes. Like he got inside of her, not just in a
sexual way, but in every way possible.

When she lay there with her body pressed against his
from head to toe, it was like they'd been fused together.
Her ribs were bumping up against his, hearts beating in
tune with one another, heat, sweat, power, need, everything. Him and her. In this together completely. Did
things like that really last?

"You're worrying again," he murmured in a deep
voice raspy from sleep.

"I'm can't help it. And I'm allowed to worry, right? I
promised I wouldn't run, but never that I wouldn't
worry."

"All right. If you insist, you can worry. But I have to
warn you, if I catch you at it, I'm going to be tempted to
distract you, and it's no telling what form that distraction
might take."

His hand pushed down the covers, baring her breast.

His fingers curled around the bottom, thumb curling
close to the pucker of her nipple, him watching as if absolutely fascinated by the sight of his hand on her.

Julie sucked in a breath, the sensation seemingly totally out of proportion to the action, especially given the way they'd spent the afternoon. She seemed to feel his touch through her entire body. Head, heart, down between her legs, all the way down to her toes. He touched her like she was the most precious thing in the world.

His thumb rubbed back and forth across her nipple, and she moaned, couldn't help it.

"It's not going to go away," he said.

"What? My left breast?"

He grinned. "The way this feels. The way we feel when we're together. It won't ever change. I won't go away. I won't change my mind. I'll always want you. Just like this. Think about believing it, Julie. Give it a chance. What if all that was true? What if you believed it? Then what?"

"I'd marry you," she said.

And he looked happier than she'd ever seen him.

"I think I'm going to enjoy the time it takes to convince you," he said, as he kneed her thighs apart and lay cradled between them, his body hard and throbbing against hers. "How about it? Feel any more certain than you did an hour ago?"

"I'm not sure," she said, opening her body to him. She was still halfway aroused from the first time, and her body was soft and welcoming.

He kissed her forehead, the tip of her nose, her cheeks, her neck, and finally her mouth, then began to push his way inside.

"There we go. Right there," he whispered in her ear, flexing his hips.

One more smooth, controlled thrust, and there he was, inside her completely, their bodies flush together, his mouth locked on hers. She squirmed and wriggled and tried to get closer, tried to simply climb inside of him. The feeling seemed to get stronger each time they did this, until she couldn't imagine being just her anymore, and not attached to him. Like she just wouldn't be complete. Like she never had been.

"I love you," he said, and she came in a rush. There was no stopping it. No control. Just pure, honest need, him coming right after her.

She felt tears in her eyes in the aftermath. The man simply overwhelmed her.

"Don't do that," he said, his hand on the side of her face, kissing her softly. "Don't. It's all going to be fine. You'll believe it, Julie. I won't quit until you do."

She lay there sniffling and trying not to cry, and he fussed over her, wiping away tears and rubbing her back and kissing the sides of her face. She finally just let it all go, all the worries, all the doubts, and let him take care of her. Let him just be here beside her, imagined always having him, no matter what.

She must have dozed, because the next thing she knew, he was dressed, mostly, leaning over her and kissing her good-bye.

"What?"

"I've got to go. Peter's going to be here any minute."

"Hmm?"

He laughed. "You have to get up, too. Unless you want to get caught like this."

"I do?"

"Yes. Up. I have to run, or he's going to see me leave, and I think he's got enough to deal with right now without being upset about us."

"Okay," she murmured.

"You'll get up?"

"Yes."

Zach laughed again.

Next thing she knew, the phone was ringing. She jerked awake at the sound, disoriented for a minute, then remembered she kept the cordless by her bed. She put the phone to her ear and said, "Hello?"

"You didn't get up," Zach said, still sounding amused.

"No," she grumbled. "I didn't. You're gone?"

"Not far," he said. "I'm right down the street."

"Oh, okay."

"I still love you. Julie. Just in case you were wondering. I haven't changed my mind."

She rolled over onto her back, pulling the covers up over her naked body, missing him already. "Just in case?"

"Yeah. I was thinking. We can do this every day. As long as you need to. Until you believe me. I'll just stay right here and keep saying it."

"Oh. Well . . . that would be good."

"Now get dressed. The kid's probably halfway down the block, and somebody's truck just pulled into your driveway."

"What?"

"A truck. Were you expecting someone?"

"You're not serious."

"I am. I'm surprised you didn't hear it."

Come to think of it, she did.

Someone was really outside? She gave a little squeak of protest. Zach laughed and said he'd talk to her later. She scrambled into her clothes, the doorbell ringing for the second time as she was running down the stairs, feeling like she might as well be wearing a T-shirt that said, SPENT THE DAY IN BED WITH THE SEXIEST MAN ON EARTH. Surely it showed all over her.

She pulled open the door and tried her best not to look

guilty. An older man with a clipboard and a pencil stood there. "Ms. Morrison?"

"Yes?" she said.

"I came to appraise the house," he said. "Sam said you needed it done right away, and I had a cancellation this afternoon . . . I tried to call, but I didn't get an answer. I was close and thought I'd take a chance. I hope I'm not . . . interrupting anything."

She turned six shades of red and swore that he wasn't, wishing that was one lie she could have told with more skill than she managed, then went on to explain as best she could why the door to her teenage brother's room was locked. The appraiser just laughed.

"He should be home soon. I'll have him open it."

With that, the man went to work. Julie looked in the mirror, seeing a little reddish mark on her neck. What in the world had Zach done to her?

Peter came home while the appraiser was still there, and, in front of the man, she had to give him a too-brief explanation of what was going on. But maybe that was a good thing. He didn't argue or smart off in front of the man. Maybe they should have all their conversations in front of strangers.

The appraiser left, saying he'd have the report for her in a few days. Julie thanked him and hadn't even shut the door when she heard Peter behind her. "What's he doing?" he asked, with the kind of belligerence he reserved only for her.

"I told you, he's an appraiser. He was here to look at the house."

"Why? You're selling it?"

"No, the bank is foreclosing on the house because the mortgage hasn't been paid in months."

He looked confused and then resigned and then bitterly angry. "So what does that mean? You're going? I'm going back to the group home?"

"No. It just means we'll have to sell the house, unless someone comes up with a lot of money fast, which I don't think is going to happen."

"And then what?"

"Zach's father offered to buy it, and if that works out, he said we could stay here for a few months at least, while he's renovating it."

"And then what?"

"I don't know. I guess we'll figure something out." Like whether they could stay in this town. Where their parents were going to be. What was going to happen with her and Zach. Her and Peter. Everything.

"Don't you have a place to live? Back in Memphis?" he asked.

"I did. But I gave it up when I came here." Okay, technically, she'd given notice because she thought she was going to be married to Steve, but she didn't have to offer that many details to a thirteen-year-old, did she? "That reminds me. I have to have my things out of the apartment in two weeks."

"You can get another apartment back there."

"I quit my job, too," she said.

"But you could go somewhere else," he insisted.

"I could. I could go anywhere I wanted. I've decided I'm staying here. I told you I took a job here. Just until after Christmas. But, who knows . . . If I like it, and they like me, it could turn into something permanent."

"You won't stay," he said for maybe the hundredth time since she'd returned.

"You don't know that, Peter. Just because I left before, doesn't mean I will again."

"You won't stay," he repeated.

"Okay. You can think that way if you want. I can't stop you. Except maybe by staying here and showing you that you're wrong."

"I'm not wrong," he insisted.

"You know, I lived with them, too," she tried. "I know what it's like, Peter. I know how you feel. I know how angry you must be. I know it changes the way you see the whole world. And I know I left you here alone with them."

He shrugged, looked like he was mad enough to spit. "I didn't give a shit."

"Sure you didn't," she said. "I was only eighteen when I left, Peter. Think about that. I was five years older than you are now. I wasn't even sure I could take care of myself, let alone take care of you and me both. You were only five. Do you even remember that part?" Sometimes she wasn't sure if she remembered that part. What could she have done at eighteen with a five-year-old? "I just couldn't take it any longer. It hurt too much to be here, and I knew it wasn't ever going to get better. But you know what? You and I aren't them. We don't drink. We don't hit when we get mad. We're so much better at managing money than they are. I know you had to be to survive all these years, right? So doesn't it make sense that we don't have to live like them, either? That things can be different for us?"

She'd seen it when she'd gone to visit her mother. She was not that woman. She got to make her own decisions, live her own life, and she chose to be here, to try to trust in the love she had for Zach and to try to find her way back to Peter.

"When I left," she said, "being away from you was the hardest part." She got nothing from him for the admission. He stood stone-faced and glaring.

"I know what it's like to be scared," she tried. "To think that because life has always sucked, it always will. To find it hard to trust anyone to stay and to love you. I know because I feel the exact same way. I don't ever think anything good will last, and it's easier to try not to get too attached to anyone, because nothing ever works out in the end.

"But you know what? That's a lousy way to live, and I'm tired of it. Aren't you tired of it, too? I'm just not going to do it anymore. I'm not running. I'm going to try to learn to trust people and to let myself love them."

"That guy, you mean? The one you're supposedly not involved with?"

"Yes, Zach."

"So that was a lie."

"No . . ." She closed her eyes, trying to find a way to explain. "You said I came back here for him, and that wasn't true. I came for you. I came because I was sick of running, sick of being too scared to face what I'd left here. But while I was doing that, Zach came back, too, and he and I . . . Things change sometimes, you know?

"He says he loves me, Peter, and that absolutely terrifies me, probably as much as it scares you when I tell you I'm here to stay and I won't leave you. I want to believe him so much, and yet a part of me is screaming that I'm just going to get my heart torn apart again.

"But he's a good man. The best. And I've probably always loved him. When I was a little girl, he took care of me when it seemed like no one else in the world really cared about me. I know he did a better job of looking out for me than I did for you, and he never left me the way I left you. He never gave up on me. But even knowing all that, it's still hard for me to trust him."

Peter turned away, and she thought she might have

seen a glimmer of tears in his eyes. "So, you know what I'm going to do? I asked him to give me some time. He's a patient man, and he's kind and determined, and he says he won't give up on me. Not ever. So I guess I'll just be here for a while, and I'll get up every morning and wait and see if he's still around. If he still loves me. And I'll try each day to find just a little more faith in him and let go of a little bit of the fear.

"And I'm hoping that one day, the faith will far outweigh the fear. And then, if he still wants me to, I'm going to marry him. Imagine that? Me and Zach . . . He has a wonderful family. They'll take us in, in ways you won't even believe. And whatever happens with Mom and Dad, we'll get through it."

"And what about me?" he asked finally.

"Well, I think it'll work the same way for you and me. I figure, I'll just stick around, day after day. And you'll keep waking up and finding me right here where I promised I'd be. And one day, you'll forget that you were so sure I'd leave you, too, and you'll let yourself love me again."

He didn't say anything about that—about loving her. He said, "But . . . you're going to marry this guy?"

"He wants me to."

"So then you'll go off and live with him, and—"

"I'm not leaving you. If Zach and I are together, you'll be a part of that. He would never make you feel like you shouldn't be."

He shrugged. None of it mattered. "You won't stay."

"We'll see, won't we? We'll wait each other out and see who's right."

Chapter 19

Two months went by so fast, it practically made Julie's head spin. The Christmas festival organizers did indeed need her in the worst way. They'd been right—no one could have come into the job cold, not knowing the town or the people or the festival, and gotten it done.

But she knew how the whole thing worked. When she was growing up, she'd alternately thought it was the most sickeningly sweet, fake thing in the world—a storybook, small-town Christmas—or looked at it with a sick kind of longing that can only come from a child who will never have a holiday like that.

This year, despite all the work she put into it, Zach made sure it was a Christmas to remember. She had to be at nearly all the events, and he insisted on coming with her and playing tourist. He claimed it would make her so much better at her job—seeing it all from a tourist's perspective—and he wanted her to be great at her job. Because he wanted her to keep it, so he could keep her here.

She knew he was worried about that—her being willing to stay—and it didn't seem so bad now.

Peter was doing okay. He went to school without

grumbling most days, did most of his homework, hadn't gotten into any fights. There'd been tough days, like the one when their parents pleaded guilty to taking the money from the bank and were sentenced to two years in jail. But they'd gotten through it.

Zach's father and brother-in-law were working on the house, and most days Zach was there with them. He liked keeping busy, and when he was growing up he'd helped them a lot on job sites. So he knew what he was doing. The house looked like a different place. She couldn't imagine how good it would look when they were done.

Zach was feeling much better, like the man she'd always remembered and yet different in a good way. She'd never forget the vulnerability she'd seen in him, never forget the fact that he'd needed her. She thought he still did, and she knew she needed him.

He'd given her the time she'd asked for.

And now, somehow, it was a mere four days before Christmas. They were going to his parents' house for a party. Peter hadn't grumbled once about it. He was smitten with Emma's oldest daughter. It was the funniest thing to watch. Awkward and sweet and scary, thinking about the difficult years to come.

Julie had promised him she wouldn't leave him again, and she thought Peter was starting to believe it.

Zach called her every morning before she climbed out of bed to tell her that he was still there, right down the street, and that he still loved her. Nothing had changed there. She was starting to believe that nothing ever would.

As they stood on the doorstep that day so close to Christmas, she found it hard to believe how much her life had changed in just a few short months, how full it was, how happy. She wasn't scared anymore, wasn't waiting for the rug to be snatched out from under her. It had been so odd at first when the fear slowly fell away, and once it was gone, she wondered how in the world she'd managed to live that way for so long.

"Is Dana here yet?" Peter asked impatiently, as they waited at the door. He'd bought her a present and hidden it under his coat. He planned to slip it under the tree for her to find when she came here Christmas morning.

"I think so," Julie said. There were cars up and down the block. It seemed like half the town was here.

Sam opened the door himself and welcomed them inside. The house sparkled with candlelight and Christmas lights. It smelled heavenly. Rachel had been baking. And there were people everywhere.

Peter went off to find Dana. Julie left her coat in the foyer and went off to admire the tree. Grace was there, having just gotten back three days ago from being away for almost eight weeks on her mystery project, and she was talking to Emma. Julie went to say hello.

"Hi. Have a good trip?" Julie asked, thinking she looked tired and drained.

"Yes."

"Are you sure?" Emma asked.

"Yes. I just . . . got caught up in the project. You know how it is. I'm getting to be as bad as Mom. Just lost in the work sometimes."

"But you had a good time?" Julie asked.

Grace nodded and smiled. Julie wasn't sure she bought it, but before she could ask anything more Grace frowned and said, "Why is the tree in the wrong place?"

Julie looked at it and thought it wasn't, that it had always been on that side of the fireplace, but Emma said, "I don't know. I asked Mom, and she got the funniest look on her face."

"I thought it had always been there," Julie said.

"Not for years," Grace said. "Like . . . I don't know. Ever since Mom and Dad replaced that old sofa with the sectional. When was that? Six years ago? Eight?"

"At least," Emma said.

"And that was such a change, it took us years to get used to it," Grace said. "Mom just doesn't change things like that. You know how she is about traditions."

Julie nodded, still thinking it looked to her like the tree was in the right place. One of Emma's daughters joined them and started complaining about the tree herself, and they all laughed.

It was a good party. Relaxed. Happy. Normal, Julie realized. This was how they did holidays in this house. This was why she used to sneak down here every chance she got and stay for as long as they'd let her.

She was feeling particularly nostalgic as the evening wore on. People started drifting off to go home. Peter went with Emma and her group for a sleigh ride afterward. Rachel's cousin owned a Christmas-tree farm and gave sleigh rides in the winter. Borrowing the sleigh got harder and harder as the holiday got closer, and this was one of the only times they could get it for a ride.

Zach asked Julie to stay, and she found herself easing into what she'd always thought of as her corner of his house. When the tree was up, she was nearly under it, beside the fireplace where it was warm.

She was thinking of those days, hiding here, soaking up the serenity, the laughter, the joy. There'd been a time when this place had been all she'd known that was good in the world, and Zach had always been here, always been a part of that. He came into the room and sat down on the floor beside her, putting his arm around her, kissing the side of her face. "Have a good time?"

"Yes. It was great. I can't believe it's almost Christmas."

It seemed like the time had flown by, and then at times, it seemed like she'd always been here. In her new life. With him. Already, she couldn't imagine doing without him.

He picked up a little package from under the tree and handed it to her. "I have special permission for you to open this one thing early."

"Special permission?" She laughed, because it was too big to be a ring box and it weighed too much. It was maybe four inches square all around, so she figured she was safe.

"Yes. My mother has strict rules about these things."

"I remember." They were a Christmas-morning kind of family. None of this opening things on Christmas Eve or earlier for the McRaes. "Sure I need to open it now?"

Zach nodded, looking at her intently, making her nervous with the look.

She got a little uneasy and started babbling instead of tearing at the paper. "We were talking about that earlier. How seldom your mother changes anything. Grace and Emma and about fifty other people commented on the tree being on this side of the room instead of the other.

"Uh-huh," he said.

And all of a sudden that made her nervous, too.

"I asked her to put it over here," he said.

That was . . . odd. Julie had a little trouble breathing all of a sudden. She managed to get out, "Why?"

"Why would I want the tree here, Julie?"

"I don't—"

"Yes, you do."

"Well . . ." Why would this matter to him? Unless, he really had noticed everything, forever. Unless he would take note of the smallest things that had ever meant something to her. Even something like being comfortable here in his house. "This is my corner," she said.

He nodded, a hint of a grin playing at the corners of his mouth.

She loved to kiss that spot on his cheeks, where the dimples were. She loved to kiss any little part of him at all, and she liked sitting in this corner of his house, by the fireplace. At Christmas it put her right beside the tree. She could nearly disappear here, and it was familiar and comforting, and he'd noticed.

And made his mother move the tree for her, so it would be the same way it had been all those years ago, when she was a lost little girl and he was watching out for her, trying to make things easier for her. Just there, when she needed him.

"Open the box, Julie."

Her hands started to tremble. Tears filled her eyes. Still, she kept telling herself it wasn't a ring. It was too heavy. "It's not even Christmas. . . ."

"You'll need it for Christmas," he claimed.

For Christmas? What did she need for Christmas that came in a box this size?

"Go ahead," he told her.

She took a breath and unwrapped it, finding a little cube-shaped white box. Puzzled, she opened the lid. He took it from her, then tipped the box upside-down so that a bundle of something wrapped in white tissue paper fell into her cupped hands. She peeled back layer after layer. Whatever was inside must be fragile. Someone had gone to great lengths to protect it. Finally, she undid the last layer.

It was a star-shaped ornament. A beautiful star made of beveled glass. Zach's mother made them. It was one of their most sacred traditions.

"You know what this means," Zach said.

Julie nodded, crying now. It had her name etched into it and a date . . . from the year she was seven.

"You've always been a part of us," he said.

Julie nodded, simply unable to say a word.

Zach turned the ornament around in her hand, and on the other side was a different date, a different name.

Julie McRae.

The date was next year's.

In Zach's family, everyone had an ornament. Hand-made, just like this one, with their name on it and the date they'd become a part of the family. They gathered together on Christmas Day and one by one hung their ornaments and those of family members long passed away, on the tree.

She'd seen them do it so many times, and it never failed to bring up inside of her the kind of longing that at times had felt like it might choke her, right there on the spot. "I've always wanted one of these," she whispered.

She'd always wanted to belong. Right here. Scarcely letting herself believe she'd belong to all of them and to him.

"There's another one. For Peter. He'll be a part of this, too."

Julie nodded, still crying. Zach would do it this way.

"I want them hanging on the tree with all the others on Christmas Day," he said.

Julie nodded. "I'd . . . I'd . . . Oh, Zach."

"Tell me. Say yes."

"Yes." She cried again, throwing her arms around him, as he did the same, holding on so tight.

"Believe it?" he asked.

"Yes."

Everything. Every good thing in the world, she believed in. All of them were coming to her.

USA Today **Bestselling Author**

TERESA HILL

THE EDGE OF HEAVEN

To Rye, the postcard-perfect town of Baxter,
Ohio, is like something out of a dream. So,
too, is Emma McRae. She seems to trust him
completely—and he decides not to reveal the
real reason he turned up at her door.

(410343)

Also Available:
UNBREAK MY HEART   (409310)
TWELVE DAYS   (201450)

To order call: 1-800-788-6262

Hill/S638

JANET LYNNFORD

SPELLBOUND SUMMER

An enchanting tale of two very different souls brought together one spellbound summer...

Confronted by a temperamental Scottish laird while collecting clay from his property, artisan Angelica Cavandish finds herself in the midst of a war over disputed land—and in a personal battle for the heart of a warrior.

"Lush and sexy...brings the romance of the Scottish countryside to life." —Tess Gerritsen

0-451-41052-1

To order call: 1-800-788-6262